TURNING POINT

Drew eased Carrie's head back against him, blazing a trail of kisses along her hairline. Still, she did not respond, except to release a sigh, like a child whose sleep has been disturbed.

"Carrie?" Drew's hand returned to her breast.

The whisper of her name tickled her earlobe. "Hmmm?"

"Are you asleep?"

Should she betray her state of wakefulness? And if she did, would it put a halt to his bold caresses? She had not yet gotten her fill . . .

"No, Drew . . ."

Immediately the trail of kisses ceased. "And you are not fleeing across the room to yell curses at me?"

A smile curved her mouth. Taking his hand, she eased it beneath the bodice of her gown. "I plan to cut out your heart, Drew Donovan," she said. "You might as well enjoy yourself beforehand."

ALLEGHENY CAPTIVE

CAROLINE BOURNE

ZEBRA BOOKS
KENSINGTON PUBLISHING CORP.

ZEBRA BOOKS

are published by

Kensington Publishing Corp.
475 Park Avenue South
New York, NY 10016

First printing: October, 1990

Printed in the United States of America

This one's for you, Dad

Gently sways
the loosely braided
tendrils
of sweet rapture's vine,
Where clings a single
rose
Unfaded.

Against your ear
I softly speak
And watch the crimson
Rush upon
Your ashen cheek

Alas, your lips!
The sweetest wine
Softly touching
Upon mine

Dare I believe
that I might tame
the passions of
an Allegheny Flame

Part One
The Dawning

Chapter One

October 1820

The mighty Mississippi spread out from Drew Donovan's steamboat in a blanket of crimson shards. Despite the playful chiding of his comrades, Drew was slow in awakening. His long, sinewy body stretched in a reluctant attempt to face the new day, then slumped lazily upon his cot. Being on the river for more than twenty days took its toll on a man's ambitions and his exuberance, he thought.

A shuffling of feet caught his attention. He looked toward the doorway as his friends approached, thankful for the cup of coffee handed to him.

"Get up, you worthless scoundrel!" Noble, his Indian blood brother, ordered, suppressing the chuckle tickling at his throat.

"Aye, why should we do all the work?" Bundy Duncan interjected, leaning in the doorway of Drew's cabin. "It's but a day's distance to your gallant port of New Orleans. And you have promised us a good time!"

In one swift move, Andrew Cynric Donovan rose to his full height of over six feet. Skimming back his ebony hair, his slate-gray eyes narrowed as he met Bundy's surprised look. "Didn't think my feet could find the deck, eh, you half-breed scalawag?"

Bundy's laughter echoed across the river. "Didn't, to be sure. Watch your tongue, white man, or the Indian half of me will lift your scalp."

"Breakfast is ready in the dining room." Noble's terse tone, when he had joined in the manly playfulness just moments ago, was oddly out of place. He took his Seminole heritage much more seriously than his half-breed brother, Bundy, and ofttimes did not tolerate his gibes.

For a moment, Drew studied his two comrades. Both were sons of the Seminole warrior Oclala, one born of a white captive, Polly McFadden, and the other born of Oclala's fierce female warrior, Black Face, so named because of a disfiguring birthmark. Neither had known their father, who had been killed along with his renegade comrades by the men of Pine Creek, North Carolina, halting the bloody northward movement of the warriors from Florida. Bundy, the elder by five months, had been raised by his mother and stepfather, Jim Duncan, and Noble had spent his early years with the embittered Black Face, who had lived her remaining five years under the careful watch of the residents of Pine Creek. The five-year-old Noble had then been taken into the home of Cole and Diana Donovan and raised as Drew's brother. Although he had been given the name of his father — Oclala — at his birth, he'd been renamed Noble, and given the surname of his adoptive family.

Diverting his attentions, Drew, owner, along with his two blood brothers, of the steamboat *Donovan's Dream*, took the position of authority. "I'd better get with the captain and make sure we have enough wood on board to complete the trip."

Just at that moment, the young lad Drew had taken on the evening before from the settlers of St. Francisville emerged from beneath a tarpaulin, stretching his arms and yawning widely. "We're movin' south'erd?" Cawley Perth asked, slicking down the scruffy peach fuzz clinging to his upper lip. Fair and blond, his smooth features would have

10

looked more proper on a girl his own age of seventeen.

Drew affectionately tousled the boy's unruly hair. "You said you were a good steamboat man, and I expect you to earn your wages. And on the way back upriver, if you decide to return here . . ." Drew pointed to the small settlement of St. Francisville in the distance behind them, "I'll skin your blasted hide for wasting my time."

Cawley grinned widely. "My pa'll skin my hide, Mr. Donovan, before you get a chance. I'll be a hidin' under that tarpaulin when we come this way ag'in. No, sir, I'll be wantin' to see Pennsylvanie, like you told me I could."

Just the night before, Drew had snatched the brutally mistreated boy from the clutches of his enraged and drunken father. He was suddenly reminded of a boy he'd known a long time ago, a boy just this age, with all the enthusiasm and patriotism of the most die-hard American soul. Drew had traveled downriver with Andrew Jackson and his men in the winter of 1814 and had engaged in the Battle of New Orleans against the British. He'd joined Jackson despite the heated objections of his parents, Cole and Diana Donovan, and had befriended a young soldier named Danny on that long, perilous journey. After the battle, Drew had returned to North Carolina with nothing more than a mosquito-bitten hide. Danny had died facedown in the Louisiana swamp.

Drew pulled himself up straight, arched his back against the warm sun, then moved toward the large dining room and the second cup of coffee sorely needed to face still another day on the river. He poured a cup, then sat at the end of the long table to nurse the brew between his fingers. No one else was about. The crew, including the captain, were all at their stations. He could feel *Donovan's Dream* being drawn into the currents of the Mississippi for the last leg of their journey to New Orleans.

After giving Cawley his list of daily duties, Noble joined Drew in the dining room. His ebony eyes caught the rays of

11

the sun breaking the timberline across the river and flooding the room from two small windows. His Indian blood brother, usually perceptive to Drew's moods, now misinterpreted his silence. "Thinking about Jolie?"

Drew looked up. The haughty face of Jolie Ward, daughter of Zebedee and Callie Ward, their longtime friends at Pine Creek, haunted his memories. "Jolie? Why would I be thinking of Jolie?"

"The girl left her home and followed you to Wills Creek to be with you. And scarcely the age of fifteen at the time." Noble Donovan spoke with a note of bitterness. He'd wanted Jolie Ward as a wife for years, and though she frequently had allowed him in her bed, she still held out for marriage to Drew.

"It was her decision." Drew's mouth pressed into a thin line as he thought of the persistent woman. "I told her I cared for her only as a family friend. I told Zebedee and Callie but, blast! The girl is as hard-headed as a mule! Why couldn't she have had Hester's good sense?"

"Speaking of my wife?"

Both men looked up as Bundy Duncan entered. "We mentioned Hester's name, aye," Drew explained. "Just wondering why Jolie couldn't have been more like her sister."

Bundy stood with his feet apart, arching his back as if it was the end of the day, rather than the beginning. "Now you know why I married Hester. Why I didn't care if she was older'n me. She's a good woman."

"Has to be," Drew replied. "Only a good woman could keep you outta trouble."

Despite his lazy drawl, Andrew Cynric Donovan had graduated at the top of his class from King's College in England. From there he had gone to reside at the family mansion in Philadelphia to help his father establish a shipping business between Europe and America. When adventure had grabbed at his heart, he had joined Andrew Jackson as a civilian scout. Returning to Pine Creek, North Carolina,

12

after the New Orleans campaign, Drew, with his friends Noble and Bundy, and Bundy's family and sister-in-law—the persistent Jolie!—had journeyed to Wills Creek Trading Post after his great-aunt's death. At the time he had not really felt that he was separating himself from his family, because his parents journeyed at least once a year to their family home in Philadelphia, the sinister Rourke House.

The last word Drew had gotten from his parents was from Pine Creek—a missive informing him that they planned to journey to Philadelphia in the spring. He might join them there, leaving his friends to run the trading post in his absence. His father had talked about returning to his native Scotland for a visit, and Drew hoped to accompany his parents on the trip.

Drew had only good memories of his childhood—he and Noble living as brothers under the watchful and loving guidance of Cole and Diana Donovan. Along with Bundy, the boys had gotten into their fair share of trouble. Drew felt that Noble and Bundy were as much brothers to him as if they had all been born of the same parents.

The three boys had lived a good life at Pine Creek, hearing stories of Diana Donovan's mysterious home in Philadelphia, of a demented cousin, Webster Mayne, whose body had never been found in the ruins of the burned east wing of the house—the same wing in which the mummified body of Webster's mother had lain upon a rotting bed for fifteen years. Had Jocelyn Mayne's brother and Diana Donovan's father Standish known that his sister had died, he'd have made Philip and Webster Mayne leave the stately estate overlooking Philadelphia. Greed had compelled the two men to keep Jocelyn's death a secret, and to keep her body hidden in her private chamber.

On every occasion spent with his parents Drew learned more of his mother's macabre family. Rourke House had more skeletons in its closets than a monastery had monks. Though he hardly played the role, Drew was one of the wealthiest men in the state of Pennsylvania. Any number of women would have stood with him at the altar, but he had yet to encounter the one who could tame him long enough to get him there.

The muscles of his chest tightened. Drew was sure that if he did not feel the supple softness of a woman against his body soon he would begin to feel like a monk.

Finishing his coffee, Drew set down his cup and rose to his feet. A southern October was different from a New England one. The sun was soothing upon his flesh, the breeze wafting across the Mississippi refreshing and warm. He and Noble moved out on deck to supervise duties aboard the *Dream*.

"Hot damn!" Drew turned quickly. Cawley hopped toward him, holding a twenty-inch thrashing, protesting field rat by the tail. "Look here what I found. Cook it or make it walk the plank, Mr. Donovan?"

Moving along the deck and coaxing the boy ahead, Drew and his good friends laughed heartily. "We're only about a hundred yards from shore, Cawley. The beast will be into what is left of our food if we don't let him swim for it."

Cawley threw the rat as far as his strength allowed. "And don't come back!" he yelled, swinging his fist at the offending creature who swam confidently toward the eastern shore. They had just reached a bend in the river when its scraggly body disappeared among the cattails along the Mississippi shore.

Three hundred miles to the south a different kind of rat had suddenly found itself emerged in frigid water. Junius Wade did not fare as well as the four-legged rat as he bobbed in the swells of the Gulf of Mexico. "Throw out a float!" he screamed at the top of his lungs. "Damn you, throw out a float!"

Actually, the crew and passengers aboard the American

vessel *Rebounder* had placed bets on how long he would stay afloat while dropping sails to circle the unfooted passenger. The crew, known for initiating bets, was taking an inordinately long time coming to his rescue. Junius Wade was a procurer of loose women; his activities included smuggling, and white slave buying and selling as well. The grotesquely disfigured man, with a hook on the stump of his left wrist and his face and scalp mottled by burning, had made life miserable for the other passengers since they'd left Haiti. He often hissed savage insults through the half of his mouth that had not been burned away.

Seeking revenge for his evil acts, Carrie Sherwood, one of the slaves he'd purchased in Haiti, had crept up behind him and pushed him overboard. Now Carrie sat in the cabin with the other women and shivered in her bravado. Her flaming red hair was loose and disheveled, and her almond-shaped eyes flashed emerald fury. Goose bumps had popped up on her milk-white skin and her full mouth had turned down in a trembling pout.

"I hope the sharks eat him!" a pretty mulatto girl hissed. "Though his putrid flesh would probably poison them!"

"Hush," Carrie softly admonished. "No matter what he is, I had no right to—"

"You had every right!" another of the women interjected hotly.

"I had no right," Carrie reiterated her prior position.

Julia, the mulatto, sauntered before Carrie, her hands on her wide hips. "The proper little English princess is ashamed of herself! You did what we all wanted to do, Flame!" She spoke the pet name Junius had given her with as much antagonism as she could muster. "Why do you scold yourself? Hopefully the bastard will die and we can all be free when we reach New Orleans."

Discordant boos erupted from the deck. Within moments, the cabin door flew open and a wet, bedraggled Junius Wade stood in the doorway, his beady eyes scanning the faces of the six slaves he had recently purchased. "Which one of you . . ." He raised the stump of his left wrist, "caused me to lose my favorite silver-plated hook! Which of you tried to kill me!"

Julia carelessly shrugged her shoulders. "Not me. And I didn't see who did."

The other girls joined in the chorus of denials. Only Carrie was silent. "Flame?" Junius Wade had given her that name because of her brilliant red hair. She was also his favorite, though he wasn't sure why he'd selected the feisty English girl—perhaps because of her spirit. "Do you know who did this to poor Junius?"

Shamed by her act of brutality, Carrie dropped her eyes. She shrugged weakly, her cheek lightly touching her thin shoulder in the coy move. The other girls would be disappointed if she confessed. "I don't know, Mr. Wade."

"Are you sure?"

Fear of the repercussions grabbed her from within. "Yes, I am sure. I saw nothing."

"Then . . ." Tucking the stump of his arm into his soaking waistcoat, Junius turned his accusing gaze to Julia. "Then you are the one who shall be punished, my little dark one. Get the lash from my cabin. The others of you shall watch."

Julia gasped in horror, her eyes cutting between Junius Wade and the girl he called Flame. Her own bravado waned. "Why me? I did not do it!" Her face was suddenly as red as the satin dress she wore. "I will not be punished for something I did not do!"

Carrie rose and moved between Junius Wade and the mulatto girl. "Julia should not be punished for something I did."

Junius sucked air through his twisted half-mouth, his eyes moistening with disappointment. "You, Flame? Your lovely, milk-white hands pushed me over the rail?"

Carrie lifted a haughty chin. "And I shall do it again if you attempt to touch me in a . . . a familiar way. I shan't

16

stand for it. Now . . ." Her full, sensual mouth trembled, "shall *I* get that whip? I hope you have recovered your strength sufficiently after your ordeal, because you will have to run me down to use it." Though bravery marked her words, she was unable to keep the tremor out of her voice.

Junius sauntered deliberately toward her. His right hand twisted through the flaming tresses of her hair and tightened. "You are much too valuable to me unmarked, Flame. As your punishment, your wares shall be sold first, before that of the other girls. And I'll make sure a boisterous, boasting swill shall take from you that which you claim no man has ever had. I'll make sure of it! You are further confined to this cabin."

His rancid breath assailed her delicate senses. Carrie's breathing ceased until his fingers withdrew from her hair and he turned away. Stepping from the cabin, Junius turned, crooked his finger at the petite Kama, and called her out to the deck. The others knew the vicious little man would take his pleasure from the fearful, wide-eyed girl who had been his bargain purchase before he returned her to the company of the other women. He closed the door with a dull thud.

"You are in trouble, Little Miss Princess, if he hurts Kama," Julia promised, her hands drawn arrogantly to the girl's rounded hips. "Will your uncle, the duke, be able to help you then?" Her deep-set black eyes glared threateningly as she joined the remaining girls for a stroll on deck, leaving the English girl alone in the cramped cabin they shared to consider what she had done.

Carrie's long, lithe body fell to the small cot in a sobbing heap. She dearly missed her uncle and wished to God she had not defied his orders and taken an early-morning walk on the beach on the Isle of Wight, where they had been vacationing together. Five months had passed since she'd been plucked from the water by white slavers and subjected to indignations no decent woman should have to suffer. They

17

had attempted to take everything from her—her pride, her courage, everything except one thing. A virgin was worth ten times as much at the white slave auctions in Haiti, and she had certainly brought top price. And now, sailing for her final destination, a filthy rat trap in New Orleans referred to as "The Swamp," Carrie was quickly regaining her courage and indomitable pride.

Why then was she lying upon the cot, a sobbing, emotional bundle? She drew herself up, the button at her tiny waist popping in the move, her supple breasts heaving against the tightness of the emerald satin gown she wore, a perfect complement to her thickly fringed eyes. The sunset tresses of her hair caught in the beads of perspiration upon her neckline, then in the pearls Junius had made her wear. Suddenly, the string broke and the floor was littered with the pearls which rolled to and fro with the movement of the ship. Carrie untangled the string and its golden clasp from her hair and dropped it to the floor. She wanted nothing the evil little man had given her. She wanted only to be free of him.

A boisterous, boasting swill indeed! How dare Junius threaten her so! He wouldn't dare attempt to sell her, Lady Charissa Sherwood, niece and sole heir of the Duke of Devonshire, to a common drunk—some uneducated barbarian one might find unconscious under a shipping dock. But then, Junius had purchased her from the white slavers. If he would purchase her, then he would sell her. It was as simple as that. She would have to find a way out of her predicament so that she might implore some good soul to pay her passage back to England.

Rising from the cot, she approached the secured washstand against the right wall. The black makeup Junius had ordered her to wear under her eyes had made dirty rivers upon her crimson cheeks. She took the soap and cloth and scrubbed at them until she was sure she had removed the top layer of her flesh. She swore that, no matter what Ju-

18

nius said or did, she would not allow herself to be manipulated by him.

Junius Wade was furious with the lovely English girl he called Flame, so furious, in fact, that his brutal sexual attack on Kama had left her lifeless beneath his grunting body. Blast! he thought. Now he would have to sacrifice valuable sleep time to get rid of the body! He had taken Kama cruelly, deliberately making every moment a living torment for her. Now he faced the problem of disposing of her!

His usual pattern was to be brutal toward the girls he purchased, but he had a soft spot for the tall, slim English beauty he called Flame. Thinking of her erased the dark fury from his eyes, leaving only a shell of disappointment. She had claimed to be the niece of a duke, had implored him to return her to her homeland, promising an ample reward. But if she were indeed well born, how had she ended up on an auction block? She certainly had delusions of grandeur, making the claims, even knowing they would bring ridicule upon her. Already, the other girls were taunting her, calling her "Princess" and making life miserable for her.

Ah, but they were merely envious! Flame was given first choice of the dresses Junius purchased for his girls, first choice of the jewelry, the best cuts of meat served at their private table in the ship's dining area. One day Flame would make a lot of money for him; she was worth the attention he showered on her, and the withholding of the brutality he inflicted on his other girls. At twenty-one she had many good years of service ahead of her. He envisioned riches beyond his wildest imagination.

He would not, however, forget that she had tried to kill him. She should have known that the pat on the rear he had given her had merely been a show of affection. If it had an-

19

gered her, she should simply have said so. There had been no need for brutality. And why had she waited half an hour to retaliate? As he changed into dry clothing and strapped on his metal hook, he reflected on his future with this pretty English girl.

He was confused and disappointed that he felt intimidated by her. She was the one who should have fed his sexual needs, not the little Kama. He would have to find a very special way of punishing Flame for her misdeed.

Junius wished he could reflect back on a more carefree existence, but he had no recollection of life before his middle years and could only guess that he was about sixty-five. He'd spent ten years in a North Carolina asylum, recovering from severe burns, a missing left hand, and absolutely no idea as to his true identity or place of birth. When he had recovered sufficiently to leave the asylum, he had taken his identity from its name—the Junius Wade Institution for the Deranged—and had moved ever southward, engaging in gambling and debauchery, eventually setting up lucrative businesses in New Orleans and Natchez with money he had won at the gaming tables. He journeyed frequently to Haiti to purchase white slaves who seldom lasted longer than a year or two—either dying of rot or running off with the paying gentlemen.

Junius felt he had gotten a fine lot of girls on this trip. Flame might possibly have found her new owner's favor and been spared the slobbering attentions of the men had she not booted him into the Gulf of Mexico. He would choose the most obnoxious "gentleman" to tame the English girl's haughty temper. Perhaps then she would be more to his liking and certainly more receptive to his personal attentions.

Junius walked out on deck. His girls, with the exception of Flame and the unfortunate Kama, hovered in a group around a particularly handsome young Spaniard. Let them have their pleasures, he thought. Upon reaching their final destination in The Swamp, the common name of a dozen blocks of saloons, dance halls, gambling dens, and bordellos in the heart of New Orleans, it would be business only with the gentlemen.

Moments later, Junius burst into the cabin where Flame sat upon her cot, her feet drawn beneath her skirts. Her face was devoid of emotion as Junius sat upon the opposite end of the cot and hid the hook that was his left hand beneath his right elbow. Then, as her eyes met his narrowed gaze he observed her defiance.

"So, you retain your spirit, eh, Flame?"

"My name is Carrie," she replied firmly, "and you've done nothing to destroy my spirit."

"We will see, my sweet one, after you have lain with the vilest of men."

Carrie was unable to keep her bottom lip from trembling, the only betrayal of her fright. "When my uncle, the duke, finds me, then you will be—"

Junius Wade bounded from the cot with more agility than one would have thought possible. "Enough of your ridiculous illusions of grandeur, Flame! I am sick of hearing about your uncle, the duke! I am sick of hearing about your excursion to the Isle of Wight where you were snatched by smugglers! I am sick to death of hearing it all!" Suddenly, Junius spun toward her, his good hand clenched into a fist, his normally light-brown eyes black with rage. "If I hear any more of this, I will whip you! Do you understand?"

Carrie eased back into the corner, then drew her trembling fingers into the folds of her skirt. "Yes, I understand," she said in a strained whisper. "Why did you come in here? I will not forget your degrading threat to compromise my honor. Will you throw it in my face at our every meeting until the vile act occurs?"

Junius smiled wickedly as he backed toward the door. "I will not compromise your honor, Flame. I will simply sell you to lowly scum and perhaps then you will crawl down from that pedestal you have set yourself upon." Touching his

21

forehead in mock respect, Junius quietly closed the door behind him.

Once again, Carrie's eyes moistened, though she did not allow the tears to touch her cheeks. She had to maintain her dignity — and her strength — if she was to survive this ordeal. Somehow, upon reaching New Orleans, she would try to get word to her uncle in England.

Her uncle's kindly face rose in her mind and her thoughts wandered back to the good times she had spent with him, to their happy lives together at Holker Hall, their magnificent home at Grange-over-Sands, Cumbria. She remembered her pleasant horseback rides over the spacious pleasure grounds, watching the herd of fallow deer lope gracefully through the woodlands, then returning to the house to be scolded by Mirabell, her childhood nanny, for staying out so late.

What wonderful, wonderful times! She'd spent many hours on her favorite garden bench, reading from the diary of Lady Willoughby that told of the civil war of the seventeenth century during which the king had been beheaded. That was a period in their history her uncle, the present Duke of Devonshire, did not want her studying. He had lost family to the civil war, and the whole affair had not turned out exactly as he might have wished.

If only she had insisted on staying at Holker Hall rather than journeying to Morton Manor on the Isle of Wight, where she and her uncle had summered since the death of her parents. Perhaps she would not now be sitting in a small, dingy ship's cabin, fearing a fate worse than death. She would never forget that last morning, when she had defied the wishes of Mirabell and crept out of the house just past dawn to swim in the ocean. She had moved swiftly through the terraced gardens and had disappeared from the house before her uncle had arisen for his early-morning ride. She'd felt a certain pleasure in her victory, knowing she was about to do something that went against the grain of her status as a lady—and as the niece of the Duke of Devonshire. To swim in the ocean at dawn with nothing on but the barest of undergarments was worth both the risk of Mirabell's chastisement and a report to her uncle of her wicked ways.

The morning sun had just broken the horizon when she reached the beach and discarded her morning dress, shoes, and accessories in a pile among white rocks. When she was sure that no one was about, she ran across the clean white sand and plunged into the gentle waves of the English Channel. Laughing at her own wickedness, she swam far out into the Channel.

She had not seen a ship in the Channel, nor a longboat, but suddenly she had been plucked from the water by thick, burly hands, and a similar hand clamped over her mouth so that she could not possibly scream. Mute with fear, she scarcely remembered being taken aboard a smuggler's ship half an hour later. Strangely, she remembered thinking that the Worsleys would be disappointed she could not make the ball at Appuldurcombe that evening.

That had been five months ago. The tears that had moistened her eyes just moments ago now clung to her cheeks. She imagined that once her clothing had been found hidden upon the beach of her beloved Isle of Wight, her uncle had believed her to have drowned.

Memorial services had probably been held, and now the Duke of Devonshire would go on with his life without her.

Oh, why had she been so stubborn and defiant! Mirabell had been outrageously authoritative that night before, forbidding Carrie to do this and to do that, and inhibiting her every move as though she were a three-year-old. This was Mirabell's fault. If she had minded her own business . . .

Carrie sighed deeply. No, it was not dear, loving Mirabell's fault. It was her own fault. Good sense should have forbade her to go swimming in the Channel. Smugglers had been known to traverse between France and the English coast ever since the days of Roman occupation, and she knew that she shouldn't have gone out alone at such an isolated hour. Had she waited an hour or two, there would have been children on the beach with their parents, enjoying the warm May morning with the slightest breeze rolling in from the Channel. But no! She'd had to do something daring and forbidden.

Her rebellion had cost her dearly. Once a maiden of high English society, she now sat upon a humble cot in an American ship, the *Rebounder*, her destination the arms of a vile American who would attack her innocence with the frenzied heat of a mastiff. If she were ever rescued from the clutches of Junius Wade, she would not be fit for her gentle England. She would be fit for a brothel instead!

Junius Wade's other girls began to return to the cabin, their scornful eyes refusing to rest upon her for even a minute. Despite their disapproval of her, a very important question needed an answer: "Where is Kama?" Carrie asked quietly.

"She is with *him!*" replied Julia, lifting a haughty chin.

"But he came here to intimidate me soon after he took her."

"Then she must have liked what she got and decided to stay."

Carrie seriously doubted that. She had a feeling none of them would ever see Kama again.

She began making plans in her mind. Somehow an opportunity to escape would present itself. Nothing would stop her, especially Junius Wade.

If her virtue was to be compromised, the compromiser would be of her own choosing.

Chapter Two

While Noble and Bundy stirred from a night of drunken debauchery in the establishments of The Swamp, Drew sat down to his journals and accounting sheets, a job he'd avoided for the past six days. He still felt the tightness of anger remaining from the night before, when a hotel manager had refused lodgings to Noble. Along Wills Creek it had not mattered that Noble was an Indian. Why then should it matter in this southern hole where most of its citizens lived in poverty? Turning away from the hotel, rather than causing trouble, they had found lodgings in the Sure Enuf Hotel, a seedy establishment in the heart of The Swamp run by a doddering old harridan named Mother Colby.

That night, Drew and Bundy decided to make the rounds of the saloons, gambling dens, and dance halls they had not visited the night before. Noble preferred not to join them. "Not because of that blasted hotel manager, eh?" Drew queried.

"No . . ." Noble tried to force a smile, but it would not come. "I'll organize the buying and see some merchants today."

"Can I go to them places?" Cawley asked.

"You're too young," Drew replied indulgently. "Remain here and assist Noble in the buying." Returning his gaze to Noble, he asked, "Sure you don't want to go, friend?"

Noble shrugged absently. "I'll remain. You two go on and

have your fun." His dark eyes lit in his first attempt at humor of the day. "And try to keep out of trouble."

"What's the sense in going?" Bundy interjected, wishing Drew was not so fond of his freckled, red-haired wife that he might relate to her a husband's indiscretions.

"You!" Noble shot back. "You keep out of the arms of a whore. I swear, if Drew does not relate your prowlings to Jolie, then I will."

"Drew won't tell you if I seek that kind of company," Bundy kidded in return.

"To hell I won't," Drew chuckled. "That's the first thing that'll come out of my mouth when we return to Wills Creek. I'll be the only one seeking that kind of pleasure tonight."

"Damn!" Bundy scratched his tousled head. "I might as well stay here, too, in that case."

"Then I can go, Mr. Donovan?" Cawley again asked, enthusiasm and hope bubbling in his voice.

"No—Bundy's going. Somebody's got to keep me out of trouble tonight."

The boy walked off dejectedly, stuck his hands in his pockets, and turned back, grinning. "Next time, Mr. Donovan—next time we come to N'awleans, I can have a good time and go to them places."

Drew laughed heartily. "The next time we come back here you might be too old to care about the pleasures awaiting a man in the bordellos."

Grinning, the youthful Cawley replied, "I'd have to be dead then, Mr. Donovan."

Drew gave last-minute instructions as to the nature of supplies to be purchased, and he and Bundy were soon walking along the bustling lanes of New Orleans. Street vendors hawked their wares—plump black women with oversize baskets precariously balanced on their heads, and muscular men carrying their weight in wares, their haunting chants advertising their specialties, "Oyster man! Oyster

26

man! Get your fresh oysters from the oyster man! Bring out your pitcher, bring out your can. Get your nice fresh oysters from the oyster man!" The thought of oysters, mingled with the nausea of too much whiskey the night before, made Drew want to turn back to that seedy hotel room.

As the chants of the oyster man faded into the early morning, Drew felt the rumblings of his stomach settle down. He set his gaze straight ahead, occasionally glancing at a comely feminine face, at full skirts with hoops, tight bodices, and well-trimmed hats. He noticed a gay old gentleman in a hat whose brim was too narrow for a fly to perch upon. Drew needed the smile that sight elicited. As his eyes picked among the various gaming establishments, he began to look forward to the arms of a pretty woman who would satisfy the primal craving inside of him.

Without warning, Drew halted; a chill crept down his spine. What had made him remember that morning of January 8, 1815 . . . a heavy fog, cool but not cold, the British columns moving forward in solid ranks. The American batteries had opened fire, the British advancing to within one hundred fifty yards of their lines. The American riflemen had opened fire, the British falling by the hundreds and only a few reaching the American breastworks.

God! Drew thought. *Why must I remember this now?* But it was as clear as if it had happened yesterday — shattered and depleted regiments retreating in disorder, the proud British Army vanquished, its bugles silenced, its colors trampled in the earth; the blood-soaked Chalmette Plain covered with dead and wounded British soldiers.

Bundy's hand brushed Drew's forearm. "Feelin' that whiskey, Drew?"

Snatched from his memories, Drew's gaze met that of his friend. He managed a half-cocked smile. "Yeah," he lied, "but I'm all right now." Forcing himself ahead, he called to Bundy across his shoulder. "Let's get me to that woman I'm aching for. That'll sure as hell sober me."

27

A face tried to form in his mind—a face without features, a blur without substance—a face he would briefly see again this evening and not recognize.

Drew wasted no time in choosing a bordello. He reluctantly allowed the black guard to relieve him of his weapons. The music wafting from the interior of the bordello helped him to make up his mind.

Stepping into the smoke-filled interior, the two men looked around. "What a fine covey here . . ." Drew's eyes moved fluidly over the comely, half-dressed girls, his gaze immediately halting on the one with flaming red hair who seemed oddly out of place in the decadent surroundings. "If the devil would but throw out his net."

"And snag only one, I'll wager." Bundy grinned lecherously. "Kind of figured you'd throw your line out for the best-tastin' one. Shame my brother wouldn't come along. He'd have liked that one over there . . ." he continued, pointing toward the golden-skinned Julia.

"Somebody's got to take care of the purchasing while we get in trouble," Drew mumbled, cutting his eyes to the approaching waiter. Within moments they were escorted to a table.

"Game of chance?" the immaculately dressed black man asked when they'd been seated. "Or shall I escort ladies of your choice to the table?"

"A bottle of your best whiskey," Drew replied, looking around the dimly lit interior. He liked to get a proper feel for a place, in the event that a quick escape became necessary. From the looks of the paneless windows draped in red satin, it appeared that some men had taken that route in exiting.

The waiter left a bottle of fine whiskey and two glasses at the table as a black dancer approached the table. He was dressed in baggy silk pants gathered at the ankles, glittering gold shoes with curled toes, and a red, wide-sleeved silk shirt. Over all this hung gold and silver chains and bangles and beads, but nothing as blinding as his bald, polished head and the large gold hoops hanging heavily from his ear-lobes.

Dancing before the two men, the black man fanned cards before them. "Magic, gentlemen? Shall Solomon demonstrate his magic?" Before Drew could decline, the man straddled a chair and drew himself up to the table. "Ah, good, you wish to see Solomon's magic!"

"I was about to say—"

Immediately, the entertainer's finger came up to his mouth to hush Drew. "Go along with me, monsieur." A wide grin exposed straight white teeth. His curiosity aroused, Drew fell silent. "Do you see the beautiful woman there? The one in the emerald dress, whose hair gleams like wildly dancing flames?" Drew's eyes cut to her. "Ah, yes, I see, monsieur, that you admire a beautiful woman." As he spoke, he fanned the cards, performing various tricks for the two men. "Do you wish to have her do your bidding for an hour?"

"What makes you think I am interested?"

"I believe you have, indeed, come here—you and your friend—not for the games of chance, but for the beautiful women who pleasure men."

"It is a whorehouse, is it not?" Drew asked indignantly.

"Bordello, monsieur," the man amended without admonishment. "We cater to better quality gentlemen."

Drew sipped his whiskey. "You are her pimp?"

"No, I am not. Merely say, monsieur, that you want Flame for the evening and I shall arrange it for you."

Drew was suspicious. He had been rolled of his money once in St. Louis, and if the burly black man dressed like a court jester was setting him up, he was in for a big surprise. "I would like to have that one," Drew said softly, slipping his wallet to Bundy under the table so the man would not see.

"You arrange it and we have a deal."

"And how much will you pay for Flame's favor?"

Drew narrowed his eyes and scrutinized the woman who sat alone on a long velvet settee. "How much are the girls getting these days?"

"Most, a picayune. But Flame, she is special. Fifteen dollars for her, no less."

"That's a pretty price. She'd better be worth it."

Smiling, the man stood. "I am sure I can arrange something for fifteen dollars."

Because Flame favored the daughter of his first beloved master, who had died, Solomon had taken to her the moment he'd met her. Unlike the others girls, the Englishwoman had befriended him and had confided in him about Junius Wade's plans for her. Seeking out his quarry, Solomon found Junius seated several feet away from Flame, keeping all men away from her until that special one came along.

"That man wants Flame," Solomon told him, nodding his head toward Drew.

"Which one?" Junius craned his head for a view of the vile male he would pair with Flame. When his eyes met Drew's, a vague familiarity flew through his head for but a moment. "That one? No, he is too good for her."

"Ah, but looks are deceiving, Monsieur Wade. He will pay twenty-five dollars for the privilege of beating one of your girls. And he wants the prettiest one."

"He wants to beat her, eh? But I had wanted a vile, despicable, smelly swine."

"But a beating, monsieur," Solomon entreated. "It will surely teach her the lesson she needs. A man who would beat a woman . . ." He had been about to finish, "knows no equal in wretchedness." Junius, of course, would take that personally, and Solomon did not want to feel the sting of the whip again so soon.

The loud music was deafening. Junius could see that

Flame had not overheard their conversation. He sensed her discomfiture in the tight-fitting dress that scarcely hid her heaving bosom, but the fear he had seen since taking her from the auction block was, for the moment, absent. That fear had to be restored if she was to be properly punished for what she'd done to him. A vile swine taking her sexually would humiliate and degrade her. But she would soon recover. Yes, a beating would be much more suitable. He would let another man do what he did not have the physical strength to do himself. It pleased him that she would accompany a fine-looking young man to one of the rooms upstairs, thinking she could safely talk her way out of satisfying his needs, and there he would beat her within an inch of her life. It pleased him immensely!

"Solomon, tell the man he has a deal. I want payment in advance and I don't want any permanent marks left on Flame."

Grinning, Solomon moved back into the gaming room and approached Drew. "Her master will take twenty-five dollars."

"Twenty-five dollars! Hell!" In the few minutes the black man had been gone, Drew had gulped enough whiskey to feel the effects. He had bargained for fifteen dollars. That he remembered quite well!

"She is the prize of the lot, monsieur, well worth the fee. And . . ." Solomon grinned, "she is unbroken, I understand."

"You got yourself a virgin," Bundy cackled, punching Drew's shoulder in boastful humor.

"Sure," Drew said caustically. "Like the cow in the bullpen. Don't be so damned gullible, Bundy."

"Why should he lie?" Bundy queried, swirling the whiskey in his glass.

A grin raked Drew's rugged good looks. "To make her worth that blasted twenty-five dollars I'm about to hand over. Give me the change purse."

Removing the necessary funds, Drew handed the cowhide purse back to his friend. He didn't want to have his pockets picked while his pants were lying in a heap on the floor. As he accompanied Solomon to the girl reclining on the settee, his eyes caught those of the man called Junius Wade. Though he did not know the reason for it, Drew felt the muscles of his chest suddenly tighten in revulsion. It had nothing to do with his evil, hideous looks. Drew was sure he had encountered him before.

Breaking his train of thought, Solomon said to Drew, "Now, you be good to that little girl. And don't you mess her up none, you hear? I shall see if your friend also wants the company of one of our ladies."

Solomon turned and placed his hand on Drew's chest to halt him. "Let me prepare her, monsieur. You will be her first."

Drew suppressed his grin. "Sure. Whatever you say."

The young woman stood when Solomon approached. He spoke to her in hushed tones, motioning toward Drew, who instantly caught the wide glance of sea-green eyes. Solomon coaxed her toward Drew, who could not help noticing her hesitation. He might have taken offense had the whiskey not made him light-headed and indifferent.

Carrie stood just outside touching distance of the man she had been sold to. His eyes raking the tight bodice of her dress, the swell of her bosom, the slim column of her neck made her shudder and fill with warmth at the same time. She had expected to be sold to a vile, slobbering drunk, not this remarkably handsome man with sable-colored hair and gray-black eyes that had yet to redden from the effects of the whiskey. He was broad-shouldered, slim-waisted, his muscular thighs straining against the tight fabric of his trousers, which were tucked into dusty black boots. Because of his appearance, she turned questioning eyes to Solomon.

"How is it that I've been sold to this man?" she questioned.

The gaudily attired Solomon smiled comfortingly. "I told Junius the man was paying for the privilege of beating you."

Carrie drew in a short, ragged breath, her fingers clutching at her neck as she did so. "Beat me?" Wide, terrified eyes cut briefly to Drew Donovan. "That man will . . . hurt me?"

Solomon whispered, "He will not hurt you. But Junius must believe that he will. Be sensible, *chérie*. Solomon is trying to help you."

"But, how—"

"Shh . . . too many questions, little one. Go with this man and do your duty. I will think of something afterward to satisfy Monsieur Wade."

Carrie trusted Solomon. He was gentle and kind and had taken an instant liking to her. She hoped he had noticed right away that she was out of her element. Lifting her head determinedly, Carrie moved toward Drew.

She paced silently ahead of him on the stairs, avoiding the beady eyes of Junius Wade. They had scarcely entered a large bedchamber draped in red and black, a large mirror anchored precariously over the velvet-covered bed, before Drew was atop Carrie on the coverlet. "Sir! Sir!" she whispered harshly, pressing her palms to his iron-hard chest. "Get off me!"

Her perfume assailed his delicate senses. His mouth moved to cover an exposed earlobe while his right hand roughly massaged the swell of her breasts. "Come on, pretty thing. I've only paid for an hour and there's much to be done. Now . . ." Boldly, his right hand cupped her firm breast, then eased beneath the scant fabric. "Out of your garments before I rip them off."

Terror filled Carrie Sherwood's eyes. "N-no . . ." Even as she stammered her protests, Drew Donovan was undoing the buttons of his trousers. A scream caught in Carrie's throat as his other hand fought with her voluminous skirts, traveled clumsily over her silken thighs, and twisted around the waist of her undergarments. Dragging them downward, he positioned his maleness against her tightly clamped thighs.

"Come on . . . come on, sweet thing," he slurred, again seeking her mouth. "I've paid good money for you. You do not need to play this coy act with me. I'll believe what you want me to believe."

Digging her fingers painfully into his hair, Carrie twisted him to his side, slipping out from under him as skillfully as a cat. "How dare you molest me!" she hissed, her eyes drawn hypnotically to his naked loins. She had never before seen a man—there!

"Molest you, hell!" Drew's eyes narrowed to mere slits as he repositioned his trousers. He could not very well reason with her with them dragging around his knees. "For the next hour every inch of your body belongs to me!"

When he dove toward her, Carrie flew off the bed. To find nothing but velvet covers beneath his hand was a slow-registering surprise to the inebriated Drew.

He became aware of the sounds of the gaming room below, and of high-pitched feminine laughter mingling with the lusty voices of men. He had been drinking off and on all day and had consumed his fair share of whiskey in the few minutes Solomon had bargained for the woman. He was not in the mood to have his quarry evade him at every turn. His animal lust was begging to be sated. Jumping to his feet in a fury, he pulled Carrie firmly against his body. "I'll not be cast aside by a Drury Lane vestal!" he hissed, employing the vulgar term for a London prostitute simply to infuriate her. "We're not playing ducks and drakes here, Princess! I've paid good money for you and I will collect!"

Because of his drunkenness, Carrie easily evaded his questing mouth. "Please . . . please, sir. You look like a sensible man—"

"Sensible, hell! I'm as drunk as David's sow. Will you keep still so I won't have to fight for that kiss I want." Running his fingers through the thick masses of her hair, Drew managed to still the evasive movements of her mouth. He smiled rakishly, his breath warm and intoxicating upon her cheek. "There, pretty lady. Flame, isn't it? Befitting you. Now, burn me with your sweet body—and if you dodge me again, I'll break your pretty neck!"

If nothing else could have sobered him at that precise moment, the renewed terror in her eyes had just that effect. His smile washed away and his eyebrows furrowed in a severe frown as fear radiated from her widened eyes, piercing him straight to the heart. "Blast it, woman . . ." he slurred. "You've almost got me convinced you haven't done this before!"

"I have not, sir," Carrie managed to whisper. "I am untouched." As the drunken glaze of Drew's eyes seemed to wane, Carrie's attentions focused once again on his masculine good looks. In the dim lights of the gaming room she thought his hair to be sable-colored, not the rich ebony that it now appeared. "Will you kindly remove yourself from me, sir?"

A sheepish smile returned. "If I do that, Princess, that sweet, soft flesh your gown could not confine will be exposed to this Yankee bastard."

He was teasing her; she could tell. Her cheeks were suddenly as crimson as the gaudy bedcoverings upon which he once again tossed her. As he moved, hoping once again for a glimpse of hidden treasures, she pulled the spread across her bodice and hid herself from his view. "Please, sir, you must listen to me. I . . . I do not belong here."

Lying beside her, he propped himself on one elbow and braced himself with the palm of his right hand. Only then did he notice her rich beauty—the full, shining, copper-colored tresses, the wide, almond-shaped eyes as crystal clear as the purest emerald, the sensual mouth, the skin as smooth as a dew-kissed rose. She was tall; he liked that in a woman . . . she was slim and graceful, even in her futile

35

attempts to fight his amorous attentions. In that moment, his actions shamed him, and he mentally retreated from the foreplay, though his words did not betray his intentions. "I paid for an hour, you've wasted ten minutes of it. I'll give you five minutes to tell me your sad tale before I take my pleasure with you."

Carrie sat upright, clutching the covers to her body. Her hand scooted beneath the coarse fabric in a feeble attempt to tighten the stays of her bodice. "Perhaps when you hear my story, sir, you might show me the mercy I deserve."

"Doubt it," Drew mumbled, his gray-black eyes narrowing to mere slits. He lay back on the bed and tucked his palms beneath his head. "You've got four minutes and fifty seconds. Forty-nine, forty-eight . . ."

Temper flared in Carrie's eyes. "Very well! Why must you be so impatient?"

"Because you are wasting my time. I want your pleasures, not a bedtime story."

Carrie pulled up the bodice of her gown, then let the bedcovers fall. She turned away from Drew, nervously wringing her hands. Scarcely a muscle moved as she told Drew her story, speaking softly so that Junius would not overhear, and taking only half the five minutes Drew had allotted her. Then she turned toward him, expecting sympathy and understanding—and possibly even his assistance in escaping from Junius Wade. But Drew's expression had not changed, except for a slight arching of his left eyebrow.

"Well, sir?"

Drew pulled himself to a seated position. Absently checking the cleanliness of his fingernails, he replied, "I'll say this for you, pretty thing, you've got quite an imagination."

"Ohhhhh!" For only the second time in her life—the first resulting in Junius Wade bobbing in the Gulf of Mexico—Carrie Sherwood resorted to physical violence. She flew at Drew Donovan, forcing him backward on the bed as her fists flayed at his chest. "I will not stand for your vicious degradations! I am a lady!"

Drew could scarcely stifle his hoarse chuckle as he grappled for her evasive fists, pinning them against the chest she had moments ago attacked. "I do believe you're going to provide me a good time tonight, you feisty English wench! Now put those energies to better use."

Suddenly, though, the trembling of her body against his own, the fear and vulnerability in her eyes and yet the strength, made him want her so desperately that he knew he could not take her like this, a man paying for a whore. He wanted her to lie with him because *she* wanted to, not because he had paid her pimp for the privilege. He wanted to blame the sudden trembling of his own body on the whiskey he had consumed, and yet he could not, in all good conscience, do that. The woman with flame-colored hair flowing across his neck and cheek was like no woman he had ever met. She made him wish he could believe her preposterous tale.

Losing his smile, he whispered huskily, "Tell you what, pretty thing . . ." As he spoke, he massaged her slim wrists, "I'll pretend to believe you've never before lain with a man, but I do not believe anything else you have told me . . ."

"But—"

"Don't press your luck. You lie beside me for the next three-quarters of an hour, and you make me feel good—"

"I will not have . . ." Carrie shuddered at her own words, *"that* . . ." She cut her eyes to his groin area, "digging at me!"

"Hell! What do you think I'm here for? Baby kisses?"

"I will lie with you, but you must not touch me!"

"I guess you expect me to tell old Junius that I've satisfied myself with you?"

Terror again filled her eyes at the thought of what he'd do if he knew otherwise. She remembered poor Kama, dragged by Junius to his private cabin to satisfy his wicked lust, then disappearing from the face of the earth. "I do, sir," she responded after a moment.

"I'm a bit of a rogue at times, I'll admit, but I don't usually lie." Taking her firmly by the arms, Drew pulled her to his side, then dragged the pillows down beneath their heads. "I think I threw away twenty-five dollars. Unless you change your blasted mind!"

Her gazed cooled. "I will not change my mind. And I trust you to be a gentleman."

Drew shrugged carelessly. "I don't mind being a gentleman. I just want my money's worth."

Without warning, Carrie let out with a spine-chilling scream that caused Drew to shoot up from his relaxed position.

"Christ, woman, what was that all about?"

Carrie propped herself on her elbow and managed her first smile of the evening. "Junius sold me to you because he wants me to be hurt and because Solomon told him you paid for the privilege of beating me. I tossed him into the Gulf of Mexico and he promised to sell me to the vilest man he could find."

Drew grinned. "And I am that man?"

"Apparently, sir. I am with you, am I not?"

"I believe I've been insulted."

"Surely not for the first time in your life?"

As they bantered insults, their gazes met, and Drew smiled again. He wanted the tall, comely Englishwoman. Perhaps when she felt relaxed with him, she would be more willing to satisfy his male needs. "Actually, for the second time," Drew replied, grinning. "I'm a nice fellow, actually."

"You're a drinker!"

Drew smiled boyishly. "Only when I take one of these trips for pleasure. Back home I hardly ever touch a drop."

"If I believe that, mister, that I'd believe in fairies."

"God! You mean there aren't any?" His playful sarcasm won him the narrow scrutiny of her exquisite eyes.

Any other man might have jumped atop her and taken

38

his pleasure with her, without prelude. The fact that Drew Donovan had not yet resorted to that violence did, indeed, make Carrie feel more relaxed. She thought, perhaps, that she might even like him, given the opportunity to be better acquainted. Perhaps too, if he liked her, he would help her contact her uncle in England if she could convince him of the truthfulness of her story.

An alien warmth flooded Carrie. She scooted to his side and propped her chin on his muscular chest, meeting his eyes. Her uncle had always referred to her as a bold little thing. "You have had too much whiskey, sir," she reminded him. "I am surprised that you will leave my virtue untouched."

"Not as surprised as I am," Drew replied, favoring her with his rakish smile. His hand went to her back and rubbed it very gently. "Hell, woman. Maybe it's all the whiskey that makes me afraid I'd embarrass myself if . . ."

Carrie's quizzical look indicated to Drew that she might possibly have no idea what he was talking about. Who would ever have expected to encounter a virgin in a New Orleans bordello?

"Where are you from, sir?"

He had closed his eyes for a moment but now opened them. "Pennsylvania."

"What are you doing here?"

"Brought my steamboat, *Donovan's Dream*, downriver to buy supplies."

"*Donovan's Dream?* Is that your name? Donovan?"

Rising to his full height, Drew bowed with grand flourish. "Andrew Cynric Donovan at your service, m'lady."

"You must be very rich to own a steamboat. Do you not have men working for you to accomplish such a menial task?"

"Actually, I made the trip myself expecting to have a good time—"

"With a woman who would do your bidding?"

"Something like that."

"Sir . . . ?" she ventured boldly. "Will you help me get back to my uncle in England?"

Easing to her side on the bed once again, Drew said, "And have your pimp hunt my hide from here to Wills Creek? Lady, if you had satisfied my needs, I might feel inclined to do something nice for you."

Shocked, she whispered harshly, "What an ungentlemanly declaration. You're something of an ass, aren't you?" Using expletives was one of the vices her uncle had often chastised her about. "If I were to lie with you and let you have your way with me, then you would help me? Sir, I'd as soon give myself to a sot."

"Right now that is just what I am." Drew's fingers rose to her pert chin to caress and hold it between his fingers. "Reconsider, pretty thing?"

"Not in a thousand—no, a hundred thousand years!"

"Then I shall report to your pimp that you are not worth twenty-five dollars."

Carrie moved to his side, her eyes wide and imploring, her mouth trembling.

Ah, what a mouth! Drew thought, fighting the urge to capture it against his own.

"Please, sir, do not do that. He will surely kill me."

"Why should I listen to your entreaties? You have not even given me one of your sweet kisses."

Her lips tightened; green fire burned in her eyes. "Were I to kiss you, sir, would you help me then?"

"I might consider it," he teased, his steady tone of voice distressing her.

"Very well." Puckering her mouth, Carrie Sherwood closed her eyes, the softness of their lavender lids capturing his full attention. His hands moved to grip her arms roughly, instantly relaxing into a gentle embrace. What a face! Smooth and unblemished, a full, pouting mouth puckered to receive his caress, rich, flaming hair clinging to the tiniest beads of perspiration across her forehead.

He had been teasing her about the kiss. Now, however, he could not deprive himself of the innocently offered reward. Slowly, lingeringly, he captured her mouth in the gentlest of kisses, pulling her close to him, massaging her slender arms through the silken fabric of the poufed sleeves, feeling the soft mounds of her breasts molded against his own hard chest.

Drew breathed intoxicatingly of her perfume, allowing it to flood his lungs and assail his senses. Suddenly, his hand was at her back, moving slowly upward to capture the sleeves of her dress once again to ease them down her arms.

The lovely lady of the evening seemed lost in his arms, giving herself completely, without abandon, allowing her body to become one with his own. Only when his right hand slipped beneath the bodice of her gown to again capture one of her breasts did she suddenly pull away, breathing heavily, her words gasping forth from between lips that had, just moments before, been his willing prisoner. "How dare you! How dare you use an innocent kiss to molest me!"

Drew grinned. "Thought you'd changed your mind and were going to earn that twenty-five dollars."

The brightly patterned Oriental rug was immediately beneath Carrie's slippered feet. She attempted to bring some semblance of order to her bodice. "Get out! I don't ever want to see you again! May hell be your destination!"

Humored, Drew rose to his feet, standing within touching distance of Carrie Sherwood. "Ma'am . . ." Returning his hat to his head, he flipped it back from his forehead with his middle finger. "I've been in this room with you for more minutes than I care to count. Hell would probably look like a picnic. Good night."

The vase she threw as he exited missed his head by scarcely a fingernail's width.

Chapter Three

During the next two weeks, Drew and his men purchased two hundred tons of the best freight to be had in the state of Louisiana—raw cotton, plantation sugar, and barrels of molasses and syrup; tobacco from the Caribbean, tallow, dried beef, and pork and cheese. With enough lumber to build a mansion and seedling trees wrapped in burlap, he feared *Donovan's Dream* might reel to a cruel fate at the bottom of the Mississippi. But the haul, which would leave much money in their pockets, was well worth the risk.

Drew decided on an early-Sunday-morning departure, hoping to outrun a squall moving in from the gulf.

"There's a fellow on the pier needin' to talk to you, Drew," Noble announced.

"What does he want?"

"Don't know. He's from the warehouse."

Dropping the ropes he'd been working with, Drew moved down the gangplank of the steamboat and approached the heavyset man waiting nearby. "Them forty barrels of molasses will be delayed until tomorrow, Mr. Donovan."

"Hell!" Drew gritted his teeth. "We were planning to pull out this morning."

"Sorry, mister."

"Can't be helped," he replied, looking across the southern horizon toward the incoming storm. "Just make sure they're

42

here first thing in the morning."

"A bit of bad luck," Noble remarked.

"I don't like delays—"

"That's because . . ." Bundy cut in with a throaty laugh, "he can't stop thinkin' about that feisty redhead in The Swamp."

Drew gritted his teeth to keep from replying and moved rapidly toward his cabin.

He had not returned to The Swamp, had not seen those exquisite emerald eyes again or touched the velvety skin, but Drew could not forget the tall, willowy Englishwoman known as Flame. His every waking moment was spent thinking of her, his sleeping moments dreaming of her. The thought of never seeing her again made him feel empty inside.

Once he had sobered up after that twenty-five-dollar encounter, he had wondered if the story she had told him was true. Had she been kidnapped from a lonely English channel and sold as a white slave? Had she been unmolested by men? And was she still? Her pimp had wanted her beaten. How had she explained an unmarked body after his departure? God! The thought of her being abused made him feel sick inside. And he didn't know why.

He wondered if she thought of him at all.

Actually, Carrie had not stopped thinking about the tall, muscular man from Pennsylvania. The memory of his hands so intimately touching her body brought a mixture of emotions. At one moment she was repulsed and ashamed and hated him, at the next, her body physically responded to the memories that were so vivid she might have been with him just that morning. The fact that he had left her untouched after paying twenty-five dollars for her gave some evidence of his character. Had he not been foggy-headed with drink, he might even have agreed to help her.

43

Immediately following Drew's departure from the bordello that night, the kindly Solomon had appeared with his makeup case, reddening her eyes, artfully applying blackening to resemble bruises, and daily altering the wounds to convince Junius of their authenticity. As Solomon had requested, she had complained to the other girls of a painful wrist, a wrenched back, a stiff neck, and headaches. Taking pity on her, Junius had spared her the attentions of paying gentlemen during her convalescence.

Today, however, he had decided to put her back into service. Her desperate pleas for further convalescence went unheeded, and Carrie was very aware of the immediate threat to her purity. With panic and dreaded anticipation pounding inside her, Carrie knew she had to act quickly. Desperate to escape from The Swamp and the vile man who would enslave her, she paid little heed to the approaching storm.

Drew's steamboat threaded its way around and between the many islands of the lower Mississippi. The wind was against him, making the pulling hard. Fog slowed progress of the noisy boat, and he feared hitting a sand bar in shallow waters.

The storm continued the following day, but they pushed on, the wind threatening to drive them against jutting crags with calmer water between them.

Three days later they had weathered the storm and steamed past the post of St. Francisville, where Cawley hid in one of the cabins lest his drunken father be looking for him from shore. Only when night had fallen and the post was half a day behind him did the boy emerge from between the barrels of molasses, fighting off bees that clung to his molasses-soaked right sleeve. The men shared a much-needed round of laughter as he flayed the air for the insects that had fled upon first attack.

Two weeks later they were riding the current fifty miles south of St. Louis, making better time than they had expected. Drew hoped to reach Louisville, where *Donovan's Dream* would sit in dock, by mid-December, sell the bulk of their supplies and make good time overland, arriving at the trading post with their loaded pack horses by early January. If the weather held up, they would be able to keep to their schedule.

Having eaten very little since the morning, Drew decided to stretch out his legs and enjoy a meal in the solitude of his cabin. He sliced bread on the wooden tray Cawley had brought in earlier and dug the lid off the pork barrel with his knife. "Damn boy!" he bellowed at the returning Cawley. "This barrel's pert near empty."

"You just don't have your eyeballs in your head," Cawley laughed, setting down a bottle of rum before moving back toward deck where Bundy stood. "Just opened that one yesterday."

Pushing over the barrel with his boot, at which time only a few scraps of dried pork spilled onto the deck, Drew yelled through the doorway at Cawley. "Then we have rats. You better get to digging among the supplies."

Dropping heavily against the rail, Cawley replied indignantly, "Ain't no rats done got by me, Mr. Donovan. I can sniff 'em a mile away."

"What you makin' such a stir about a barrel of pork?" Bundy asked. "We have plenty for the trip. Hell! We have plenty of everything since we bought supplies."

"I might as well worry about the pork. Just about every time I bring a plate of food to my cabin and leave it for any amount of time, something crawls in and eats it!" Drawing his hands to his narrow hips, Drew's eyes picked among the food items in his cabin, then toward the boy. Shrugging his shoulders as if the loss of the pork did not really matter, he stooped to pry the lid off still another barrel. Finding it full, he removed several strips and sat down to his meal. Soon

45

joined by Noble and Bundy, he forgot the missing pork.

From her hiding place between the lumber and the bales of cotton, Carrie had heard the men bantering words back and forth. Guiltily she looked down at the scraps of pork she had taken from the barrel during the night, then gathered them into the grease-stained folds of her gown.

She ate her stolen meal in silence, listening to the pleasant voices of the men, and, occasionally, a rather off-color joke, usually told by the man named Bundy. But salacious jokes aside, Carrie could not believe her good fortune. She had slipped aboard the large steamboat the night before its departure from New Orleans, and she still had not been discovered. She was pleased with her success as a stowaway. She prayed she could remain hidden until they docked at a city where some kindly soul might take pity on her and help her return to her uncle. She had heard the men speaking of a place called St. Louis. Perhaps there would be an efficient police authority there who might listen to her story.

Carrie looked forward to the evening and the men snoring loud enough to wake the dead. They usually gathered with the crew in the main dining room, giving her the opportunity to sneak into Drew's cabin, eat whatever food he'd brought there during the day, and take a much-needed bath. The boy, Cawley, always kept the cabin stocked with barrels of fresh, clean water. She had not bathed in three days and, despite the coldness of the unheated water, she could not wait to feel it against her skin, though she still longed for a hot, soapy bath in a tub large enough to stretch out in. She was surprised she had not come down ill in the foul nights, bathing in ice water and shivering the night away beneath a scant shawl and the canvas covering she had managed to pry loose from one of the bales of cotton. She longed for the warm comfort of Drew's cabin, where she often watched, through the open door, the men guzzling from a shared bottle of whiskey. She longed to join in their laughter, to be spoken to and noticed, to share a meal that might not be begrudged her, rather than having to sneak every parcel of food she put in her mouth.

But what would Drew Donovan do if he suddenly found her on board? Put her ashore in a remote forest along the river, where she might find herself surrounded by hostiles? Carrie shuddered at the thought. She had managed to stay hidden these past two weeks. They would reach St. Louis in a couple of days and he would be rid of her without ever knowing she had stowed away.

After eating the remains of the pork, Carrie lay back on her mattress of cape and canvas and tucked her hands behind her head. Though it made her cringe inside, she found herself thinking once again of Junius Wade. Oh, how furious he must have been to have found her missing! She still could not believe her luck that night. One of the other hotels had caught fire and all the men had gone to extinguish the blaze. She had fled along the narrow streets with nothing on her back but the dress she had been wearing and the thin matching cape that now lay in shreds beneath her slim body.

Once she had escaped from The Swamp, it had not taken long, asking directions and following leads, to find Drew Donovan's heavily laden steamboat. While the crew had slept, she had crept in, thanks to the drooping eyelids of the young night guard and had found her hiding place for the long journey ahead.

Wrapping her arms around her slim body to ward off the cold, she felt the grime-stiffened remnants of her emerald dress. How she had grown to hate green. Green, green, green! Junius had made her wear it constantly, because it complemented her eyes and her flaming hair. When she returned to England, she never wanted to see the color again! Not even on the trees or the shrubbery or the grass! She would confine herself indoors except during the winter months! If she ever saw green again, she would lose her stomach! Her eyes fluttering closed, Carrie enjoyed a much-needed afternoon nap.

As the sun began to sink in the west, chilling both the air and her bones, she awoke and began her patient wait for the men to settle down. This time of the evening they usually began to drink—men could be such vile creatures!—and soon afterward would seek their separate sleeping accommodations here and there about the steamboat, with no evidence of their existence except their loud snoring. The man Donovan, however, did not share that rude vice. She had never once heard him snore. Why did he insist on being so different from every other man?

Because his cabin was visible from her hiding place and he always slept with the door open, Carrie had been able to watch him nightly, his long, slim, well-muscled body reclining, his forearm resting lightly across the bridge of his straight, narrow nose. Oftimes, watching him made her blush furiously, as she remembered the exposed maleness of him pressed to her tightly clamped thighs, the silence of his gray-black eyes scorning her lack of cooperation. Warmth flooded her body at the memories—a strange, alien warmth with no visible source. Her thoughts and feelings and desires humiliated and degraded her, and yet filled her with a longing. Why did she have to wonder what it might have been like to have had him . . .

No, no, she couldn't think like that. She was Lady Charissa Sherwood, virtuous and clean, saving herself for the man her uncle would arrange for her to marry—a man deserving of her, a man bedecked in the latest finery of London's fashionable high society, who knew how to respect and love a woman, who would father her children and perform all the duties of a husband, a man who was rugged and handsome and—

Rugged? Well, that did not exactly fit into the mold of high London society. Rugged was for mountain men and common laborers, Americans . . . perhaps even an arrogant, self-centered Pennsylvanian who rode steamboats along dirty, swollen rivers —

Carrie was not sure why she felt the need to berate him for simply being what he was — a man. He had attempted to molest her that night in The Swamp, but he had thought he'd paid for the privilege. Perhaps it was time to forgive him . . .

Forgive him? Never! He could have helped her that night. He should have been sensitive to her truthfulness. He could have cared enough to have asked the name of her uncle and agreed to let him know where she was. Rather, he had worried about his lost twenty-five dollars!

Well, that was what he got for not knowing when he was in the company of a true lady. He had deserved to lose his money. He was an arrogant, egotistical bully, and she wanted only to be rid of him!

Carrie sniffed indelicately. Nightfall gave her the moment to move closer to the entrance of her hideaway. Soon the expected bottle of whiskey was making the rounds between the men who moved toward their rendezvous in the dining room. She had only to wait until she heard their boisterous laughter to slip into Drew's cabin.

The sky blazed red across the horizon. Hearing the snoring of some men and the laughter of others mingling with the faraway cries of the night creatures, Carrie crept from her hiding place and closed the door to Drew's cabin. She liked the masculine smell of him wafting among the heavy wood furnishings, and to touch his stationery upon a cluttered writing desk, and —

But enough! Locating the blue ewer, she began to fill the iron tub from the water barrel in the corner. Then she removed her tattered gown and underthings and slipped into the frigid water. She had learned to suppress that first startled gasp as the water threatened to lower her body temperature to fatal limits.

She stayed in the water just long enough to clean the grime from her delicate skin and wet her hair. Stepping out, she gripped the sides of the tub and sent its contents swooshing onto the deck. As always, the river of bathwater moved out onto the deck and was soon lost among the cracks. Hastily pulling her undergarments over her wet skin, she picked up her dress and moved stealthily toward her hiding place.

Suddenly, a shot rang out from deep within the steamboat, simultaneous with the piercing cry of a man. Hearing the men stir from within the dining room, Carrie scooted back into hiding.

The masculine cry of pain sobered the men and brought them to their feet. "What the hell was that?" Noble asked, scratching his dark temple.

"Probably a card cheater among the crew," Drew replied, arching his back against the stiffness.

"We in danger?" Cawley asked, genuine concern reflecting in his youthful gaze.

"Not unless you cheated the man, too." Drew's laughter eased the worry in the younger man's eyes. "I don't think we're in danger, but we better see where that shot came from."

But there was no need to investigate. One of the crew emerged from below deck clutching a bleeding hand. "Shot my blasted hand cleaning my gun!" he hollered. "Just goin' to bandage it, Mr. Donovan, and get back to my station."

Despite the reassurance that it was nothing more than an accident, Cawley set about gathering the weapons and checking them for fresh ammunition. Clumsily, he dropped a box of rifle balls. Falling to his knees he began gathering the slippery things into a knothole in the deck. Then, in the light of the single lantern he saw something alien between the bales of cotton, red and shiny and wet, lying upon the deck in limp strands. Hopping to his feet, he began to yell at the top of his voice. "Rats, Mr. Donovan. I done found me a big, wet, floppy rat over here!" Instantly, the wet tresses disappeared into blackness among the freight.

Drew laughed heartily, drawing his hands to his narrow hips as he did so. "You and your blasted rats, boy! Couldn't you have the common decency to see beautiful women instead?" He dragged his foot onto a small keg and watched the boy bounce about.

From her hiding place, the wide-eyed and terrified Carrie Sherwood's breathing had all but ceased. What if Drew Donovan investigated Cawley's claim? What if he dragged out the bales of cotton and the lumber and found her curled into her bundle in the darkness? What if he threw her overboard without a prayer? What if—

Too many *what ifs!* He wouldn't dare hurt Lady Charissa Sherwood! As a woman, she knew she had to have a certain allure, and she could, if she so desired, forget that she was a lady for a moment in order to win him over and humble his egotistical attitude. But would she resort to her feminine wiles? He was a man, she was a woman . . . If she could not coyly plead herself out of his disapproval, then she had not been properly tutored. She had eyelashes to flutter at him, a mouth that could pucker and tremble on cue, and tears that could flow freely if she so willed it. She had her ammunition at hand. Why then should she be so fearful of discovery?

Quickly, she eased herself into the remnants of her only gown, careful not to make a sound lest Cawley begin squealing again about his ridiculous rat. She heard the murmurings of the men, an accomplishment in view of the wild pounding of her heart, her eyes darting among the shadows of her hiding place for a niche where she might scoot to avoid being discovered.

Carrie clamped her hand over her mouth to still her breathing when bales of cotton and lumber began shifting beneath the hands of the searching boy.

51

"I'm sure he's in there, Mr. Donovan," Cawley said, dragging out a long length of board which threatened to bring the rest of the pile down on Carrie.

"Forget the rat," Drew ordered, a touch of annoyance lacing his voice. "He's probably got a wife and a litter to support and is doing no harm. Perhaps he's just trying to get back to Louisville with his ass in one piece."

"No, sir, that's a N'Awleans rat and I'm gonna git him. My pa never said much good about me, but he always said I was the best damn rat catcher east of the Mississippi."

"I said forget it," Drew responded on a note of finality. "I'm getting some shut-eye."

Carrie saw his highly polished black boots moving back and forth on the deck, his dark-brown pants tucked carefully into them. She watched the boots pivot and their wearer move in long strides along the deck of the steamboat. As his cabin door barred them from her view, all around her the lumber was shifting precariously. For the first time in two weeks, Carrie feared for her life.

Junius Wade stood at the small, dirty window of his room and looked out over The Swamp, at the shacks with their low-gabled roofs, built of rough cypress planks and lumber from old flatboats. He'd been so blasted angry these past few days that just last night he'd let a flatboat man have a drink, a woman, and a bed for the night for the ridiculous sum of six cents. From the teeming cesspool of iniquity that was The Swamp, Junius vowed to find his prize—his fiery English beauty—and bring her back where she belonged. He'd already had his slave Solomon punished for allowing her to escape, but what he'd gotten could not compare to the punishment in store for Flame. He had one last lead to follow. One of the saloon owners on Tchoupitoulas Street believed he might have seen a woman fitting Flame's description fleeing toward the docks on the night in question.

In a city whose population had swelled to almost twenty-eight thousand, finding one red-haired woman had proved to be quite a trial. He had only to wait until his courier returned to know in which direction to search for Flame. He would find her, even if he had to travel to the ends of the earth to accomplish it.

Pinching his chin, Junius snapped a "Come in" when a rap sounded at the door. One of his guards, a big, burly man, entered. "What did you find out?" The question was spoken with a razor-sharp edge.

"It was, indeed, Flame he saw, Mr. Wade. I made inquiries at the dock and spoke to a man who saw her board a steamboat."

Junius pivoted as sharply as his bent body would allow. "A steamboat? Which steamboat, man?"

"He wasn't sure. Said only that it departed the following morning."

When he paused, looking blandly at Junius, the elderly man spoke rudely. "Well? Is that all the information you have for me?"

"Two steamboats paid up their dock fees that morning and moved out—the *Vesuvius* and a privately owned steamboat, *Donovan's Dream*. The *Vesuvius* is sitting in dock at Natchez, the latter is traveling upriver."

A lost memory clicked in Junius Wade's brain . . . Donovan. Donovan! Donovan! "Philadelphia," he mumbled between his twisted lips. "Tanner, send Solomon to me!"

"Mr. Wade, something wrong?"

Flipping his one wrist, Junius scowled. "Just get him!"

Tanner backed into the corridor and momentarily returned with Solomon. Despite the lashing he had gotten shortly after Flame's escape, Solomon stood his full height before the man who owned him. "I am here, master."

Junius clicked his tongue in fury. "Solomon, the man who beat Flame . . . was his name Donovan?"

"I believe that is what she said."

53

Junius turned formidable eyes to his slave. "Tanner tells me she might possibly be aboard Donovan's steamboat bound upriver. Tell me, Solomon, why do you think she might feel safe in the company of a man who beat her?"

"I do not understand women myself," Solomon responded quietly, and certainly would not confess that she hadn't been beaten at all. "Is that all, master?"

The man's one hand raked the air. "Get out." He could scarcely contain his temper. "Tanner!" The man immediately appeared. "Hire a steamboat, no matter the cost, and a good crew. We're going upriver."

Tanner was preparing to withdraw from his brooding employer when both men heard a commotion from the gaming room. "I be danged if I ain't a yellow bantam pullet, but I seen that fella deal a keerd from his sleeve!" a voice proclaimed.

A declaration like that was usually followed by gunshots. Tanner stalled until the expected volley, followed by a heavy thud, reverberated through the walls. "I'll call for a doctor or lay out the bodies, whichever is appropriate," he said, before departing.

If Junius had heard Tanner, his features gave no sign. He continued standing at the window, stroking the stubble of his chin, thinking thoughts that could only be bred by a demented mind—blackened walls crashing in, pain shooting through his arm as he suddenly found his hand separated from him by several feet . . . his flesh sizzling against the flames . . . his lips afire . . . burning clothing searing into what was left of his flesh.

Junius shivered, but not from the November chill. *Philadelphia*. Why had that historic city popped into his mind along with his gruesome thoughts? And why did it linger so? Had he visited there at some time before his memories had been lost? And the name . . . Donovan. Why had the mention of that name caused him to grit his teeth so tightly pain had shot through his jaw?

Junius felt sick at the pit of his stomach. He might have fallen if he had not dropped heavily into the nearest chair. Despite the chill, sweat popped out on his brow. His forehead creased, deepening the pits in his grotesquely scarred flesh.

Fearing the nightmares that had been cruelly plaguing him lately Junius fought sleep that night and worked himself into a terrible state. A gurney had to be employed the following morning to transport him to the stern-wheeler *Racer*. His state of half-consciousness did not prevent him from barking orders, though they were not sensible enough to obey, and Tanner confined him to a large cabin to be cared for until he reached some degree of reasonable recovery. By midmorning, *Racer* had moved fifty miles northward on the mighty Mississippi.

The falling lumber immediately halted the probe of Cawley Perth's long, bony fingers. He scooted backward on his rear just as the neat stack of lumber crashed to the deck with a mighty clatter. Every man above the engines responded to the explosive noise, including a very irate Drew Donovan.

"Damn it, boy, I told you to stop digging for that rat! Now look what you've done. I ought to throw you out into the current!"

"I'll clean 'er up, Mr. Donovan."

Drew began snapping his fingers at the air in a most irritable fashion. The crew gathered and began putting the lumber into some semblance of order. Drew was just returning to his cabin when one of the men called out, "There's something here, Mr. Donovan . . . God, it's a body!" Immediately, the long lengths of board began hitting the deck.

"Damn, Cawley! Didn't you see anyone about when you were rat hunting?" Drew asked in irritation.

"N-no, Mr. Donovan," the boy said softly, scratching at

his head. "I swear, weren't nobody about."

"Well, who ever it is in there didn't come out of thin air!"

Drew stood to the side, taking the boards handed to him and stacking them in a neat pile behind him. A very slender hand, streaked with blood, came into view. It lay there, lifeless, connected to an arm covered with tattered green satin. Drew got to one knee and touched the hand. The blood had come from a small puncture wound on the underside of the index finger.

Within moments, the men gathered around to view the limp, lovely form of the stowaway. "My God," Drew exclaimed. "It's the English girl from The Swamp!" Bundy had made a point of telling the crew about the twenty-five dollars Drew had wasted. The men now took advantage of the opportunity to tease him about his folly, but Drew pretended to hear none of it. "What the hell is she doing here?"

Even as he spoke harshly, Drew picked Carrie up tenderly and cradled her within his strong arms. As he moved toward his cabin with her, he yelled at Cawley. "Get the captain over here. He claims to have some medical expertise." Several of the men moved toward the cabin behind him, still guffawing. "You fellows better get on back to work before we hit a sandbar."

Dropping to one knee, Drew placed Carrie gently on his cot. Sweeping the hair back from her forehead, he said softly, "So you are the little rat who has been sneaking in and eating my meals." His fingers traced a path across her temple, feeling the shallow throb there, then down the slim column of her neck. Noticing a tiny trickle of blood at her hairline, he investigated and found a small cut and a nasty bump. At that moment, the captain, short of stature and wide of girth, strained to get through the doorway.

"What have we here, Mr. Donovan? A stowaway?"

"An injured one," replied Drew, rising from his knee. "She has a nasty bump to the head and a cut on her right hand."

The captain bent over and touched his hand to the area of the first wound. "Quite a pretty stowaway, eh?"

"As pretty as they come, I would imagine," Drew replied, trying unsuccessfully to portray indifference. "Is she all right?"

A shallow moan suddenly came from Carrie's parted mouth. Her head moved slightly and she tried to touch her hand to her face. Captain Wyatt took her hand and roughly patted it. "I think she'll recover, Mr. Donovan. I'll dress her wounds and . . ." Briefly touching the tattered fabric of her gown, he continued. "Perhaps that boy of yours will go through the ladies' garments you purchased for your trading post and find something suitable for her."

Since he felt personally responsible for causing her accident, Cawley had been waiting just outside for news of the pretty stowaway's injuries. "I'll find something, Mr. Donovan," he said, excitement and relief raising the pitch of his youthful voice.

Captain Wyatt had brought a small brown bag with him. He used whiskey to clean the two small wounds, salved both, and bandaged her hand. In departing, he grinned widely and said, "I leave the young lady in your able hands, Mr. Donovan. It is, after all, your steamboat, and stowaways are your problem. Besides, one of the crew tells me she owes you."

Drew gritted his teeth and did not respond to the captain's boisterous laughter as he exited. He looked down at the pretty girl the man Solomon had called Flame. Her waist-length hair was damp and disheveled, her tattered clothing scarcely able to cover her slim body. The soft, supple swell of her most feminine curves heated his body through and through. Trying to put his thoughts elsewhere, he wondered how she had survived the frigid weather in her hideaway of boards and raw cotton.

Drew sat on a small stool beside the cot. Propping his elbows on his knees, he linked his fingers beneath his chin.

How fair and lovely the English woman was . . . and how determined she must have been to escape The Swamp that she would hide these past two weeks aboard his steamboat, with no luxuries and having to steal every morsel she'd eaten. Why couldn't she have trusted him? Did she think he'd have thrown her overboard without a prayer? Had he been such a loathsome creature that night in the gaudy chamber that he had left that impression on her?

Touching his fingers lightly to her hairline, Drew whispered, "My little British beauty, where do you propose that *I* sleep tonight?"

"Not with me" came her very shallow reply. Drew, thinking she had been unconscious, wrenched his fingers away. Carrie's almost translucent eyelids opened, revealing her exquisite emerald eyes. "That boy and his rats . . ." Her tone did not change, "just about done me in."

Drew smiled. "True English ladies don't say 'done me in'."

"But true English ladies have scullery maids who do." Carrie's hand lifted weakly to the wound atop her head. When she flinched, Drew took her hand and held it warmly.

"Are you going to toss me overboard, sir?" she asked.

Drew shrugged lightly, favoring her with his easiest smile. "What else should I do with a stowaway?"

Their eyes met and held . . . emerald ones and gray-black ones, so very close and yet so far apart. She wondered why he was not angry with her. He wondered why she had been so desperate to escape. Cutting her eyes from his own, Carrie said quietly, "You could be a gentleman and help me return to my uncle in England."

"Is it the only way I'll be rid of you?"

"Is getting rid of me something you desperately wish to do?" Her gaze lifted teasingly . . . seductively . . . to his features.

A grin raked Drew's chiseled, masculine features. "Not really." Carrie attempted to sit up, but pain grabbed her head. Then, noticing her bandaged hand, she asked, "Am I injured badly?"

"Not too badly, Flame," he replied.

"Carrie . . . my name is Carrie Sherwood. Did you forget?" The warmth in his eyes startled her. These past two weeks she had often seen him on deck, barking orders, engaged in games of chance with the men, enjoying the lewd stories told by some, and drinking himself into insensibility some nights. Why then, did he have a strangely soft look in his eyes? Attempting to change the mood of the moment, Carrie managed a small smile, "Sir, I hope you don't intend to collect from me that which you did not succeed in claiming before."

Rising, slapping his knees as he did so, Drew laughed. "Pretty thing, you read my mind. But you must be prepared to pay your passage in some fashion."

Carrie drew in a shallow breath, even as the prospect of paying her passage in such a fashion appealed to her adventurous though virginal spirit. "You are jesting with me, surely."

Drew approached the cabin door, then leaned lightly against the facing. "You wonder about that . . . and keep on your guard. Men are lecherous creatures who will take their pleasures at almost any cost."

"Including you, sir?"

Smiling, but failing to respond, Drew pulled the door shut.

Carrie managed to sit up, noticing only then that she had been in so great a rush to pull on her gown that it scarcely concealed her breasts. Crimson touched her otherwise pallid features. The musky, manly aroma of Drew Donovan permeated the chamber. She breathed deeply, enjoying the lingering fragrance of him.

That he would probably return in a few minutes filled her with excitement, and a warmth that took the chill out of the November air.

Chapter Four

Carrie suddenly found herself the center of attention aboard *Donovan's Dream*. Cawley had brought her several fine dresses and accessories from the lot Drew had purchased for his trading post, and a special place stood reserved for her in the dining room. The following day she was flattered to find the men vying for the privilege of sitting next to her at the meals and accepting a draw from the cards to determine the winners.

Drew Donovan, however, had taken up residence in a smaller cabin and had yet to make an appearance for the day. At midafternoon, she found the attentions of the men a bit overwhelming and retired to the cabin where Drew had taken her the night before.

Neither of her wounds had been disabling, and nothing more of her ordeal than an annoying headache and stiffness in her cut finger lingered.

She had just rebandaged her hand when a rap sounded at the door. Thinking it might be Drew Donovan, she hopped up, only to find the youthful face of Cawley Perth grinning at her from the doorway. Tipping his hat, he asked, "Anything I can git you, Miss Sherwood? Mr. Titus done made some fine buttermilk biscuits."

"No, nothing, thank you." Again tipping his hat, Cawley turned away. "Cawley." The boy turned back at the mention of his name. "Is Mr. Donovan about?"

"He's working on the books in the other cabin, since you put him out of his own. Don't want to be disturbed, he says."

"Oh, I see."

Carrie was disheartened. Last evening he had seemed almost pleased to have her aboard, had joked with her and, upon returning to her following her rest, had reminisced pleasantly about their first awkward meeting. Was he now avoiding her? Surely he'd had these past two weeks to work on ledgers. Why would he choose to do so today?

Carrie stood for a moment, feeling the chill upon her shoulders. He'd said he didn't want to be disturbed. Well, that was too bad. Lifting her skirts slightly, Carrie moved briskly toward the cabin where he'd confined himself.

She started to knock, then hesitated. Gathering her courage and thinking that perhaps he wouldn't be so bold as to bite her, whatever his mood, she knocked gently at the door. From within, a masculine voice called, "Enter!"

Slowly, Carrie pushed the door open. Drew Donovan turned his head, and his eyes narrowed as they pierced the semidarkness toward her. She suddenly wished she hadn't bothered him.

But she did not see what Drew Donovan saw. He'd narrowed his eyes against the blinding brightness of the afternoon sky and the light that had ignored the fabric of her skirts as if it did not exist. The slim outline of her body had been revealed to him, her loose hair had become a flaming halo wavering in the cool breeze now wafting toward him. Her features were little more than an indistinguishable blur, but beauty radiated there. Drew Donovan's body was flooded by a wondrously painful need.

"Miss Sherwood," he greeted, rising to take her hand. "I am pleased by your visit."

"I thought perhaps you were angry with me."

Drew's dark eyebrow arched in surprise. "Why would you

61

think that?"

"You left me last evening promising to look in one more time and say good night, then I did not see you again. When the boy brought the dresses for me, I changed into one I thought you'd like and awaited your return. But you did not return."

Drew released her hand, surprised that she would want to please him. "But I did, Miss Sherwood. After our talk, I returned several times while you slept to make sure you were all right."

A tiny frown touched Carrie's forehead. "You saw me . . . in my undergarments?"

Drew laughed, turning away to pour a sherry into a delicate crystal goblet, which he handed her. "You were well covered, Miss Sherwood, I assure you. I saw nothing you would not have wanted me to see. Now . . ." Drew crossed his arms. "What is it you wish to see me about?"

Carrie looked into his mellow eyes. She remembered last evening when she had wondered if he would be so cruel as to drag her from her hiding place and cast her into the swirling current of the Mississippi. Now he was being cordial and polite and acting as if he was pleased to have her aboard. Suddenly suspicious, she wondered what his thoughts truly were.

"Sir, I have stowed aboard your steamboat. You must be terribly irritated with me."

"Why must I be?" asked Drew. "You're causing no hardships. If you had a problem with Mr. Wade, then I am the last person who would expect you to stay with him. I believe in people being free and doing what they wish to do, not doing someone else's bidding. I would not, however, want Mr. Wade to track me down because you are aboard. But if he does, I will handle it."

Carrie had considered that possibility but had put her fears at the back of her mind. They now came forth, clouding all other thoughts. "I would not wish to jeopardize you,

Mr. Donovan. I shall disembark in St. Louis and seek out a kindly soul to help me."

"There is no need."

"What do you mean?"

"If you will graciously accept my assistance, I shall see that you return to England."

Releasing a delighted squeal, Carrie threw herself into his arms. "Sir, you would do that for me? You will help me return to England?"

"I will even pay your passage."

Frowning, Carrie drew away from him. She was terribly suspicious of his motives and wondered what manner of beast might lurk beneath that gentle facade. "Why would you help me? Do you now believe what I told you about my uncle, and about my being kidnapped from the Isle of Wight."

Drew turned slightly, poured himself a sherry from the decanter and lifted it to his mouth. He did not mean a thing he was about to say but, God, she was beautiful when angry, and he felt a playful urge to drag out that becoming state. After all, it was very vital that he keep her constantly on her toes, wondering as to his true motive. "My dear lady, I am no fool. But again, I am not concerned with the reason you wish to flee to England. If it is your pimp, so be it, or one of your paying customers who felt cheated—with whom I certainly sympathize—that is your problem."

Carrie's goblet crashed to the floor. Before Drew could protect himself, her slim hand had viciously attacked his face. "I should have known that an American couldn't be a gentleman! I should have known that beneath your gentle exterior lurked the black heart of a snake!"

Drew rubbed his stinging cheek and spoke with as much sweet sarcasm as he could muster. "You said you were a lady, my dear."

Stomping her foot in a childish fashion, Carrie's body stiffened defensively. "I *am* a lady! How dare you insinuate otherwise!"

She turned to storm from the cabin when a loud explosion rocked the boat. It keeled starboard, throwing Carrie backward into Drew's arms. Black smoke bellowed over the decks and a frantic masculine voice yelled out, "Volcano in the engine room! Volcano in the engine room!"

Rising to the alarm, and placing his priorities elsewhere, Drew merely pushed Carrie away from him. "Damn, the engine blew! We'll take this up later, woman."

Carrie sat back on her bustle on the wide cot where he had pushed her. " 'Woman'!" she sniffed. "Whatever happened to 'Miss Sherwood'?" Then it took only a moment to place her own priorities, and she didn't relish the idea of becoming ashes aboard a burning steamboat.

Drew had run into a panic on deck. Men rushed to and fro with buckets of water drawn up from the Mississippi, and rolling black smoke made it almost impossible to see more than a few feet in any direction. Drew spied Captain Wyatt. "Anyone hurt?" he asked.

"There's a man dead. Don't know who."

Drew felt his heart skip a beat. Just an hour ago Noble had been in the engine room. He set about in a frantic search for his childhood friend, eventually running into Bundy. "Have you seen Noble?"

Bundy formed one link in the line of men bringing water up from the river. "Haven't seen him for about an hour, Drew."

On the shore a crowd was gathering . . . men, women, and children. Boatloads of men, including the local Indians, moved through the current toward the steamboat. With their help, the fire was brought under control and, afterward, three dozen exhausted men scattered about on the deck to rest. Noble still had not made an appearance, and Drew feared the charred body being brought up from the boiler room was that of the man who had been raised with him as a brother. He was repulsed by the sight, and took a moment to pray the poor fellow had died instantly.

As Drew returned to his cabin and dropped wearily onto the cot, Carrie appeared at the doorway. "Did you find your friend, Mr. Donovan?" she asked.

Drew looked up, scarcely able to see her through the blur of moisture-sheened eyes. "No, I didn't." Flicking the tears away before she could know their true nature, he feigned an explanation. "That blasted smoke . . ."

Carrie started toward him, but he quickly arose, turning almost rudely away from her. Her slim hand fell to his shoulder. There were no words she could speak in comfort. "I apologize for striking you. I should have known you were teasing me," she offered.

"Yes, of course I was," he replied with forced gruffness. "You didn't hurt me, so don't let it bother you." Turning toward her with recaptured composure, he said politely, "I would like to be alone."

After she had closed the door, Drew dropped to the small table where he'd been catching up on his ledgers. Linking his fingers, he drew them to his forehead. "Noble. God, Noble, how could you do this?"

"Looking for me, Drew?"

Drew came out of the chair so quickly one might have thought he'd been shot. Noble stood in the doorway, dragging a dirty handkerchief across his grease-soiled forehead. Quickly closing the distance between them, Drew roughly embraced him, then lifted him off the floor. "You blasted scalawag! I thought you'd been killed!" Releasing him, Drew shook him firmly by the shoulders.

"That was poor Cullen," Noble replied. "The fire and smoke trapped me the other side of the boiler room. But I damn well thought I'd be joining the unfortunate fellow."

Drew gritted his teeth as he thought of the unfortunate young Canadian. "But thank God you're alive, my friend."

Noble arched a dark eyebrow. "I would have thought with the English girl aboard you wouldn't have given me a second thought."

Drew managed a soft chuckle. "My friend, I would have been concerned for you had there been a thousand English girls aboard."

Noble poured himself a brandy from Drew's private stock. "What will Jolie think if the Englishwoman is still with you when we return to the trading post?"

Upon reaching her cabin, Carrie remembered something else she had meant to ask Drew and immediately turned back. When she heard the word "Englishwoman" spoken she hesitated just outside of Drew Donovan's cabin, only a little ashamed that she eavesdropped on the two men. She had not heard Jolie Ward's name mentioned in their conversation, and assumed they spoke of herself.

Pressing herself against the wall, she turned her right ear to their voices.

"I couldn't care less what she thinks," Drew Donovan replied to his friend's question. "I need to get rid of her. She is a burden to me, Noble. How about you? Will you take the woman off my hands?"

Carrie clamped her hand over her mouth, shocked yet curious as to the handsome Indian's response. "Hell," Noble barked, sipping at his brandy. "The woman takes to my . . ." The fact that he had never told Drew of their sexual liaison halted Noble's words. He quickly amended himself, cringing from his lie. "The woman wouldn't take a full-blooded Seminole to her bed. She thinks she's a lady. We both know it is your bed she is waiting to crawl into."

"What she wants and what she will get are two different things. You either marry her, Noble, or I'll send her packing. It's as simple as that. The woman is a millstone around my neck. I never wanted her around to begin with, and when she suddenly appeared . . . Well, you know how I feel. Let us drop the subject before I work myself into a heated sweat."

Hearing the men approach the door, a very shocked Carrie Sherwood moved swiftly toward her cabin, closing the door the instant the two men appeared.

Clasping Noble's shoulder, Drew said, "Let's see what damage has been done and arrange to bury Cullen." He found himself searching along the deck for Carrie Sherwood. Try as he might, he could not get her out of his mind.

A mixture of emotions flew through Carrie's brain—shock, anger, humiliation, hurt. How could one man be so outrageously egotistical to even think that she—Lady Charissa Sherwood—was anxious to hop into his bed? Since being discovered aboard *Donovan's Dream* yesterday, she had tried not to be any trouble and certainly had not conducted herself wantonly. Drew Donovan had said she was a millstone. How could that be? She hadn't even been in his life long enough to become a certified nuisance. All her pent-up emotions suddenly flooded her heart and she dropped facedown upon the small cot. She thought of her uncle and home and the vile American slavers who had kidnapped her, of Junius Wade and his whorehouse, and now, Drew Donovan, the one man she had thought would ultimately help her, and who had even offered to do so. He did not want to help her. He wanted only to be rid of her.

Why then had he lied to her? He had said he would assist her in any way he could. Even as he had teased her unmercifully he had been every bit a gentleman, except, perhaps, for that first night in The Swamp. That episode she could easily blame on his state of inebriation, though. He had expressed doubts about her motives, yet he had offered to pay her passage back to England. What a strange, strange man he was! As hard as she tried to force herself, Carrie could not cry in her disappointment. She'd gone through five months of pure, unadulterated hell since being forcibly taken from her beloved England. She wanted only to be rid of this untamed American land and now the Pennsylvanian who would offer her in marriage to his Indian friend.

If he wanted to be rid of her, then so be it! At that moment she realized she was simply too angry to cry. She would play his dirty little game. He would find that she could swing her moods left and right with the same success as he.

Late that afternoon, with the help of a family of locals, the men of *Donovan's Dream* buried Ira Cullen on the banks of the Mississippi River. Thereafter, an estimate was made of the engine's damage and a tally taken of the parts needed to make her seaworthy once again. The smoke had made the damage seem insurmountable, and, though extensive, repairs could be made. It would take some time and a bit of money.

Drew decided to journey along the river to St. Louis to arrange for the transport of parts and to begin proceedings at the Bank of St. Louis to have the necessary funds sent from Philadelphia. That would take at least several weeks.

As he prepared to begin the trip the following morning, Drew was furious that their return to Wills Creek would be delayed. The snows would have set in by the time they returned, and travel would be slow. Sitting back in his chair, with the front legs perched precariously above the deck, he covered his closed eyes with his forearm.

"Mr. Donovan?"

Drew's eyes opened at the sound of the only feminine voice aboard, but he did not remove his arm. "Yes, Carrie?"

Though she was angry with him, she liked the sound of her name on his lips. "I would like to travel with you to St. Louis."

The chair legs hit the deck with a resounding thud. "It is

a fifteen-mile walk."

"Surely the locals would lend horses."

Drew normally did not discuss this weakness in his character. "Horses are for pulling wagons and freight. I ride the river and walk the land. I do not ride horses. Besides, why do you wish to journey to St. Louis?" His brief but very heated argument reminded him of that terrifying moment in his childhood when a skittery horse, purchased as a gift for his tenth birthday, had backed him in the corner of the stable, crushing him. When he had emerged from a seven-day coma, the horse had been taken away and he hadn't liked the beasts much since, riding only when it was absolutely necessary.

"I want to return to my uncle and—"

"I told you," Drew huffed, clenching his fists into balls, "that I would assist you in returning to England once we reached Pennsylvania." He was not sure why he was allowing her to irritate him.

How dare he say one thing to her face and another behind her back! Carrie bit her lip to keeping from giving him a good piece of her mind. "I am in the way here."

Why was she provoking him? Drew had enough troubles without her becoming one of them. Taking long strides, he approached and gripped her arms firmly. Seeing a moment of pain flit across her face, his grip relaxed into a gentle embrace, relaxing, simultaneously, the anger he had felt. Threatened by an overwhelming desire to kiss her, he shook off the urge. He was not partial to having his face slapped again. "Has any man here threatened you?"

"No."

"Has any man here been less than a gentleman?" He smiled. "Besides me?"

Carrie shrugged. "No."

"Why then are you being argumentative?"

Gently extracting herself from his arms, she wanted to scream her indignation, to confess that she had eavesdropped on his conversation with Noble. But she was too much a lady to make such a despicable confession. "Mr. Donovan—"

"My friends call me Drew."

"I am not your friend." Carrie instantly regretted that declaration. Though he had teased her about her English roots, he had never been unkind to her. She turned away, trying to fight the exasperation and the strange warmth rising together from somewhere deep inside her. Why couldn't she remember that he did not want her around? "Please forgive me, Drew," she said quietly, indulgently. "At times I have no manners."

Rather than respond with anger, Drew approached and folded her within his strong arms. "You called me Drew. I hope this cumbersome Mr. Donovan and Miss Sherwood formality is at an end. And . . ." When she gently attempted to extract herself, he turned her to face him, adding, "you may accompany me to St. Louis, if that is what you wish."

How easily she had gotten her own way. Miffed by his concession, she did not reply. Rather, her full, moist mouth parted, then trembled oh so slightly. Her fingers closed over his forearms and tightened, her eyes narrowing to meet his own, transfixed. There were words in her heart that would not form on her lips. She wanted to scream her indignation, and at the same time, she wanted to tell him how he made her feel—warm and sweet and womanly.

Drew was suddenly curious. He had agreed to allow her to accompany him to St. Louis. Why then was she being so obviously sensual? Her breasts moved lightly against the fabric of her plain blue gown, and the cream-colored shawl she had been wearing, fallen to the floor at her skirts, was absently ignored.

Drew did not release her, even when a silent, grinning Cawley Perth appeared at the cabin door. Without taking his eyes from Carrie, he addressed the boy. "Cawley, bring me one of those shirts and a pair of the britches you bought for yourself in New Orleans."

The tow-headed lad scratched at his ear. "What for, Mr. Donovan?"

"The lady is traveling along the river to St. Louis with me. She will need sensible clothing for travel."

Carrie dragged in a deep, surprised breath, immediately easing herself from his grasp. "Britches! I would never wear men's britches! It's . . . ungodly!"

"But you will, Carrie," Drew said quietly. "I won't have you tripping over skirts for fifteen miles along muddy banks. And, Cawley . . ." Ignoring the emerald fury in her eyes, Drew looked across her shoulder. "Bring her a pair of boots—small ones. And a warm coat."

Cawley walked off, scratching his head and laughing lightly. "Boy, I sure gotta see this!" His words drifted painfully back to Carrie Sherwood.

Her eyes flashed fury as they bore into Drew Donovan. Why was he attempting to humiliate her? "I will *not* wear men's clothing!"

"You will," he countered, sober-faced, "or I'll undress you and put them on you . . . even if you squirm and protest and scream your lungs out. I don't care how long it takes me to accomplish the task."

"You wouldn't force me." Carrie's voice was deliberately sure and calm. "I dare you."

Drew managed a half-cocked smile. "Pretty thing, it might interest you to know I have never in my life passed up a dare."

Meeting his steady gray-black gaze, Carrie imagined that she'd met her match. She had always been one to seek adventures—after all, hadn't she gone swimming off the coast that fateful morning in June in nothing but her unmentionables? If he wanted her in men's clothing, then she would wear them. He was probably trying to get an argument out of her anyway. And she had no doubts he'd humiliate her by

71

dressing her in the clothing himself if, indeed, she attempted to wrestle against the demand. "Very well," Carrie replied after a moment, her chin lifting haughtily. "I will wear the clothing, as long as it is clean." Without awaiting his response, Carrie pivoted on her heel and quickly left his cabin.

Though they would not depart until the following morning, Carrie forced herself to put on the clothing within moments of Cawley bringing it to her. The trousers, made for a man's body, clung to her feminine curves. She moved a small mirror Drew used for shaving up and down her slim body, trying to see how she looked in the outrageous garb. If not for her long, flaming hair, she might very well have been mistaken for a prepubescent boy. How shocked her uncle would be to see her dressed so!

She was disappointed that Drew Donovan felt this need and was not willing to let him think he had gotten away with humiliating her. She tucked her thumbs into the pockets of the tight-fitting pants and made herself stroll out on deck.

Within moments, a crowd of men gathered around her. She laughed deliberately loud in response to their gentle chidings so that Drew Donovan would hear her. The ploy worked and his tall, well-muscled frame emerged from the darkness of his cabin.

His eyes narrowed as they scanned the group of men. Had Carrie's long, flaming hair not caught his eye, he might have thought she was one of the crew. He moved in long strides toward her, his eyes narrowing almost threateningly. "What are you doing, Carrie?"

She smiled her widest smile. "Why, Drew, darling," she responded with heavy sarcasm, "I was showing the men my new attire." Turning in a circle with her arms outstretched, she asked, "What do you think?"

Rather than respond, Drew's right hand went out and locked around her wrist. He pulled her from the ranks of the men. "Come with me."

Carrie attempted to free herself from his brutal grasp and looked imploringly toward the group of men. "What are you doing?"

When he had pulled her into his cabin and closed the door, he released her wrist. "Keeping you from making a fool of yourself," he explained irately. "Those trousers are too tight. Don't wear them in front of the men."

To keep from smiling, Carrie arched a copper-colored eyebrow and pressed her mouth into a thin line. Linking her fingers at her back, she kicked an imaginary stone against his shinbone. "You don't like my trousers, Drew? I thought they were charming."

"I did not say I didn't like them. I said 'don't wear them in front of the men.' "

"You are a man."

"I won't deny that. But if they make *me* look twice, imagine what they do to the others."

Unlinking her fingers, Carrie moved them deliberately up Drew Donovan's clean white shirt. Clasping his shoulders, she lifted arrogant eyes to his own, noticing the nervous tick in his right cheek. She had gotten to him; that pleased her. "Whatever do you mean?"

Again grasping her wrists, Drew brought her hands down from his taut shoulders. "Don't play games with me, Carrie." Her mouth trembled so close to his own. He was not sure whether she was stifling humor or tears, but her full, sensual mouth was like a siren calling to him, inviting his full attention.

Carrie was suddenly staggered by his touch, soft and gentle, yet magical and volcanic, threatening her equilibrium as nothing ever had before. She might have given in to her impulses if she had not remembered the conversation she had overheard earlier wherein Drew and Noble had deemed her nuisance at best.

She turned away from him, then wriggled free of his

hands that gently clasped her arms. She was very aware of his bold eyes casting glances up and down her mannishly attired frame, which made her look almost more sensual than the scantiest of ladies' gowns. "I don't want you to wear those clothes," Drew said quietly.

She spun back, defiance lifting her chin. "What do you mean? You are the one who suggested—no, ordered—that I wear them?" To emphasize her resolve, she sniffed. "I'm going to wear men's clothing from this moment on!"

A smile curved Drew's ample mouth. "You are a stubborn little Lymie, aren't you?"

"You have your geographics confused. I am not a Lymie."

Drew again sat back in his chair. His boots rose to a desk scattered with journals and papers. "You do not argue with being stubborn. Good girl."

Carrie tried not to respond to his smile, but it was like asking the sun not to shine. Still, in the back of her mind she knew he did not want her around and that had to take precedence over the moment of humor they shared. It seemed natural to banter playful insults with him. If he wasn't so outrageous, they might be—

The word "friends" almost finished her thought. But he was not the kind of man a woman could be friends with. They could be either enemies or lovers, nothing in between. Strangely, the idea of Andrew Cynric Donovan as the latter did not curdle her blood.

Carrie paid no attention to the hum of conversation from the deck of *Donovan's Dream*. She was sure the men were discussing her unexpected manner of dress. That Drew Donovan might be jealous of the men's attentions gave her a sense of challenge. "Well, I'd better check with the rest of the men and see what they think of my britches."

A flash of irritation lit Drew's silvery eyes. He came up from the chair in one swift move. "If you insist on wearing that getup, stay in your cabin. The men have work to do and need no distractions."

She could bear it no longer. She spun back, laughter clinging to her crisp English accent. "You *are* jealous, Drew Donovan! Why? You have no designs on me. I am not your woman and it should not matter one way or the other if men look at me! After all, I am a burden to you. You should be glad to be rid of me once we reach St. Louis."

His expression was incredulous. Then, to mask his surprise, he smiled a deliberately sarcastic smile. "Jealousy is for a child wanting the toy of another. You think too highly of yourself, Princess." God! How had she so easily read him. He *was* jealous. Rage blackened his heart at the thought of the crew enjoying her curves outlined by Cawley's tight-fitting trousers. He wanted her out of them, even if he had to remove them himself.

Somehow, Carrie knew that. Though the twinkle of humor stayed in her sea-green eyes, the smile passed from her lips. "Shall I ask Cawley for looser trousers?" she asked, attempting to remedy the moment. Pointing to the exterior, she added, "I could go in search of him now."

Drew stepped around her, blocking her path to the door. "You stay here. *I* will find Cawley, and *I* will approve the trousers that you wear."

Carrie's mock salute followed his declaration. "Aye, aye, Cap'n," she mumbled with mock severity. "Your little 'cabin mate' will stay right here . . . aye, aye."

"Are you ridiculing me?"

Carrie's efforts to suppress her smile resulted in two tiny, matching dimples in her cheeks. When a frowning Drew Donovan closed the cabin door, she whispered, "Aye, Cap'n." The smile dissipated as she added, " 'Tis cat-and-mouse we play, when other games might be more delightful."

Chapter Five

By midmorning of the following day, Drew and Carrie had moved three miles through verdant marsh meadows and past acres of yellow water lilies couched on blue-green leaves. Ghostly cypress stumps and flat, lightly wooded banks formed the backdrop to what had been a silent journey thus far. Carrie was weary of matching Drew's rapid pace but much too proud to suggest that they stop and rest. Drew kept up his pace, carrying in a pack on his back the few provisions they needed for the journey. Occasionally a slider turtle dropped into the water from the log where it sunned, causing Carrie to drop back from the quickly pacing Drew Donovan in order to catch sight of other activity on the river. She found the American scenery fascinatingly barbaric, and yet so beautiful no words could describe it.

At noon, with still no words spoken between the two, Drew dropped his backpack beside the wall of a long-abandoned cabin. Carrie lowered herself wearily onto a small, rickety stool beside what had once been a barn, where blacksmith and carpenter tools lay among dead shards of grass and weeds. A harmless garter snake slithered between her boots, but she merely nudged it aside, eliciting a sideways glance from a surprised Drew Donovan. If he had expected her to leap hysterically into his arms he didn't know her very well.

"Didn't know you liked snakes," he mumbled.

"I don't," she sniffed indelicately.

Turning from his smiling eyes, Carrie studied a small, covered bridge crossing a wide creek. The clearing, with its cabin and barn, accessible by both the bridge and the trail from the forest, seemed peaceful. She wondered why the occupants had fled it, leaving their tools and other domestic items behind.

While Drew searched his bag for the food items Cawley was to have packed, Carrie entered the dim, dark interior of the abandoned cabin. It had only two rooms parted by a shredded curtain, with dusty furniture lying about, the remains of a woman's prized china littering a table and benches, a kettle and cauldron hanging in the hearth. Then, through a window she saw the reason for the abandonment—a row of graves, two long and three short ones, graced by simple wooden crosses held together by rotting twine.

How very sad, Carrie thought, turning swiftly away from the sight. Then the aroma of beef and biscuits once again drew her to the outdoors.

The Missouri air was cold, a breeze wafting across the river and the marshland penetrating her thick coat to chill her to the bone. She became aware of the coarse fabric of the trousers rubbing between her legs and took the moment to be thankful she hadn't been born male.

Dropping to her knees just mere inches from Drew, she took the biscuits and beef he handed to her.

Drew offered a canteen of water. "You'll need this to wash it down," he commented.

Carrie took the canteen and rested it against her left leg. Across the clearing a white-tailed deer moved along a narrow trail, unaware of the presence of the human pair. Carrie watched in wonder as the doe quenched her thirst at the creek, then moved off into the woods.

The American wilderness was strange and unknown to her and, thus, an exciting challenge. Every day of her life in England had been guided by tutors and nannies and matrons chosen by her uncle to arrange her social schedule. She could not honestly say she missed her domestic regimen and her uncle's unrelenting desire to protect her from eligible courters. At twenty-one years of age, they had still treated her like a giddy child.

But here, surrounded by the wildness of unsettled land and a mighty, challenging river, Carrie felt adventure clutch at her heart. Now that she was safely away from Junius Wade, she did not miss her uncle so much. She would see him soon enough, but for now she simply wanted to enjoy the adventure of being with the gentle, if not somewhat somber, Drew Donovan for a day and a half.

Tomorrow she would be in St. Louis, preparing for her journey overland to the coast, then across the Atlantic to England. Her eyes lifted to study Drew Donovan's strong profile. He ate his meal of biscuit and beef as if he really didn't want it, quiet and thoughtful, with a darkly veiled face that hid his emotions. Carrie wondered what he was thinking or feeling.

Cutting her eyes from her companion, she felt mischievous. What would he do if he looked around and found her gone? Would he stop to look for her or continue the journey without her? She smiled, unaware that he watched her intently.

"What is so amusing?" Drew asked, tossing a few crumbs of bread into the woodline.

A crimson hue crept into Carrie's cheeks. Had he read her thoughts? "I was thinking how lovely the woods are," she easily lied.

"Aren't you cold?"

"Just a tad."

Drew leaned back, linking his fingers across his chest. "I

have a feeling you're up to something."

"I am not!"

Without warning, Drew took her arms and dragged her against him.

"What are you doing?" Her struggles to free herself from him were futile.

"Wondering why I put up with you," he replied, his smiling mouth mere inches from her own.

The color in Carrie's cheeks deepened dramatically. She sat up straight and craned her neck away from him. "Release me, or I shall have to resort to brutality." The warmth of his breath assailed her flushed cheeks, even as his smile widened in his laughter.

"Brutality! Spare me, my pretty."

Pressing her mouth into a thin line, Carrie studied her traveling companion in annoyance. "Why are you teasing me? I'm not being a bother."

"Because, pretty thing, we have traveled for hours without so much as a word. Why don't you just enjoy a moment of playfulness?"

She hated the fact that he was devastatingly handsome, that his smoke-colored eyes held her attention, and that his mouth continued the teasing, playful smile. But would she rather he was dark and brooding and somber? She didn't think so.

She would have to play his game in order to extract herself from arms that made her feel warm and excited inside. She felt a tightness in her abdomen like nothing she had felt before, and her breasts swelled against his iron-hard chest.

Suddenly, his grip tightened almost painfully. His eyes narrowed as they bore across her shoulder. "You're hurting me, Drew."

His grip tightened even more. "Don't move!" Scarcely half a dozen inches from her boot a snake coiled, ready to strike. This time, it was not a harmless garter snake. The offending creature baring hollow, venom-injecting fangs was a deadly cottonmouth.

Carrie had no chance to react, because in one swift move Drew had slung her across his body and out of danger, the calf of his left leg taking the full brunt of the attack. Tearing his knife from its scabbard, he swiftly decapitated the pit viper. Carrie sat in shock upon her haunches as Drew fought to free the leg of his trousers from his boot, exposing puncture wounds that were already swelling.

"Christ!" he bellowed, attempting to position his leg to see the wound. He knew he had to act fast, before the venom flooded his veins. "Damn, woman, do you have any sores in your mouth?"

Carrie looked at him in shock and surprise. "Of course not. Why?"

Clamping his jaw, Drew dragged the smooth edge of the knife across both puncture wounds to form an X. "Because you're going to have to draw out the poison or I'll die right here."

He had expected her to hesitate in horror, but she did not. Instantly, she took the clean white handkerchief he handed her and wiped away the excess blood. She tasted the bitter poison as it flooded her mouth just before she spit it into the dirt. When she finally tasted only the saltiness of his blood, she cleaned the wound with water from the canteen, removed the narrow belt from her trousers, and tightened it just below his knee. Only then did she look up into Drew's face. His face was ghastly white and, despite the cold, sweat ran down his forehead.

"It's going to be rough," he mumbled, fighting for every moment of consciousness. It was inevitable that some of the poison would escape into his bloodstream. "I'll sit here a while."

"Shouldn't you rest inside?"

"No. In just a few moments we will resume our journey." Perspiration dotted his brow and he grimaced from the pain in his leg, then tightly clamped his jaw. He did not want to appear weak in the presence of Carrie Sherwood. What she thought of him mattered very much.

Carrie drew up her legs and wrapped her arms around her knees. He looked anguished and yet she knew he would not want her to make a fuss over him. Over the course of half an hour his breathing became more labored and the perspiration now saturated his face. His eyes crept open and, though there were no words spoken, his plea for help reached out to her.

"Come . . ." she said firmly, easing to his side and attempting to lift him against her body. Carrie struggled to get him to his feet. "There is a bed inside. We must get you there."

"Thank you for what you did."

"I didn't do anything," she replied.

"If I live, I'll have you to thank for it."

Scarcely had they entered the small, dim cabin before he collapsed onto the bed. His features contorted in pain as Carrie dabbed at the perspiration upon his brow. "I've never seen anyone snakebitten," she said quietly. "Please, tell me what to expect."

"It all depends on how much poison got into me."

"Then give me the worst that can happen."

"I could die."

Carrie shuddered visibly. "Besides that."

Foggy darkness enveloped Drew Donovan. He heard Carrie's voice, but it was far away, as if she were deep in a cavern — soothing words echoing against the walls until nothing reached his ears but a scarcely audible whisper.

He was only vaguely aware of her movements, the door creaking open, and the invasion of sunlight upon his pained face. Then he felt the heaviness of a blanket covering him.

"How has this happened?" Carrie whispered brokenly.

81

"One moment we are enjoying a meal, and the next you are near death upon a dusty cot."

Instantly, Drew's hand covered her own. "Do not worry for me, pretty thing. I am . . . going to sleep . . . a few hours . . ." His words became softer and softer, fading into nothingness, and the pain playing upon his moist brow became a mask of unconsciousness.

Carrie wanted to flee into the brisk midday air, to be far away from his suffering. But no one had ever needed her the way Drew Donovan needed her then. It was all that kept her close to him, knowing that without her he was helpless.

Her emotions were in utter turmoil. As the hours of afternoon passed, she found a quandary of thoughts flooding her head. What had happened to the carefree English girl who'd once had the riches of the world at her fingertips? What had happened to the playful exchange of insults with a rigid but loving nanny, the excursions to the park with a doting uncle? What had happened to lush satin dresses and envied bonnets, shoes with ribbon lace-ups and reticules carrying a woman's accessories? What had happened to indifferent complaints about the weather and fluttering eyelashes at a bold young suitor who'd managed to slip into Holker Hall beneath the watchful eyes of her overprotective uncle?

Carrie felt that she'd aged a thousand years in the past five months. Swallowing the lump that suddenly formed in her throat, she eased her fingertips toward Drew's forehead. He moved ever so slightly, his features, even in his state of half-consciousness, strong and virile. She almost expected him to come bounding off the cot and reprimand her for wasting valuable travel time. Instead of the smooth, deep voice, only an occasional grunt escaped his mouth. It was almost as if he was berating himself for the untimeliness of the moment.

Carrie was suddenly desperate to hear his voice. Her

softly placed fingertips upon his brow now became daggers at his shoulder. "Drew? Drew, is there anything I can get for you?"

He did not open his eyes. "Nothing. Just a few hours . . . sleep."

He'd already been sleeping for hours and she didn't want him to sleep a minute longer. She feared that if he did so, he would not wake up. Where were his sarcastic little insults when her ears ached for them? Where was his humored and baiting gray-black gaze when she longed to match her will against his own?

A gentle wind suddenly permeated the room, teasing at her flame-colored hair and casting it full upon Drew's chest. Carefully, she dropped her head so that her cheek lightly touched his shoulder. "You're a devil of a man," she whispered, "but, oh, I am so worried for you."

The wild pounding of his heartbeat frightened her, yet she was obsessed with listening to it. All other sounds were drowned out — the music of a songbird, the splash of a beaver in a pond fed by the Mississippi, the wind whistling through the forest. She did not even care that her back ached horribly from bending over him all afternoon.

Dear God, was the pace of his heart slowing? Carrie jerked her head up, her eyes wild with fright, her hand moving timorously toward the buttons of his shirt. She was scarcely able to undo the protesting little things so that she could press her palm to his heart. Yes, there it was — thump . . . thump . . . She wanted to shake him to full wakefulness and make him aware of her fright. He couldn't die. She could still taste the bitter venom in her mouth, feel the heaviness of his body next to her own as she'd sought comfort for him in this poor, pitiful, abandoned shanty.

Carrie felt a sharp pang of shame. She knew, however, that focusing on the sacrifices she had made for him was merely a cover for her fear. She wasn't insensitive and self-centered. Surely, he would understand the confusion of her thoughts.

Slowly withdrawing her hand from his bare chest, Carrie suddenly became aware of the masculine allure of him. He lay unconscious upon the cot, fully at her mercy, the length of him available to her scrutiny. Her eyes moved slowly down his slim, well-muscled body, the gentle rise and fall of his chest, the trousers pulled tightly across his groin. At that point, curiously, she wanted to touch him. Without conscious thought, her fingers, with only the slightest hesitation, gently touched his hip, instantly withdrawing when he took a long, deep breath.

She was sure the crimson of embarrassment had impaled her cheeks all the way to the bone. His eyelids had fluttered. Placing her hand upon his forehead, she leaned over him, waiting for his eyes to focus and transfix to her own. When they did not, she asked softly, "Are you awake, Drew?"

To which he replied, in a hoarse whisper, "No."

Gentle laughter played upon her mouth. "You've been asleep most of the afternoon."

His eyes crept open. Once again, humor twinkled in them. "I've been half dead most of the afternoon. But not too dead . . ." Drew took her hand and held it to his chest, "to miss the curious little explorations of this pretty thing." Gently, he squeezed her fingers.

"I was just feeling your heartbeat," she said quietly, hoping he would not pursue the matter and thoroughly humiliate her.

Drew, however, was unwilling to pass up such a chance. She was even more lovely and sensual with the crimson flooding her cheeks. "At my hip, Carrie?"

"You are a scoundrel, Drew Donovan!" Even as her words were deliberately harsh, her mouth curled into a warm smile. "I do hope you're going to be all right so that I will not be stranded here alone. And . . . I don't relish the idea of calluses in the palms of my hands from having to bury you."

"Come here . . ." Drew outstretched his hand, inviting her to sit on the cot beside him. "Come . . ." When puzzlement touched her features, he waved his fingers. "Here, put your face close." When she reluctantly obeyed, he touched his mouth oh so briefly to hers.

"What was that for?"

"You saved my life. Most women would have hesitated to do what you did."

"Pooh!" Carrie attempted to rise, but his arm was clamped across her legs. She felt obligated to add, "I am not most women. It was only a little blood and snake venom." An attempt to cut her gaze from his was also unsuccessful. "Will we resume travel?"

"We'll rest for the night and begin afresh in the morning."

"Will you be up to it?"

"I'll be up to it, Carrie Sherwood. But aren't you hesitant to spend the night alone on a strange river, with a man you loathe? Don't you fear me?"

"Pooh!" She thought she'd broken the habit of using that silly word her uncle abhorred so. Nervousness always brought out her worst habits. "I handled you quite well when you physically attacked me in New Orleans."

A mischievous grin creased Drew's strong features. "Ah, but I was drunk then, m'lady. I am not now."

"You are weak from snakebite," Carrie reminded him, waving a slim finger before his face. "You really mustn't tease me so."

Carrie could not read the look in his eyes. Had she known they smoldered with passion, she might have fled into the cold of late afternoon. She set about tidying the blanket she'd placed over him earlier, and did not hesitate to slap his hand away when he attempted to keep her from withdrawing from him. His smile betrayed that he'd taken no offense.

Over the next half hour, Carrie brought in firewood from the back of the cabin. Drew watched her in silence, fighting with the brimstone, fanning the spark she'd begun with her fingers only to have the damp papers she'd been using snuff the weak flame. She tried again, using straw she'd gathered outside, and soon had a fire burning. "There. I do believe I could survive in the wilderness if I had to."

Drew turned to his side. "A fire does not a pioneer make," he reflected. "Could you, indeed?"

Carrie wiped her sooty hands on the sides of her trousers. "Of course I could. I can be quite resourceful when faced with a situation." Smiling sweetly, she continued. "In the panic, our remaining foodstuff was left out of doors and now is a feast for the ants. Beneath the busy little beasts, however, I found a fishing hook and line . . ." Bringing it up from the pocket of her trousers, she held it out to him. "I've found a nice stick to use as a fishing pole and shall go down to the pond to catch our supper, which I shall cook on the grill I found and cleaned while you were sleeping." Carrie rose to her feet and moved toward the door.

Picking up an old jar, she added, "And I dug a few worms while you were out cold."

Drew watched her retreat, her rounded hips swinging in the loose-fitting trousers, her flaming hair bouncing at her back. "Don't fall in," he called after her, managing a hoarse chuckle.

"If I do, you'll starve," she laughed in return.

She had not closed the door. Drew watched her move onto a wide trail, then ease down a slippery bank toward the pond they had passed earlier. He wished he'd warned her to beware of snakes. He wished he'd warned her to look out for strangers. He wished . . .

Blast! he thought, turning to his back yet keeping his

86

eyes peeled toward her slender frame against the backdrop of the Missouri forest. He wished to hell she wasn't so anxious to leave him in St. Louis. He was growing fond of her and he liked having her around. She was a welcome change of scenery from the men and crew aboard *Donovan's Dream,* and her alluring beauty brought out a gentle side of him he had suppressed for years.

He really didn't know why. His parents, Cole and Diana Donovan, had been and were still deeply in love and he had been raised beneath their loving scrutiny. He had always hoped for a love of his own to parallel that of his parents', but he had long ago given up hope of finding the woman who could fulfill his dreams. Was the English beauty on her knees at the pond, patiently attempting to catch a fish for dinner, the woman he had been waiting for? Certainly it was not Jolie Ward. Her bold pursuit of him had destroyed any interest he might have had in her. Once he returned to Wills Creek, he hoped to ignite her interest in Noble with another of his good swift rejections. If he could get the woman married off, perhaps then the pursuit would end. He suspected that she frequently went to Noble's bed—or he to hers—though both sought to protect their secret trysts from the residents of Wills Creek. Ofttimes, Drew felt that Jolie was responsible for keeping other women out of his life. She could be devious and cruel and as underhanded as a pickpocket.

But Carrie Sherwood . . . Flame . . . Lady Charissa Sherwood—whoever the hell she was—the mystery of her was an aphrodisiac, stirring him physically and mentally, tormenting him with an allure that compelled him to beg at her feet. He almost believed she was worth the humiliation if it would win her heart.

God knew, he wanted her . . . wanted her with a painful awareness that made him ache. But what could he do in a day? Tomorrow she would leave him, leave herself vulnerable in a land with which she was not familiar, and he could not protect her. He still did not know why she had insisted on traveling with him to St. Louis when she had so readily accepted his offer and had agreed to travel with him to Pennsylvania. He wondered if one of the men had said something. But which one? They had all been enthusiastic about having the English beauty aboard *Donovan's Dream*.

A woman's mind was as quick to change as the weather. There was probably no logic to her reasoning. Therefore, he would have to help her see the error of her ways. He did not want to delay his arrival in St. Louis, because the necessary equipment had to be sent downriver for repair of the *Dream*, but he was not ready to lose Carrie Sherwood. She was, possibly, the woman for whom he had been looking for many years. He would have to defeat her illusions of grandeur and social importance and convince her that America would be a happier place to live than England.

She would have him believe she was a virgin. That was a laugh! She'd lived in a brothel in The Swamp, and only God knew where she'd been before that. Still, there was something sweet and innocent and yet provocative about her. She was probably a damned good actress. He could imagine her on the stage, stepping high, slinging her head of flame-colored hair and making claims that any man would fall at her feet believing. What was it about her that grabbed at his heart? Or was he still wanting to get his twenty-five dollars' worth?

Ah, she had caught a good-size fish. Drew tucked his palm beneath his tousled head and watched her approach, a proud grin curling her full, sensual mouth, her gait longer and more confident. She burst into the cabin, holding out a flopping bream at the end of her line. "Told you I'd catch supper," she laughed, moving toward the flat grill. "I guess I just place it here and rest it atop the burning logs . . ."

"Aren't you going to gut it?"

Carrie's eyebrows met in a puzzled frown. "Gut it? What do you mean?"

"Slice him open underneath and pull out his innards."

Carrie's face became a grimace of pain and disgust. "Innards! Fish have innards?"

Drew stifled the laugh tickling at his throat. "Everything has innards."

Dropping the fish with a look of disgust, Carrie propped her hands on her slim hips. Sniffing stubbornly, she said, "Well, I won't remove them! That's filthy, Drew Donovan! Besides, it's still alive!"

Feigning weakness, Drew said, "It is all right to put him over hot flames alive, but not all right to gut him alive?"

"I was going to hit him on the head first."

"I didn't think you'd be able to gut a fish, Carrie," he challenged, his voice deliberately calm. "But if you can manage this small task, don't forget to scale him."

That was all it took . . . to say she couldn't do something! Picking up the fish and turning on her heel, Carrie moved to the backpack outside the door and found Drew's big knife. Again she dropped the now-lifeless fish, fell to her knees in front of it, and, hesitating only a moment, opened it up underneath. She groaned as she forced her right hand into the cavity, dug out the soft, moist innards, and deposited them on the ground. Scaling the beast was the easiest part, but she still didn't enjoy doing it. The scales popped off, and several adhered to her ashen cheeks. When she reentered the cabin, her face was a sickly white.

"That was disgusting," she said quietly, her equilibrium threatened by the gruesome act she had committed. "I'm not sure I'll be able to eat this creature."

"Then he died for nothing. Never kill anything you don't intend to eat."

Feeling sick to her stomach, Carrie wanted to return to

the sweet-scented air. But she did not want Drew Donovan to think she was a simpering female so she tossed the fish on the grill and placed it upon the logs.

Approaching Drew, she started to put her hand on his forehead. "You've got fish blood on your hand," he reminded her. "And scales on your cheek."

So she did! Carrie poured a little water from the canteen over her hands, then wiped them dry on her trousers. With one fingernail she pried the scales from her face.

Returning to Drew, she touched his forehead. "You feel warm."

He did not respond to her understatement. He felt like a boiling cauldron inside, and it had nothing to do with the snakebite. Her sensual nearness flooded him; he wanted to reach out, grasp the back of her neck, and pull her mouth to his own. He had never before exhibited such control. He wanted her. Even the weakness produced by the snakebite did not dent the iron-hard passion swelling within him. His body physically responded to her nearness; he only hoped she would not notice. Or did he?

"How are you feeling? Really?" she asked, smoothing the backs of her fingers across his cheek. She could not possibly have known what her innocent movements were doing to him.

"I may need an extra day to recover," he lied. "I feel that my veins have been opened and my blood let in huge quantities."

"I guess a delay won't hurt, though I thought you were anxious to get to St. Louis and be rid of me."

"I am anxious to reach St. Louis and get those parts for my steamboat shipped downriver. I am not anxious to get rid of you."

Carrie pressed her lips to keep from snapping a rebuttal. She had heard his conversation with the man named Noble and was well aware that he considered her a millstone. He was probably furious that the snakebite had delayed his arrival in St. Louis. He probably loathed the idea of having to spend even one more day with her.

Her mood changed dramatically. She rose swiftly from the cot and gave him full view of her back. She turned the fish on the grill, then set about locating two unbroken plates which she took down to the pond and washed thoroughly. By the time she returned, the fish was sizzling on the grill and a very puzzled Drew Donovan had propped himself on his palm to study her intently.

"What are you looking at?" she merely barked the question.

"You, English. You look as though you could pounce and kill."

How right he was! She wanted to stay with him all the way to Pennsylvania and was furious that he was anxious to be rid of her. She wondered if he now considered her more of a helpmate than a millstone since she was, after all, cooking him a meal—her very first ever. And to have gutted and scaled the creature! She was surprised that she would have done this for him. She should have abandoned him, let the venom worm its way through his bloodstream so that he would writhe away his life in pain. She should have moved into the darkness of the timberline and watched the horror of it!

Without warning, Carrie Sherwood bellowed, "I hate you, Drew Donovan . . . Do you want your dinner now?"

It went without saying that he was at a loss for words.

Chapter Six

Carrie washed their two plates, then turned to face Drew Donovan, only to be met by an engaging smile. Drew had accused her earlier of being up to something. Now she wondered if *he* was the crafty one. "I thought you were ill, Drew."

"As weak as I am, I can still manage a smile for the prettiest girl this side of the Mississippi."

Carrie lifted her chin and looked down at him. "I feel like the *only* girl this side of the Mississippi. You are an outrageous man, Drew Donovan. Whatever am I going to do with you?"

In a moment of faltering strength, he dropped the hand he was stretching out to her. "Sit by me, pretty thing. Tell me about your life in England."

"Why?" Carrie sauntered toward the cot, then dropped to the edge of it. "You think I am daft and made the whole thing up about my life there."

"Prove to me you're not daft. Convince me you are a princess. After all, I might listen to conclusive proof. I am a reasonable man. I assure you of that."

"You are already being outrageous, Pennsylvanian. I never said I was a princess, only that my uncle was—is— the Duke of Devonshire."

"Does that make you a duchess?"

"I never considered myself so." Meeting his humored gaze, Carrie shrugged her shoulders. "Why do you tease me so? Why do you dislike me and consider me a millstone?"

Drew's eyebrows met in a puzzled frown. Even though he felt weak and dizzy, he swung his boots to the floor and sat beside her. "A millstone? Where did you get an idea like that?"

Should she tell him she had eavesdropped? Such people were said to have no character; she couldn't bear to be placed in that category. "Well, don't you? Surely I am in the way. Being the only woman aboard your steamboat, I have caught the attention of some of your crew. Perhaps you even blame me for the accident that has disabled *Donovan's Dream.*"

"That is preposterous!" Drew attempted to rise, but the pain in his calf made it impossible. He felt wretchedly ill — a mixture of the venom in his blood and the fish churning through his digestive system. "The men are well disciplined. They would not sacrifice duty to look at a pretty face."

At just past six that cool December evening, night was already falling. The thin triangle of light at the window became shapeless shadows as the trees absorbed the remaining sunlight that had, moments before, glimmered upon Carrie's flaming hair. Drew was held in awe of the magnificence of her standing there by the small, paneless window, her willowy beauty almost radiant, one slim hand resting absently upon the other as if she had suddenly allowed some deep thought to take her far, far away. Even though she stood a mere few feet from him, Drew felt the distance parting them. Was she thinking of England and the ocean separating her from home? He wanted to approach her and enfold her within the comfort of his arms, but he knew if he made such a move his weakness would send him staggering. He remained attached to the security of the cot, bracing himself with his palms firmly upon the thin mattress, looking at Carrie as if he were seeing her for the first time. His imagination wandered, and he wondered what she looked like beneath the manly clothing he had made her wear. His hand had felt the silkiness of her thighs, mauled the waist of her undergarments in an attempt to join himself to her, and yet his eyes had seen little more than the swell of her breasts above a tight-fitting bodice, a slim ankle, an erratic pulse in the slim column of her neck.

Forcing the arousing thoughts from his mind, Drew gathered the strength necessary to attend to human needs. He eased up from the cot, gained his footing, then moved toward the cabin door. Only then did Carrie come back from her momentary trance. "Do you need my assistance, Drew?"

He gave her a cockeyed grin, cutting his eyes briefly to her. "I believe I'll manage this on my own."

The meaning of his words flooded Carrie, bringing a moment of embarrassment. Her shoulders moved in an absent shrug. "Watch out for snakes."

While Drew was outside, Carrie moved around the small cabin she would share with him that night. She found a child-size lap desk with papers still inside, the large, bold printing obviously done by a very young child. Also inside was a porcelain doll scarcely larger than her hand, a doll belonging to a little girl — her life cut tragically short, buried now with her parents and siblings in the simple graves outside.

Seeking to banish the melancholy her discovery had elicited she quickly thrust the lap desk aside and began slapping at the dusty mattress where Drew Donovan had rested that afternoon. She recalled the warmth of his body and enjoyed the manly aroma of him clinging to the very fibers of the room.

She shot up like a lightning bolt when Drew returned to

the cabin, immediately depositing an armload of firewood on the planked floor. He appeared to be strong; Carrie, therefore, did not understand their delay in traveling. Why did he need an extra day to rest? She became wary of his motives.

Sensing her suspicion, he suddenly began limping on the snakebitten leg. "I've brought extra firewood for the night, and for tomorrow, since a storm is moving in from the north."

At that moment, thunder rumbled across the far horizon. At least he wasn't lying about that. "We don't want to delay long, at least not beyond tomorrow."

Drew tossed her pack across to her. "Here are your dresses. Why don't you get out of those clothes and don something more comfortable?" When her look narrowed, he continued. "Lord, woman . . . you are outrageously modest, aren't you?" When she failed to respond, he suggested, "You might change behind what is left of that curtain."

As Carrie moved toward the dark corner, Drew sat stiffly upon the cot. Though he had familiarized himself with it by sleeping on it that afternoon, he still eyed it critically. Was it large enough to accommodate him and the English beauty? Or would she insist that he sleep on the floor while she wallowed in comfort? He imagined the latter would apply.

He leaned back and watched the flutter of the curtain across the small room. Soon the trousers were deposited into a pile, exposing a shapely calf through the tear in the drapery. He hadn't realized what slim feet and ankles she had, the prettiest he'd ever seen. When she emerged from behind the tattered fabric she was wearing a simple white loose-fitting dress. Her bare toes emerged from the hem.

Catching the direction of his gaze, Carrie explained. "I forgot to pack shoes, and the boots didn't seem to complement the dress."

"At least get a pair of socks from my pack."

"Socks! Heavens no. I did pack stockings . . . if you insist that I wear them."

Never had Drew expected to be rewarded with such a sensual sight. Her simple dress might well have been a bedgown, and the slight pucker of her mouth was like that of a woman-child emerging from sleep. Spasms jerked from his body, spasms Carrie mistook as symptoms of his snakebite. She was immediately at his side.

"Are you suffering?"

"God, yes! But not from what you think."

Arching a fine eyebrow, she queried, "Whatever do you mean, Drew?" For one fleeting moment, she truly did not comprehend the meaning of his reply. Then it hit her and she bolted from him, burdening him with a contemptuous look. "Don't you dare attempt to compromise me. I'll have none of it."

Having always considered himself a proud man, Drew Donovan would never take that which was not willingly offered to him. He watched her body quake. Had he frightened her that badly? Would she be anxious to leave him—a barbaric American—and return to her dreams of fine, debonair gentlemen back in England?

What he did not know was that something strange and alien and wonderful was tugging at Carrie's restraint. She had never been alone with a man such as Drew Donovan, and a flood of emotions rose from deep within her, compelling her both to flee into the cold night and pounce into his warm, inviting—and very willing—arms. She was sure he would not cast her aside like so much rubbish, but for the moment her pride was one degree stronger than the flood of desires moving within her.

"Come, pretty thing . . ." Drew ordered lightly. "You can sleep in the cot and I'll take the floor."

"I'm not tired." All the stubbornness and determination bubbled to the surface, slapping him in the face with her tart words. "I will sit by the window and watch the storm come in. You sleep in the cot since you are the one who had a bad turn today."

"Come here, Carrie." She resisted, crossing her arms as her right toe patted the floor. "I will be gallant and not compromise you. I want only to assure you that you are safe with me. Now . . . come lie beside me, unless you are afraid of me."

"And if I do not?"

Dropping his head to the pillow, Drew replied, "So be it."

That he did not care one way or another compelled her to take him up on his offer. She approached, sat midway upon the cot, then stretched stiffly along the length of his body. His left hand gripped her arm just below the shoulder, but otherwise he made no move. Perhaps he was a gentleman after all.

But was he? Carrie was suddenly consumed by the masculine heat of his body, by his groin resting lightly against her buttocks. Did he press himself more firmly against her, or was her imagination playing tricks on her? Strangely, she felt no compulsion to flee; rather, she wanted to ease more securely into his arms, to feel the length of him firmly against her body.

She no longer wanted to be a wall of virginal granite. She wanted to be warm and exciting and desirable. She wanted to be loved. Oh, but she'd dreamed about being with a man—not just any man, but a man like Drew Donovan—for as long as she could remember. Would she deny herself the pleasure now because of the puritanical conventions she'd fought at every turn? She remembered dear Mirabell, her nanny, saying, "It's a wedded woman's duty to let her man dig at her with his privates. Only a brazen hussy enjoys it. A decent, virginal girl like you must keep your knees clamped together. Hear me, missy?"

"Yes, yes, I hear you, Mirabell."

97

Drew lifted his head. "Who are you talking to, Carrie?"

Her eyes flew open; that becoming blush rose in her cheeks. "Oh, I . . . I was thinking of my nanny back in England." Carrie's pulse raced wildly. Deliberately she shrugged her shoulder so that Drew's hand fell and grazed her right breast.

When she did not protest, the bold Pennsylvanian did not remove his hand. Seconds that seemed like hours passed, and his fingers, as if possessing a will of their own, began to gently massage the soft mound of flesh through the scant fabric of her gown. Her eyes were closed, her lashes fluttering delicately, her breathing relaxed. Was she asleep and unaware of his boldness?

Carrie had always been drawn by adventure and unexplored terrain. She wanted to know what it was like to have a man touch her. What better ruse than sleep to experience the unknown and yet not have to be ashamed of it? She enjoyed the gentle massage of his hand upon her breast. It was all she could do to keep from taking his hand and guiding it to further explorations. So she was stepping on dangerous ground! It was her body; she would be able to draw the line when it became necessary. She could control his strokes and manly caresses that, for the moment, suited her needs and desires.

Carrie Sherwood was so lovely to look upon that Drew's breath flew away with the wind. For the first time that day he was unaware of the pain of the snakebite; the pain in his groin held his full attention. Moving his hand up from her breast, he eased her head back against him, touching his ample mouth in a trail of kisses along her hairline. Still, she did not respond, except to release a moan like a child whose sleep has been rudely disturbed.

"Carrie?" His hand boldly returned to her inviting mound of soft, feminine flesh.

The whisper of her name tickled her earlobe. "Hmm?"

"Are you asleep?"

Should she betray her state of wakefulness? And if she did, would it put a halt to his bold caresses? She had not yet gotten her fill. She wanted to know what she had missed. What of it! she thought. Awake or asleep, he was a man she could control. "No, Drew . . ."

Immediately, the trail of kisses ceased and his hand lifted slightly from her breast. "And you are not fleeing across the room to yell curses at me?"

A smile curled her mouth. Taking his hand, she eased it beneath the bodice of her gown. "I plan to cut out your heart, Drew Donovan. You might as well enjoy yourself beforehand."

"I will not touch you if you do not wish it," he responded with husky need. "Tell me to stop and I will." Even as he spoke, his fingers popped open the stays of her bodice and released the swells of her rose-pink breasts. As his mouth closed over first one peak, and then the other, he breathed in the deliciously sweet breath escaping from Carrie's lips.

Suddenly he was atop her, holding her wrists gently to the pillow, his mouth teasing her with hot, moist kisses. "I am — what is your favorite word? — *compromising* you, Carrie," he whispered hoarsely. "What are you going to do about it?"

"When I wish this to stop, then it will stop . . ."

Gruffly, he pinched her wrists together. His glaring eyes bore down into her emerald ones. "There is a point, Carrie Sherwood, when a man does not stop. It will either be now, or it will not be at all . . . not this night. Are you afraid, little girl, of the wolf in man's clothing?"

Carrie pressed her lips together to keep from betraying the tremor resting there. How dare he call her a little girl! Were her breasts not sweet and supple enough for him? Her body not fiery enough? Were her kisses not honey enough for his taste? Perhaps she should make him stop now while there was still time. But her body burned with wanting. If she did not find out this very night what the bold attentions of a man led to, she feared she would never find out. She couldn't bear the thought of being eighty years old and still a virgin. She had a choice. It was either stop now, or not at all.

While her mouth tried to scream at him to get off her, her heart clutched her protests and held them deep within the recesses of her flaming body. The words simply refused to form, and because of it, Drew Donovan smiled a small, knowing, and almost devious smile.

Drawing himself to his knees, he pulled her up to his body. She stiffened, arching her back, as his mouth again sought the sweet agony of her pale rosebud breasts. His hands moved roughly to her back and held her rigid against him. Carrie felt the throbbing of his groin against the apex of her thighs.

Her illusions of man and woman together were being tested at an accelerated speed. Suddenly she was frightened. Digging her fingers into his cloth-bound shoulders, she whimpered, "Stop . . . stop, Drew. Don't do this."

Instantly, his movements ceased. "Very well, I will stop."

She was surprised. Her eyes widened into saucers and her mouth parted seductively. "No, don't stop. I don't want you to stop."

"Which is it, Carrie?" Exasperation edged into his brusque voice, even as his hands moved to the hem of her skirts and eased the offending material upward. A grin raked his features as her knees parted upon the mattress and her body once again arched, offering herself fully to his masterful caresses.

She moved with the seduction of a harlot. How dare she try to convince him she was a virgin! Drew teased the soft mound of her breast against his mouth until it was a hard, thrusting peak, then gave equal attentions to the other.

Carrie's fingers dug into his ebony hair, clenching, her mouth gulping air as her chest heaved against his mouth, his tongue, his bold caresses. The scoundrel! He would have ceased this wonderful torment! He would have withdrawn from her and left her unsated and curious about this unknown world of passion. How could he even consider it!

Good sense told her to stop now, but her body would not allow it. As his fingers wrapped around the waist of her undergarments, she wriggled her buttocks in an attempt to help him remove them. Soon, he was dragging them under her knees and her feet and they became a ragged pile upon the cabin floor. In the red glow of the hearth she saw his moist eyes—narrow, lust-filled, greedy! Did they match her own? she wondered.

As she was eased backward to the bed, Carrie heard the clinking of his buckle, of trouser buttons, then the coarse material being impatiently raked down his muscular thighs and discarded along with his shirt which he dragged from his arms. He had ripped her gown from her, and it lay beneath her body, becoming an irritating ball of fabric which she whisked away with her hand.

His first look at her naked form seemed to last hours rather than the few seconds it took to lower himself to her. He did not immediately enter her but perched above her, easing her thighs apart with his knees and trailing wet-hot kisses along her heaving torso.

Carrie was not sure why she felt the torment and pain in her abdomen. It was pleasant and wonderful and scandalous. Her fingers gripped the edges of the thin mattress so that her hips could arch violently against him.

"You lusty little wench," he growled, playfully nipping at her bottom lip before joining his tongue to her own seeking one.

Her face flamed as hotly as her body. Why did he hesitate to join to her? Could he not see that she was ready for him? Perhaps he needed more time. Venturing a look downward, Carrie was suddenly apprehensive. He had not been that large just moments ago.

Panic rose within her. She wanted to scoot quickly from beneath him, but something told her the moment he had warned her about—the moment that was beyond the stopping point—had arrived. He would probably take her against her will if she tried to hold on to her virginity for even a moment longer.

Well, she couldn't think of anything better to leave in America. She had been snatched from England a maiden; what better way to return than as a woman?

"Are you ready for me, Princess?" Drew's hoarsely delivered question snapped her from her thoughts. She met his gray-black gaze and bit her lip to keep from trembling. Without reply, her boiling, anxious body rose to him. He released a humored chuckle. "I imagine that you are."

Drew's fingers gently plunged into the moist depths of her. She gasped, but his mouth instantly covered hers. Even as her features looked almost pained and embarrassed, her thighs spread, then closed impatiently over his hips. In that very moment, Carrie felt his penetration, so very carefully initiated it surprised her. She had grimaced, expecting excruciating pain, but it was nothing like that—merely a fullness and a wondrous aching in her abdomen threatening to explode into a million shooting stars.

Then, without warning, Drew Donovan drove himself into her with full, unexpected force. His mouth, covering her own once again, swallowed the protests his first, violent thrust had torn from her throat. Her body jerked convulsively and stiffened. Tears flooded her eyes.

Clamping his hands brutally against her temples, Drew remained embedded deep within her. As her cry became a tiny whimper, he whispered brokenly, "Blast it . . . you *are* a virgin!"

"I . . . I told you that I was," she wept, clinging to him as the pain faded away.

"Forgive me . . . I didn't believe you."

"I know," she murmured.

Several times Drew had looked into her eyes only to see shimmering ice. Now they were moisture-sheened, making him feel like the most selfish, insensitive bully who ever drew breath. How could he have so totally misjudged her?

Even though he felt guilty as hell, his need to satisfy himself coaxed his hips into movement. That she easily matched his rhythm and pace managed to somewhat quell the guilt, and he clasped his fingers through her flaming hair. She took tiny gasps, her translucent eyelids closed, her mouth trembling yet accepting his caresses.

Her body was heaven to the Pennsylvanian. He felt her breasts burning into his chest. The passion of the night, and Carrie Sherwood, was something he never wanted to forget. Tonight he was taking the treasures of a woman he was determined would one day be his wife . . . England and Duke of Devonshire be damned!

Carrie clung desperately to him. After that brief moment of pain, there was only ecstasy, and she had never imagined that being with a man could be so wondrous and fulfilling. She would gladly remain joined to him forever like this until the sun faded from the heavens and the earth itself died. His hips ground against her own, the movements growing in intensity, her mouth sought over and over by his own, his tongue thrusting between her teeth, his hands firmly beneath her buttocks to lift her upward, upward until nothing lay beneath them but the stormy skies and the dim light of the moon scarcely able to penetrate the swiftly moving clouds. She did not feel the coldness of the winter night; she felt only the heat of his body enveloping her, drawing her deeper and deeper still into the cauldron of his intensity and his passion until there was nothing left but the explosive spasms of man and woman together, fusing like liquid gold.

At that point, the walls of the cabin returned to surround them, and a winter breeze stirred the embers of the hearth. Her breathing slowing to match his, Carrie clasped him to her, enjoying the fullness of him within her in the aftermath of their love. She had tasted the ultimate pleasure that night. She was hopelessly addicted.

Drew lifted his eyes and held her gaze lovingly. Cupping her face between his palms, he said, "You are quite a woman, Carrie Sherwood." The expected downpour began to pelt the roof of the small cabin. Drew instantly found his back attacked by a steady stream of raindrops. He moved swiftly to Carrie's side, laughing as she gulped air when the startlingly cold drops filled her navel. She moved so quickly they both fell from the cot, Carrie straddled across his naked form. Dropping her cheek against his own, she joined in his laughter.

Grabbing the blanket from the cot before it got wet, Drew tossed it before the hearth and moved onto it, taking the weight of Carrie's body with him. Holding her close to him, feeling the downy softness of her flaming hair upon his chest, they fell asleep together, dreaming the dreams their night had created.

In Philadelphia, that same night, Diana Donovan sat in a wing-back chair across from her husband in the large parlor of Rourke House, her ancestral home. Hardly enough gray strands to count on both hands had violated the rich spun gold of her loose hair. Looking up from her reading, the slim beauty, who scarcely appeared old enough to have a thirty-two-year-old son, met the loving gaze of her husband Cole, whose own dark hair had tackled the invasion of gray across his temples with youthful flair.

"I am anxious to see our son again," Diana remarked, closing the book with a thud as she decided it was time to retire. "I hope Hester will not forget to give him our letter telling him we will be in residence here until the summer."

"You must stop treating Drew like a child," Cole admonished without true feeling. "He takes off on these trips to escape your motherly affections and remind himself he is a man rather than a boy." Cole Donovan rose to a height matching that of his only son, showing a muscular frame that had evaded the ravages of time. "Come, pretty lass . . ." Thirty-five years in America had gently faded his rolling Scottish accent. "It is time that we retire."

Diana found her footing, but did not immediately move into the wing of her husband's waiting arm. She looked around the large, high-ceilinged room, at the family portraits staring hauntingly toward her. "I wonder what happened to him?" she asked for perhaps the hundredth time in so many days. An unsteady finger pointed toward the portrait of the evil, maliciously smiling Webster Mayne, her first cousin.

Cole folded his wife within the crook of his arm. "Why are you so obsessed with Webster?"

Diana shuddered against him. "Because, Husband, I know in my heart he is still alive, even to this day. He is out there somewhere. I know one day I will look around and his twisted cruelty will be staring into my eyes, threatening me like he did that night so many years ago."

Twice, her cousin Webster had tried to kill her. Diana knew that so much evil could not possibly have died in the fire that had razed the east wing of the house that night, the second time he had tried to take her life. She had been young, scarcely twenty-three.

Cole squeezed his wife tightly. "If you don't stop talking like that, lass, you'll have nightmares."

"I know he will return, Cole. I've felt it so strongly these past few days. It is almost as if I feel him moving toward this house, closing the time and the distance as if it has never existed. I am frightened, not only for us, but for our beloved son."

"Blast it, Diana!" Anger surfaced in Cole's voice. "I am

going to have the portrait removed."

"No, don't!" Diana was terribly confused by her hesitation to hide the offending likeness. She thought that the portrait hanging there as a constant reminder would perhaps halt the arrival of the personification of the devil she was sure was destined to invade Rourke House. Or perhaps she was just being silly. "Let it hang there. I promise I won't mention this again."

As they moved up the stairs toward their bedchamber, Cole held her close to him and guided her to the inviting warmth of their bed. How slim and youthful she was, he thought, taking her robe from her to lay across the back of the chair. She was every bit as beautiful as the day he had first seen her, fleeing from him on a narrow mountain trail with a friendly bobcat dogging her heels.

Cole could not hate Webster. Had it not been for his murdering Diana's father so many years ago, he might never have fallen in love with her. Webster had framed him for that murder, then, because he had looked like a deceased ancestor, had purchased him from the Walnut Street Prison before his execution and forced him to masquerade as the dead man to drive Diana insane. His plan had backfired, Cole had fallen in love with the evil man's innocent victim, and Webster himself had been caught in his own web of treachery.

Had Webster died in the fire, leaving nothing but his dismembered left hand to be scraped up from the ashes? Or had he escaped the inferno and fled the lifelong home he would have taken from Diana? It was a mystery that had haunted Philadelphia—indeed, all of New England—for more than thirty years. Men were still discussing his disappearance at the taverns, and voicing their own morbid speculations.

Diana was aware that she had set her husband to thinking about Webster, something that always made him dark and somber. He had suffered badly at the hands of her cousin, and he had not needed her insensitive reminder of that day long past. She attempted to set a better mood in which to retire. "Do you think our son will ever find a wife?"

Cole laughed heartily. "Lass, another of the reasons the lad avoids us is your determination to get him married off."

"We're getting older," she sniffed, "and we need grandchildren. Besides, Drew is not a lad; he is almost thirty-three."

"Be patient, lass. He'll surprise you one day with a daughter-in-law and bairns to spoil." Undressed now, Cole eased into the bed beside his wife. "Promise that when our son journeys to Philadelphia you will not nag him about getting married."

"I cannot promise that. My son would think I was ill and would call in a physician."

Her attempt at humor pleased him yet did not eradicate the gruesome subject she had brought up just moments ago. The specter of Webster Mayne had certainly put a damper on his evening. Cole feared that he would be the one to suffer nightmares before the dawn.

Chapter Seven

Carrie awoke the following morning to find Drew bending over her. His eyes held her awakening features with teasing affection, the corners of his mouth turned up by that boyish half-grin that was so appealing.

"Good morning, sunshine," he greeted, smoothing her disheveled hair back from her cheek.

Carrie stretched lazily, then dropped her hands to her flat stomach. Looking across Drew's body, she saw that a new fire burned in the hearth. He must have been terribly careful not to have awakened her when he'd slipped from beneath the blanket they'd shared.

How lovely she was, Drew thought, with the innocence of sleep still clinging to her emerald eyes, her twilight moment of half-wakefulness puckering her mouth as she tried to form a greeting this chilly morning in the Missouri wilds. She needed help in awakening, and Drew gently touched his mouth to her own.

As he put the shallowest space between them once again, she asked, "How is your wound?"

"Ah, the leg . . . the swelling has gone down." Tracing his finger along the graceful curve of her collarbone, he asked, "And you?"

Carrie smiled timidly. "I believe I shall recover from any damage that was done." Turning into his arms, Carrie laughed. "Drew Donovan, why do you tease me so?"

"Because I love to see the color rise in your cheeks, Princess. And because I feel comfortable with you. Teasing is my way of showing affection."

"Not the only way!" she retorted playfully, her reply instantly erupting into soft laughter. She was not sure why she'd given her virginity to him last night. Perhaps because she would return to England and never see him again. After all, she was a millstone around his neck.

Oh, why did his conversation with Noble keep popping back into her memories to spoil her mood? Last night when she had lain with Drew, giving to him what no other man had ever had, she had been deliriously happy. Though she would inevitably return to her uncle and take her rightful place as his niece and heir, she had wanted to enjoy the newness of America and see sights she might never get a chance to see again. Her uncle had said America was a barbaric land, not fit for a lady, but that made it all the more challenging to her adventurous heart—a heart whose desires she would not have a chance to follow because Drew Donovan, the only American she felt was suitable as an escort, considered her a millstone!

"What are you thinking about, Princess?"

When Drew's hand gently grazed her cheek, Carrie slapped it away and sat upright. "What do you care what I am thinking about, Drew Donovan? I am merely a woman, a millstone, someone you are anxious to be rid of! Hand me my dress. If you didn't rip it in your lustful frenzy, that is!"

An exasperated frown lined Drew's forehead. Damn, the woman was moody! Turning, he grabbed the edge of the dress and flipped it across his body toward her. "There, Princess." As she tried to pull on the dress while holding the blanket to her nakedness, Drew's hand fell to her busy one. "Do you really want to put this on?"

Carrie jerked the garment over her head. "Why

wouldn't I want to get dressed?"

Ignoring her sudden abrasiveness, Drew traced his finger down her slim arm. "I thought perhaps we could—"

"Well, you are wrong. We need to reach St. Louis so that we can each go our separate ways."

That was all it took. Wearing only his trousers, Drew jumped to his feet, and his hands fell to his hips. "Before we start throwing insults back and forth at each other, I demand to know why you are riled up."

"I don't like you," she snipped.

"You liked me fine last night!" Dropping to his knees, he firmly gripped her arms, drawing her to him. "Damn, Carrie, why do your moods swing like a dead snake on a windblown branch? One minute you are almost serene, the next minute you are spitting venom. Either tell me what I've done, or I'll . . ."

Narrow green eyes locked to gray-black ones. "Or you'll what?"

Drew didn't like being backed down. Of course, he would do nothing. "Just tell me what is troubling you, Princess?" His voice softened, even as irritation clutched at his insides.

Well, they were back to her lack of character again, her rare moment of eavesdropping! She wondered what explanation he would have, if, indeed, he could come up with one. "I heard you speaking with your friend in your cabin the day the boiler exploded. You told him I was a millstone."

"What?" Drew's hands left her arms and settled lightly upon his thighs. "I have absolutely no idea what you are talking about. I've never said anything of the kind."

"You said you needed to be rid of me because I was a burden. Then you asked the Indian if he would take me off your hands, and he said it was your bed I wanted to crawl into. Somewhere at that point in the conversation you said I was a millstone around your neck! That is when I decided I would leave you the first opportunity that arose. When you made plans to travel to St. Louis, I asked if I could come along. You very easily gave in. Yes, I made love with you last night. I did it because I want you to miss me when I'm gone, and to feel guilty for speaking so cruelly of me. I want you to desire me and beg me not to leave you in St. Louis!" Oh, why was she saying such things? Last night had happened because she had wanted it to happen. She'd had no selfish motives. But she wanted to hurt him for being anxious to get rid of her!

Drew had quietly absorbed her words. When he did not speak, she looked up into his hooded eyes, their piercing silvery depths full upon her face. Slowly, his hands circled her wrists and drew them against his bare chest. "My little princess, it was not you I was speaking of. It was a woman named Jolie who is helping run my trading post on Wills Creek while I am away. She is my millstone, not you. Noble loves her, but she will not have him as a husband. Her pursuit of me has made my skin crawl for ten years."

Dare she believe him? She had expected him to come up with an explanation, but something lame and transparent, not something that almost sounded sincere. She met his gaze. If he had lied to her, he would look away. But he did not. "I heard you speak of me," she said quietly. "In your conversation with Noble. I did not hear this woman's name—Jolie, is it? I heard 'Englishwoman,' and I considered that to be me."

Drew's thoughts flew back to that afternoon. He remembered that Carrie had just left his cabin when Noble had made an appearance. They had embraced and exchanged words. He'd told Noble he was worried about him, and Noble had replied something to the effect that he was surprised he would even think of him with the English girl aboard. Noble had asked him what he thought Jolie would think if Carrie returned with him to Wills Creek . . .

"Damn, English," spoke Drew affectionately, "if you're going to eavesdrop on a conversation between two men, don't miss the vital part of it. It *was* Jolie I was speaking of, not you!"

No . . . she couldn't allow herself to be that gullible. She would have to forget about the wonderful moments she had spent with him last evening. When she arrived in St. Louis, he would go his way and she hers. Dropping her eyes, she said, "It is time we moved on so that we can part company, don't you think, Drew?"

"Is that what you want?"

Her bottom lip trembled. If she journeyed with him to Pennsylvania, she would never be able to leave him. She knew that for a virtual certainty. There would be repeats of last night, and she knew she would be powerless to stop them. Her uncle expected her to become the wife of a nobleman and take her place in society. A liaison with a rugged American like Drew Donovan would not be accepted. Her heart and her good senses were acting separately as she replied softly, "That is what I want."

He was gravely disappointed. "Very well, Carrie. Does it matter to you that I wish you would stay with me? I will take care of you and see you safely to Pennsylvania. If you wish to sail from Philadelphia, I will arrange it aboard one of my father's ships."

"Your father is a seaman?"

"No, he invested in a shipping company. He and my mother might be sailing for the Isles sometime after the New Year. If you need an escort, I could recommend no one better."

Carrie fought the urge to throw herself into his arms, to tell him how very much she wanted to remain with him. But he was a threat to her future as the niece and heir of the Duke of Devonshire. She cared not a whit for an arranged marriage and the ultimate possession of Holker Hall. She cared not a whit for the prestige of being a lady of society. She wanted Drew Donovan, even if he never wanted her for anything more than a consort. Last night had awakened a sensuality she would never experience with another man.

But she could not stay with him. Duty and England called. She had to return to Holker Hall, even if the rest of her life was spent in misery.

"Thank you," she said in response to his offer, "but if you will pay my passage east, and thus to England, I will see that repayment is sent to your bank."

"I do not want repayment. I want you to remain with me, Carrie, until we reach Pennsylvania." He wanted to add *and forever,* but rather continued. "Let me protect you."

Tears moistened Carrie's sea-green eyes. She swiftly turned away from Drew Donovan and delicately cleared her throat. It was imperative that he see no emotion. "Thank you, no. Your protection until St. Louis will be quite adequate to suit my needs."

Suit her needs! Drew sucked in a ragged breath. *Very well, Princess!* he thought. *I wouldn't want to get in your way.*

Wasting no time, Drew pulled on his boots and shirt, then picked up his firearm. He said nothing to Carrie as he left the cabin to hunt for breakfast, nor during the meal of stewed rabbit an hour and a half later. At just past seven that chilly morning, he and Carrie resumed their journey northward toward the village of St. Louis. He did not even bother to complain about her leaving Cawley Perth's clothing back at the cabin in the Missouri woods. And she did not complain about leaving her maidenhood there.

Drew found lodgings at a small tavern of brick and

mortar near the docks on Main Street. The normally bustling village was quiet this Sunday morning; he and Carrie had both slept late . . . in their separate rooms.

Carrie sat upon her bed with her ear pressed to the wall, hoping to hear some movement from the room where Drew slept. He'd been strangely formal with her since their arrival the night before and had not even asked her if she wished to share a room. After all, it wasn't as if they were strangers. As she continued to listen for him, her eyes absently scanned the large room — its ceiling arched to accommodate the canopy bed upon which she lay, a blue jam cupboard filled with lamps and extra bedding, an upright wing chair with splayed legs. The geometric quilt beneath her was downy soft, the hooked rug running the length of the bed giving the room a country air. The painted and grained blanket chest at the foot of the bed had served as a desk earlier in the morning when she'd written a hasty letter to her uncle at Holker Hall but then decided not to mail it.

The proprietor had said the room was the best in the house. It did not even remotely compare in luxury to the room of even the lowliest servant at their spacious mansion at Grange-over-Sands, a place Carrie had been thinking less and less about these past few days. She was sure the handsome Pennsylvanian was responsible for her state of remorse and hesitation to contact her dear uncle.

Drew had arisen early, and now she heard a gentle rap at the door, followed by the familiar voice calling her name. She rushed to the door, preparing to welcome Drew with a smile and a "good morning." But his face was dark and somber and his eyes narrowed as if he loathed the very sight of her.

Thrusting papers into her hand, he said brusquely, "A ticket for public transportation to Baltimore, Maryland, and enough money to pay passage to England and for meals and incidentals you may need along the way."

Handing her a package wrapped in brown paper, he explained. "Decent shoes for travel. The stage leaves tomorrow morning at seven. You will not be seeing me again."

Before she could respond, Drew had pivoted on his heel. It was just as well; if she'd called him back, she would have begged him to let her stay with him. England called, and she had to answer.

That silent summons in her head did not prevent her, however, from throwing herself on the wide, spacious bed and weeping. She wanted to be strong and independent and yet follow the path of least resistance. That path led to England, without looking back. But she couldn't bear the thought of not seeing Drew Donovan again—that stubborn, prideful, egotistical American who had won her heart and soul, even as she'd tried to hate him!

Why couldn't she just forget him? He had given her passage all the way to England and money to spare. Absently, she picked up the package Drew had given her and untied the rough twine. At least he had good taste, she thought, carefully looking over the highly polished lace-up boots with sturdy walking heels. They appeared to be a perfect size. Swinging her feet over the edge of the bed, she pulled one on, then the other, laced them, and stood, pulling her skirts up for a better view in the cheval mirror.

A knock sounded at the door. "Drew . . ." With a delighted squeal, she quickly traversed the room and pulled the door open. But rather than the tall, brooding Pennsylvanian, she faced a pale, slim boy carrying a tray of covered dishes. "Mr. Donovan said you'd be needing some breakfast, miss."

"Of course." Disappointment trembled in her voice. "I'll get some money."

"No need." The lad placed the tray on the table just inside the door. "Mr. Donovan paid for it. Paid for all your meals today. Said you wouldn't be venturing out."

Carrie's eyes suddenly flashed green fury. How dare he be so presumptuous! "Oh, did he?" But her fury was wasted on the tavernkeeper's son, for he was not responsible for the audacity of Drew Donovan. She shrugged her apology. "Forgive me. I'm a bit on edge."

"That's all right, ma'am," the boy grinned as he retreated. "The English are always a bit on edge."

The door closed; he did not see Carrie draw her slim hands to her hips in silent outrage.

Throughout the day she lounged about the large, comfortable room. It was just as well that she rest up for the first leg of her long journey back to England. Drew Donovan did not want to see her again and she was prepared to honor his wishes. She did not want to see him again, either. Oh, what an outrageous man he was!

She left her room only to venture to the water closet at the far end of the hallway and to use the iron bathtub with its ugly claw feet. The luxury of hot water flowed freely when a brass chain was pulled.

Carrie scarcely touched her dinner that evening. The room had become boring and suffocating, but she was hesitant to venture out into the night. The dim chants of drinking men drifted toward her; she wondered if Drew was one of them.

Andrew Cynric Donovan! Why would she even waste her precious thoughts on a man who would have her think he had been well born? He certainly did not deserve a thought! Or two! Or three!

Oh, but who was she fooling? She missed his egotistical yet winning ways, the way the corners of his eyes crinkled when he laughed, the iron-hard command of his body against her own . . .

She shouldn't think such thoughts. She'd lain with him in unabandoned intimacy and she would have to live with that folly.

116

The following Monday morning, Drew Donovan moved among the various mercantiles at the dock. He knew he'd have a hard time finding someone to order the parts he needed. It had been only four years since the first steamboat had moved into dock at St. Louis, and many people were still skeptical of their importance in shipping freight. Finally, though, he met a man at a café where he breakfasted who knew a merchant who could order the parts.

At just past seven, Drew was feeling heavy-hearted. He looked at his pocketwatch. Carrie Sherwood would board the stagecoach in less than fifteen minutes. He ached for her long, slim body, the full mass of flaming hair that had covered his chest just three nights ago, her gentle laughter and emerald eyes. God! Why had she been so blasted stubborn!

Suddenly Andrew knew he could not bear to see her go. He rose so swiftly he almost upset his cup of coffee, hastily threw a coin on the table, and moved into the cool morning. He looked first one way, then the other, and his long strides began to close the distance to the stage depot. He had just reached the boardwalk where the passengers normally gathered when the wheels of the coach for Baltimore stirred dust on the wide road in its hasty retreat.

"Damn!" He quietly hissed the word, looking at his pocketwatch once again. The blasted thing would have to leave five minutes early!

Carrie Sherwood was gone; he would just have to accept that. Turning slowly, he ambled back to the small café which now teemed with life — women in fashionable eastern dresses chatting with bankers and boasting politicians, common men from the docks, and common women from bawdy houses.

He was sick at heart that he'd missed the coach.

Quickly gulping his second cup of coffee, he had just paid his bill when he turned and, surprise registering unchecked in his eyes, faced Carrie Sherwood. Even as he wanted to embrace her, here and now for all to see, his gaze narrowed suspiciously. Pride would not allow him to betray his elation. "What are you doing here? Sleep late and miss your ride?" he asked coolly.

Carrie was so happy to see him, but she could not let him know that. He was already outrageously egotistical. "You can't be rid of me that quickly. I want to travel with you to Pennsylvania. I will feel safer with you than traveling alone to Maryland." Carrie couldn't have cared less that she'd drawn an audience. Her eyes were only for the Pennsylvanian. Yet he stepped around her and began a retreat, which didn't settle well with her at all. "Drew Donovan, don't you turn your back on me!" Drawing her hands to her hips, she tapped her toe in outrageous indignation. "You can't do this!"

Deliberately ignoring her, even as he fought the impulse to take her in his arms and tell her how happy he was, Drew stepped out to the boardwalk.

Carrie's eyes desperately scanned the room, settling on a big, burly seaman who had wandered in for breakfast. If there was one thing she'd noticed about American men it was their chivalry, regardless of how vulgar they appeared on the outside. Without hesitation, she rushed up to the seaman and clamped her slim fingers over his broad shoulder. "Sir, sir, you must help me. That man— see, the one standing on the boardwalk—he is my husband and he is attempting to abandon me and our two little daughters. Please, I implore you to help me."

The man rose, startling Carrie with his enormous height of almost seven feet. "Sure, little lady. That varmint there, you say?" Wiping gravy from his beard with his sleeve, the man moved toward the entrance. Stepping out to the boardwalk, he clamped his hand brutally across

Drew's shoulder. "Ain't nice to abandon a little woman an' your two young'uns. Now you git on in there an' you gather up your family."

"You must have mistaken me for someone else," Drew mumbled, attempting to pry the man's fingers loose from his shoulder. "I have no wife and children."

When Drew attempted to leave, the man's fingers tightened. Drew yelped, more in anger than in pain. He did not see Carrie emerge from the small café, but the sailor did. "This your man, eh, little woman?"

"He is," she replied, suppressing the grin tickling at her mouth. "He has paid passage for me back to England and is taking my babies away from me to give to his barren sister! I don't want to lose my babies."

Drew had planned to drop his mask of indifference and invite Carrie into the warmth of his embrace. He had planned to tell her how happy he was as soon as he'd enjoyed the teasing indifference of her that had drawn him out to the boardwalk. Now, however, he was furious that she'd recruited help from the patrons of the café. "Get your hands off me, man!"

"You'll be wantin' this rogue to take care of you?" the bargeman persisted.

Carrie feigned a frail and pained look. "Oh, yes, sir, I do! He's my husband! I only want him to see reason!"

"She's not my wife!" Drew bellowed, clutching firmly at the wrist of the man who surely outweighed him by a hundred pounds. Just as he swung at the large sailor, the town marshal and one of his deputies approached the cafe.

"What's going on here?" the taller of the two men inquired.

"This here bastard's attempting to abandon his wife— that poor little missy there. Just trying to make him see reason."

"Let him go," the marshal ordered. As the sailor did so,

Drew angrily straightened the front of his coat. "Are you trying to abandon your wife?"

"She isn't my wife," he replied as patiently as possible.

Even as she realized the scene was going much too far, Carrie Sherwood broke out into a most hysterical wail, taking all the men off guard. When she dramatically flailed her arms, adding emphasis to her feigned despair, the short, wide-girthed deputy took her wrists to control her.

"Be calm, miss. We are here to protect and to serve."

Had it been any other moment in her life, Carrie might have rolled her eyes at the platitudinous declaration. While the deputy made some effort to comfort her, the marshal continued to question Drew. "What is your name, sir?"

"Andrew Donovan."

"And why are you in St. Louis?"

"To buy parts for my steamboat that's crippled about fifteen miles downriver."

"Why are you abandoning your wife?"

"She is not my wife!"

The marshal took immediate offense at his vicious tone. Instantly, manacles were removed from his belt and clamped on Drew's wrist and his sidearm was confiscated. "Mr. Donovan, you are under arrest."

"What is the blasted charge?" Drew bellowed, his eyes cutting furiously to the now-quiet—and stunned—Carrie Sherwood.

"Criminal abandonment for now," the marshal announced, taking him firmly by the upper arm.

Carrie's little prank had gone awry. She certainly had not intended for Drew to be arrested. As she walked quietly along with the deputy while the marshal escorted Drew Donovan to jail, she wondered how she was going to get out of this situation. She knew she'd have to resort to some of the skills her uncle so loathed in her.

Moments later, they entered a small redbrick building. The manacles were removed and Drew was shoved into one of two small cells. He turned. If looks could have killed . . .

"Earl, you do what you want with the fellow," the marshal said to his deputy. "I'm going over to the café for my breakfast." Tipping his hat, his eyes sympathetically held Carrie's. "Sorry about your troubles, missy."

The marshal, whom Carrie had instantly judged to be a little smarter than the deputy, soon closed the door. It was time to act before this went any further.

"Aaaa-owwww!" Carrie wailed in the most dreadful voice. " 'E'll be pinchin' me off without a farthin', 'e will. 'E treats me beetle-'eaded, 'e does, an' me with a belly full ag'n! 'E promised me a round sum, 'e did to come over 'ere an 'itch with 'em, 'e did. The 'en-'earted 'ector is me ol' man, 'e is, an' me an' me chits, we'll starve, we will!"

Drew folded his fingers around the cold bars of the cell. Was there a single vulgar term the "well-born" Englishwoman did not know? That must be some scullery maid on the loose at Holker Hall. Patiently, Drew replied, "I do not consider her to be dull-witted, nor is she with child. I did not pay her to come here and marry me, I am not a cowardly bully, and there are *no* chits, I mean . . . babies, to starve!"

Carrie hopped from the chair where the deputy attempted to comfort her. "Aaaa-owwww! See 'ow 'e lies, 'e does! Have mercy, Bobby, 'e ain't much, but 'e's all me an' me chits 'ave."

The deputy folded his plump arm around Carrie. "There, there, girl, don't you worry none. If you want the rogue back, well, who am I to argue . . ." Cutting a humored look meant only for Drew, Carrie wailed again. The cell keys came up from the deputy's belt. The marshal had, after all, told him to handle it as he saw fit, and he couldn't break the poor little lady's heart.

While he fumbled to unlock the cell door, Drew asked tonelessly, "Did you really fall for that pitiful act?"

"Shut up, mister." He was obviously enjoying the authority the marshal had given him. The door opened. "You get out of here with your little woman. If I hear any more complaints about you and if you cause any more trouble in St. Louis, we'll have a private collar-party back in the alley."

A furious Drew Donovan grabbed up his sidearm, reholstered it, then moved in long strides out to the boardwalk. He rubbed his wrists, one of which had been slightly bruised by the heavy manacles. Silently, Carrie Sherwood stepped out behind him. "Are you angry with me?" she asked.

Drew turned swiftly back. "Why the hell aren't you on that coach?" He would never admit to her that he had sought to intercept the coach with one last plea that she remain.

Her shoulders made a delicate move, and her mouth pouted prettily. "I didn't want to go."

"Why the hell not?"

"I want to stay with you, at least until we reach Pennsylvania." Proudly, she held his money out to him. "This is most of it. I cashed in the stage ticket."

Drew snatched the wad of bills from her and stuck it into his inside coat pocket. "Blast it, woman!"

Carrie remained undaunted by his fury. "What are you going to do with me, Drew? Leave me to the mercy of America without proper funds?" Drew's fingers closed tightly over her right wrist. He began dragging her down the street, paying no heed to her protests. "What are you going to do to me, Drew Donovan?"

"There's only one thing I want to do when I'm mad enough to kill."

"Wh-what is that?" she stammered, ignoring the surprised glances of the group of ladies Drew dragged her past.

"It doesn't require clothing!" he hissed.

Carrie's feet became brakes upon the boardwalk, but he was much too strong for her. Had she not decided to stumble along once again, she was sure she'd have seen smoke at her heels. "Let me go, Drew Donovan! You can't treat me so!"

"Why not? Didn't you call me a hen-hearted hector? Well, English, if it's a cowardly bully that does what I'm about to do, I'll have to live with that character assassination!"

Carrie wanted to solicit help from the many people watching the embarrassing spectacle. But she could not make a sound. She'd never imagined that a man like the Pennsylvanian could be so furious.

And certainly he would not take her against her will!

Would he?

Chapter Eight

Carrie realized how deliberate Drew's actions were when he dragged her down a narrow alley to keep from walking in front of the café where the marshal breakfasted. Drew obviously gained immense pleasure from embarrassing her, and she wouldn't give him the satisfaction. She stopped protesting and matched his long strides with obvious mimicry.

She held her head high as they entered the hotel on Main Street where she had maintained her room. "Is Miss Sherwood's room still available?" Drew bellowed at the clerk behind the counter.

Before the clerk, astonished by his vicious tone, could answer, Carrie said curtly, "I have paid up through the week! With your money!"

Drew's dark, hooded gaze locked to her own. Again, a smile turned up his mouth. "Then, little wife . . ." He spoke so that only Carrie would hear. "Shall we bed ourselves?"

"This man is assaulting me," Carrie said, her statement indifferent and weary.

To which the clerk replied somberly, "That, madame, is your problem."

As Carrie was ruthlessly dragged up the narrow steps, a thought occurred to her that almost robbed her breath.

She had made love with Drew Donovan, and, by all intents, he now planned to take her by force. After her adventures in America, she planned to return to England. Suppose her union with Drew Donovan had planted the seed of a child within her. Dear Lord, why hadn't she considered that very viable possibility? She had been ignorant, conducting herself like a giddy schoolgirl. She was the niece of the Duke of Devonshire and she might very well be impregnated by this American's seed. Her dear, sweet, kindly uncle would never live down the disgrace!

Having submitted to his brutality just moments before, Drew was surprised that she now fought him at every turn of the stairs. "Let me go, Drew Donovan! I'll file charges. You cannot rape me!" She hissed the words at his back, then kicked him in the calf with her left foot.

He did not physically respond to the attack. But once he had thrown her into the large, airy room, he replied, "How can I rape my own little wife? Isn't that what you told the marshal? That you are my wife?" Drew tucked his thumbs into the waist of his breeches and released a throaty chuckle. "Why, we even have chits! What are they? Two girls? Two boys? One of each? No, my darling, you are going to lie in my arms . . . and your body will be mine for as long as I want it!"

Harsh, cruel reality struck her in the face. So, he *would* take her against her will. She had misjudged him. In a strangled whisper, she begged. "Please, leave me unscathed, Drew Donovan. I shall not resort to dramatics to stay with you. If you do not want me, I shall leave in the morning. I swear this to you!"

Suddenly Drew found her sweet entreaty a soothing balm. The anger that had rushed upon him like a wild, uncontrolled flood now became a thin veneer of mere frustration. She'd brought false charges against him and had seen him thrown behind bars. It had been for only a few minutes, but it had happened nonetheless. She deserved his wrath. He was relieved she hadn't gotten on the stage, but he wouldn't let her know that. It might give her the upper hand.

"Unclad yourself, woman." He mouthed the words as if it really didn't matter one way or the other if she obeyed. "I'm not in the mood for restrictive bindings." When she stalled, looking at him in a mixture of shock and horror, he growled, "Well, get to it, woman!"

Carrie's arms stiffened; her slim hands became tight balls. "I will not!" she gasped, her finely arched eyebrows moving stubbornly upward. "I'll admit that what I did was ghastly, but you have no right to treat me like a common harlot! My uncle the—"

"The duke!" He spat the finish to her sentence with unbarred sarcasm. "If he does indeed exist, he is thousands of miles away." Coolly, calmly, Drew approached her, stood close for a long, silent moment, then gripped her arms and dragged her toward him. Her gentle breath, the subtle fragrance of perfume that he had not purchased for her, sweetly assailed his senses. "What have you been spending *my* money on, m'lady? You are like a flower in my arms."

Did she note his sarcasm, or were his tenderly spoken words sincere? Why was she not pulling away but standing like an awestruck girl in the arms of the devastatingly handsome Pennsylvanian?

Every time Drew was near the Englishwoman, he found his body wanting her, needing her, clinging to the tenuous hope that she wanted him as much. She'd humiliated him by having him thrown behind bars, and yet he could not remain angry with her. She'd proven her desire for him. She'd wanted to remain with him badly enough to have made a fool out of herself by acting irrationally and talking like the lowliest gutter snipe in London.

Carrie was making a deliberate effort not to look into

his eyes; her coy innocence was certainly intended to divert his intentions. That annoyed him because he did not want her to think for a minute he could be so easily sidetracked. In one swift move, Drew loomed over her, gripped the bodice of her lavender gown, and pressed his knuckles against her soft flesh. "Are you going to remove this? Or shall I?" Stubborn pride sparkled in her eyes. Drew pressed his mouth into a thin smirk even as his fingers slightly loosened and his knuckles absently grazed her breasts beneath the fabric of her gown. "What is your choice, m'lady?" he asked on a note of finality.

Instantly, a small derringer pressed into his ribs. He did not remove his hands. A nervous tick at the corner of his left eye relayed his surprise. "The choice, Drew Donovan," she hissed between tightly clenched teeth, "is yours. Either you live or you die."

Drew managed to control his reaction to the derringer she had apparently purchased with his money, though he did not understand her need to be armed. So, she had more up her sleeves than soft, ivory skin! Was he willing to let her back him against a wall?

"So the choice is mine," he murmured patiently, his body moving closer to her own. The snubbed barrel of the derringer dug between his ribs. "Then fire your little weapon, Princess, because not only is the choice mine, but *you* are mine as well."

His sweet, warm breath assailed Carrie's crimson cheeks. She was in a quandary; she had been so sure that the derringer she had purchased that morning would quell his male intentions. What was she to do now that he had made his choice? Didn't he care that, for all intents and purposes, she intended to shoot him?

"Well, Princess?" Drew's hands moved up to grip her slim shoulders beneath the fabric of her bodice. In one swift move, he tore the gown down her arms, dislodging the weapon from her trembling fingers and sending it

127

clattering to the floor.

Carrie held the heavy material to her breasts with one hand and struck out at his cheek with the other. But Drew took both wrists and pinched them together. "Let me go, Pennsylvanian!"

"Certainly, Princess." As he released her wrists, he pushed her backward to the bed. She lay there, her mouth gaping in surprise, bracing herself with her elbows on the smooth covers. Kicking the little derringer across the room, Drew approached, dodging the foot that kicked out at his shin. "Since you didn't get out of your clothes, I will have to do it for you."

When he lowered himself to her, Carrie found her voice. Her hands pressed firmly against his shoulders in a weak effort to remove him. "Get off me, Drew Donovan! How dare you assault me like this!" Trembling in a mixture of fury and desire, she hissed at him. "You cannot have your way with me every time you're in the mood! Bastard!"

"Shut up," he ordered brusquely, his hands circling her wrists to pin them to the bed. "And don't be so vulgar."

"Please . . . please, Drew . . ."

"And don't beg so pitifully, my sweet. I have every intention of satisfying you."

"Only your death would satisfy me!" Carrie wanted desperately to dispel the passion surfacing from deep within her. She could not allow his assault; he would think she liked it this way. How egotistical he was, even as he teased and taunted her, trying to turn the cards so that she would appear to be the seducer. She had to beat him at his own game. A man wanted most what was not easily offered to him. And with that in mind, Carrie ceased her protests. Her body lay limply beneath his.

He was at once surprised, then suspicious. His grip relaxed, and the sarcastic smile left his mouth. Carrie held his gaze, transfixed. She did not protest as his mouth touched her own, but she did not respond, either. Even when his hand slipped beneath her bodice and roughly caressed the soft mound of flesh hidden there, she did not react. Even her breathing had slowed to virtual nonexistence.

"What is this game you are playing, Carrie?"

"If you want your way with me, then have it and be gone." All the willpower in the world could not have been a match against his masterful caress, as the dark crest beneath his hand peaked with desire. A surge of excitement rippled through her. She drew in a long, steady breath, wishing to the Almighty that he would withdraw from her before she humiliatingly responded to his maleness—and her own need.

Drew, however, had seen through the dramatics. If she thought he would leave her simply because she had gone limp in his arms, she was sadly mistaken.

But who was he trying to fool? He would not take a woman if she were not willing. With an irate groan, he withdrew his hand and pushed himself up from her. The move manifested itself in her eyes as stunned surprise.

"Hell, English!" Swiftly, he put his clothing back into some semblance of order. "I'm getting out of here!"

He had scarcely retreated a half dozen steps before she sprinted from the bed and landed full at his back. He spun around, grappling for her flailing wrists, anger twisting at his mouth. Then he saw the tears moistening her eyes and the tremble wracking her body.

He pulled her tightly into his arms. She did not fight, but slumped defeatedly against him. "Why do you treat me like this, Drew?"

Silence. Coaxing her face to his shoulder, Drew's hand gently twined through the thick, rich masses of flaming hair. "Why are you so emotional, Carrie? I would never force myself on a woman who does not want me! You think I will make love to a woman who lies there like a slab of marble?"

The tears became salty rivers upon her cheeks. Her voice, cracking with emotion just moments before, now became soft and sultry. "You knew I wanted you! You withdrew from me simply to punish me! I am a person and I deserve a little respect."

Her calmly delivered words stirred Drew to shame. It did not matter what had happened that morning at the St. Louis jail. It did not matter what had happened just moments before on the comfortable bed that now lay crumpled and empty where they might have lain in wonderful fulfillment, if not for her blasted theatrics! As far as he was concerned, her statement deserved his consideration. She had said nothing that wasn't true.

"What do you want of me, Carrie? From this moment on, what is to be my role in your life?"

Carrie removed herself from his embrace. With the back of her hand she smoothed away her tears, then tugged at her bodice loosened by his bold caresses. "I want to feel safe with you. Now that I am away from Junius, I want to enjoy America and her adventures. After I have had my fill, I want to return to England and my uncle."

His dark, hooded eyes narrowed. Crossing his arms, a moment of thoughtful silence fell to his features. "I see. You want a protector in a strange land, and a tour guide to see you safely on your adventures. Then you want to board a ship and return home, taking nothing more than exciting memories of the great American wilderness."

Dare she admit to anything more personal, like the emotions and the longing swelling within her for him? She could not risk being trapped in America by her feelings for him. She had to force herself to remain aloof, to use him to her advantage just the same as he used her. With that in mind, she tartly replied, "Of course, what more could it be? Surely, you wouldn't expect me to remain because I care for you. That is preposterous!"

Try as he might, he could not disguise the pain springing to his eyes. Because the emotion in those dark orbs took Carrie by surprise, she felt an immediate need to let him know where he stood, and at the same time, deny her own feelings. But even as she spoke, her heart bled. "You are an American. I am English, and I have a life awaiting me in my homeland. You are physically stronger than I, and I am sure that if you wish to take advantage of that fact, you could take to my bed any time you wished. Just remember that if you ever do, I will loathe you."

Calmly, deliberately, Drew approached the far wall and bent to retrieve the derringer. Taking long strides back to her, he opened her hand and pressed the weapon into her palm. He said nothing as he stepped away from her, met her haughty gaze for a moment, then opened the door and disappeared into the corridor.

Carrie restrained herself from rushing after him and pleading for his forgiveness. Balling her hands in a fit of frustration, she threw herself facedown on the bed. The musky manliness of him clung there. She breathed deeply and longingly of it.

Carrie certainly did not expect him to brood miserably for days. When he dined with her he said nothing except to solicit her food order, and nightly he left her at the door to her room with not so much as a parting word. She would hear him leave the hotel, destined for one of the many saloons dotting the village of St. Louis. Thereafter, she rested with the derringer under her pillow, waiting for the familiar sound of his boots clipping toward his room beside her own, frequently pausing at her door before disappearing toward his lonely bed. His steps were often unsteady, the gait of a drunk.

This night, however, four long, tense days following their heated encounter, she heard not only his familiar steps but giddy feminine laughter as well. Hopping from the bed, she fought the urge to tear open the door, electing rather to press her ear firmly to it.

Vinna McMurtry had not expected to be noticed by so handsome a visitor to her lifelong village of St. Louis. She appeared much older than her actual age of twenty-eight, and had frequented the saloons, soliciting the attentions of men with money, for ten years now. She'd built a reputation as the easiest woman this side of the Mississippi, a reputation she was very proud of. It gave her an edge over the other women who frequented the saloons. She hoped the tall, unprepossessing stranger with his arm locked across her shoulder was not too drunk to provide her a good tumble but drunk enough to have his pockets picked clean afterward. She had a feeling it would be a very profitable night.

"Velda . . . here . . ." Drew stumbled into the doorway of his room, forcing the door open on its rusty hinges.

"It's Vinna," she said, her throaty whisper betraying her poor breeding. "You've got some memory, mister."

"Sorry, Verna."

"Vin—" Vinna shrugged her shoulders; what the hell did a name matter? He could call her anything he wanted, as long as the night was profitable. "Come on, mister, let's get you in here."

Drew could not remember a time in his life when he'd been drunker. Certain points of his memory were sharp, though. He knew *why* he was so drunk—that high-and-mighty she-male right next door who would treat him like a servant!

Drew stumbled against his bed, then fell upon it face-first, his hands stretched above his head. When he heard the door close, he attempted to roll over, but he was trapped by his own heaviness and could not accomplish the task. The woman's hand fell to his shoulder and, with her coaxing, he tumbled over, his gaze meeting her own in the semidarkened chamber.

"Velma, honey," he slurred. "Come here to me. You gonna make me feel real good tonight."

"Sure, mister," she whined. "Vinna will make you feel so good you'll know she was here when you wake up in the morning."

The coarse, dark-haired woman paid little heed to the creak on the floorboards just outside the door—probably one of the other guests coming or going, she thought.

The intruder upon their privacy was, however, Carrie Sherwood. She had donned her robe, grabbed up her freshly loaded derringer, and stood just outside the door, listening to the intermingled masculine and feminine voices from within.

Carrie was not sure why she was so furious. She wanted to charge into the bedchamber and rip the woman's hair out by the handful, then put the derringer to Drew Donovan's heart and pull the trigger. How dare he carry on so shamefully! It was one thing to drink himself into insensibility, but to take a cheap, vile woman to his bed was an outrage. After he had lain with a real lady, how could he be so despicable?

The door had not closed completely. Carrie watched the shadow that was the saloon whore swarming over the half-conscious Drew Donovan. It was all she could do to keep from pouncing in for the kill.

Vinna tugged at Drew's shoulders, attempting to dislodge him from the bed. "C'mon, mister. I thought we were going to have a little fun, eh, lovey?" The coarse voice had become insincerely sweet. When she realized he'd passed out from drink, her long, bloodred fingernails began to dig into his pockets, depositing to the covers first his expensive watch then a few coins from his coat, then a sterling silver flask, and finally the small, leather purse containing his money.

Carrie watched as the woman sifted through the items, selecting what she wanted, then dropping them into the cleavage of her full bosom.

Pushing the door open just enough to accommodate her slim form, Carrie crept up behind the woman. As the small derringer dug into the base of her skull, she released a startled cry. "What're you doin', mister. I ain't doin' nothin'!"

"I'm no mister," Carrie whispered in her sweetest voice. "And the man you're robbing belongs with me. Put back what you've taken or I'll tear your heart out—"

"I didn't take nothin'—"

"Put it back!"

The woman fumbled nervously in her bosom and removed the valuables she had taken from Drew Donovan. She tossed them in such haste the money scattered to the floor. "Can I go now, lady?"

Carrie drew in a deep breath, digging the derringer more firmly into the woman's neck as she did so. "You get out of here. And if I ever see you with my man again, you'll have to wear wigs for the rest of your life!"

The woman spun on her knees and stumbled from the room. Even as she clambered down the corridor with steps loud enough to wake the dead, Drew did not stir from his sleep.

Carrie wanted to pounce upon him and dig his eyes out. She'd never been so angry. How could he lie there looking like an innocent babe when just moments before he'd dragged a whore to his bed?

Quietly, she gathered his valuables into a pile and deposited them on a tray on the bureau. He was sprawled upon the bed with his boots hanging over the rail; she tried to tug him up to his pillow, but he was much too heavy for her. She managed only to move him a few inches. Locking her fingers beneath his torso, she again attempted to budge him. Alcohol fumes wafted across her cheek, nauseating her.

Suddenly, his arms locked around her back and held her close. "You're still here, Valda. I thought you'd left . . ."

Carrie tried to pry his fingers loose from her back, but he was more determined to hold on to her. In one swift move, he pulled her to his side, and his fingers wrapped among the strands of her hair.

Even in his half-consciousness, Drew was surprised. The locks of hair tangled through his fingers were soft and silky, not stiff with the curling pastes that had repulsed him in the saloon. "Washed your hair, eh, Vixie?"

"Let me go, Drew!"

Had he noticed the crisp English accent in the terse order? His hand moved the length of the bedgown covering her slim figure, eliciting a groan of protest from her.

Even in his drunkenness he was too strong for her. Carrie found herself on her back with him hovering over her, his mouth clumsily searching for her own. Immediately he felt the victory of her body's erotic betrayal beneath his clumsy caress. In the moments that followed, Carrie could not extract herself from his powerful arms, even as he fumbled to free himself of his trousers. Without prelude, she was filled with him—a violation that, strangely, did not repulse her. Drunk and delirious, he was uncommonly gentle, though a tad clumsy, with the woman he thought he'd picked up in the saloon that night. Even though his only thought at the moment was satisfying himself, Carrie locked her slender legs around him and moved with him, matching his fervent rhythm and pace.

She fought an unsuccessful battle trying not to respond to the sensual excitement grabbing her in its powerful clutches. As his hand roughly moved up and down her thighs, she enjoyed his deepening thrusts. She responded achingly to him. He plummeted again and again, claiming his treasure as his mouth roved teasingly over her tightly pressed one. She traitorously enjoyed the playful teasing of his kisses.

Her body continued to match his tempo. She closed her eyes tightly so that she would not see mocking victory in his eyes. Oh, but there was none of that there. She might have enjoyed his look if she hadn't deprived herself of it so blatantly and stubbornly.

Her hands moved to clutch at his shoulders, and her hips moved faster and faster still until the pinnacle of passion was just beyond their grasp—the anticipated treasure, delayed so that the full enjoyment of sensuality could be savored and tasted, like the richest of honey.

The sweet agony of his final thrust elicited a tiny moan which was immediately caught up in Drew's kiss. When at last they lay locked in exquisite fulfillment, she could not be angry with him.

Drew turned over slowly, pulling up his trousers, and stared at the feminine form upon the bed. "That was real good, honey. Come here . . ." He held out his hand. Hesitating only a moment, Carrie eased into his embrace. "How much do I owe you, Princess?" Carrie drew in a deep breath and held it for a long, silent moment. So! He called all his women "Princess." It was not a special endearment for her. He treated all women the same and expected each and every one of them to be at his beck and call to satisfy his primal needs! How dare he! "How much, Princess?" he repeated, drawing her close and nuzzling against the disheveled masses of her hair.

Even as she wanted to hate him, she looked forward to the moments when she lay in his arms. In a quiet but strangled whisper, tears sheening her emerald eyes, she replied, "Twenty-five dollars."

"Ever going to give me bargain rates, eh, Princess?"

That was not something he'd have asked the common Vinna whom he'd apparently met just that night. Startled, Carrie asked, "Who do you think I am, Drew?"

"My princess . . ." he mumbled, the flicker of his long lashes tickling at her cheek. "My princess with the flaming hair . . . whose blasted temper could split a squealing hog."

Her tears were immediately of joy as she turned into his arms. Waves of pleasure and relief soared through her as she looked forward to a long, wondrous night sleeping in his embrace.

But would he want to see her face in the morning when he was sober? Should she slip from his room in the predawn hours so he would not know *she* had provided him his pleasures that night and not the woman named Vinna?

Closing her eyes against the darkness, she decided she needed a few hours' sleep before attempting to answer the questions. Within the security of his arms wrapped so possessively around her, she quickly let sleep overtake her.

The predawn hours, however, found her fully awake, gently extracting herself from his embrace. Slipping from the bed, she moved quickly toward her own lonely room and lay there until the sun crept slowly upward on the horizon.

Through the walls separating them, she soon heard a curse and a grumble as Drew forced himself from his bed. Carrie imagined that he'd have quite a headache and certainly no memory of the night before. He would never know that she had lain with him.

But she was so wrong.

First, his door came open, then her own. He stood in silhouette in the doorway, looking at her. She could not see his eyes, but she imagined they were hooded and angry. She could see his mouth forming curses and damnations as he prepared to berate her for her deception.

Rather, he said, "Why did you leave my bed?"

To which she replied, "What do you mean? You brought a woman from the streets to your bed."

Drew sauntered slowly and deliberately toward her, fighting for the steadiness his previous night of unabandoned drunkenness had robbed him of. He sat on the bed and brutally dragged her into his arms. His rapid breath assailed her senses. *"You* were in my bed!" he hissed, twisting his fingers painfully through the rich, disheveled masses of flaming hair. "My princess. Don't you think I can tell one woman from another, even when I'm drunk?"

"I wouldn't know," she whispered, her gaze locking to his own.

"You allowed me to have my way with you. You could have broken from me. I was drunk out of my mind!"

Stubbornness pinched her mouth. "You were too strong for me, Drew Donovan," she argued.

"You *wanted* to lie with me! Admit it, Princess!"

She could deny it to hell and back. But he knew better, and she knew he knew it. In an effort to save face, she said, "You were so drunk, you needed protection, Drew. The harlot was going to rob you!"

"Why would you care?"

"Because."

"Because why?"

"Because I just do!" she spat out, attempting to pry her wrists from his firm grip.

"You care for me, don't you, Princess?"

A certain sinking defeat settled into her stomach. She could sling denials and degradations at the man who held her in his arms—this kind, gentle man she had hurt with bitter accusations and insults just a few days ago. She wondered how he could stand to be near her, let alone have loved her last evening. It was time for the denials to

138

end, at least for a little while . . . at least until she returned and took her place in English society. "Yes, Drew . . . I do care for you, as I have never cared for another man."

His blackening gaze held her with doubt and indecision. He wanted to believe her, but was he that gullible a fool? He remembered their discussion a few days ago. Did she want him simply as a tour guide and protector? Or as a lover? Possibly even as a husband? The idea was not repulsive to him, but he also could not imagine her putting forth the effort to be a wife. She was young and free-spirited. Was she worth his time and trouble?

Drew pulled her into his embrace. He said nothing, but held her for a long, long while.

Perhaps she was worth his time. He decided to see what lay ahead in the future.

Chapter Nine

Junius Wade looked out over the swelling currents of the Mississippi, his monocle clamped firmly in the wrinkles of his right eye. A cold wind blew down from the north, rustling the dry gray wisps of hair across his mottled scalp. Three weeks had passed since the churning, volcanic stern-wheeler upon whose deck he stood, had left port in New Orleans. Within days they would reach St. Louis, where supplies would be restocked before they continued toward Louisville, the home berth of *Donovan's Dream*.

Since Carrie had disappeared five weeks earlier, Junius Wade's mood had blackened treacherously. He'd cursed the sun for rising and the night for falling. He'd cursed the wind for blowing; it had not borne Carrie's fragrance upon it.

He was standing so deep in pity for himself, it was little wonder he didn't drown on the spot. He didn't know why he was obsessed with recapturing Flame. He'd lost girls before and had given them scarcely more than a second thought and a curse of eternal misery.

But something tugged unmercifully at that black vortex within him that should have carried memories . . . memories he ofttimes felt were so lost they'd never be found again. Hatred churned like a sweltering sea within him,

140

spewing up tiny fragments of memory that could form into nothing he could grasp with any degree of certainty. Fire . . . a gloomy old house . . . a mummified corpse — a corpse for God's sake! . . . a peaceful creek winding through immaculate lawns . . . the bells of a church pealing across a cold, cloudless night . . .

For one moment something that might otherwise have been pleasant flashed within the blackness of his mind . . . a tall, willowy, golden-haired woman . . . and the vision rushed hot and cold down his spine. He stood upon the deck and shivered, not from the cold but from that vile, fleeting whisper from his dark past. Murderous, maniacal rage sprang into his eyes but darted away before his crippled body could react.

Diana Donovan shot up from her sleep like a person viciously struck, her body drenched in a cold sweat, her bedgown clinging damply to her body. She trembled so violently her husband, caught unawares by her sudden emotion, pulled her tightly into his arms.

"Diana, what is wrong?" he whispered against her still-golden hair. "Are you ill?"

As foolish as she felt, Diana could not prevent the tears that escaped her violet eyes. "It is he, my husband. He crawled across my flesh like a cold, deadly wind . . ."

"Who?" Cole held her tightly. "Who are you talking about?"

Diana pulled back, terror rushing into her eyes as they met his bewildered gaze. "Our son is in danger. What can we do? Our Andrew . . ."

Caught in a moment of frustration and rage, Cole shook his wife. "Dammit, are you speaking of Webster Mayne again?" His Scottish accent was stronger now. "He is dead, lass! How many times must I tell you this? Our son is *not* in danger! You are just upset because tomorrow will be our first Christmas Eve without him!"

She hadn't given a moment to Christmas; the terror had completely taken away all sensible thought. If she had retained any senses at all, it did not reflect in her wild-eyed gaze. Even securely tucked into Cole's embrace, she felt the cruelty of that other man — that vile, despicable gorgon from her past . . . from Cole's past — emerging upon them from the black hole of hell. "Hold me, husband. I am sick with fear."

Cole wished to God Andrew would return to Wills Creek and send a message to them that he was safe. Diana had suffered a brutal nightmare, and she would not be consoled by his reassurances. *Where are you, son?* Cole thought desperately. Though Diana was not aware of it, Cole trembled inside. As long as he'd known Diana he'd known her to be blessed — or cursed — with the gift of insight. Secretly, he was as fearful for their son as she was.

On this cold December morning, Carrie tucked herself comfortably into the crook of Drew's arm. As he slept she watched his strong profile for some signs of life; he seemed reluctant to stir from the warmth of their shared bed. With the edge of the sheet she tickled his nose, but he merely flicked it away in his sleep with nothing more than a low grunt.

The past two weeks had been wonderful. They'd reached a mutual understanding and had not had a single argument since that morning he'd come to her room. They wouldn't be in St. Louis much longer. It was simply a matter of time before the parts necessary for repair of *Donovan's Dream* arrived and began their downriver trek.

The fire had burned down in the predawn hours and a chill crept over Carrie's exposed flesh. Drawing herself beneath the covers, she eased her arm across Drew's shaggy chest. Her more vigorous movements stirred some life into him. His thick, dark eyelashes fluttered against his cool cheek but still his eyes did not open.

"Awaken, sleepyhead," she murmured, watching a tiny smile appear at the corner of his mouth. "I am lonely for you."

His failure to respond beyond the smile gave her a moment to reminisce over their last weeks together. Theirs had been almost a mutual acceptance of each other's needs. Not once had he gotten angry over some thoughtless act on her part and he had been tolerant of her moods and haughty airs. Carrie felt safe with him; the mere presence of him was like a soothing balm in this wild, free country that was America.

A rap sounded at the door. Still, Drew did not stir from his sleep. Easing from the warm covers, Carrie pulled on her robe and opened the door just enough to see the caller. A young boy, appearing to be no more than ten, stood there, rubbing sleepy eyes and holding a bit of paper folded in thirds. He smiled lazily when his eyes met Carrie's questioning ones.

"From Mr. Curtis," he explained.

Carrie took the letter, aware that the sender was the man who had ordered the parts for *Donovan's Dream*. She opened the short note and read: "Parts arrived this morning. Please present to dock and pay additional shipping costs." Gathering her robe about her, a suddenly playful Carrie rushed toward the bed and threw herself upon Drew's sleeping body. With a loud, startled groan he came fully awake, grasped her arms, and pulled her firmly to his body. "Damn, Princess! If I'd had a gun I'd have shot you!" Carrie tucked her chin on her crossed hands and met his sleepy gaze. When he saw the paper held loosely in her fingers, he took it from her. "What is this?"

"That was just sent by courier. The parts are in for *Donovan's Dream*."

143

"It's damn near about time." A smile played upon Drew's mouth. "And what am I to do with a feisty female who throws herself upon a sleeping man?"

Carrie shrugged absently. "Oh . . ." Her whimsical expression widened his smile. "Get dressed and take her out to breakfast?" she suggested.

"Sounds good to me," he replied, lightly flicking her pert chin with his index finger. "There is just one problem . . ."

"What is that?"

"I have this godawful heavy load upon me!"

"Ohh!" Carrie chuckled good-naturedly. "I'm not heavy, Drew Donovan! I'm as thin as a rail—not an ounce of fat upon these bones!"

Clasping his arms around her slender back, Drew turned on the bed with her. Resting above her, he gently touched his mouth to hers in a good-morning kiss. "And were your bones as plush as leather seats, I would still desire them!" He smiled warmly. "Shall we take care of our stomachs and our business this morning and make arrangements to travel downriver?"

An unexpected frown touched Carrie's eyebrows. "What will the men think when I return?"

"They will think . . ." His mouth touched hers in playful, teasing kisses, "that I was so smitten by you I have taken you my prisoner."

"Noble will be furious that you've brought me back."

"He will be elated." Drew murmured the argument. "If you return with me to Wills Creek, it will greatly improve his chances of winning Jolie's hand."

Carrie's frown deepened. She did not want Drew to get too accustomed to having her around. After all, ultimately she would have to return to England and resume her position as mistress of Holker Hall. Even now, their parting would be difficult. How much more difficult would it be in a few weeks or a few months?

Forcing away the gloom that had settled upon her, Carrie managed a smile. "I am starving, Drew Donovan! Shall we dress?"

"In a little while," Drew whispered huskily, trailing kisses upon her cheek and each of her translucent eyelids. "In a little while . . ."

The captain saw the crippled steamboat on the sandbar from a distance and sent word to the sleeping Junius Wade. The grotesque man who had paid four thousand dollars to lease his stern-wheeler for the chase appeared within moments of the summons and joined the captain in the wheelhouse. Turning control over to his junior, he moved with Junius to the hurricane deck for a better view of the beached steamboat ahead.

"That's her!" Junius exclaimed. "That's *Donovan's Dream*. How close can you get?"

"A few hundred yards," the captain replied. "I'll not be wanting to end up on the sandbar beside her."

The men of the *Dream* had taken places along the boiler deck when the northern-bound stern-wheeler's smokestack had been spotted. Other river travelers had stopped in the past two weeks to offer help, but somehow this one was different, perhaps because a hideous, twisted man stood at the stern, watching their every movement.

"Good God!" Bundy exclaimed to Noble. "That's the English girl's pimp! Come lookin' for her, to be sure!"

Quickly, Noble pulled the men together. But by the time Junius Wade and several of his men had taken a rowboat to *Donovan's Dream*, the crew had dispersed, leaving only Captain Wyatt, Noble, and Bundy to greet them.

Bundy was first to offer his hand to the aging man struggling up the ladder, fighting the urge to release the limp appendages slithering against his palm. "If you fellows are offering help, we are awaiting parts from St. Louis. There's really not much your men could do."

Junius Wade's feet landed precariously upon the deck. "We, *sir*, have no desire to assist you. I am looking for property that I believe to be aboard your steamboat."

Noble scratched at his neatly trimmed black hair. "We have forty tons of freight on board, mister. We bought everything legal-like, but you're welcome to see our bills of lading."

"What I am looking for," Junius Wade quipped rudely, "does not require proof. One of my girls escaped. I have reason to believe she stowed away aboard your steamboat."

"No women aboard the *Dream*," Bundy said. "We don't take on passengers—"

"I said a stowaway!" he clarified. "I wish to see the owner of this craft . . . Mr. Donovan, I believe." He merely hissed the words between his deformed mouth.

The gathering of the men earlier had resulted in a plan, though Bundy's suggestion had not been to Noble's liking. Lying did not settle well with him, nor did he understand why Drew Donovan should be endangered by the presence of the creature standing a few feet from him. But, deferring to his half-brother's lack of character, Noble informed the man, "We had a boiler explosion a few weeks back. Mr. Donovan was killed below deck. And my friend here . . ." Noble's hand fell to the shoulder of his half-brother, not as an act of affection but to relay his displeasure at being put on the spot, "he didn't lie about your girl."

"You're a full-blood, eh?"

A deeper shade of bronze marked Noble's features. "I am. Do you have trouble with that?"

He chose not to reply to Noble's direct question that he felt was clearly intended to start trouble. Damned Indians! Junius thought. The world would be better off without them! "Then you will not mind my men having a look around?"

"I consider it an invasion," Noble remarked indifferently. "But I am sure that will not matter to you. Go ahead and have your look around. Then I want you out of here."

Noble scarcely contained his fury and frustration as Junius Wade led his men into every cabin aboard the *Dream*, spied beneath, between, and betwixt the freight, and slithered through the crippled steamboat looking for his lost property. When nothing turned up on first inspection, Junius sent the men again. This time, a big, burly man Junius had referred to as Tanner dragged a protesting Cawley Perth out of hiding. He held the boy's collar in one hand and a ball of green material in his other.

"Caught the boy sneaking off to throw this overboard." He handed Junius the tattered and soiled gown. It had been tied into a ball with twine and weighted with a rock.

"This is Flame's gown." His lethal gaze turned toward the wide-eyed boy. "Where did you get this?"

Noble pried the man's gnarled fingers loose from Cawley's collar. "Leave the boy alone. If that's what you want, you take it and get out of here!"

As Junius raised his hook, the men he had brought aboard with him produced weapons. "I want what was *inside* this! I want the woman called Flame!"

The hot-tempered Cawley yelled, "She ain't here. She's done gone with Mr. Don—uh, I mean, Mr.—uh, Cullen, to St. Louis."

Junius Wade's eyes narrowed maniacally. "So! Your Mr. Donovan was killed in the boiler room, eh?"

Junius Wade must have been insane to believe that seven men with weapons could stave off twenty-four. Instantly, he and his group were surrounded, top and sides, by the now-armed men of *Donovan's Dream*. The cocky Junius remained undaunted, though his men lowered their weapons.

"You get out of here," Noble ordered. "I'm in charge."

"I did not know Indians lied so easily," he smirked. "Are you not the one who told me Mr. Donovan was dead?"

"I do what I have to do."

"I know now why you felt the need. When will he be back?"

"None of your business."

"And my girl? Is she with him?"

Noble crossed his arms, his feet apart in a careless stance. "You ask a lot of questions for a man surrounded by hostile guns."

"Is my girl with him?" Junius repeated, showing unusual restraint.

"She was with him three weeks back. She accompanied him to St. Louis so that she could take a coach for the East Coast. Now, are you going to get off this boat or do you want an official escort?"

"Talk like a white man, *don't* you, blood?"

"I'll put it like this . . ." Noble replied indulgently. "I was raised by white men, so I talk like white men. You don't like it, that's fine with me. Because you and me are about to put distance between us."

"You do not control the river, blood," Junius hissed. "We will tie up in the river and await Donovan's return. I guarantee you that if I lose my girl, Donovan will lose his head."

Junius Wade's stern-wheeler sat off their portside, only a hundred yards into the river. While the men of the *Dream* watched their activity, Noble sat in Drew's cabin and wrote a hasty message to his friend informing him of the dangers awaiting him if he returned. Thank God he'd gotten rid of the Englishwoman by now. He could take the stagecoach back to Pennsylvania and avoid an unnecessary confrontation with Junius Wade. He shuddered to think, however, that Drew might welcome such a confrontation. He wasn't one to back down from danger.

Noble folded the letter, then summoned Cawley from the deck. "Boy, I want you to slip into the water on the starboard side . . ." Noble pressed a few twenty-dollar gold pieces and the letter into his hand. "You buy the best horse you can find from one of the locals and you hightail it for St. Louis. You can make it by midafternoon, but don't wind the horse. And . . ." Gripping the boy's shoulder roughly, he ordered, "you keep that letter dry."

"Then what, Mr. Noble? Should I stay with Mr. Donovan, or head on back here?"

"You do whatever Mr. Donovan tells you to do."

"But what about the *Dream?*"

"You don't worry about us. When Drew sends those parts downriver, my brother and I will see to the repairs and make sure everything gets to Louisville." The boy nodded. When he began his retreat, Noble's hand again fell to his shoulder. "You make sure when you slip into that river that none of those men from the stern-wheeler spots you. You scramble up into those cattails and you be gone. And—take care of yourself."

Cawley grinned widely. "Sure will, Mr. Noble. I'll be a wantin' to see Pennsylvanie."

The following day was Christmas. Carrie made excuses to Drew that she wished to do some shopping, then set off among the few shops and mercantiles in St. Louis. The town was abustle on Christmas Eve. Decorations and flickering candles encased in hurricane globes dotted the streets, store windows were gaily dressed, and children sang Christmas carols on the boardwalk.

After two hours of shopping, she had only two purchases to show for her efforts, both gifts for Drew—a painted pine storage box embellished with an eagle and the American flag and a warm wool scarf to be worn around his neck on these brisk winter mornings. She'd chosen a tweed of gray and black, to match his startling eyes. After another hour of shopping, she'd purchased heavy cotton shirts for Bundy, Noble, and Cawley, and boxes of cigars to be shared among the crew of *Donovan's Dream*.

Before returning to the hotel, she stopped at the butcher's to purchase a turkey. The portly gentleman brought a young hen from the back of his shop. When the creature released a panic-strickened gobble, Carrie took a step back, eyeing the bird with surprise and trepidation. "Oh, dear, I'd wanted it ready to be cooked," she said.

"I got a fine ax out back and a boy who's the fastest plucker north of New Orleans."

"Oh, dear . . ." Carrie did not like the look in the turkey hen's eyes—a pleading, desperate look that almost seemed human. She imagined she herself might have had that look when she'd stood on the auction block. "Well, all right, I guess I . . ." The butcher turned.

"No, wait! Oh, go ahead. No, wait . . ." What was she to do? At home at Holker Hall, she'd never seen a turkey that wasn't cooked, stuffed, garnished with parsley, onions, and boiled eggs, and served on a silver platter. She'd never really been sure what one looked like in its natural state. It was rather an ugly bird, but the preferred holiday poultry of England's wealthy.

"Well, ma'am. Do you want this turkey for your Christmas dinner or not?"

A labyrinth of emotions flooded her winter-cooled features. Oh, dear, what was she to do?

When she slipped through the rear door of the hotel, she spotted Drew's long, lanky form at a corner table in the small dining area. He nursed a cup of hot coffee between his palms and stared across his hands as if in deep thought. Quickly, Carrie moved up the stairs, deposited her purchases to a hiding place beneath the bed, then returned to the dining area. Drew looked up and smiled when she stood silently before him.

He stood and did not return to his chair until she had taken one across from him. "Did you complete your shopping? Have any of your money left?"

"A little." Carrie smiled warmly, dropping her chin to her linked fingers. She remembered, in that same moment, Mirabell's oftspoken lecture about elbows on the table, but still did not remove them. "How did you spend your morning?"

"Saw to the parts and arranged to send them downriver by barge." He did not admit that he'd done a little shopping himself. "We'll be returning to the *Dream* day after tomorrow."

"We will be able to spend Christmas together then? Just you and me?"

A waiter approached and stood silently by. "Are you hungry?" Drew asked Carrie.

"I'm famished," she declared. "I'd like a plate of beef like that lady over there is eating."

As the waiter departed, Drew took her hand across the table and held it tenderly. "So, tell me, have you arranged with the hotel to use the kitchen to prepare our Christmas feast tomorrow? I'm hardening my constitution for it."

"Pooh! Why should the kitchen be empty tomorrow? Since the staff is given the day off to celebrate Christmas with family, it needs to be put to some use! Thank goodness the café down the street will be open or the other hotel guests would be expected to starve!" Carrie teasingly withdrew her hand. "You'll see, Drew Donovan. I'll have you know we're having a turkey for dinner!"

"Indeed?" Uncertainty froze upon his brow. "And my little princess is going to stuff, prepare, and serve a turkey all by herself? Did you learn all this from the same scullery maid who tutored you in the vulgar tongue—and tutored you well, I might say?"

"The cook taught me to prepare many fine meals. And yes, I'm going to stuff her and I'm going to serve her. And I'm going to stuff and serve you, too!"

A humored Drew Donovan took her hand and squeezed it lovingly. "This I've got to see, Princess!"

Drew, who had lunched earlier, chatted pleasantly as Carrie enjoyed her meal. Later, they sauntered leisurely through the streets of St. Louis, enjoying the revelry of Christmas carolers and the fireworks that lit up the cold, overcast sky. They had just retired to their hotel when an exhausted Cawley Perth charged into Main Street atop an equally exhausted and recently purchased sorrel gelding.

Cawley had absolutely no idea where to begin his search for Drew Donovan, but he moved toward the most logical place, the marshal's office. He entered a dimly lit interior where a big, burly man reclined with his boots propped on a narrow desk. "What can I do for you, boy?"

"I'm lookin' for a man," Cawley said, removing his hat in respect to the law officer's authority.

"Lots of men about. Any particular one?"

"Yes, sir. Mr. Andrew Donovan. He's—"

"Don't know him. Sorry."

"Got to find him, Mr. Marshal. It's real important."

Only now did the marshal's boots hit the floor. It was

152

Christmas Eve; he was not in the mood to have a missing person's report filed when it was almost time for his relief to come on duty. "What does this fella look like?"

"Bout so tall . . ." Cawley gestured Drew's height. "Black hair, about thirty years old—"

"Sorry—"

"He was with a real fine-lookin' lady with red hair a few weeks back . . ."

Recollection clicked in his head. "Fine-lookin' lady, eh? About twenty, twenty-two? English?"

"Yeah, that's her! You know where I can find 'em?"

"Boy, I got better things to do than keep up with visitors. I ain't seen your man since I threw him in jail."

This declaration both startled and awed Cawley Perth. Nervously, he crushed his hat against his chest. "You threw Mr. Donovan in jail? That man's wealthier than this whole state. What'd he do?"

"Wealthy man, you say, eh? Your Mr. Donovan tried to dump his poor little wife in St. Louis without a penny in her pocket. And took her two babies away from her."

Cawley giggled nervously. "Mr. Donovan, he ain't married. What makes you think he had a wife?"

"She told me. Real distressed she was. An' that fella, he was treatin' her like he just really didn't give a damn. Boy, if you're wantin' to find him, try the hotels and the boardin' houses. That's all I can suggest."

Cawley backed to the door. "Thanks, Mr. Marshal."

"An' stay out of trouble in St. Louis, boy. My jail's empty tonight and I'd like to keep 'er that way."

"Yes, sir, Mr. Marshal."

When Cawley opened the door to leave, the marshal said in a throaty tone, "Merry Christmas, young fella."

Cawley stepped out to the boardwalk and scratched at his head. He looked up and down the street, then dragged up his collar when a blast of cold wind assailed him. "Well, Mr. Donovan . . ." he mumbled. "Where the

153

heck am I going to find you?" Taking the reins of his horse, he said, "Least I got enough money to bed us down for the night, old boy."

Chapter Ten

Lord Penley Seymour sat quietly in his favorite chair this early Christmas morning, watching the flames shimmer in the massive hearth and thinking of the many Christmases that he'd spent with his beloved niece. He puffed absently on a freshly filled pipe, its aroma drifting through the great hall, and stared at the window where they normally would have erected the grandest Christmas tree to be found in all of England. The massive ceilings had accommodated beautifully decorated trees that required ladders for completion, and the silk-and-porcelain treetop angel that had always graced its highest bow had customarily been put there by Carrie's hands. As he sat staring at the vacant space where only the misty dawn could be seen outside the window, he could almost hear the ringing gaiety of Carrie's voice. Christmas had always been her favorite time of year.

Never a day passed that memories of Carrie did not fill Penley's heart. He always thought of her alive, never dead, smiling and happy, never lost to eternity. He'd never forget the day an early-morning search of her had yielded only her damp clothing, deposited carefully on the beach behind a rock, and her slim footprints leading into the tide. He would never forget his stunned grief. He would never forget the memorial service that had been held—a service attended by His Royal Majesty, King George IV. England's current monarch, the unrestrained and extravagant son of their former king who had spent his final years in madness, had been fond of Carrie to the point of ridicule among his royal circles.

Carrie's death had turned Penley's life upside down. Once a confirmed bachelor, at the age of forty-six he had decided just two months following that tragic June morning to take Lady Anne Wallace as his wife, hoping that her companionship would serve to quell his grief and perhaps provide him the heir that Carrie had been. His acquaintances were shocked that he had not spent the customary year in mourning. His marriage to Anne had provided his first public scandal and might very well be the first time he'd deliberately allowed society to frown upon him.

Anne's life very closely paralleled his beloved Carrie's. Carrie's parents had died in a fever epidemic many years ago, shortly after they had sent their tiny daughter to safety with friends in the Scottish Highlands. It had taken Penley two long years to locate his only living relative, and she had been his constant companion ever since. Anne had been raised by a maiden aunt after her parents' ship had gone down in a gale while en route to New York to visit relatives.

The slim arms of his pretty wife moved gently down his shoulders from behind the chair. She was gracious and soft-spoken, her hair pulled up and held by simple ivory combs. Her cool, pale cheek coming to rest against his own elicited the tiniest of smiles. "I wish you'd have allowed a tree to be erected," she said wistfully. "It might have helped a bit to have carried on as usual."

Penley took her hand and coaxed her around to him. When she knelt to the thick rug, he placed his pipe on a small table and tenderly folded her hands between his own. "You're a kind and dear woman, Anne. I'll never understand why you married me when any number of young men were vying for your hand."

Anne smiled warmly. "I am twenty-four years old, Penley. Haven't you wondered why I haven't married before now?"

"I have, indeed."

"Because I wanted you. I was just a girl, scarcely thirteen years old, when you and Carrie visited my aunt at Chillington. I knew one day that you would be my husband."

Penley favored her with a smile. "I'm not particularly handsome."

"You are as handsome now as then, Husband. I am very pleased to be seen with you."

So warm and sincere was she that Penley felt guilty about depriving her the enjoyment of Christmas. He could not expect her to live in the shadow of his gloom. "About the tree, perhaps next year . . ."

Anne met her husband's gaze and noted with compassion his moisture-sheened eyes. She wanted his grief to end. It had been six months since the death of his niece and her friend, and it was time for life to go on. She hoped—dear God, she hoped!—that the Christmas gift she had for him might provide the miracle cure for his bereavement.

"Husband, though there are no visible signs of Christmas at Holker Hall this year, and though you forbade it, I do have a gift for you, if you will but accept it."

He was a little annoyed. Though she was twenty-two years his junior, and still moved by childlike curiosities, he had expected her to obey this one small request not to celebrate Christmas this year while he grieved for the loss of his niece. "What is this gift, Anne, that must be important enough to have gone against my wishes?"

Taking his hand, she lightly placed it on her abdomen. "The gift, my lord, is the seed of your child growing here within me."

What Anne thought was a frown was actually a fleeting moment of bewilderment. It took that long for the news to register in the brain of the dour, melancholy man. "Are you sure, Anne?"

"The physicians were here yesterday while you were in London. Yes, Husband, they are sure."

Penley squeezed her hands between his own. "And on what day is this blessed event expected to occur?"

Anne visibly shuddered. She had hoped he would not be so precise. "In June," she replied, her eyes lowering.

"In June," he reflected. "And did your physicians pinpoint a date more accurately?"

Silence. Her pale, powder-blue eyes raised to his clean-shaven features. The nostrils of his aquiline nose slightly flared, as though he were annoyed that she hesitated in answering him. "On June 12," she answered after a moment.

"June 12. That is the day—"

Anne's finger touched his mouth. "Yes, I know what day it is, Husband. But all the melancholy and grief will not erase that day as if it had never happened. Your dear Carrie is gone. My heart breaks, also, for she was my very dear friend. We spent many happy moments together, and I bless you for allowing our friendship when we were parted by so much distance. It is time for us to go on with the future, and to cease dwelling on the past. It is doing no one any good. Not you, not me . . . not the dear people who serve Holker Hall and grieve for your loss and weep for your tears. Please, dear husband, please let life go on. I cannot bear to watch your torment!"

She was right, of course. It was time to cease the grieving. Anne was his wife now, and by the end of spring she would give him a child, a new heir. He had selfishly and thoughtlessly dictated his wishes insofar as

Christmas was concerned, giving no thought to the needs or wishes of anyone else, including his new wife.

She had been patient and tolerant; she had allowed him to live in his shadow and exclude her from his life. She had never been less than a lady when she'd had every right to abhor him for his selfishness.

Something clicked inside him. Fixing his gaze to her own loving one, he recalled her softly spoken entreaty. Coaxing her to her slippered feet, he called loudly to his butler. "Artemas! Artemas!" The butler, who had brought him a tray with coffee just moments before Anne had arrived, immediately answered his summons. "Artemas, have a man cut that cedar behind the stables. And I want it decorated before noontime."

Anne released a delighted cry and threw herself into Penley's arms. "Oh, thank you, thank you, Husband!"

Artemas turned to leave but Penley spoke his name. "Artemas, send a message to Mr. Telford to open up his shop this morning and inform him that I shall pay him for his troubles. Lady Anne and I will be wanting to make Christmas purchases. Please direct Walwyn to have a carriage ready by the hour of nine."

A very bewildered butler moved toward the brisk outdoors, sure that Lord Penley had finally lost his mind.

"I must go upstairs and make a list," Anne bubbled enthusiastically. "It'll be a grand day." Taking her husband's hand in her moment of departure, she said, her voice softening to suit the occasion, "I shall summon the minister this evening to speak a tribute to our dear Carrie."

Penley smiled, but it was a sad, brief smile. "That is very thoughtful, Anne. Perhaps then we can all go on with the future."

At that moment, in the large village beside the Mississippi River, Carrie was thinking about Christmas at

Holker Hall. She remembered the past Christmases, the spirit and the gaiety, her uncle Penley's adorations and generosity, as their traditional tree had teemed yearly with brightly wrapped presents waiting to be opened by Carrie, the servants, and their families. Last Christmas more than a hundred people had enjoyed the festivities at Holker Hall. Carrie wondered how her "death" had affected Christmas this year.

Quietly, so as not to awaken Drew, Carrie sat at the desk beside the window and began a short letter to her uncle.

Reading it over to make doubly sure she hadn't said anything to worry him, she folded the note, addressed it, and tucked it into her handbag. Then she slipped from the room and made her way downstairs. Approaching the morning clerk, she handed him the letter and a coin, asking politely, "Will you see that this is posted tomorrow?"

"Of course, madame."

Carrie moved toward the kitchen at the back of the dining room and the cold box where she'd stored her food purchases from the day before. All through the morning she busied herself, toasting bread and crumbling it, adding seasonings and onions, fresh butter and eggs, and cooking rice for pudding. Occasionally she moved toward the back entrance and looked out into a fenced yard. Several times the clerk, drawn by the aroma of cooking food, deserted his desk to sample her dishes. Before half the morning had passed, Carrie had invited the clerk and a half dozen hotel guests to share their Christmas dinner. After all, the spirit of Christmas was in the sharing and the giving.

Recruiting the aid of a young woman named Maude to assist her with the meal, Carrie, revitalized by the joy of Christmas, bounded up the stairs toward the room she shared with Drew. Bumping into him at the platform of the stairs, she was immediately drawn into his arms.

"You are full of vim and vigor today," he murmured, humorously flicking a lump of dough from her nose. "Making biscuits?"

"Everything is ready. I was just coming to fetch you."

Tucking her into the wing of his arm, Drew accompanied her on the stairs. He was surprised to find the front desk abandoned and close to a dozen people lounging at the tables in the dining room. "What have we here?" Drew chuckled.

Carrie hastily explained. "It is Christmas, and I've prepared so much. I thought it would be nice to share with the other guests."

"And I admire you for it," Drew replied sincerely.

Carrie led him to the table she had reserved for them. "Sit here. Maude and I will bring out the plates."

Over the course of the next few minutes, plates filled with food were brought out and set on the tables. Fresh milk was poured and plates of biscuits and fresh butter put on each table.

Drew eyed his plate. Stabbing his fork into the poultry, he said, "This is chicken. I thought we were having a turkey for dinner."

Carrie blushed violently, smiling as she did so. "We *are* having a turkey for dinner . . . in an odd sort of a way," she managed in a small voice, backing from him toward the rear door of the dining area. Momentarily, a plump, clumsy turkey hen stumbled into the room and made its way among the tables. "I didn't have the heart to order the butcher to do her in." Stunned silence followed among the guests. "We won't go hungry!" she quipped in righteous indignation, meeting Drew's startled gaze. "I roasted half a dozen chickens." Carrie was immediately surprised and wary of the laughter slowly erupting among the dinner guests, including her own Drew Donovan.

At that very moment, watching her scamper like a playful child after the friendly bird, the tall, hungry

Pennsylvanian fell deeply in love with the kind-hearted niece of an English duke.

Her illusions of grandeur were not doing him any harm; why deprive her of them?

At the age of ninety-eight, Hambone wondered what kept him going year after year. He sat on the wide, airy porch of the Wills Creek Trading Post this cold December day, watching a snow goose take to flight across the timberline. He thought of his dear wife, Rufina, dead these ten years, and wished she could be with him on this, what could possibly be his final Christmas. A tear came to his eye, but a gruff cough forced it back.

A furry head scooted beneath his hand. Sweet Boy, grandson of the bobcat raised by Diana Donovan, looked up at him with a question in his eyes. "What's the matter, boy?" Hambone asked, rubbing his arthritic hand clumsily over the affectionate head. "Still miss your mama, eh?" He'd always blamed the cat's moods on a mother he'd forgotten years ago. For a moment, the keen mind of the old man remembered that day twenty-five years ago when Honey Boy, Diana's pet, had returned to the trading post with a scratching, hot-tempered she-cat clamped firmly between his teeth. They'd named her Honey Girl, and five years later, she'd given birth to Sweet Boy. Shortly thereafter she'd been killed in a fight with a wolverine, and Sweet Boy, who'd shown very little interest in mating, was destined to be the end of the line. At twenty-one years of age, Sweet Boy was probably about as old as Hambone, in his cat years. He might possibly live as long as his grandfather, who had died only four years before at the age of thirty-five, an almost unheard-of age in the life of a bobcat.

In his usual fashion, the aging bobcat fell lazily across Hambone's rawhide boots, then began chewing on the edge of the blanket across his knees. Hambone stared at the trail disappearing into the woods, almost as if he expected Drew to emerge and scold him for being out on such a cold day. He missed the boy; in Hambone's mind he was eight, rather than thirty-two. Hambone had hoped he'd return to the trading post by Christmas, even though, before departing, Drew had not held much promise that he would.

Jolie Ward entered the porch, hugging a thick woolen shawl to her slender frame. She stood for a moment, staring across the bleak, gray-cast sky, then dropped her hand to Hambone's thin shoulder. "Why are you out, old man?" She spoke affectionately, squeezing his shoulder as she did so. "Thinking of Drew, I suppose."

"Bah! I've better things to think about than that wayward boy!" He'd spoken sharply, but Jolie did not take offense. It was just his way. "What do you want, woman? Nothing better to do? If you'd rid yourself of that haughty air and take a husband, you wouldn't be so bored you'd have to check on me constantly."

A warm, somewhat humored smile turned up Jolie's full mouth. The gaze of her dark almond-shaped eyes absently scanned the timberline rustling beneath the strength of the wind, and her hand moved up to tousle the brittle strands of the old man's hair. "No man is brave enough to take me to wife," she replied after a moment. "Besides, Hambone, how could I worry you to death if I had to clean up after another man?"

"Bah!" Hambone pursed his thin lips, his piercing eyes locked in a mass of wrinkles as he glanced up at her lean, lovely features. "You don't take a man because you want my Drew!"

Though his sarcasm prickled her, Jolie managed a small laugh. "Indeed I do!" she shot back with equal ferocity. "And old man, you mark my word, I'm going to have him."

If he'd had enough strength, Hambone would have laughed himself. Rather, he tightly crossed his arms, vowing that Andrew Cynric Donovan would rue the day that he took that feisty wench to his bed. Did she think Drew had held out for his health? Jolie Ward had wasted her youth—she was twenty-five years old—hoping to wed a man who looked at her as an annoying little sister—and she was going to have to look elsewhere for a husband.

"What are you thinking, old man?"

Hambone glanced up at the woman who took care of him. "Wondering why you're out here wasting time when you should be seeing to my Christmas dinner!"

"Don't be ornery, Hambone. Hester is quite able to see that the meal is put on the table. After all, most of those eating it are her spawn. She must think she's a brood mare!"

"Talking about me, Jolie?" An unsmiling Hester stood in the doorway, rubbing her hands on a large white apron. Her wheat-colored hair was streaked with flour from her baking. "Or are you simply being your sweet old self?"

Jolie shrugged her shoulders, caring little that her sister had heard her cruel words. "Don't be so sensitive, Hester. Some of us are put on this earth to have children. Some of us have more glamorous pursuits."

I imagine, Hester thought. *Like trying to trap a man who doesn't want you.* Rather than reply as she might have liked, Hester announced somberly, "The dinner is on. Bring Hambone back indoors, Jolie. Have you seen my children about?"

"You round up your own little brats today," Jolie quipped. "I didn't give birth to them, and I'm not going to be responsible for them. I will not be the keeper of my sister's uncontrollable offspring!"

"I didn't ask you to round them up," Hester replied patiently. "I simply asked if you'd seen them."

164

"No! Come on, old man, unless you want to starve this Christmas day."

How she could be so patient with the aging Hambone, and so vicious to her older, sweet-natured sister was a mystery. Most people thereabouts imagined that it was because Jolie reacted more favorably to men. Women, even older sisters, simply prickled her nerves. As usual, Hester just shrugged her shoulders and moved about the trading post, solicited the assistance of her oldest girl, Dora, and gathered her rambunctious children. She wished her husband Bundy would return soon. Jolie was always easier to get along with when Hester had backup forces.

After their dinner, Jolie accompanied Hambone to Rufina's grave, a ritual he performed only once a year, on Christmas Day. Jolie had journeyed to Wills Creek with Drew from their home in Pine Creek, North Carolina, after Rufina's death, so she'd never met the old woman. Everyone in the region spoke fondly of her, and the thought that Drew had dearly loved her was enough to bring emotion to Jolie as she stood silently with the old man. Drew's emotions were her own; it was only right that they ultimately be together.

Why she suddenly thought of the Indian, Noble, when Drew had filled her thoughts, bewildered her. She was well aware of the Indian's feelings for her. After all, he was the only man, thus far, who had enjoyed the pleasures of her body, and her rejection of him had nothing to do with his looks. He was tall and bronze and darkly handsome, and he had shown a white man's gentleness that would make him a perfect husband. While she had rejected Noble as a husband, she had yet to reject him as a lover. He made love to her with an Indian's passion and yet spoke the tender endearments common to the white man. Jolie hated her traitorous body for not being able to turn him away when he came to her bed.

165

"What are you thinking, woman?"

Drawing in a freezing breath of air, Jolie cut her glance to Hambone's narrowed eyes. Color rushed into her winter-pale cheeks. "What do you mean, Hambone?"

Hambone shrugged his shoulders away from the protective arm of the young woman. "I feel that heat, woman! When you're like that, my boy Drew is inside your head."

"I was not thinking about Drew," she pouted. "I was thinking of Noble!"

"Bah!" Hambone began to mumble under his breath. He enjoyed bantering with Jolie; it kept her on her toes, wondering whether he liked her or not. Of course Hambone liked the haughty young woman. If he'd ever had a daughter, he imagined she'd have been a lot like Jolie, and not like her timid sister, Hester.

Crossing his frail hands upon his cane, Hambone looked down at the carefully tended grave of his dear Rufina, then at the massive marble monument Drew had specially ordered from Philadelphia. An angel with outstretched hands, as if embracing Rufina's soul in that netherworld, met the old man's gaze.

"Jolie, could I have a moment alone with Rufina?" he asked the young woman. When he stood alone, his tall, thin frame only slightly stooped, he smiled warmly as he read the words of endearment chiseled into Rufina's monument: "Rufina Chambers, beloved wife of Hambone, beloved aunt of Diana Rourke, beloved great-aunt of Andrew Cynric Donovan, beloved friend to all. Resting peacefully in the hands of heaven, died July 26, 1810, aged 68 years, 2 months." The old man sighed, remembering how Rufina had tried to entreat him to betray his true name so that she would not have to continue carrying the name of her first husband.

"My dear wife . . ." Hambone greeted her, "what can I tell you about this past year? Our Drew has journeyed to the South and I pray daily for his safe return. He still has not taken a wife and I worry that he never will." A voice almost a century old cracked with exhaustion. "I am still with the earth, and only God knows why. I think of nothing but resting against the bosom of my dear wife. Rufina, it will not be long now . . ."

He almost felt the breath empty from his lungs. The bitter December wind pricked at his throat and chilled him to his brittle bones. Jolie started to return to him but he waved her back with an impatient fling of his left wrist.

He wanted to think about the past; it was important to him right now. Not the present, not the future—there wasn't much of that left for him. He recalled the day he'd sat on the front porch of the trading post, rubbing absently on Sweet Boy's head and wishing that a trader would emerge from the forest. The trading post had not been visited in more than two weeks, and eight months following Rufina's death, he had been feeling a might lonely. Then a raggamuffin lot had suddenly materialized from the dark forest trail . . . a lot that had compelled him to take up his musket which had been resting against the wall within his reach. But in the following moments he had found himself embracing his twenty-two-year-old Drew, whom he hadn't seen since he was a lad of fifteen, accompanied by his Indian friend, Noble, and Noble's half-brother, Bundy. Two women had made the long trip with Drew—Bundy's wife, Hester, and her sister, Jolie, as well as Bundy and Hester's two older children. The other two were destined to be born in the back room of the Wills Creek Trading Post within a five-year period.

A grand reunion had followed. What Hambone had thought would be a summer-long visit became a permanent resettlement of the young people who had left their lifelong home of Pine Creek. With the blessings of his parents, who had remained behind in Pine Creek, Drew had been determined to help Hambone run the Wills Creek Trading Post. Noble and Bundy, and Bundy's family, had decided to accompany him to Pennsylvania and make new lives for themselves and the fifteen-year-old Jolie, who, Hambone was to learn over the months, had made the trip, not to be with her older sister but to be near Drew. Ten years had passed before Hambone's watchful eye, and Drew had never shown more than a sisterly interest in Jolie. The old man often thought that her infatuation with him was an annoying burden, and Drew had often spoken of Jolie marrying his good friend, Noble. Ten years had passed, and it still had not happened.

Hambone didn't figure it ever would . . . not until Drew himself had taken a wife. Perhaps then Jolie would forget him and go on with her own life. But would she? Hambone had been on this earth too long to believe a woman as passionate as Jolie Ward would forget a man simply because he had married.

Hambone had to give the young woman credit for one thing. She truly loved Drew Donovan. He had lived a simple life at Pine Creek, never betraying the wealth that stood behind his family, and the youthful Jolie had fallen deeply in love with the man, not the luxuries he could provide her. Even now that she was well aware of his finances, it mattered not a whit . . . She wanted Drew.

Standing solemnly before Rufina's grave, Hambone protested with a groan the fact that his body was not as strong as his mind. He waved Jolie to him, and the young woman took his arm. "How can you leave an old man standing alone?" he admonished.

"You silly old fool!" she shot back without true feeling. "You wanted to be alone, so don't you fuss at me. I'll drop you over a precipice and allow the vultures to nibble at your withered old bones!"

Taking her strong young arm, Hambone chuckled

hoarsely. "Woman, you wouldn't do any such thing! You adore these whithered old bones!"

Jolie joined in his laughter. "I do, indeed, old man. God only knows why!"

That evening, Hambone sat quietly in his rocking chair before a blazing hearth and allowed the children to lull him to sleep with softly sung Christmas carols. He dozed off with visions of the laughing Drew ambling through his mind, of Christmases past, and Rufina gathering every vagabond from the region to share in their Christmas festivities. He thought back to that time long ago when his beloved Diana had been a gangly young woman, scrambling over the boulders and through the forest with Honey Boy nipping at her heels . . . He remembered when she had gone away to Philadelphia, vibrant and curious about her past, and had returned to Wills Creek a woman deeply in love with a Scotsman named Cole Cynric Donovan.

She'd been like a daughter to him, and Drew was like his grandson. If anything in the world could keep an old man alive far past his time for dying, it was his desire to see Drew again and to know that he had returned home from his latest adventure, safe and secure in the peaceful forest of the Wills Creek Trading Post.

Chapter Eleven

Had Christmas not customarily been a day for home and family, Cawley Perth might never have found Drew Donovan. Drawn from the quiet streets by the laughter of people in the St. Louis hotel, as well as the aroma of food drifting into the cold air, he easily recognized Drew's voice mingled with the gaiety of the mood. He entered the empty hotel lobby and made his way toward the laughter and the music of a violin being played by an elderly, bearded gentleman sitting in the corner of the dining room.

Cawley's eyes scanned the seated crowd, and when his gaze locked to Drew Donovan's, there was immediate surprise from both men. Drew came to his feet and put his arm out to the younger man, giving him an affectionate hug. Cawley did not immediately see Carrie, who was with the woman named Maude in the kitchen.

When Drew recognized the urgency of Cawley's visit in his stiff stance, he casually motioned him out of the hotel to the boardwalk. Wearing only a thick woolen shirt, Drew was immediately assailed by the bitter wind and crossed his arms across his chest.

He was just about to ask Cawley his reasons for venturing to St. Louis when the younger man took the letter from his jacket pocket and handed it to Drew. "What's this?"

"It's from Noble," Cawley answered. "We got some real problems back at the *Dream*."

"Just don't tell me she's on her side."

"Naw, Mr. Donovan." Cawley tucked his hands into his pockets. "It's worse than that."

Suppressing the alarm he felt, Drew flipped open the letter and read the bold handwriting:

"Drew, we got trouble. A man named Junius Wade is anchored to port waiting for your return. He knows the Englishwoman was on board the *Dream*, and he's bound and determined to get her back. Says if he don't, you're a dead man. Send the supplies downriver and travel on to Wills Creek. I'll take care of things here." The missive was signed "Noble Donovan."

"I'll be damned if a deranged little man will keep me away from my boat!" Drew mumbled.

"He said he'll kill you, Mr. Donovan. He's all fluffed up in the brain, but there's an evil in him. Mr. Noble, he's got the best idea—"

"I will *not* be controlled by threats!" *Didn't this turn out to be a fine day!* Drew thought, his eyes suddenly glazing over with the blackest of anger.

"Good thing the English lady is long gone, Mr. Donovan."

"Someone mention me?" Carrie stepped out to the boardwalk and joined the two men.

"Miss Sherwood." Cawley was visibly surprised. His eyes were like saucers. "Thought you'd be halfway home by now. That man back—"

Drew's hand clamped over the boy's mouth, but he instantly removed it and roughly patted Cawley's shoulder. "What the boy was saying is that it's a real shame poor Cullen had to get killed in the boiler room."

A dubious look crossed Carrie's face as she looked from one man to the other. "Indeed?"

171

"Cawley . . ." Drew squeezed his shoulder. "You go on in and have one of the ladies fix you a plate of food."

"Don't mind if I do, Mr. Donovan." The boy ambled off.

"Now why, Drew Donovan, would Cawley bring up Cullen? What was he really saying?"

Drew's hooded eyes narrowed. Silence penetrated the December air. He was scarcely aware of a coach filled with laughing children passing on the street behind him. It occurred to him that while he wanted to go back to the *Dream* and face Junius Wade, his bravado would place Carrie in danger. She was the one the demented man really wanted. It was time he thought of someone besides himself. "I'm afraid this is my fault," Drew said after a moment. "You see, Carrie . . ." He pulled her into his arms. "I've never entrusted Noble with anything really important. The boy journeyed upriver just to tell me that he and Noble were talking, and Noble said he wished he could see to the repairs of the *Dream* and take her up to Louisville. So I'm thinking that you and I could travel overland to Wills Creek after I send the parts downriver. What do you think of my plan?"

An attractive pout turned down the corners of her mouth as she extricated herself from his embrace, crossing her arms beneath her dull gray cape. "What do I think, Drew Donovan? I think you've gone mad, that's what I think. Since you are not partial to horses, I must assume you're planning to walk all the way to your Pennsylvania and Wills Creek. Well, I'll simply have none of it. If you wish to walk, then do it alone. I'll travel downriver with Cawley and the supplies for *Donovan's Dream* and I'll meet you there in a few weeks. Now, what do you think about that?"

Try as he might, Drew could not be angry with her. He admired a woman with spunk and enough bravado to stand up against a man. Carrie Sherwood had never ceased to amaze him. Still, the fact remained that she was in danger—a danger he could not, in all good conscience, relay to her—and just this once he would insist his decision prevail. "We *will* travel overland together, Carrie, and if you do not come along peacefully, I will throw you across my shoulder and carry you."

Her shawl flared out like wings as Carrie drew her hands to her hips. Oh, how outrageous he could be! There were any number of ways he could give his Indian friend responsibility without requiring them to walk to Pennsylvania. She wondered if Drew had other motives. "Don't make me regret not getting on the coach a few weeks back," she said quietly. "I will not accept a feeble explanation that Noble needs to assume responsibility. I am perplexed by your motives to travel overland, Drew, and I believe I am entitled to the truth."

Dare he tell her what she wanted to know? Would the truth reduce her bravado to fear and apprehension. Would she constantly watch over her shoulder for the presence of the demon she thought she had escaped? The very thought of fear darkening her lovely green eyes sickened Drew. He would protect her with his life, if need be, but he would not willingly allow her to exist under a cloud of fear. His mind was made up. "After Cawley leaves in the morning with the boiler parts, I'll book us passage aboard the coach to Baltimore," he informed her evenly. "From there we shall sail to Pennsylvania aboard one of my father's ships. Then, if you wish, I shall arrange passage to England."

Alarm blazed in Carrie's suddenly widened eyes. A hot rush flooded her body as she moved into Drew's arms. "No . . . no, Drew, you said I could go with you to Wills Creek, to your trading post. You said I could stay with you as long as I wished and that you would arrange my travel to England at a time of my choosing! Don't you want me anymore?" When he did not answer, she repeated in a weak and trembling voice, "Oh, Drew, don't you want me?"

How sensual she was, how she could take away his anger with a simple moistening of her emerald eyes. He felt his body physically responding to the nearness of her. He scarcely felt the brisk winter wind digging its icy fingers into his thick, disheveled hair; he felt only the whisper softness of her warm breath upon his cheek and heard the desperate entreaties emanating from her sweet mouth.

Dare he admit to her that her return to England was the last thing on the face of the earth that he wanted? She was in his blood; that he would ever be parted from her, for even a day, made him feel empty inside. He had once thought bachelorhood was a disease that would accompany him to his grave. If there was a miracle cure, Carrie was it. That was a truth he could no longer deny.

Drew's strong hands came up to caress her arms beneath the thick folds of her cape. He cared not that Christmas travelers passed along the street, that discernful eyes turned to them. "Will you obey me this once, Carrie Sherwood, and travel overland with me?"

"Is it really so important to you, darling?"

Drew smiled; that was the first time she'd used such a sweet endearment. Because he cared so much for Carrie, he was able to lie effectively, "I believe my friendship with Noble will suffer if I do not entrust him with the responsibility of the steamboat. I wish my friendship with my blood brother could be as important to you as it is to me."

"I do know how important Noble is to you, Drew. Do you think I am so insensitive?"

"I wouldn't want to think so, Carrie, nor would I want to know I had so wrongly misjudged you."

Carrie felt that she deserved the disappointment she detected in his voice. "You haven't misjudged me, Drew. I just don't want you to be less than truthful with me. If

174

there is some other reason we are not returning to the steamboat . . ."

Drew gently shook her, halting her words. "There is no other reason. I simply want my friend to take the *Dream* to Louisville."

"But she's your responsibility, not Noble's."

"Noble and Bundy both own shares of her, as do my parents." Her continued argument was severely trying his patience. Drew felt that he should part from her before she detected his anger. "Won't you retire to your room, Carrie, while I journey to the docks?" Carrie held his strong hand in hers for a long, silent moment. Their eyes met. The gray-black anger was there, a tremendously powerful thing that seemed able to reach out and take her prisoner. She wanted to say, "Don't be angry with me, Drew," but the words would not form. Then their hands parted and he cut his gaze from hers. Carrie stood on the boardwalk and watched him amble down the wide street, tucking his hands into the pockets of his cream-colored trousers.

Noble had been brooding for two days. This early Monday morning, he stood at the stern of *Donovan's Dream*, staring at the stationary stern-wheeler sitting a hundred yards out in the river. Though crimson streaked the horizon, the sun had not yet risen.

His thoughts were in a quandary. He knew that nothing would dampen Junius Wade's malevolent intentions to recapture his white slave and see Drew Donovan dead. Noble knew in his heart what had to be done. He had considered every alternative and his thoughts always returned to the same solution.

His nerves jumped as Bundy crept up behind him, then slumped across the rail beside him. "Damn, Brother, you don't sneak up on a thinking man!"

"Need I ask what your thoughts are? You're worried about Drew. And you're thinking of that bastard over there."

Noble's dark eyes hooded. Many years ago he had made a moral commitment to honor the life given to every being on the face of the earth. Now, he had to make a choice . . . to go against the grain of his commitment or to allow Drew's life to be placed at risk. The only choice—dictated by common sense—made him tremble inside. "You know, Brother, there is only one thing to be done."

Silence. Bundy linked his fingers so tightly he felt pain. Drew was in trouble. Junius Wade sat across the river, patiently waiting to wreak his vengeance. Bundy, Noble, and Drew had grown up together at Pine Creek, then had moved together to Pennsylvania. Drew was as much a brother to him as was Noble. There was nothing in the world he wouldn't do for a brother. "Let's do it, Noble."

Noble gritted his teeth. "Are you sure?"

"Sure as I'll ever be. Let's get it done before the sun comes up."

Noble moved into the darkness of the steamboat. Several minutes later he returned, a length of rope looped over his left shoulder, rawhide strips tied to his wrist. He was bootless and bare to the waist. As he waited in tense silence, Bundy prepared to slip into the frigid waters of the Mississippi with his brother.

The two swam silently through the water, ignoring the cold, closing the distance separating them from the stern-wheeler on which they hoped Junius Wade slumbered peacefully. Very little movement could be seen on the deck, and a young man, posted at guard duty, was about as watchful as a blind coyote. Stealthily, the two men slipped over the rail, pressed themselves into the darkness of a cabin wall, and spied Junius Wade through the partially open door of his sleeping quarters.

Within moments the unsuspecting man, caught without his hook that could have served as a most effective weapon, was bound and gagged and weighted down by an iron skuttle used as a doorstop in his cabin. Before any man aboard the stern-wheeler could be the wiser, Noble and Bundy had returned to the river as quickly as they'd emerged from it, taking their quarry with them into the icy current. Halfway between the two boats, they released the squirming, terror-stricken man who hadn't a prayer for survival and watched his body catch in an undertow that immediately dragged him below the surface. Noble would never forget that final horrified gaze as the grotesque face disappeared into the blackness.

Though Bundy, who'd always been the wilder of the two, could not make such a claim, Junius Wade was the first man Noble had killed. As he dragged himself up over the rail of *Donovan's Dream* he felt sick to his stomach. Berating himself for the flurry of emotional weaknesses he blamed on a lifetime of white culture, he moved toward his cabin and closed himself in. He would not see another man, including his brother, for two days, nor would he eat a meal.

Five men of the stern-wheeler had just left *Donovan's Dream* when Bundy knocked at his brother's door. "Noble?" He tried the door, finding it bolted from the other side. "Noble, the stern-wheeler's turnin' back to New Orleans."

Silence. Bundy stood back as the bolt slipped on the other side. Dark, piercing eyes met Bundy's through the crack of the door. "What do you mean, they're turning back?"

"They've given up hope of finding Mr. Wade. The cap'n thinks he had too much whiskey under his gut and fell overboard. They're giving up the search." When Noble seemed hesitant to permit his entrance, Bundy forced the door open. "What the hell's wrong with you, Noble?"

"We killed a man!" he hissed. "And it doesn't settle well with me!"

Bundy took his full-blooded brother by the shoulders and shook him viciously. "Hell, you act more like a white man every day, Noble. I'm only half Indian and I show more strength than you!"

Noble had always been the studious one, the kind-hearted one. He had been an enigma to the people of Pine Creek where he'd been raised. They'd expected him to be more like his fierce Seminole warrior parents, but he had never shown the inclination. "Remembering that man's face as he went under makes my skin crawl," Noble admitted.

"That weren't no man, Brother," Bundy retorted. "Just a real mean creature that needed to die."

Noble didn't want to talk about it any longer. The horrible deed was done. It was best to go on with the future. Bringing his hand to his stomach, Noble remarked, "God, I'm hungry. What kind of grub we got to eat?"

Drew had just seen to the shipment of the boiler parts aboard a flatboat bound downriver. Cawley, wanting to remain with Drew, had reluctantly accompanied the shipment, which would reach the stranded steamboat by noon. Drew didn't like leaving the ominous chore of getting the boat back in the current to his two good friends, but in view of Junius Wade's presence on the river, he had no choice. He and Carrie would depart for Baltimore early Wednesday morning. All travel had been suspended for the two days before and after Christmas, and they had to await the Wednesday departure.

Having spent most of that Christmas night playing cards with other hotel guests, Drew retired to the room he shared with Carrie for a long, peaceful morning of sleep. She had gone out early that morning with the woman named Maude to take care of shopping needs and would not be back until later. Arching his back to relieve his tension, Drew sat on the edge of the bed and picked up the wooden box with its carved patriotic symbols that Carrie had given him. It was well made, and perfect for storing the gold pocketwatch his father had given him. Setting it on the small table, his hand brushed the thick woolen scarf she had also given him. He wasn't sure why her thoughtful gifts made him think of the stories she'd told of a life back in England, but he found himself suddenly absorbed with her tales. She was so precise and so sincere in relating her English background. He wanted to believe she was simply embellishing what had probably been a simple and very boring life, and yet in his heart, he knew she was a true lady.

Drew frowned. He'd often been on the receiving end of Carrie's idle chatter and yet there was a certain spontaneity in many of her responses that hinted at truthfulness. Her precise details made her stories almost believable.

Sighing deeply, Drew stretched his full length as he lay upon the bed, tucking his palms beneath his dark head. Then, just as he might have gotten comfortable, a thought came to him. He was having to flee overland with Carrie because of Junius Wade's threat. She was out in the streets of St. Louis, shopping with a friend and unaware of the dangers just fifteen miles to the south. Suppose the evil little man should . . .

Drew shot up so quickly pain grabbed at his forehead. He took up his firearm and moved quickly into the corridor and down the narrow stairway, soon emerging into the overcast morning. He looked first one way and then the other, eventually settling on a southerly course toward the shops Carrie frequented. His heart raced like the wild wind.

How could he have been so stupid as to have let her

out of his sight for something as frivolous as shopping? Drew moved swiftly along the boardwalk, entering then exiting each shop along his path. His piercing gaze studied the main street and its side streets and alleys, looking for the royal-blue velvet gown and accessories he had purchased for her as a Christmas gift. He had been sitting in the dining room when she'd departed the hotel; she'd looked so exquisite in the tight-fitting bodice and billowing skirts that he'd felt the pride many husbands might have felt in seeing a comely wife so fashionably attired.

A husband! What had made him compare himself to such a lucky fellow? Carrie Sherwood was a sweet yet fiery, innocent yet passionate woman . . . the kind of woman Drew had hoped truly existed. She was everything he wanted in a wife. And the very idea that he might have allowed her to walk into danger almost made him physically ill.

It seemed more like a lifetime rather than the fifteen or twenty minutes it took to locate Carrie in a millinery shop where she was trying on a hat. The portly matron approached him when he entered, but he simply said, "I have come in search of the lady."

Carrie turned, giving him her widest smile. "How do you like this one, Drew? Or do you think the dove a bit much?"

Cutting his gaze from the matron, who had already decided to disapprove of his opinion, Drew approached, touching his index finger to the beak of the realistic-looking ornament surrounded by peach-colored silk blossoms. "It isn't something I'd have chosen for you. Where is Maude?"

"She returned to the hotel a while ago." Carrie snatched the bonnet from her head and turned to others displayed on a carefully arranged shelf. "Which bonnet, then?" Taking up a narrow-brimmed traveling hat, she perched it atop her head and looped the chiffon ties beneath her chin. "How do I look in red?"

A very alarmed matron, moving faster than her portly frame should have allowed, eased to Carrie's side. "Madame, that is not a suitable bonnet. The ladies who buy them . . . well, they cater to the rabblerousers."

"What do you mean?" Carrie's eyes narrowed quizzically. Instantly, recognition stirred in them. "Oh, you mean the ladies of the evening . . ."

"Yes, madame. That fribbling lot of lusty sows comes in here all the time, expecting to be waited on like they were a decent sort. Me! Wait on the lot of them!"

That was all it took to rile Carrie Sherwood. She cared not a whit what some of the women of St. Louis had to do to survive. Who was this woman to condemn them?

While a very surprised and crimson-cheeked Drew looked on, Carrie chuckled mischievously. "What do you think, Drew? Shall I buy a red dress to match the red hat? And perhaps even a pair of red shoes to complement both?"

"Madame!" The matron was shocked. "Surely you are jesting with your husband."

Carrie's finely arched eyebrows shot up. Looking first toward Drew, she took great pleasure in meeting the wide-eyed expression of the matron. "Madame, this man is not my husband. He is my lover. By the way, darling," she continued, meeting Drew's stunned gaze, "did you get a good price when you sold our three children to that woman on the river?"

The shop matron promptly fainted. Had Drew Donovan not caught her, she'd have hit the wood planks with an alarming thud. As it was, he saw her to a chair, poured her a glass of water from a pitcher sitting on a narrow counter, and assured himself that she would be all right. Then he turned a swift, disapproving eye on Carrie. "Why did you do that?"

"Because she is a narrow-minded witch!" Carrie shot

back, removing the hat and slinging it back to the shelf. "You mollycoddle her if you wish. I am returning to the hotel!"

Carrie marched away, leaving Drew with the teetering woman. When she recognized Drew Donovan she viciously flicked her wrist at him, forcing him to retreat from her. "I just wanted to see that you were all right," he explained apologetically.

"Leave my shop or I shall call the police!"

"If it is any consolation, madame, the woman and I have no children. She was just having a little fun."

"Out of my shop!" she ordered, trying unsuccessfully to find her footing.

Another customer entered. Drew met the pretty brown eyes of a young woman and asked quietly, "Will you take care of this poor woman? She has had an episode."

Exiting the shop, Drew moved quickly through the streets toward the hotel, thinking that Carrie Sherwood was the most outrageous woman he'd ever met.

Drew entered the hotel and took the stairs two at a time. When he pushed open the door to their room, Carrie sat quietly on the edge of the bed, her elbow propped on her knee and her chin upon her fist. Staring blankly at him, she watched him slowly close the door.

He was broodingly quiet as he sauntered toward her, his arms crossed, his hat still on his head but pushed back from his forehead. He looked terribly grim, holding her gaze with the blackest of moods reflecting in his slate-gray eyes. He looked as though he could pounce and kill without giving it a second thought.

When he stood before her, she picked her chin up from her fist and met his scolding gaze. "Why are you looking at me with such scorn, Drew Donovan?" she asked flippantly. Rather than reply, Drew took her wrists and literally dragged her to her feet. "Ohh! You hurt me, Drew!"

Instantly, his rough grasp became a gentle massage.

Taking her hands, he guided them to his back and gently planted them there. "Now doesn't that feel better than putting a damned red hat upon your head?"

Carrie's fingers moved tenderly over the taut muscles of his back, then found a resting place beneath the waist of his trousers. "Red isn't my color," she quipped without feeling. "Doesn't go at all well with my hair."

"Do you know what does go well with your hair, Carrie?"

She shrugged. "What?"

Touching his mouth to her hairline, he whispered, "Me. When you rest your head upon my chest, and I feel its flaming softness there, I cannot imagine being with any other woman. Just you, Carrie. And damn, you do frustrate me!" His movements were not as harsh as his words. His fingers moved to the stay at the front of her cape and unfastened it, slinging it away like a swirling cyclone. It landed in an almost perfect circle on the dark carpet.

Dropping her forehead to Drew's chest, Carrie whispered, "Why did you come looking for me?"

Of course, he could not tell her about the threat of Junius Wade. "I was about to take a nap since I was up so late last night, and I missed you."

"I bedded early, so I am not tired."

His sweet, warm breath descended upon her cheek. Tenderly, he filled both his hands with the long, loose tresses of her flaming hair. "And I am not tired, either— at least, not now," he responded after a moment. "You can make me so blasted angry that I come fully awake." His features were not angry as he brought the silken tresses to his lips and caressed them.

Carrie's hands moved fluidly over his back and came to rest upon his shoulders. "And are you still angry with me, Drew Donovan?"

"Angry enough to—"

"To what?"

Instantly, he pushed her backward to the coverlets of the bed, tasting the sweet breath of laughter his action elicited. "To take you, Carrie Sherwood, here and now. Blast that it be the morning. Blast that you're a fiery wench badly in need of taming. Blast that the door is unlocked . . ."

"I'll not be taken like a common wench!" she threatened in a teasing voice. "Ah'm a laidy, Ah am . . ." Her scullery-maid diction brought a cockeyed grin to his masculine good looks. "Andrew Cynric Donovan! You are crushing my new velvet frock!"

"Blast your frock!" Playfully, his right hand eased to the hem of her gown and dragged it upward, exposing a long, slim leg. Holding her daring look, he began to unfasten the stays of her high-heeled boot. "Blasted thing," he mumbled. "Why can't women wear sensible boots!"

"Something a rogue can unceremoniously drag off!" she laughed, "along with my new Christmas frock! Well, I'll have you know I've got on my tightest corset, and it might as well be a medieval chastity belt against your invasion!"

"We'll see about that, woman!" Drew inhaled deeply, his cunning gaze scanning her ivory features melded in humor. One by one his fingers popped the ridged stays at the front of her gown, exposing her delicate underthings, her supple curves . . . everything, except corsets. Such a slender build did not need the restrictive bindings of torture devices. No one knew that better than Drew Donovan.

His hot, masculine smell rushed into Carrie's senses. She was suddenly drawn into the passion of the moment, his sinewy body resting lightly upon hers, moving occasionally to accommodate the deft movement of his fingers as he rid them both of their clothing, the direction of his gaze upon her supple breasts, the flat plane of her stomach, and lower.

"You are an exquisite woman, Carrie," he muttered, touching his mouth to her own, then trailing kisses over her flushed cheek. "You torment me . . . you enflame me."

"I do not mean to," she responded demurely.

Drew crushed her to him in a protective embrace, enjoying the heat of her body melting into his, the rapid race of her heartbeat against his own, the way her leg lifted to squeeze against his narrow hips. Every time his hands moved over her body, there were new and exciting discoveries, caresses that brought kittenish moans from her soft, inviting mouth.

She was suddenly like a sensual river of fire beneath him, caring not that the door separating them from the hallway, though closed was unlocked, and that anyone could charge upon their private moment. Without prelude, without those tender, exquisite moments normally preceding their joining, he filled her with the proud evidence of his gender, easing her body upward on the bed, then tossing the offending pillows here and there about the immaculate room.

The ecstasy of his thrilling caresses became a mirror to her soul . . . joining her to him in a fervent need for eternal union. In that moment, Carrie could not imagine the existence of another human being outside the intensely exciting vortex that imprisoned them together. In that moment, as they shivered together in rapturous fulfillment, England, Holker Hall, and Lord Penley Seymour ceased to exist.

Home was a simple log trading post in a remote area of Pennsylvania called Wills Creek.

Part Two
Full Bloom

Chapter Twelve

The trail emerging from the forest into a wide clearing was mantled by sparkling white snow. Shards of ice clung to the eaves of the trading post roof, occasionally dropping to the frozen ground and shattering into a million splinters. One of those, almost two feet long from tip to base, missed claiming Carrie's life by a mere half inch. An icicle, after the long, arduous, and for the most part uneventful trip overland from St. Louis, Missouri was her welcome to Wills Creek. Carrie wondered what else the seemingly quiet countryside held in store for her.

First the icy shards had chilled her to the bone. Now she faced a tall, slim woman with mouse-brown hair, whose eyes made the lethal daggers of ice look like harmless feathers.

Jolie Ward drew her hands to her slim hips and tapped her right foot in an outrageous fashion. Any other time she'd have thrown herself into Drew Donovan's arms and welcomed him home with the enthusiasm of unrequited love, but now her furious gaze cut from one to the other.

"Who is she?" she hissed at the man who'd filled her dreams nightly.

With an angry glare, Drew ignored the biting jealousy of Jolie's inquiry. "She is—"

Carrie extended her hand from the protection of her

cape, an act to which Jolie did not respond. "I am Carrie Sherwood." Rather than allow the woman to intimidate her, Carrie dropped her hand as if the woman's rudeness did not matter. "My, but it's warm inside."

"That's what fires usually do," Jolie continued in her sarcastic tone, turning her attentions to Drew. She was so happy to see him, but so infuriated by the company he had brought with him. She wondered what the woman was doing here, and what her relationship to Drew was. "Where are Bundy and Noble?"

Hester chose that moment to emerge from behind the curtain separating the foyer from the living quarters in the rear. "Yes, where are my husband and his brother?" Wrapping her arms around Drew's neck, the older woman gave him a sisterly hug. "Welcome home, Drew."

As Drew explained the circumstances delaying the other men, Hester's children began to emerge from the living quarters. Introductions were made between Carrie and the residents of the Wills Creek Trading Post. While Drew and the children were getting reacquainted and he was promising gifts from exotic New Orleans, Carrie thought of the long trip from St. Louis. They'd arrived in Baltimore after a three-week trip aboard a bumpy public coach, then by schooner along the coast to Philadelphia. There, a very disappointed Drew had learned that his parents had made a trip to West Virginia and would not return for several weeks. Exhausted from their journey, she and Drew had stayed three days and nights in the eerie family mansion, with the very strange servants to tend their needs, overlooking Philadelphia, then had traveled from there by horseback to Wills Creek. As the voices of Drew and the children drifted off into silence, Carrie thought of Drew's vehement argument against the horse she had personally chosen for him from the Rourke House stables. She had been determined that his child-hood fear of horses would be lost once he had gained the confidence of the twelve-year-old gelding she had chosen from the rich stock. Unfortunately, the beast had spooked just five miles from Philadelphia, throwing Drew on his rump in a thick patch of snow, and he had chosen to travel the next few miles on foot, leading the contrary beast behind them. At her gentle chiding, he had given the gelding another try, and the last leg of the trip had been uneventful. Just before reaching the trading post, he had spoken fondly of taking her horseback riding when the spring thaw came.

Suddenly she was aware that Drew had spoken her name several times. Embarrassment rushed into her cheeks as she met his questioning gaze. With Jolie looking scornfully on, Drew took Carrie's hand and coaxed her to the back of the trading post. "Come, I want you to meet Hambone, my oldest and dearest friend."

When she was again alone with Drew, Carrie inquired about Jolie. "Is she always like that?"

Drew chuckled. "I told you how she was. It is merely one woman's jealousy of another. I wouldn't give it a second thought."

"She could make my life miserable," Carrie reflected quietly.

"And she could find herself booted back to Pine Creek, North Carolina." Drew spoke with vehemence. "She knows how much I will and will not tolerate."

Within moments, Carrie stood before a seated man of ancient age, whose dark eyes danced as introductions were made. Hambone took Carrie's hand and held it affectionately. "And are ye, young lady, that one in a million who shall tame my Andrew?"

Color rushed into Carrie's cheeks. "I believe, sir," she laughed, "that it is he who shall tame me!"

"Ah, an English lass," the old man reflected. "Aye, indeed, ye'll be a needin' a little tamin'. Children, where are my other two boys?"

191

"Noble and Bundy remained with the steamboat below St. Louis. Trouble in the boiler room."

Surprise brightened the old man's gaze. "And ye didn't remain with 'er, too, Andrew?"

Drew chuckled nervously. He had never mentioned to Carrie the menace of Junius Wade on the river, and knew he'd have to choose his words carefully. "Noble can manage just fine. Besides, I wanted Carrie to meet you, and I couldn't wait for the repairs to be made."

Just at that moment the bobcat, Sweet Boy, ambled lazily into the room. Carrie bent and touched her hand to the wide space between his ears. As if on cue, Sweet Boy fell lazily to his back and nuzzled his face into the folds of her skirts, just as had been his grandfather's habit. "Isn't he beautiful?" She felt that she knew not only the bobcat tugging at her gown but also his mother and grandfather, of whom Drew had spoken fondly during the weeks of their travel. There was almost nothing she didn't know about the people of Wills Creek. Drew had, whether deliberately or not, greatly understated the affections of the woman, Jolie, toward him. Carrie imagined that making friends with Jolie Ward might prove something of a problem.

Panic boiled inside Jolie. She felt a tremble begin in her knees and travel upward, enveloping her body all the way to the crown of her head. How could Drew do something like this? She had worked for ten long years to convince Drew that he loved her; she could not understand why he would suddenly bring home a flighty English tart. It mattered not that she was beautiful, that the thick masses of her flame-colored hair made Jolie's look like mangled hemp. As far as Jolie was concerned, the woman was trouble, and she owed it to Drew to protect him from such a scandal.

Her mind began revolving at an incredible speed. The first thing she had to do, though it would be very difficult, was to change her attitude toward Carrie Sherwood. She breathed a long, deep sigh, then moved to the wide parlor where she had left Hambone sitting before the fire. The lovely Englishwoman was sitting on a stool beside him, holding the old gentleman's hand. Jolie was immediately envious of the affection Hambone was showing for the stranger.

Drew looked up as Jolie approached. His eyes dared her to be troublesome. Rather, he saw a timorous smile touch her mouth, a smile with the power to coax Carrie's gaze up to her own. "I owe you an apology, Miss Sherwood," Jolie said in a barely audible whisper. "I acted abominably. Will you forgive me?"

Carrie hesitated only a moment before taking Jolie's proffered hand. "I hope we can be friends, Miss Ward," she replied, coming to her feet.

"Jolie . . . please call me Jolie."

"And I am Carrie."

Jolie returned her smile with sticky insincerity. "Come, let me show you to your room."

"She'll not be taking a room here," Drew informed her. Jolie suppressed an expression of surprise and anger. "Carrie will share my cabin."

A thousand hours of stormy anger filled the few moments since he had spoken. Jolie's eyes lowered. "Very well, Drew."

It was all she could do to keep from pouncing and killing as Drew and his English consort slipped their arms around each other's waists.

In the weeks to follow, Jolie seethed with the rage of a woman possessed. In the cold late-winter nights, she sat alone on the wide porch of the trading post and watched the dance of lights through the window of Drew's cabin. Occasionally a shadow would pass by the thin curtain, followed by another, then the shadows would mingle and ease gradually toward the floor—the space of floor where a thick bear rug lay in waiting for their entwined bodies.

Perhaps when Noble and Bundy returned, she could get a clear picture of the circumstances that had cast the woman into Drew's arms. Then, perhaps, she would have the tools necessary to drive them apart. For now, all she could do was bide her time and hold her tongue.

What did the woman have that she did not? Jolie wondered with a childish pout. True, she was pretty, with her emerald eyes and her flaming hair, but she was still just a woman, with the same anatomy as every other woman on the face of the earth. So what attracted Drew to her? Was she wealthy? But that wouldn't matter to Drew. Her wealth could not possibly match his own. Was she able to warm his feet on a cold winter's night? Jolie's mouth pressed into a thin line of frustration and rage. She could have warmed his feet—and anything else in need of it— just as successfully as the Englishwoman.

Jolie might have brooded all night if the door to Drew's cabin hadn't opened and he stepped out into the darkness. Rising sharply, hugging her thick shawl to her shoulders, Jolie met him at the woodpile where he gathered up logs for the hearth.

"What are you doing outside, Jolie?" he asked, stacking the logs on his left arm.

With one swift move, Jolie dragged the neat stack from the crook of his elbow. Before he could react, she had thrown herself into his arms. "Oh, Andrew . . . Andrew . . ." She pouted prettily. "How could you bring that English tart to Wills Creek? I am the one who adores you. I am the one who should warm your bed! Not her!"

Taking her by the shoulders, Drew shook her roughly.

"Why the theatrics, Jolie? You've always known I cared for you as a sister, and nothing more. You wouldn't want to lie in the bed of a man who does not want you. Good God, woman . . ." His rough grasp relaxed. "Noble wants you, Jolie. He would make you a kind, loving husband, if you would but give him a chance!"

"Noble! Noble, that full-blood! He is good for nothing but satisfying my needs when you will not!" Ripping herself from Drew's arms, she turned her back to him. "You've brought that English creature here just to tease me—to taunt me! That's all! You do not care for her. You could not possibly love her!"

Tenderly, Drew's hand dropped to her shoulder and coaxed her to face him once again. When her brown eyes lifted to his gray-black ones in the scant light of the winter moon, he saw the gleam of tears. He gently flicked them away with his thumb. "Listen to me, Jolie, and listen well. I have not brought Carrie here to tease you. I have brought her here because I do, indeed . . ." Dare he say the words to Jolie that he had yet to say to Carrie? Dare he trust his emotions that clung to him like fiery ice, warming him one moment and frightening him the next? "Because, Jolie . . ." he began afresh, "I love Carrie Sherwood. If she will have me, I will take her as my wife."

Even in the semidarkness, Drew saw the horror darken her eyes. "No . . . no, Andrew, you can't. She doesn't love you. She can't possibly love you, not the way I do!"

"You love what you cannot have, Jolie. Please do not make me feel discomfort in my own home. If just once I look at you in the future and I see loathing, I will send you away from here. If you ever do anything to hurt Carrie . . ." He left the threat unspoken. Touching his fingertips briefly to her tear-moistened cheek, he hastily restacked the logs and disappeared into the inviting warmth of the cabin he shared with Carrie Sherwood.

He had just dropped the logs before the hearth when Carrie emerged from the shadows of the curtain behind which she'd been bathing. She wore a thick woolen bedgown gathered at the wrists, the one tie at her neckline undone, half exposing the roundness of her firm breasts. Her hair clung damply to her ivory skin, and she laughed, trying to pull the long hair from between her gown and torso.

"Here, let me help you, Carrie." Drew approached. Turning her away from him, his fingers eased beneath her hairline and coaxed the recalcitrant locks upward. When he had freed them, he touched his mouth to the slim column of her neck. "You smell fresh and sweet," he remarked. "Like gardenias on a summer day."

"For you," she cooed, turning into his arms. "You were outside a bit long to have gathered those few logs."

"I was talking with Jolie."

"Oh?" A copper-colored eyebrow moved upward. "She is not causing you any problems, is she?"

"No!" Drew hadn't meant to speak the single word so harshly. Immediately softening his tone, he apologized. "It isn't anything she and I haven't discussed before. The only difference is . . ." He touched his mouth to her damp forehead, "before, she didn't have you to deal with."

"That she dislikes me immensely would be an understatement." Carrie forced herself to laugh lightly. "Were I to turn my back on her I might possibly find a knife stuck in it."

Suddenly, Drew couldn't have given less than a damn about Jolie Ward or knives or petty jealousies. Carrie Sherwood was like a flame against him, her flesh melting into his own through the thick threads of their garments. When Drew's hand moved gently around her hip, Carrie looked at him with mock surprise. "Andrew Cynric Donovan, what do you think you have on your mind?"

"Think, hell!" he mumbled, pulling her ever so close. "I

know what I've got on my mind."

With a whisper of a laugh, Carrie allowed him to pick her up in his strong arms and move with her toward the large feather bed they shared.

This one night would stand out from all others that had seen them together. Tonight fate would intervene in their lives, and England would be as remote to Carrie Sherwood as Tibet.

Tonight would bind her in eternal love to the tall, commanding Pennsylvanian whose mouth and body would claim her own once again.

Jolie was furious. Though midnight approached, she could not bear to return to her bed at the rear of the trading post. Rather, her shoes crunched through the frozen snow toward the spring-fed lake a quarter of a mile down the trail. In the summer the rhododendrons and laurel would bloom in profusion; she would try to picture their beauty rather than the travesty being carried out in Drew Donovan's cabin. *She* should be in Drew's arms, not the English tart!

Soon she dropped to the bank of the frozen pond, scarcely able to see a gleam of moonlight in the heavy winter darkness. She wanted to cry, but she was afraid the tears would freeze upon her cheeks. She wanted to scream, but she feared dislodging an avalanche of snow from the thick orchard of firs surrounding her. She wanted to kill Carrie Sherwood, but she could think of no better way to lose Andrew forever.

She dropped her face blankly against her drawn-up knees and sat there for minutes that became an hour in the blink of an eye, then two hours, and three hours. Frozen dew formed a blanket over her thick shawl. Pins and needles grabbed at her feet through her boots and socks. She knew she should return to the trading post, but she almost wished the winter night would claim her and carry her far, far away into a netherworld where memories of Drew Donovan did not exist. If she could only start anew, like a newly born babe, and avoid the Drew Donovans of the world! It wasn't fair that he had never loved her. She'd done everything possible to let him know how much she cared for him. Perhaps if she hadn't tried so hard, but had let nature take its course . . .

"What are you doing, Jolie?"

Alarmed, she spun on her knees, her hands melting into the blanket of snow upon which she sat. A tall, unprepossessing form stood against the dark timberline, his familiar voice now silenced as he awaited her reply. "Andrew?"

A deep, masculine sigh filled with annoyance drifted across the darkness. "No . . . it is Noble. We have just returned." He approached, dropped to his knees before her, and clasped her shoulders between his gloved hands. "What are you doing out in this bitter cold? You'll catch your death."

His concern was so genuine; why couldn't it be Andrew caring so much for her? "I wish I would," she remarked sullenly, meeting the piercing blackness of his eyes. "I have nothing to live for."

Noble roughly drew her to him. "My poor little Jolie! Drew arrived with the Englishwoman and you feel that you have been left out in the cold. When are you going to realize Drew does not want you? *I* want you, Jolie."

"But you've always known how I feel."

Noble moved from her. His annoyance hung heavily in the space between them. "I have just returned from a long trip, Jolie. I will not argue with you this evening. I would rather . . ." His fingers clasped around her right wrist, "show you just how very much I have missed you."

With petty indignation, Jolie tore her wrist from his grip and crossed her arms. The cold that had seized her all evening suddenly drifted off with the wind. She felt the heat of the tall, bronze Indian radiating toward her, enveloping her within the aura of adoration he held for her. He had always been so kind and considerate toward her, and had always gone out of his way to prove his love. She had missed him terribly these past few months, despite the prickle of annoyance dampening her mood. Noble, son of Oclala and Black Face, was tall and well built, his masculine features pleasing to a feminine eye, and his gentleness unmatched by almost any man. But he was not Drew Donovan.

The perceptive Noble knew exactly what revolved through her head. It was in her eyes—a strange and possessive love, and certainly a love that was not reserved for him. "He will not have you, Jolie. He wants the Englishwoman. I am the one who will take you to my heart—"

"And to your bed!" she shot ferociously at him. "You have returned to Wills Creek after your long sojourn to New Orleans! If I know you as well as I think I do, you did not make yourself available to any white woman in your travels! But good old Jolie is here, isn't she? Good old Jolie whose favors you have enjoyed before!"

Noble had expected theatrics. He had not, however, expected the flood of tears that followed her angry outburst. As her body wracked with sobs, he pulled her into his arms and held her comfortingly. "You are the only woman I want, Jolie. I am willing to accept you, even knowing you are in love with my blood brother. I will take you to my bed and to my heart. I will go through the ceremonies of a white man's wedding, if that is what you want. Call me a sentimental fool, if that is what you think, but I am willing to take you as my wife, even if you save the love of your heart for Drew."

Jolie drew in a deep, surprised breath. She tried to see some emotion in the Indian's eyes, but she saw nothing but fathomless wells. The moon had slipped away into a black, cloudy night. "That is not normal, Noble. You will take a woman who loves another? And what would you do if I were to look at Andrew with love in my eyes? Would you spring and kill in a mood of rage and jealousy, as any normal man would do? Or would you shrug your shoulders and believe my feelings for him would pass? What you are saying is mad."

"Perhaps," he replied tonelessly. "I said I would accept your love for Drew, as long as you are my wife. How you look at him is strictly your business. I am willing to accept that you do not love me now. But I believe one day you will." Jolie suddenly exploded into a torrent of curses. She flailed her arms so violently that she lost her balance in the crisp snow. As she landed firmly on her buttocks, Noble knelt beside her, enfolding her within his powerful embrace. "Is your little rage ended?"

"No. How dare you! I hate you, Noble Donovan! May you rot in hell for all time to come!"

"I will gladly do so, Jolie, if you will be my wife and give me many happy years beforehand."

"Ohh!" Jolie would have clenched her fists if they hadn't been cold with pain. "You're an outrageous man, Noble!"

"Then you will marry me?"

Her voice softened; of course she wouldn't, but there was something she wanted from him that required a certain allure on her part. Resting her cheek back against his waiting one, she said, "Have you warmed your cabin?"

"It is warm and awaiting you, Jolie."

"Then take me there. If you please me tonight, Noble . . ."

As he welcomed her into the protection of his arm, he was certainly suspicious of the sudden softening of her voice, her body, her eyes meeting his in the darkness. What was it the white woman wanted from him? Or had she simply missed the pleasures they enjoyed together as man and woman?

Jolie was glad that Noble's cabin was set off from the main settlement of the trading post. He had built the one-room, L-shaped cabin of split pine logs with a square porch in the bend of the L. His horses, his pride and joy, stood in a lazy huddle in a large pen to the right, with two new ones added to the several that Jolie had been taking care of during Noble's absence.

"My horses look good," Noble remarked.

"Two of the mares will drop foals in the spring."

Entering the warm cabin, Noble smiled. "The black and the sorrel?"

"Yes." Turning into his arms when the warmth of the hearth enveloped her, Jolie pouted prettily. "Let's not talk about horses, Noble. Tell me about your trip to New Orleans. Tell me of your indiscretions . . ."

Noble pulled her close. His breath was winter-cool upon her cheek. "There were no indiscretions. I want no woman but you."

"Didn't I say you would take no white woman to your bed?"

"You weren't entirely truthful."

Her pale-brown eyebrows eased slowly upward. "What do you mean? You just said . . ."

With a hoarse chuckle, his ample mouth covered her own. When a breath of space separated them once again, he reminded her, "In the summertime you are so Indian brown that I believe you forget *you* are a white woman. "Now . . ." Taking the edges of her shawl, he moved it down her arms, "you are winter-pale, a white woman . . . my white woman."

Assailing his cheek with her sweetest kisses, Jolie whispered, "Do you want me, Noble? It has been so long."

"Of course I want you, Jolie," he responded, dropping to his knees and taking her with him. "Why don't you want me? I can give you everything a woman could want. I can give you love, I can give you happiness . . . children. Jolie, I can give you forever."

"Forever!" The word caught cruelly in Jolie's throat. Forever was something she wanted from Drew Donovan, not the Indian holding her sincerely against his heart. She wanted only one thing from Noble. She wanted everything else from Andrew Cynric Donovan, including love and children.

Ignoring his declaration, Jolie's fingers wrapped through the thick locks of his hair cut in the white man's style. "Make love to me, Noble. Make me forget everything else in the world. Make me forget that my heart breaks, that my soul is as black as your hair."

Grasping the material of her bodice, Noble ripped it asunder, baring the inviting twin mounds of her breasts. How sweet she was; well worth his sacrifice of all other women. He hadn't realized how much he'd missed her as the frenzied moments robbed them both of their clothing, his brown, sinewy body entwined with her slim, milk-white one. He had positioned himself for possession but had yet to enter her; she enjoyed the teasing ecstasy that brought her body to arousing heights. Her back stiffened as she offered her breasts to his stimulations. Her hands grasped his with trembling excitement to guide them over her passion-sensitive flesh.

When the tight, exquisite pain fused their bodies as one at last, she cried out in sweet agony, her hips immediately convulsing against his own, inviting his thrusts deeper and deeper still. As her hands clutched at his black hair, she imagined that the powerful body covering and claiming her own was Drew's, that his hands stroked her flesh, that his mouth claimed hers again and again. Closing her eyes, gulping breath as though she drowned in the sea of passion surrounding them, she whispered hoarsely, "Drew . . . Drew . . ."

Noble's movements suddenly ceased. Wrapping his fingers through her hair, his body relaxed in frustration and quiet rage. At that moment, he could have killed his blood brother. Regaining the moment, his piercing black eyes lifted to her stunned ones, and he hissed, "I am Noble! Do you hear me, woman? I am Noble!"

His movements commenced with a driving, insane frenzy, so hard and quick that she was unable to match his pace. Jolie could tell by the sudden stiffening of his body that fulfillment was near. Bracing her palms on his dark shoulders, she attempted to wriggle from beneath him and screamed in horror, "No . . . no, Noble . . . you have promised . . ."

He failed—or refused—to heed her entreaty. As she cried out in such fear that tears flooded her eyes, he drove himself deeply into her, filling her with his seed. That was a fulfillment he had always sacrificed before, because she—the woman he loved—had wished to avoid becoming pregnant.

Though the victory was his, Noble sank heavily in defeat upon her slim body. She was too stunned to attempt to free herself from him. She lay beneath him, attempting to still the maddening pace of her breathing, failing to feel his heaviness, her hands loosely entwined through his coarse hair. Then, as the realization of what he had done pumped through her veins, she began flailing at his face with her clenched fists with such brutal force that with only a few blows his face was covered with blood. He did not attempt to halt her attack.

When at last she lay in breathless exhaustion, Noble moved to her side and pulled her to him. Several minutes passed before she whispered brokenly, "Why did you do that? Damn you, Indian!"

His mouth was already swelling from the strength of her blows, his eye cut at the corner where her gold ring had caught. "If my child grows within you, Jolie, you will have to forget Drew."

"I will never forget him!" Pulling herself into a sitting position, Jolie spun on her buttocks, preparing to verbally lash the Indian who had just made love to her. But she saw what she had done and, stunned by her own brutality, silently poured water from the ewer into the bowl. She began to clean the blood from his battered face. His arms stretched out upon the rug, his right knee drawn up, he allowed her to tend his wounds and deliberately did not flinch. His little white woman was very strong when riled. She'd had every right to vent her rage against him.

"Will you forgive me for hurting you, Noble?"

"There is no need."

Brushing her mouth lightly against his bruised cheek, she murmured, "You should hate me, Noble. Why don't you? You are a handsome man; you could have any woman you want. Why me?"

His dark gaze met her questioning one. The flames of the hearth flickered in golden paths across his naked bronze flesh. As his eyes lovingly caressed her slim, pale body, he felt the renewed arousal of her nearness. Putting his hand to her tiny waist, he coaxed her body to cover his own. Jolie propped her chin upon his hard chest and held his gaze, transfixed. Noble was an enigma to her. His Indian brothers—even his true half-brother, Bundy—showed a temperament that Noble did not. He was gentle and good and tolerant. Damn, but he was tolerant! Any other woman in Jolie's position would have found herself the victim of the brutal attack that she had dealt him instead.

"What are you thinking, Jolie?" he asked after a moment.

"I am wondering why you put up with me, Noble."

"I want you to be my woman."

She jerked up. Her body stiff and naked, she snarled down at him, "Yes! Even if you must win me through trickery! If your seed produces a child, I will never forgive you!"

Without anger, he asked, "And would you destroy my child, Jolie?"

She drew in a short, ragged breath, raising her hand to her throat as she did so. "What do you mean?"

"I mean, Jolie, would you cause my child to be ripped from your body?"

Stunned silence. Jolie was well aware of his meaning. Rumor had circulated through the region of an old hag living in the forest who would remove a developing child from its mother's womb. The thought appalled her. "What kind of woman do you think I am, Noble?"

His smile caused pain. When his face contorted, Jolie's hand fell sympathetically to his forehead, but he merely took it and brought it to his swollen mouth. "There are only a couple more hours before the dawn, Jolie. Remain with me. The fire is warm, though were it not, my love would warm you."

Despite the turmoil of her emotions, that was an invitation Jolie could not refuse. As she lay in Noble's arms, her body aroused by his loving caresses, she forgot, for those few short hours of winter darkness, that Andrew Cynric Donovan even existed.

Chapter Thirteen

Holker Hall, March 26

Lord and Lady Seymour had returned just the day before from a two-week sojourn to Cholmondeley Castle at Cheshire. Since Anne had grown increasingly weaker during their absence from Holker Hall, at the advice of her physicians she had now been confined to her bed for the duration of her pregnancy. Anne was determined not to brood over her confinement; she took with her to her bed her baskets of needlework and tatting.

Lord Penley was overwhelmed by the correspondence that had arrived during their short absence. His accountant had set aside the bills and public notices for perusal at his employer's leisure, and this early morning Penley sat at his large writing table. Set at an angle against the window that afforded him a wide view of the lawns, he could almost see the gentle transition from winter to spring taking place. Returning his thoughts to the tedious regimen he had neglected the past two weeks, he opened each letter one at a time, penning his answer before moving on to another.

He worked through the morning, finally reaching the last of the letters in the stack.

"What is this?" Taking the sheet of paper folded in

thirds, he studied the flowing hand that had written his name and address on its exterior. A quick, burning feeling hit him in midchest. How familiar was the handwriting, so familiar, in fact, that moisture sheened his eyes. His first thought was that the American writer wanted help for a relative confined to a British prison; he'd gotten several such requests during his tenure in Parliament. The familiar scroll had caused a tremble to settle in his hands and he was scarcely able to unfold the short letter. Quickly, his eyes scanned the greeting: "Dearest Uncle Penley . . ."

The usually staid man cried out in horror and disbelief, to which his accountant immediately responded. "Lord Penley?" the short, wide-girthed man queried. "Are you ill?"

His hand trembled so violently he dropped the letter. Picking it up with some difficulty, he held it out to Onslow. "I have read the salutation and am gripped by emotion," he whispered. "Read this to me."

A befuddled Onslow took the letter and began to read: " 'You will think that your eyes are deceiving you, but it is your adoring niece—" His words immediately halted. "My God . . ." Onslow's voice was scarcely a degree stronger than Lord Penley's. When he looked toward his employer, the distraught man merely flicked his wrist, a silent order that Onslow carry on. Picking up where he left off, he continued. "—who writes this letter with all the love and loneliness of one who has been rudely parted from her dear heart. I was taken from the waters of Wight by white slave smugglers, but I assure you, my dearest, that I remained unscathed during the horrid ordeal and am now safe from all harm and danger.

" 'I am being protected by a Pennsylvanian of means who has promised to see me safely aboard ship bound for you and home and my beloved England.

" 'Please do not worry for me. I will be home soon, perhaps by early summer. Today I shall enjoy a quiet Christmas with my companion and think of you with love in my heart.'" The missive was signed, "Your adoring niece, Carrie."

"Tell me, Onslow, that this is someone's idea of a cruel and vicious joke."

Onslow studied the letter, the stamp of an American town called St. Louis, the flowing curves of Carrie's writing, then reread the words as if he might have missed something vital. "Sire, as your accountant for fourteen years, and considering myself familiar, also, with Lady Sherwood's hand, it is my opinion that she, and no other, has written this letter to you. Lord Penley, your niece is alive."

Extending his trembling hand, Penley Seymour waited for the single sheet of paper to touch his palm. He read the letter for himself, again and again, scarcely aware that Onslow had slipped from the parlor. The chill of the morning penetrated the windowpane and touched his shoulders, causing a tremor to work its way through his spine.

His mind almost blank of thought, he arose, moved mechanically across the Caucasian dragon carpet with its brilliant greens and yellows and reds, then, regaining some degree of calm, took the spiral stairway by storm. Charging into his wife's private suite, he dismissed her handmaiden with a wave of his hand, then tossed Anne's needlework hither and yon so he could take her hands gently in his. In the move, Carrie's short letter was crushed between their entwined hands.

"What is this, Husband?" Anne's soft brown gaze held the crinkled sheet of paper.

A moment of silence followed her query. Then Penley Seymour touched his mouth in a brief kiss to his wife's pallid cheek. "It is, dear wife, a letter from . . ." Dare he say it, lest it be trickery? Should he reread the letter once again, lest evil magic have worked its way through the unsuspecting Holker Hall? No, it was true. The sensible

Onslow had confirmed it. "What I have here . . ." Penley began anew, smoothing the single sheet, "is a letter from our dearest Carrie."

Closing her eyes, Anne took a deep breath, then again met her husband's gaze. "Say that again, Penley."

He released a throaty laugh, scarcely able to restrain his exuberance. "Our Carrie . . . our dear Carrie is alive! She has sent a letter from America!"

Disbelievingly, Anne took the letter and quickly scanned the words Carrie had written. Oh, how many letters she'd received written in this familiar hand—the hand of her dear friend, her husband's beloved niece. Caught up in the joy of rediscovery, Anne crushed the letter to her satin-clothed bosom, then allowed her husband to hug her until their tears blended together in sweet happiness.

"Your dear Charissa," she murmured. "Soon she will be home. Thank God for the generosities and kindnesses of the Pennsylvanian! Your girl is safe, Husband. She said so herself in her letter."

Yes, safe, Penley Seymour thought, holding his wife tenderly and emotionally. But what might have happened in the few months since she had written the letter? Had her circumstances changed? Had she walked into new dangers, or was she still safe with the man her letter indicated she trusted? Was he old, young, a man of means, a vagabond, a lovable dandy with no ulterior motive except seeing her safely home to England? Penley knew he would not be able to simply wait until she showed up on the steps of Holker Hall. He would have to instigate acts to locate his dear niece. He would arrange to have notices sent to the place called St. Louis, and to the state of Pennsylvania. He would offer a reward for her safe return. And if that man she was with . . .

No, Carrie had said she was safe. He would have to trust her judgment that the Pennsylvanian was a man she could trust, implicitly.

The Pennsylvanian in question was trying to get a reaction from Lord Penley Seymour's lovely niece beneath the single sheet of their bed. Carrie slapped Drew's hand in her half-sleep, then smiled when his warm palm slipped around her waist. Leaning her head of disheveled flaming tresses against his inviting mouth, she whispered harshly, "Go to sleep, Drew Donovan!"

He growled inwardly. She'd been a bit preoccupied lately, discreetly moody, often parting from him with a shrug of annoyance when he touched her intimately. Perhaps she exhibited those notorious womanly moods that men were not meant to understand. He touched his mouth to her temple and whispered in return, "Sweet dreams, Princess."

Sleep overcame Carrie Sherwood much more quickly than it claimed Drew Donovan.

Carrie was still sleeping when he slipped from their bed many hours later. He sat there a moment, looking down on her peaceful features, her translucent eyelids moving ever so slightly in her dreams, her mouth curled in a smile so slight it scarcely existed at all. Her flaming hair was like a pillow beneath her head, her fingers gently entwined among the disheveled strands. Without awakening her, Drew touched his mouth in a tender kiss to her temple, then smoothed back the locks of hair from her forehead to grace it with another kiss. Then, with the sun still sleeping beyond the timberline, he moved out into the cool March morning.

Cawley Perth was up and about, chopping firewood for Hester's breakfast hearth. Drew approached the boy cautiously, since the ax he wielded was almost as long as he was. "How do you like my Alleghenies?" Drew asked the younger man. "Or have you been here long enough to form an opinion?"

Cawley grinned boyishly. "I'll be a likin' your mountains real good, Mr. Donovan. And I'll be a likin' Miss Hester's Dora, too. That girl, she's a might purty thing. Reckon Miss Hester'll mind if I come a callin' with wildflowers for her?"

"Hester wields a mean broom." Drew laughed the warning. "I'd be real gentle in the way you show interest in her Dora. She's only sixteen."

"Hell, Mr. Donovan . . ." Cawley Perth scratched his copper-colored head, "I'm only seventeen."

"Seventeen going on forty." Patting the boy's shoulder, he moved off into the darkness, the echo of his laughter following after him.

Moving onto the porch of Noble's cabin, Drew knocked lightly at the door. The door opened, and a robed, sleepy-eyed Jolie Ward met his gaze in the semidarkness. "He's up," she informed him, her voice unusually brusque. "Come in." A silent Drew stepped into the small, tidy cabin. "Care for coffee, Drew?"

"Wouldn't mind," Drew answered. "A little sugar—"

"I know how you like it!" she retorted.

Noble emerged from the curtain parting their bed from the living area, pulling on his dark shirt. Having heard Jolie's sharp reply to Drew's simple statement, he cut her a disapproving glance. "Ready to ride into Philadelphia?" he asked, a thought instantly coming to him. "We are going to ride, aren't we, Drew?"

"We are," he chuckled without embarrassment, accepting the cup of steaming coffee Jolie handed to him. "And you can thank Carrie—" Ignoring Jolie's narrow, supercilious gaze, he continued undaunted, "—for my change in attitude toward the four-legged beasts. I'd better take the gelding back to the Rourke stables. He's Tuxford's favorite, and the man is probably up in arms about him being gone so long."

"That odd bastard's still at the stables!" Noble remarked,

211

pulling on his boots. "Any sensible man would have moved on after spending fifteen years in prison."

Drew frowned. Tuxford had spent most of his life at Rourke House as a servant, and had been an accessory to Webster Mayne's—his second cousin—larceny and attempted murder. It was, indeed, strange that he'd have returned to Rourke House after his long confinement, since Drew's own dear mother had been the victim of Webster's crimes. But the ugly man-giant had promised his late mother, their housekeeper, Mrs. Sanders, that he would return to Rourke House to look out for Claudia, his sister. Though Claudia, at fifty, had the mentality of a prepubescent girl, she had managed to snag a husband and give birth to four children, all but the eldest Liddy—because of her blindness—positioned as servants in Rourke House.

Tuxford had gentled in the years of his confinement. He showed nothing but loyalty to the Donovan family now, and did not hesitate to protect his sister from the rages of her drunken husband who served Rourke House as gardener when he was able to maintain his footing. Many in Philadelphia wondered if Tuxford knew what had happened to Webster Mayne. Even Diana, Drew's mother, often voiced concerns that he might secretly be keeping in touch with her evil first cousin, though she hadn't spoken of it in several years now. Drew had grown up with the stories of Webster Mayne; he believed the fire that had razed the east wing of Rourke House so many years ago had left nothing but ashes—and the dismembered left hand—of the man who had been his mother's nemesis. But that was only his opinion. Some Pennsylvanians felt that true evil would not die so easily.

Jolie nudged Drew's boot, coaxing him from his thoughts. "I've prepared a basket of food for your trip," she informed him. "Noble says you'll be taking one of the pack horses."

Drew tried to smile at the embittered woman, but her

contemptuous look made it almost impossible. "Thank you," he said simply, rising and setting the untouched cup of coffee back on the table.

Jolie seemed hesitant to let them go. She stood in the doorway before the two men and did not move. Noble was aware that she did not want Drew to leave, but rather than allow Jolie to humiliate him, he enfolded her within his arms and touched his mouth to her forehead. "Do not worry about us. We'll be back in a week or so."

I couldn't care less about you, Noble! Jolie thought, her mouth turning down into a pout. Rather, she said, "Of course I won't worry about two grown men!" and made her reply deliberately abrasive.

During the next few minutes, both men saddled horses and loaded the packhorse. The rays of the sun cast a golden halo upon the horizon, and the settlement of Wills Creek slowly began to come to full wakefulness. Hester moved out to the porch to throw out a bowl of dirty water, the children gathered around the well, washing themselves as was their usual custom before breakfast, and Bundy joined Cawley in the chore of chopping wood. Two friendly Shawnees rode up to the trading post with furs to be traded for white man's goods; a pregnant woman sat atop one of the packhorses. When the Shawnee moved into the trading post, leaving the woman to struggle down, Noble immediately went to her assistance. The pretty, dark-haired woman looked at Noble with a mixture of embarrassment and surprise. It was not the Indian custom to assist a woman in any manner. Even great with child, the woman was expected to demean herself before her man and engage in her subservient duties. She was nothing more than a brood mare to him. That was one thing about the Indian ways Noble frowned upon.

"I'll go over and tell Carrie we're heading out," Drew remarked, unable to read the scorn in Noble's eyes. He thought perhaps he was upset with Jolie.

"Don't be long," Noble replied.

Drew had just mounted the steps to his cabin when the door opened and Carrie flew into his arms. "If you had left without telling me good-bye, I'd never have forgiven you!" she scolded with a pout. "After the way I treated you last night, I thought for sure you'd never speak to me again."

Drew held her warmly, eliciting a pretty smile. She had only halfheartedly pulled her brush through her waist-length hair and it was matted at her hairline. Her emerald eyes reflected the innocence of a newly awakened babe. "You can't get rid of me that easily, Princess."

"Drew?" A dark eyebrow arched as he awaited her query. "Are you going to tell your parents about me?"

"Tell them! I'm going to have it posted in the Philadelphia *Gazette* for all eyes to see. Andrew Cynric Donovan, favored son of Philadelphia, embraces his favorite princess!"

How sincerely and warmly his arms held her, and tightly, as if he could not bear to be parted from her. What a lucky woman she was to be cared for by this tall, commanding Philadelphian. He made her feel truly like a princess—his Allegheny princess. "Then you are going to tell them?" she questioned proudly.

"Indeed I am, Carrie Sherwood. I wish I could take you with me this trip, but Noble and I have much business to attend. I will take you soon, when better weather fully settles in and you can be the center of my attention. You deserve nothing less."

Resting her head against his chest, Carrie listened to his heart's rapid pace. It pleased her that she affected him this way. When his palms gently touched her temples and his mouth brushed hers, she wished he did not have to leave, that they could reenter their cabin and rest in gentle love in each other's arms.

But he soon parted from her, held her hand briefly in his, then allowed their outstretched fingers to slowly separate. It seemed that hours passed in the short spanse of time it took him to turn, widen the distance between them, and mount the horse whose reins Noble held. He stopped a moment to speak to Bundy, eliciting his protection of Carrie against the viciously mischievous Jolie.

Carrie absently hugged the rough-hewn porch support as the two men disappeared into the early-morning forest. She could not imagine life being more perfect.

How the angry little man ever reached Louisville, Kentucky, after his ordeal bordered on a miracle of divine origination. How well he remembered being dragged along the undercurrents of the Mississippi and being pushed into the upper currents just long enough to gulp air. Then the heavy iron scuttle had been ripped from his bindings by the horn of a cow carcass traveling the same undertow. His body had bobbed into the upper currents of the great river less than a half mile from the stern-wheeler where he had, less than two hours before, been peacefully sleeping.

Thank God he had fallen asleep that night with his pockets full of money . . . and thank God the old blind hag who'd found him unconscious on the bank hadn't picked him clean. He had to be grateful to her. She'd spent six weeks taking care of him. During his recovery, his quarry had escaped, the crew of his stern-wheeler must have presumed him to be dead and returned to home port in New Orleans. He'd been left with no choice but to travel northward alone. He was more determined than ever to find Drew Donovan; it wasn't just Flame now, it was something more, something he couldn't quite put his finger on. There was also an Indian and a half-breed to deal with—the murderous pair who had tried to drown him in the river. Ah, yes, he had seen their blasted renegade faces!

In the following weeks, he pressed his money into

greedy hands in exchange for transportation upriver. Once he'd reached Louisville, he'd had no trouble locating *Donovan's Dream* in her usual berth. Lucky for him that, because of the twenty-five-foot falls, the steamboats could not travel the Ohio farther than Louisville. Perhaps the travel of his prey had been slowed.

Setting up his home base at a modest boardinghouse across the Ohio River in a small Indiana settlement called New Albany, Junius Wade scoured the saloons and hotels on both sides of the river, looking for clues as to the destination of Donovan's party. He spoke with a New Yorker whose eyes startled with recognition at mention of Drew's name, but quickly he had denied any knowledge of the man. He would have to keep his eye on that lying bastard and watch where he went.

The grotesquely disfigured Junius Wade was remembered everywhere he traveled. Women swooned in horror, children gaped in innocent curiosity, and everyone sidestepped him as if he crawled with disease. His pompous manner might have gotten him beaten brutally on several occasions if men hadn't withdrawn from him in revulsion. That was one of Junius Wade's few advantages.

He'd been in Louisville almost two weeks and, except for the New Yorker, had not met a single man who knew the Donovans of Pennsylvania. He used his wiles on the docks where the *Dream* was berthed to learn of a family home in Philadelphia and, planning a final night of sleep in the boardinghouse, decided to resume his trip overland the following morning. He'd purchased a good horse, and the weather was just right for traveling.

As badly as he needed his sleep that night, it did not come easily to him. He felt phantom pains in his missing left hand, his leg still ached where it had been pierced by debris beneath the waters of the Mississippi, and his burn-scarred flesh itched like fire. When at last sleep did envelop him within its torrential vortex, he was plagued by

216

nightmares, and tossed and turned and relived memories he did not have. Images swam in the darkness. Again, the slim, golden-haired woman who made his skin crawl with loathing . . . and mirrors, many, many mirrors . . . portraits on dark-paneled walls of silently scorning, dark-eyed men . . .

A late-night breeze wafted through an open window of the upper floor—a breeze that carried on it the faint and nauseating odor of fire . . .

Junius Wade jerked from his sleep. Despite the coolness, sweat poured down his features, puddling in the deep, pitted burn scars that mapped his face. Mindless in the fury he had dragged with him from his dreams, he screamed in a half-delirium, "Damn you, Diana Rourke . . . you haven't seen the last of me!"

What was left of his eyelids suddenly pinched in confusion. Who was Diana Rourke?

Sitting half-asleep in her favorite chair before the hearth, Diana Rourke Donovan suddenly began to tremble. Cole, deeply engaged in financial ledgers at a large desk across the room, looked up only when she came unsteadily to her feet. He saw ashen horror reflected in her face, and scarcely had the time to rush to her side before she dropped limply into his arms.

He called sharply to Claudia. When she responded quickly to the alarm in his voice, he barked, "Claudia, send Tuxford for the doctor!"

"No . . . no . . ." Diana weakly grasped her husband's arm. "Take me to my bed. I will be all right."

"Claudia, send him for the doctor!" Cole repeated, the dark, worried eyes cutting between the two women leaving no room for argument.

Cole Donovan moved up the stairs with the agility of a man half his age. He gently put Diana upon the mound of

217

satin pillows and adjusted them beneath her head. When she looked at him with gentle reproof, he said more sharply than he had intended, "These episodes are coming much too frequently, Diana. It is time the doctor saw you."

"But it is almost midnight. Couldn't Edwin be sent for in the morning?"

"No," he replied on a note of finality. "I pay him enough of a retainer for his services that he can come tonight." Cole was not normally so demanding, but this was a matter of his wife's health.

Diana sighed deeply. How could she tell her husband no physical malady affected her? The vile face that had suddenly flooded her mind while she had sat peacefully before the fire had taken her strength and thrown it to the wind. She wanted to see Andrew. His short missive had said he and Noble would arrive in Philadelphia today. Was the appearance of the ghoul in her mind an ominous premonition? Would she see it every time something horrible happened in her life?

"Are you all right, Diana?" Cole asked, smoothing back the strands of her wheat-colored hair.

I saw Webster Mayne, she wanted to say, replying instead, "Don't worry so, Husband. It was nothing. Really, it was nothing."

The fire burning in the hearth reflected upon the strands of gray gently touching his temples. She had spent many happy years with this man and, foresight or not — Webster Mayne or not — she planned many more with him. She could not worry him simply because she had seen a monster in the darkness behind her closed eyes.

Edwin Redding arrived within the hour. Like his father, their family physician before him, Edwin was short and stocky, with dark, hooded eyes that seemed to reflect doom as he examined Diana, pinching his mouth in a worried frown when he finally put his medical instruments away.

"Well, Edwin . . ." Diana managed a small laugh. "Are

218

we going to be able to tell my dear husband waiting outside the door that I shall live?"

"True, I find no physical malady, Diana," the portly gentleman said, "but you are losing weight, I can see by the tiredness of your eyes that you do not sleep well, and your physical health will, ultimately, deteriorate. I must recommend a sleeping potion."

"No!" Horror flooded her violet eyes. "No, I must not sleep, Edwin. I must not!" Softening her voice, she continued. "I will be just fine when I see my son. He is due at any hour."

Edwin smiled his pleasure. "Andrew is visiting Rourke House again so soon?"

Her brows met in a puzzled frown. "What do you mean, again?"

"He was here in early February while you and Cole were in Virginia. Didn't you know?"

"No, I didn't. Claudia didn't mention it."

"Claudia wouldn't remember her name if she didn't hear it every day. They had journeyed overland from St. Louis."

"They? He, Noble, and Bundy?"

"Drew and a lovely young Englishwoman. From what I gather from Tuxford they spent three days in residence before taking a couple of horses from your stable and returning to Wills Creek."

"Oh, what a terrible time for them to have visited, Edwin! The house was in disarray. All the portraits were at Mr. Samson's being cleaned and some of the part-time staff had been given leave to visit their families during our absence. I do hope my son wasn't inconvenienced." She was terribly curious about the young lady who had accompanied Andrew but too much of a lady to press the issue.

Edwin, however, being a friend to both the elder Donovans and Andrew, could see the curiosity behind her gentle gaze. With a soft chuckle, he replied, "My information is that your son is very fond of the young lady. They probably were not downstairs long enough to notice missing portraits or the absence of half the staff."

Diana blushed furiously. "Are you saying, Edwin, that my son and the young lady—"

Shrugging, Edwin cut her off. "I am merely relaying what Tuxford told me. Now! Are you going to take the sleeping potion, or must I inform your husband of your stubbornness?"

If Diana had heard Edwin's question, her dreamy look did not betray it. She was thinking of her beloved son, a pretty woman he was extremely fond of, and, hopefully, marriage and grandchildren in the couple's future!

Eventually, she replied, though absently and without emotion, "Leave whatever you'd like, Edwin. I'll consider its need later."

Edwin was pleased with his choice of topic. If something dark and sinister was affecting Diana's health, the possibility of a love in her son's life seemed to be the proper remedy. She scarcely noticed that he'd left a small bottle of laudanum on the side table before exiting the room.

Cole was waiting just outside. "Don't worry, Cole," Edwin said. "I can find nothing physically wrong. I believe the problem is that she is not sleeping, and I've left a potion. See that she takes it."

Cole accompanied the doctor to the foyer. "Did she say anything about nightmares?"

"She said nothing."

"She's been having them frequently for the past few months. I believe they're at the root of her problem."

"Has there been any tragic occurrence to have caused such an upset in her life?"

"Nothing. She is obsessed with her cousin Webster, though."

Turning in the foyer, Edwin tucked his thumb into the waist of his trousers. "Her dead cousin?"

"Her *only* cousin, Edwin. His body was never found. I

thought perhaps her fears were because Andrew had journeyed to New Orleans and she was worried about him. But she has never reacted like this before. She honestly believes Webster Mayne is going to return to Rourke House."

Edwin frowned. He had never handled a disease of the mind before. "Perhaps when Andrew arrives, she will put these fears aside. Let us hope so." Taking his hat from Claudia, Edwin moved toward the door.

Edwin had just reached the road to Philadelphia when two mounted men approached. Halting his carriage, he immediately recognized Drew Donovan and the Indian, Noble.

"What are you doing at Rourke House this time of the night?" Drew questioned.

"Seeing to your mother."

Panic flashed in Drew's eyes. "Is she all right?"

"She is fine. A little tired and worn down. You might want to assure her that everything is well in your life. You might even . . ." Edwin could not prevent his smile, "tell her all about your pretty Englishwoman." Embarrassed that he had not acknowledged Drew's friend, Edwin said, "It's good to see you again, Noble. My wife and I will be dining with you tomorrow."

The two weary travelers took their leave. Drew dismounted the horse before it had halted and half ran into the foyer of Rourke House. Quickly greeting his father, he rushed up the stairs to his mother's chamber and soon enveloped her within his embrace. "Mother, what is this about Edwin having to see you?"

"I am fine," she replied, tears sheening her eyes. "Everything is fine because you are here. Now . . ." Putting a breath of space between them, she smilingly asked, "Tell me about your lady. And why haven't I heard about her before?" The admonishment was without true feeling. Drew held her hands warmly and told her all the details.

"The reason you have not heard, Mother, is because I

221

have not seen you since meeting Carrie. You were supposed to be in Pine Creek. Imagine my surprise to arrive at the house earlier this year and find that you and father had journeyed to Philadelphia."

"Oh, enough of your parents' flightiness! About this young lady . . . Will there be wedding bells, and grandchildren?"

Drew laughed. "Mother, one step at a time. I've never even told her that I love her."

"But you do, don't you?"

Drew grinned boyishly, pleasing his mother. "Love her? I *adore* her. Now! You get some sleep and we'll talk tomorrow."

"Noble accompanied you, didn't he?"

"Yes, he's downstairs with Father."

"Oh, but I should see him before I retire!"

Drew patted his mother's slim hand. "He'll wait until tomorrow. Good night, my sweet." Touching his mouth to her forehead in a tender kiss, he arose and allowed their hands to part.

His mother's smile accompanied him as he gently pulled the door closed.

Chapter Fourteen

As spring wreathed the rolling Allegheny hills surrounding Wills Creek, the nesting warblers filled the air with their musical calls. Upon the horizon this early April morning a single falcon rode the gentle winds.

A laughing Drew Donovan stood firmly upon the bank of the pond, wrestling with a large tiger muskie at the end of his fishing line. "He isn't in a mood to be our supper," he chuckled at Carrie. When her eyes continued to gaze downward as though she hadn't heard, he pulled in his fish and hooked it to his line of trout and shad, then lowered himself to the blanket beside her. His fingers moved beneath her chin, coaxing her gaze upward. "What is wrong, Carrie?"

A lump settled in her throat. She fought to restrain the tears resting just behind her eyelids. "I don't know, Drew. I feel—"

"You aren't sick, are you?"

She shrugged. "I just feel odd." Favoring him with an unsolicited smile, she took his hand and held it warmly. Reaching deep inside herself for an emotion that would please him, she continued with feigned ebullience. "But didn't I tell you that every year I am affected just so by the spring? Uncle says the pollen from the trees and flowers growing in abundance on the lawns of Holker Hall gets into my lungs and makes me feel poorly. I'll be all right in a little while. Now you go on and catch plenty of fish. Hester's children eat like little horses!"

She had mentioned her uncle and Holker Hall. Was she homesick for England? Blackness suddenly glazed Drew's eyes. It had been weeks since she'd spoken of home—if, indeed, he could put any stock in her claim of gentle birth. He had hoped she might put away her illusions of grandeur—if, indeed, that was what they were—and be content to make her home with him on Wills Creek.

The last thing he'd wanted to think about that morning was losing Carrie. Now, her melancholy and her mention of an uncle he had tried to pretend did not exist brought back that possibility. Scarcely three months had passed since he'd brought Carrie to his beloved Alleghenies, and he had hoped that her being with him in his home might make her forget her past roots.

Who was he trying to kid? She was here only for the adventures of America . . . only because she trusted him to take care of her and he had promised to send her home when she desired to go. A frown suddenly marred his masculine good looks. Silently, he arose from his knee and moved back to his fishing pole. For the next half hour, as his sport netted four more large trout—plenty enough for supper—he did not again glance at the seated Carrie.

Carrie was suddenly confused by his melancholy. Surely he wasn't worried about her spring fever. She tried to recall if she'd said anything else to bring on his mood. Had it been when she'd mentioned her uncle and Holker Hall? Though he had never spoken of love and marriage, her feminine heart hinted that it might be on his mind. She was not sure how she'd handle his declaration, when and if it was tendered. She was not sure how she'd handle a proposal of marriage. She had always intended to return to Holker Hall. But even as her intentions might have been good, she had, nonetheless, fallen in love with Drew

224

MORE PASSION AND ADVENTURE AWAIT... YOUR TRIP TO A BIG ADVENTUROUS WORLD BEGINS WHEN YOU ACCEPT YOUR FIRST 4 NOVELS ABSOLUTELY *FREE* (AN $18.00 VALUE)

Accept your Free gift and start to experience more of the passion and adventure you like in a historical romance novel. Each Zebra novel is filled with proud men, spirited women and tempestuous love that you'll remember long after you turn the last page.

Zebra Historical Romances are the finest novels of their kind. They are written by authors who really know how to weave tales of romance and adventure in the historical settings you love. You'll feel like you've actually gone back in time with the thrilling stories that each Zebra novel offers.

GET YOUR FREE GIFT WITH THE START OF YOUR HOME SUBSCRIPTION

Our readers tell us that these books sell out very fast in book stores and often they miss the newest titles. So Zebra has made arrangements for you to receive the four newest novels published each month.

You'll be guaranteed that you'll never miss a title, and home delivery is so convenient. And to show you just how easy it is to get Zebra Historical Romances, we'll send you your first 4 books absolutely FREE! Our gift to you just for trying our home subscription service.

BIG SAVINGS AND FREE HOME DELIVERY

Each month, you'll receive the four newest titles as soon as they are published. You'll probably receive them even before the bookstores do. What's more, you may preview these exciting novels free for 10 days. If you like them as much as we think you will, just pay the low preferred subscriber's price of just $3.75 each. *You'll save $3.00 each month off the publisher's price.* AND, your savings are even greater because there are never any shipping, handling or other hidden charges—FREE Home Delivery. Of course you can return any shipment within 10 days for full credit, no questions asked. There is no minimum number of books you must buy.

Donovan. She was not sure she would ever be able to leave him and had even entertained the thought of his accompanying her to England where they could live in happiness together. But that was a dream. He would never leave his Alleghenies, and she wouldn't expect him to.

Propping his fishing pole against the tree, Drew took up the heavy line of fish, then went to Carrie and assisted her to her feet. A constant, gentle splash of water over a dam into a mountain stream was the only sound to penetrate the stillness as they moved along the forest trail. A rich, blinding green clung to the trees all about them and, overhead, white cumulous clouds moved lazily northward. Soon, they crossed the narrow bridge over the gently flowing Wills Creek and entered the clearing of the trading post.

Noble chopped wood, his hard, bronze muscles glistening with sweat, the locks of his dark hair clinging to his forehead. He looked unusually foreboding this early evening. "Need some help?" Drew offered, giving the line of fish over to Dora, the eldest of Hester's four children. Drew hadn't really taken time to notice the girl before. Though tall and gangly and pig-tailed, she had very pretty features. Drew smiled. When Dora became aware of Cawley's interest, she'd probably give up the pigtails for something more feminine. He could imagine her wheat-colored hair long and loose and flowing. He could also imagine the enamored Cawley Perth following at her heels like a sick and lonely pup.

"I can manage," Noble replied brusquely, allowing enough time to have passed to properly relieve his ugly mood.

"What is bothering you?"

The ax suddenly halted. Noble dropped it to the ground beside his foot. "You tell me! Jolie is like a damned attacking she-cat. She won't tell me what is wrong. I can't even look at her without her jumping down my blasted throat!

Women, bah! I've just about had my fill of them!" Nodding apologetically to Carrie silently standing by, he said, "Pardon, Carrie."

"Shall I talk to her?" Carrie offered.

"I don't think it would help, Carrie," said Noble, cutting his gaze back to Drew. "But she might tell you what the problem is." When Drew gave him a confused look, Noble continued with haste. "Drew, if speaking to Jolie is asking too much of you—"

Drew's hand went up. "No, I'll talk to her. Where is she?" Any woman besides Carrie would have been displeased with his offer. But she was not; she was that sure of his love for her.

"She's washing clothes in the back."

Drew gave Carrie a brief look that solicited her understanding. When he'd left her standing alone with Noble, she asked Drew's Indian brother, "Is Jolie your only problem, Noble?"

Noble's hooded gaze met hers. "What do you mean?"

"I saw you talking with Bundy and a stranger this morning and all of you seemed upset. I have a feeling you and Bundy have been hiding something these past few months."

Dare he tell her about Junius Wade? Dare he not? Unknowingly, she had placed Drew's life in danger. Noble knew the Englishwoman loved Drew, and he knew, also, that she would do anything to protect him. With that in mind, Noble responded, "Yes, there is something, Carrie. I guess it is time that I told you."

As Carrie sat on a wide oak stump, Noble dropped cross-legged to the ground before her. She listened intently to his deep voice.

"Do you remember when Cawley rode into St. Louis and Drew decided that the two of you would travel overland to Wills Creek?"

"I remember," she replied quietly.

"Did Andrew give you a reason?"

226

"Not one that I believed."

"The true reason was because Junius Wade was sitting aboard a stern-wheeler a hundred yards out from *Donovan's Dream*. He found your tattered dress aboard, and he was going to wait for Drew to return. He said if he didn't get you back he was going to kill Drew."

"I see." Carrie was sure her heart had stopped beating. A chill rushed through her veins. "You sent word to Drew so that he would not return to his steamboat?"

"I did, Carrie, because I wanted to protect him. We thought you would already have left for the East Coast."

"And what happened to Mr. Wade? Why didn't he follow the *Dream* to Louisville?"

Noble inhaled a long, deep breath. "Me and Bundy swam over to that stern-wheeler, Carrie, and we dragged Junius Wade into the Mississippi current."

Closing her eyes tightly, Carrie thought she would faint. She could not imagine the gentle Noble dragging any man to his death. "You killed him, Noble?" Her eyes slowly opened. "You and Bundy killed Junius Wade?"

Noble's trembling hand rose to his forehead and swept back the long, damp locks of hair. He felt sick to his stomach as he replied, "We thought we had, Carrie. The man who rode in this morning was coming across from Louisville. He said a man fitting Junius Wade's description had made inquiries about the owner of *Donovan's Dream*. Don't know how long it'll take, but he'll be showing up here. Damn! If the Mississippi didn't swallow that bastard, then nothing of earth can kill him."

Terror and dread stirred within her. "Noble, I cannot endanger Drew's life. I must leave."

"He loves you, Carrie."

"He has never told me so."

"A man confesses to a friend—a brother—what he cannot confess to the woman he loves."

A painful tremble settled into Carrie's chest. She imag-

227

ined that death would be easier to face than separation from Drew. "Noble, whatever happens, do not question my motives, and do not suggest any to Drew. I love him very, very much. If I have to hurt him to save his life, I will do just that." Carrie took Noble's hand for support as she rose to her feet. "Thank you for telling me this, Noble. You must help me protect our Drew. I could not bear it if something happened to him because of me."

When Drew rounded the corner of the trading post, he had found both Hester and Jolie at the washtubs. When Hester looked up, Drew mouthed the words, "I need to talk to Jolie in private." When the older woman moved toward the rear entrance of the living quarters, he approached Jolie, who worked at the washtub with her back to him. She jumped when Drew's hand suddenly gripped her upper arm.

Spinning toward him, she nearly lost her footing. "You startled me so, Andrew."

"Do you have time to talk, Jolie?"

She was surprised. Since he'd returned to Wills Creek with the Englishwoman, he had avoided her, almost rudely at times. "What do you want, Andrew?"

"Come . . ." Taking her arm, he coaxed her toward a fallen log against the timberline. "You haven't been yourself lately, Jolie." He spoke as if he had personally made the observations rather than repeating what Noble had noticed. "You've been short-tempered, and that isn't like you."

Planting her palms upon the log, Jolie kicked at a stone with her right foot. "I am sorry if my actions displease you."

"I am not displeased, Jolie. I care about you. If something is wrong . . ."

"It is nothing."

"It must be something, Jolie."

The pretty, brown-haired woman wrapped her fingers tightly through the locks lying against her tightly drawn temple. How could Andrew dare to question her moods when he knew bloody well what was wrong with her? She wanted him, and yet now a misfortune had entered her life that made him as distant to her as the farthest point in the universe. Whatever hopes she had held out had flown to the wind. She had no one to blame but the Indian bastard Andrew called a brother.

With sudden, unprovoked fury, Jolie shot to her feet. When she spun back toward Drew, her arms flailing madly and tears filling her eyes, she half-shouted, "I am carrying a child, Andrew! Noble's child! And I hate *you* for it! It should be your child! *Your* child, not his!" She slumped in broken sobs against Drew, who was quite taken aback by her rush of emotions. She made a feeble attempt to strike his chest with her fists. "I hate you, Andrew . . . I hate you."

Drew calmly took her wrists and held them to his chest, allowing her to lose her tears in the folds of his shirt. He had never seen her like this. She was distraught, not because she carried a child, but because the child was not his. When her sobs became numb silence, Drew smoothed back the disheveled brown tresses that had scattered in her rage. "Noble loves you, Jolie. Do you plan to tell him?"

"What choice do I have?"

"You have no choice. Noble has every right to be a father to his child . . . his legitimate child."

After a few moments of silence, Jolie's head moved from the damp folds of his shirt so that her eyes met his. "Are you saying that I must marry him?"

"I am saying you could ask for no better husband or father for your child. If you wish to take my words as an order rather than a suggestion, then so be it."

Jolie could not halt one last, desperate entreaty. "An-

229

drew, don't you want me? Oh, please, I adore you so!"

Shaking her roughly, Drew said, "I love Carrie and I plan to ask her to be my wife. Get this foolish notion out of your head, Jolie. You will be a wife to Noble, and a good one. I demand it."

Ripping herself free from him, she turned her back. "And if I don't?"

"Then I will personally escort you back to Pine Creek. Do you want Zebedee and Callie to see you grow great with child with no man to support you?"

Ashamed, she turned to face him once again. The tears still clung to her ashen cheeks. "My parents would never understand, Andrew, if I did not marry a willing father. If it is what you wish, I will marry Noble."

"I shall summon the circuit preacher," he offered. "You tell Noble that you will be his wife, and that you bear his child. And see that you deliver the news in a way that will make him happy. So help me God, Jolie, if you hurt him . . ."

"Hurt him!" she hissed. "He has planted his seed within me! *I* am the one who has been hurt. I am the one who will swell to the size of a melon. I am the one who will have to spew forth a half-breed Indian bastard—"

For the first time in his life, Andrew Cynric Donovan slapped the face of a woman, though not really hard enough to cause any physical damage. Her eyes wide with shock and disbelief, Jolie drew in a quick, short breath, too stunned to draw her fingers to her stinging cheek or to object to his cruel treatment of her.

"I'll summon the preacher," he repeated, regaining his calm. "I believe you can arrange a suitable ceremony by Saturday."

With that declaration, he turned away, leaving her sulking upon the fallen log and wondering if he would ever forgive her vicious words.

Drew had not stopped thinking about Jolie's confessed pregnancy. How could he have been so blind that he hadn't recognized the similarities between Jolie and Carrie's moments of brooding silence and unprovoked tears? He lay upon the thick feather mattress, his hands tucked behind his head, and watched Carrie scoot about preparing to retire for the night. She had brushed her long hair until it gleamed like fire, had donned her favorite bedgown, and had warmed a glass of fresh milk, which she brought to the bed to share with him. She sat upon her knees beside him, melancholy almost to the point of tears. When the glass was empty, she placed it on a small table and slipped beneath the covers. Her finger traced a path across his fur-matted chest. She would have to be a very good actress tonight. Circumstances demanded it. Still, she could not pass up the opportunity for one final, wonderful moment with the man she loved.

"What are you thinking about, Drew?"

He'd been thinking of Jolie. He could not, however, make such a confession to Carrie. "You," he remarked shortly.

"Me?" A sad smile curled her mouth. "Tired of me, Drew Donovan? Wanting to be rid of me before I become more of a pest?"

Drew bent over her, touching his fingers to her chin, then tracing a line along her smooth jawline. While he had been thinking about Jolie, he had been comparing her moods and unprovoked antics to those Carrie had been exhibiting these past few weeks. "About this illness you blame on the spring, Carrie . . ." Her narrowed eyes met his own. "There are certain normal processes that affect a woman's body on a regular basis. Have you . . ."

Forgetting momentarily what she had decided to do, a sudden quizzical expression marred her brow. "What are you asking me, Drew Donovan?"

Color poured into the sharp lines of his high cheeks. "What I mean is . . ." His fingers withdrew, then spread upon the coverlet between them. "The nights that you and I spent together, in each other's arms . . ."

Carrie sat forward so quickly he had to dodge to avoid a collision with her. "Are you asking me, Drew Donovan, if I bear your seed?"

Regaining his physical composure, his mental one quickly disintegrated. He felt the heat of embarrassment burning upon his face, and his heart began a wild, erratic beat. "Yes," he said shortly, "that is what I am asking."

Actually, Carrie had never considered that possibility, and the very idea made her shudder. What she knew about the consummation of relationships between men and women and the various and sundry signs of pregnancy she had learned from Mirabell. Half of what her beloved nanny had said she had quickly discounted as myth; the other half she'd never been entirely certain about. "Well, of course, there are changes in my body," she said after a moment, returning to her prone position, "but I have been taken from my homeland and there are bound to be mental and physical changes when one has been tremendously affected. The environment here is so different from England, and you must remember that I lived briefly in the south of your country where it is very hot. My body would normally react to so drastic a change."

"You are telling me, then, that there have been changes?"

Carrie shrugged absently. "And I explained why," she quipped, snatching at a sheet to drag over her thin bedgown. "Drew Donovan, take those lustful eyes off me! And stop entertaining the idea that I carry a child! Wherever would you get such an idea?"

Folding her to him, Drew enjoyed the softness of her hair against his cheek. "Jolie is carrying Noble's child."

Carrie fell to her back and met his gaze. "Jolie? But

how? Why . . ."

Drew chuckled. "How? The same way we might become parents, Carrie."

"Pooh!" Carrie dropped her linked fingers to her abdomen. It felt no different than before, except that it might be a little firmer, a little rounder. No . . . no, she could not consider such a possibility. She had to leave Drew Donovan and Wills Creek. She had to save him from the malevolent menace stalking his trail. She suddenly thought of the letter she'd written to her uncle. He should soon be receiving it, if he had not already, and would expect her to return to England. Regardless of her feelings for Drew, she could not afford the burden of a pregnancy. Holker Hall would sink into a mire of shame and ridicule. Could she do that to her staid, dignified, and very conventional uncle? "Go to sleep, Drew Donovan."

Surprise creased his brow. "Go to sleep! You must have lost your mind!" Playfully, he turned her into his arms. Glaring disapproval halted the kiss he would have given her. "What is wrong with you, Carrie? When is the last time we just . . . went to sleep?"

"Tomorrow," she retorted, turning from him, "ask me that question again, and I shall reply, 'Last night'!"

Throwing his hands up, Drew rolled away from her. "Yes, ma'am," he said with mild sarcasm. "Don't let me get in your way, ma'am. Just tell me when you want me to drop dead, ma'am."

"Oh, go to sleep, Drew Donovan!" Even as humor laced her words, tears came to her eyes, which she shielded from him. But tears shed into her pillow could never compensate for the loss she would suffer that night. She could turn her back on everything in the world, as long as Drew was with her. He made her forget England and Holker Hall. He had held her and loved and comforted her for months now, and she felt safe and secure in his arms. Carrie suddenly felt like the condemned prisoner with only one night

233

left to live; tomorrow she would find herself placed against a wall, her life snuffed from her by the shattering volley of Junius Wade's obsession. And like the condemned prisoner lusting for that last moment of life, she dried her tears and turned into Drew's arms.

"You gave up too easily, my love." As he perched again on his drawn-up palm, she favored him with a teasing smile. "I thought you didn't really want me tonight."

"And I, my love . . ." he mocked her in return, "was simply waiting for you to beg for my favors."

Tonight must be wonderful, she thought, forcing back the tears sheening her eyes. It would have to be the foundation of memories to build her lonely future on. "Drew?"

His mouth touched teasingly upon hers. "Hmm?"

"Do you care for me?"

His amorous movements ceased. "What kind of a question is that?"

"Oh, I don't know." But she did know. In her heart, she wanted to hear the words, "I love you," but if he answered he was only playing a game with her, what she had to do would be so much easier.

She would have to savor this night and hold it forever in her heart. In just a few short hours, before the dawn, he would hate her. She had to make sure of that. But for now there was only herself and Drew, together in their cabin of love.

"You are so thoughtful tonight," Drew murmured, eliciting a whimper of desire from her. It was all the betrayal of her arousal he needed to imprison her willing mouth against his own. She felt his body mold to hers with heated urgency, and she could scarcely bear the moments it took to free herself of her cumbersome bedgown. The sensual invitation of her softest curves drew his hands to further explorations. They embraced as if there was no tomorrow, their legs entwined, the hardness of him pressed against her abdomen. Stroking her with long, gentle caresses,

Drew's mouth moved masterfully over her passion-warmed cheek, the slim column of her neck, plunging between her full, peaked breasts. Carrie eagerly responded to his hungry kisses. The night was young . . . the night was old. There would be no others . . . the night marked the end of their togetherness. A vast emptiness consumed her and filled her with a yearning to make lasting memories, to make it a night to place into the heaven of memories she would have to take with her back to England.

Within moments his hand moved across the delicate spread of her hips and found the wanton treasure it sought. His restraint was scarcely in tow; Drew found that he could not wait another minute to have her as he lifted her hips to allow for his entry. His eyes closed tightly as he savored their sweet joining, and his mouth sought hers in the semidarkness of love's chamber.

Each time he joined to her was a new experience. Her rapturous response pleased him as she matched his cadence and pace with unabandoned and equal fire, the fervency of her body molded to his damp one so exquisitely warm that he never wanted to part from her. When at last his passion peaked and she shuddered beneath him, he relaxed with her, a willing prisoner to her passion-heated flesh.

The pureness of their lovemaking left Carrie weak and unable to move as he eased to her side. Was his look one of smug satisfaction, or was it a look of love? Cutting her gaze to his own lustrous eyes, she did not see the satisfaction of an egotistical male. He looked at her as if she were his most precious treasure on earth.

Touching his mouth to her own in a final kiss, Drew closed his eyes, pulled her close to him, and soon drifted off to sleep. He was content and happy; the most beautiful woman in Pennsylvania—indeed, in all the world—lay quietly in his arms.

An hour later, when she was sure he slept soundly, Carrie donned her gown and slipped from their bed, took up a blanket, and exited the cabin into the cool April night. As she moved along the trail toward the pond, she was suddenly aware of the friendly old bobcat dogging her trail. When, a few minutes later, she spread the blanket on the ground where she had sat earlier that day, the cat moved toward nocturnal prey in the darkness of the timberline.

Carrie linked her fingers and hugged her drawn-up knees. Moonlight shimmered on the still pond; occasionally, a trout would leap, beginning an eternal swirl of circles that melded into the bank just a few feet from her. All about her, the breeze rustled the spring-green oaks, catching in her flame-colored hair and whipping it upon her tear-stained cheek. Her thoughts were in a quandary. She had every reason to believe that Drew's child grew within her, and today she had to learn that his life was in danger. Had it not been for her, a maniacal, obsessed Junius Wade who could sneak in and out of lives with the fleetness of a shadow would not be dogging his trail with blood in his heart. Junius had dictated the time for her to return to Holker Hall, and she hated him with a murderer's passion.

As she sat alone in the darkness, Carrie tried to justify her reasons for returning to Holker Hall. It was spring, a good time for traveling. She was her uncle's only heir, and one day she would be a duchess. Oh, why . . . why hadn't her beloved uncle married and had a child of his own—a child who could be the heir she did not now wish to be? She loved Drew Donovan with all her heart and soul and she wanted nothing more than to be his wife and live with him on Wills Creek. She wanted nothing more than to be the mother of his children.

But she was rambling insensibly. Even if her uncle had another heir, she had still placed her beloved Drew's life in danger. Regardless, she had to leave him. And that was the hardest thing she would ever do in her lifetime.

So, she would bring disgrace to Holker Hall. Perhaps,

though, extenuating circumstances would make her pregnancy less of a disgrace. She had, after all, been taken against her will from the Isle of Wight. She had suffered through the humiliation of bringing the highest bid at the white slave auction, and had been sold into service as a prostitute by a despicable little man named Junius Wade. She should have known his obsession would destroy her life. That she had been taken beneath the wing of the tall, gentle Pennsylvanian was the only good thing to come out of her American adventure. Though he had never spoken the words, she knew that he loved her.

She would return to England and never see Drew again. But if she were, indeed, carrying his child, then she would have a constant reminder of him. She knew that she would never marry but would dedicate her life to being a perfect mother to his child.

How would she survive without her beloved? Tears once again flooding her eyes, Carrie dropped her face into the thick folds of her gown.

She showed no alarm as a gentle hand came to rest upon her shoulder. The familiar male smell of him wafted into her senses and she turned tearfully into Drew's strong arms. "Forgive me. Forgive me, Drew."

"You've done nothing, Carrie. Why this emotion?"

Drawing slightly back from him, she met his gaze. The reflection of the moon mirrored in his eyes. "I must return to England, Drew. I wish to journey to Philadelphia and begin my trip."

Panic seized Drew. He grasped Carrie's arms and pulled her to him. "No, you cannot leave, Carrie. I love you. I want you to be my wife."

God! He had said those magical words — I love you. But she could not respond now as her heart wanted to. It was imperative that she be strong and aloof — and cruel, too, if that was what it took.

Carrie knew what she had to do. If there was a time in

her life when it was vital that she be hated, it was now. She knew what had to be said to build that loathsome emotion within the gentle Drew Donovan. The pain she had to inflict on him made her want to die.

"Your wife, Andrew Donovan?" she asked in a carefully controlled tone. "You expect me to be your wife?" Forcing a high-pitched, sarcastic laugh, she continued loathsomely. "I did pull one over on you, old boy! I wouldn't marry an American if my life depended on it. I have had my enjoyment with you, and now you are no longer needed!" The dark glare of his hooded gaze cut her like knives. She had, indeed, evoked the proper, and very bitter, response. "I shall wait until after Saturday so that stupid Jolie will marry your Indian friend. After all, would she marry him knowing you are still available? Then I wish to commence my trip to England." Again she forced a laugh, even as pain wracked her insides. "I can't believe you seriously believed I could care for you, a common American!"

There, it was done. Hatred glazed his eyes. He released her arms as if tangible revulsion had suddenly crawled across his skin. "I see," he said in a controlled tone. "You were playing a game—"

"And you fell for it!" she shot viciously, putting space between them as if she found his touch repugnant. "I would have played out this charade a little longer, but I am bored. Bored with you! Bored with this land! Bored with your friends! I wish to return to England where a decent man might take me to his bed!"

Andrew Cynric Donovan stood ramrod straight. His arms hung limply at his sides. Lifting a haughty chin, Carrie defiantly met his gaze. The pain she saw there almost destroyed her reserve. "I will arrange travel for Sunday morning and request that Noble accompany you."

"No!" Carrie shot to her feet. "No, I will not travel with that . . ." Oh, but she had to come up with something he would find offensive, something he would want to protect

238

his best friend from, "that Indian savage! I'll not be seen with him. You take me to Philadelphia, Drew Donovan, or I'll remain here and be a thorn in your side. You wouldn't want me to remain, would you?"

Without hesitation, he replied, "No," and soon disappeared among the shadows of the trail.

With a lump the size of a boulder choking in her throat, Carrie managed to find her voice . . . but not soon enough to call him back. Succumbing to the blanket below her, Carrie's sobs wracked the haunting sounds of the night.

She had done what had to be done.

The man who had disappeared into the Allegheny forest, with his pride crushed, had taken Carrie Sherwood's heart with him.

Chapter Fifteen

In the few days before Noble's marriage to Jolie, the tension between Drew and Carrie escalated to an unspoken hostility that set the mood whenever the two were together. They remained in their shared cabin only so that Jolie would not be aware of their problems and have second thoughts about marrying Noble. Nightly, when Carrie slipped into the bed she and Drew had shared in their moments of love and tenderness, he moved into the cool April forest and found a comfortable spot beside Wills Creek. The bobcat usually accompanied him, sleeping on the blanket at his feet and keeping away any would-be predators.

She had hurt Drew deeply. He was not able to meet her melancholy gaze, even when required to speak to her in order to keep up appearances. Noble suspected that Carrie's actions had caused this rupture, and he said nothing, except to berate himself for his and Bundy's failure to destroy the man dogging their trails. The children became victims of the quiet hostilities between the two adults, their own happy moods sorely affected.

That Friday evening, with most of the residents of Wills Creek deeply engaged in preparations for the wedding, Drew moved into his solitude on the banks of Wills Creek. Tonight, however, Carrie could not tolerate the brooding silence between them. She was annoyed by the absurdity of it all. She should have given Drew credit where credit was due and believed that he could successfully handle Junius Wade, when and if he showed up as a threat to them. But Junius was not just an old, grotesquely disfigured man. The malevolence of him had thrown Carrie into action against her beloved Drew. And that evil still hovered over them, as surely as the thunderclouds gathering overhead, promising a storm to parallel the one existing between them.

Carrie stood in the darkness of a towering oak, watching Drew spread the single blanket upon a smooth area of ground. The bobcat had not accompanied him this evening, no doubt perceptive to the coming storm, and she sank back against the smooth bark, tucking her hands in the curve of her back. The moonlight piercing the gathering clouds glimmered upon the gentle current of Wills Creek and cast a golden glow upon Drew's chest. He had balled his shirt into a pillow beneath his head and lay ever so still, one arm at his side and the other resting lightly across the bridge of his nose.

Tears gleamed in Carrie's eyes. Completely shadowed by the timberline, she was content to look at him, this man who was her love and her life and who would be the father of her child if indeed she was interpreting correctly all signals from her body. The hardest thing she would ever do in her lifetime was take Drew's child three thousand miles away from him.

A nearby rumble of thunder was followed immediately by a steady pelting of rain upon them. Drew did not attempt to shield himself from the downpour and Carrie, partially protected by the thick foliage of the trees beneath which she stood, was drawn into the vulnerability of him lying there, a willing victim to the storm, caring not what happened to him at that precise moment. Guilt rushed upon her and she was scarcely aware of a trickle of rain running down the slim column of her neck and into the bodice of her simple gown.

She had made no sound, but now she was very aware of Drew's gaze turned directly toward her. Though hidden in darkness, he had somehow managed to detect her presence. "What do you want?" he barked in annoyance. Carrie did not move but remained nervously passive, pressing herself against the tree as if she thought she might be absorbed by the solid strength of it. "I asked what you wanted," he said again, sitting up and raking the raindrops from his forehead.

Carrie stepped from behind the tree and into the steady downpour. Her linen gown clung damply to her slim figure, a stunning sight that for a moment held Drew's attention with sweet remembrance rather than loathing.

She had hoped the tree would shield her from his view, that she might be able to stand in secrecy and simply watch him. But now her hiding place had been betrayed, and there was absolutely nothing she could say to him that might remedy the tension between them. She had to maintain her determination to leave him and return to England in order to protect him from the foe that should be hers alone. Any sentimentality now — or change of heart — would only serve to make her look flighty and foolish.

"I want nothing," she replied. "I happened along to find you here and then could not leave without fear of detection. I was merely going to wait until you had fallen asleep."

Running his fingers through his thick, dark hair, he replied, "Only an insane man sleeps with rain pelting his body."

His softly spoken words took her off guard. He seemed strangely passive himself, as if he could not bear to keep up the front of bitterness and hostility. The deep fear suddenly returned to Carrie — a fear borne of her love for the embittered man standing in the semi-darkness before her.

She remembered Noble's tale of trying to drown Junius in the Mississippi. He had not been claimed by the waters of the Gulf of Mexico when she had pushed him over the rail or by the Mississippi some weeks later. Was he invincible? Evil incarnate who could not be destroyed by mortal means?

Shivering in the coolness of the late night downpour, Carrie stepped backward into the shadows of the oak. Even in the half-light, in the glimmer of the thunderous storm upon Wills Creek, she saw Drew's eyes darken and narrow.

"Come here, Carrie." When she did not respond, he said more harshly, "Come here!"

She moved timorously toward him. He had drawn up his knees, and his wrists hung limply across them. Her footsteps halted when she stood just off the blanket but within touching distance of him. Without warning, he grabbed her wrist and pulled her down between his knees. His hands roughly held her arms. "You said you would never marry an American! You said I was no longer needed! You said you were bored with me, Carrie Sherwood!"

He had been drinking; his liquored breath assailed her senses. "So I did," she murmured.

"I don't believe you, Carrie. I don't believe you meant any of those cruel things you said."

Beyond his desperately pleading gaze she saw a vision of him . . . murdered at the hands of the evil Junius Wade. She grappled with her emotions, wanting to fling herself into his arms and proclaim her love for him and yet to flee from him, confirming her loathing for him, a loathing that did not—could not—exist.

"Let me go, Drew Donovan!" she hissed, fighting for control of her own body. "Get your hands off me!"

Her efforts to free herself caused him to accidentally tear her gown. As her tender flesh was assailed by the

243

blinding rain, his mouth sought the sweetness of the rose-buds suddenly exposed to him. She continued to fight to free her wrists, but the half-delirious man wrenched them to her back, forcing her down upon the blanket beneath him. "I know you love me, Carrie . . . I feel it every time you look at me. I don't know why you said the things you did, but there must be a reason. There must be!" His hands lowered to drag the skirts of her torn gown upward to expose her slender thighs. When his fingers twisted in the waist of her underthings, she wrenched her hand free and attempted to remove his hand from the intimacy of her body.

But he was too strong for her. His hand slid lower, ripping her undergarments, finding the moist warmth of her most intimate place, and roughly assaulting her. She wanted to scream her outrage, but a thousand delights penetrated her rebellion, unconsciously coaxing her thighs apart to allow for his drunken explorations. His mouth easily claimed her evasive one again and again, trailing rough, assaulting kisses along her hairline, each translucent eyelid, down the slim column of her neck to plummet into the womanly cleavage that had, just moments ago, been covered by the gown that now lay at her side.

Ecstasy throbbed through her, robbing her of sensible thought, driving her fingers deeply into the thick, tangled masses of his dark hair. She expected to hear the sound of buttons popping on his trousers, then the coarse material being roughly dragged down his hard thighs. Rather, his mouth trailed kisses across her rain-soaked torso, his tongue plunging between her breasts, then teasing a trail across the flat plane of her stomach. The moments that followed made her gasp with wanton surprise as he showed her new ways that a man could love a woman — ways that made her abdomen rush with hot, liquid desire.

When at last he covered her, she was mindless in her enchantment, in the total possession of her body by this wickedly sensual man. His powerful hips drummed against her . . . again and again and again until, in her exhaustion, she was unable to keep up with his pace. When, at last, glimmering lights filled her brain and her body in one delightful burst of energy, she forgot that his actions might be construed as rape. If he had done it again, oh, so much more slowly, she would not have fought him, not even a little.

His possession of her was the most erotic and wildly wonderful experience she had ever imagined—his maleness filling her while the rain beat down upon their passionately entwined bodies. Now they lay in exquisite exhaustion, and had she possessed the strength to move, she doubted she would have made the effort. Her body had been rent asunder by the male power of him, like the thunderous storm that roughly hugged the heavens above them.

Then, as if his inebriated mind suddenly realized what he'd done, he shoved himself from her and quickly drew his trousers up. Surprised, Carrie did not at first move but allowed the heavy droplets of rain to pelt upon her passion-burned flesh.

The anger returned to his eyes. Roughly, he took the shirt he had balled to use as a pillow and threw it across Carrie. "Cover yourself, woman!" he demanded. "And then get out of my life."

Tears invaded Carrie's reddened cheeks as she grabbed up her gown and ran brokenheartedly along the rain-soaked path. He did not go after her, even when a painful sob broke from his throat at the hideousness of his words and the vile, drunken attack he had made upon her.

Noble and Jolie were married in a simple ceremony at ten o'clock the following morning. Though banquet tables had been set up for enjoyment after the ceremony, only the preacher and the children seemed to have appetites for the many plates of food Hester had prepared. Hambone scarcely ate enough to call it a meal but took the napkin-covered plate of cookies Hester's youngest son slipped into the folds of his blanket, promising to eat them at bedtime when his warm milk was brought to him.

A silent Drew wasted no time in preparing horses for his and Carrie's travel to Philadelphia. If he remembered the moments they had shared on the banks of Wills Creek the night before, his indifference toward her did not indicate it. He treated her as if he loathed her.

The only possessions she planned to pack were the dresses Drew had given her from the merchandise he'd purchased in New Orleans. She'd have left them for one of the other women, but she did not think Drew would have wanted that. He had been pleased to see her in the simple, practical gowns. She vowed that when she returned to England, they would be all she wore.

For two long days and nights of traveling, he spoke scarcely a word to her, and then simply to warn her of a low-hanging branch or a sunken hoofprint on the trail that might trip her horse. Once he'd almost pointed out a wild blossoming of laurel and rhododendron far off in the woods but had returned his gaze to the trail.

The nights on the trail were dreadful. Though he saw to her comfort, he chose to be parted from her by the thickness of the underbrush, and when she bathed in the stream in those twilight moments between daylight and darkness, he sauntered off in the other direction, absently chewing a bit of straw.

They arrived in Philadelphia on the morning of the third day. Drew's father, who had been inspecting the horses, emerged from the stables when the exhausted pair rode up. As Drew dismounted, Cole Donovan put his hands up to the slim, expressionless girl, who hesitantly moved into his arms.

"You were not expected, Son," Cole Donovan said, "and

this must be the young lady we've heard so much about?"

When Drew merely grunted a wordless response and began tending the horses, Carrie offered her hand. "I am Charissa Sherwood, sir."

Cole Donovan frowned. The tension surrounding them was an ugly, impenetrable fog. "And am I to assume that you two young people have had a bit of a tiff, lass?"

Carrie felt warmed by his subtle Scottish accent, tamed, she was sure, by his years in America. Her grandfather had been a Scot, and she remembered his rolling laugh capable of wrapping all who heard it in its exuberance and sincerity. She immediately liked Drew's handsome father. "It isn't a tiff at all," Carrie lied. "It is merely that I'll be returning to England. Your son said that you could arrange my travel aboard one of your ships and the kind hospitality of lodgings in your home until one so sails."

This was not at all what Cole and Diana Donovan had anticipated of their first meeting with Carrie Sherwood. In the last few weeks, Diana had spoken affectionately of the woman who might finally take her son to the wedding altar. And now, the only candidate to come along wanted only to return to England. Cole would ask no questions. It was, perhaps, a subject to be discussed between the ladies.

Diana had been sitting in the parlor, reading a volume of Master Shakespeare's works, when Drew and Carrie had ridden up to the stable. She held her skirts slightly up from her ankles and moved swiftly over the spring-green lawns. When she reached the stable, she reflected only quiet dignity as she stood before the group. Pride gleamed in her eyes as she looked at the travel-weary Carrie Sherwood.

Carrie smiled warmly, then extended her hand to the woman she scarcely believed old enough to be Drew's mother. Diana said quietly, "Enough of that stuffiness. I'll take a hug instead," and embraced Carrie Sherwood. "How lovely you are," she murmured. Looking across to her

247

stern-faced son, and yet ignoring his expression, she said, "She is as lovely as you said."

Had tears moistened Drew Donovan's eyes? If they had, they were lost in the duties of taking care of the horses as Tuxford emerged from the stables and Diana and a somber Carrie moved slowly up the lawn toward the massive old house overlooking Philadelphia.

Carrie entered the house dreading the anticipated interrogation of Drew's mother. The older woman, however, spoke pleasantly, exchanged opinions on domestic trivialities, and did not embark upon the subject of Carrie's relation to her son. As they enjoyed morning tea and delicate apple cakes, Carrie found herself feeling much more relaxed. She recalled the stories Drew had told her of his parents' first meeting, and the often tumultuous development of their love. It pleased her to see them so happy all these many years after their marriage. She hoped one day that Drew would be blessed with a good woman and a happy marriage. He deserved nothing less.

Melancholy became a dark, brooding thing hanging over her head in the wide, spacious parlor of Rourke House. Diana's pleasant words seemed to drift away, leaving a silent, empty void. Carrie felt a rapid flutter deep within her, threatening her footing. Suddenly the tea was a thick, black dregg and the sweet cakes worm-filled biscuits. The blood seemed to drain from her body, leaving a deathly pallor which alarmed the unsuspecting Diana Donovan. Carrie became aware of the lady standing over her, wrapping her hands around her shoulders.

"Are you all right, Miss Sherwood?"

Carrie smiled weakly. "It must have been the long travel," she replied weakly. "I feel very ill. I feel . . ." Her hand trembled as it moved to her mouth. "I feel as if I will be sick."

Moments later, an ashen Carrie emerged from an upstairs water closet to meet the concerned gaze of Diana

Donovan. "Perhaps you'd better lie down, Miss Sherwood."

"I'd be ever so grateful if you would call me Carrie."

"Very well, Carrie." Affectionately embracing her shoulders, she lightly ordered, "Come this way. I knew I'd eventually have the chance of meeting you, so I have kept a room prepared. I hope you will like it."

Supporting her against her own slim body, Diana Donovan escorted the younger woman down the corridor and soon pushed open one of many doors leading into the bedchambers. She had surely chosen the most enchanting room for Carrie. Before the quiet hearth sat a carved mahogany firescreen showing a parrot and squirrel in French rococo style. The room was as elegant as any in Holker Hall, with its commode inset with Chinese lacquer panels and a pink marble top, a *bureau à cylindre* writing desk veneered in a marquetry of various woods, a pair of Queen Anne modified bodice-back armchairs flanking the hearth. A settee covered with cross-stitched pillows sat against a draperied floor-to-ceiling window through which a gentle wind filled the room with the aroma of wild honeysuckle. Carrie, however, was drawn immediately to the large but simple pencil-post bed covered by its linsey-woolsey spread and coverlet. It was there that she wearily dropped herself.

Closing her eyes, she was scarcely aware of the exit of Diana Donovan.

A while later—she had no concept of time—she heard muffled voices far down the hallway . . . a woman and two men. They sat in a small, private parlor; though Carrie heard her name, everything else of their conversation was a blur. It was still enough enticement, though, to draw her up from her bed.

Drew had put off disappointing his parents long enough. Though he did not intend to tell them the whole truth, he had to put to rest their hopes that he and Carrie would ever be married. He would not even admit that he loved her.

"I thought you cared deeply for this woman," Cole said with husky disapproval and accusation. "You have not compromised her honor and then decided you did not want her?"

"No, of course not," he claimed irately. "It is a mutual thing. She wishes to return to her home in England, and our relationship is not strong enough to hold her here. It has developed no further than extreme fondness, and now we are simply getting on each other's nerves."

"Well, we were hoping, Son—"

Drew patted his mother's hand, halting her words. "Don't give up on me. I'm still a young man and the world is filled with fine ladies who might take a liking to a scalawag like me!"

"It isn't your age I'm worried about," Diana laughed, though without feeling. "I want grandchildren while your father and I are still young enough to enjoy them!"

"Mother, I assure you that if Carrie Sherwood was the right woman for me, I'd make every effort to get her to remain. As it is, there is nothing I want more than to see her board ship for England. And good riddance to her!"

A sob erupted from the doorway. His eyes dark with disapproval that his son had spoken so cruelly, Cole Donovan rose immediately to his feet and approached Carrie Sherwood. Diana, too, arose, though she remained beside the table where they'd been sitting. She loathed the gloating look of satisfaction riding her son's handsome features. For the first time in her life, she wanted to slap him.

Drew tried very hard to justify his actions, wanting to believe that he had dealt Carrie the same stunning blow that she had dealt him. He still hurt from the bite of her declarations, and now perhaps she might know how it felt. Still, hearing her footfalls heading eastward into the corridor, away from the comfort his father's arms would have afforded, Drew felt a pang of guilt seize him. He made a pretense of enjoying inflicting pain on her, and yet the very act made him tremble with revulsion.

When his father started to go after her, Drew jumped to his feet. "No, I caused her emotion, I will make it right," he said, stifling his annoyance and yet feeling the pain of hurting her. Meeting his mother's faltering gaze, he assured her, "I will not say anything further to upset her. I promise."

Carrie had just slammed the door when Drew's knuckles rapped gently at the hard wood. "Carrie, open the door," he demanded in a quiet tone.

"No," she replied, leaning heavily against it. "And if you are a gentleman, you will not enter uninvited."

Swiftly the door came open, its weight spinning her away from his dark, moody frame filling the doorway. "I did not say I was a gentleman," he reflected quietly, closing the barrier that would have separated them. Moving in long strides toward her, he roughly gripped her arms and dragged her to him. "How dare you make me look bad in front of my parents! How dare you!"

"I said nothing."

"You whimpered!" he accused, the smell of wine sweet upon his breath. "You played the poor, tragic, misunderstood little girl being victimized by the big, mean bully! Suppose I should tell them what you have done, how you have deceived me, slept with me and used me, and planning all along to return to your blasted England! You would have them think you are lily-white and their son the black villain! Damn you, Carrie Sherwood!"

His anger stunned her. She had not meant to portray him as a beast to his parents. She had simply come upon them sitting together when something especially painful had been said by the man she loved. In her heart, she wanted Drew to speak words of endearment to her, not cruelties, hold her gently, not like a bear trying to smother its victim. Oh, please, please, she thought, let his father's ship sail soon for England! She simply could not bear the torment of another day in the same house—indeed, in the same city—with the man she adored and have him loathe her so.

Before Carrie could react to his accusation, Diana Donovan stood in the doorway. Drew immediately relinquished his brutal hold on Carrie's arms. He turned, smiled wryly at her, and said, "I have apologized to the lady, and she has forgiven me." Approaching his mother, he continued. "She is anxious to return to England. When will one of Father's ships next sail?"

"Thursday morning," she replied softly. "She doesn't have much of a wait."

That was two long days away. Drew's eyebrows met in a stilted frown. "Do you mind, Mother, if Carrie remains here with you? I must return to Wills Creek posthaste. We are planting corn this year and have yet to till the acreage."

Diana looked from one inanimate face to the other. She wished she knew what had happened between these two young people. "Of course she shall remain with us," Diana replied after a moment. "And I am sorry you cannot stay for a longer visit."

"Perhaps after the planting is completed," he replied somberly, refusing to meet Carrie's gaze.

Listening to the echo of his boots disappear down the corridor, Diana Donovan, with more strength than Carrie would have imagined, swiftly slammed the door. "Young lady, I do not normally interfere in my son's affairs, but I demand to know the source of the tensions between the two of you."

Even as Diana Donovan's question demanded an answer, Carrie moved swiftly to the window looking down over the awning of the porch. Presently, Drew emerged from the house and moved swiftly toward the stable. Carrie heard Diana's patient sigh, but she could not take her eyes away from the stable, not until she saw the tall Pennsylvanian she loved with all her heart angrily coax his

252

horse into a gallop and disappear from view.

At that point, Carrie turned, then dropped wearily onto the settee among the delicate pillows that had been stitched by loving hands. She held one against her bosom, then raised her tear-sheened eyes to those of Drew's dear mother. She certainly deserved an explanation; she had, after all, gotten her hopes up for a relationship between her and Andrew. "Very well," Carrie said quietly, watching Diana ease into the comfort of a wing-back chair, "I must return to England because I have placed your son's life in danger." Before the dear lady could ask questions, Carrie quickly told the story of her kidnapping, of Junius Wade, his pursuit up the Mississippi River after Noble and Bundy had thought they'd drowned him, and his being seen in Louisville. On a final note, she added, "Mrs. Donovan, please believe that I dearly love your son, enough so to leave him. I will not see him hurt by that man because of me."

Silence. Diana Donovan rose, approached the settee, and sat beside the young woman with her tear-sheened eyes and her loose flame-colored hair. Taking her hand gently between her own, she said, "And how would my son feel, Carrie, if he knew you did not trust him to take care of both of you?"

"But you don't understand." Carrie gently shook her head, closing her eyes to regain a composure that was quickly waning. "Junius is not a normal man, Mrs. Donovan. He is vile and despicable and obsessed. I almost do not believe he is human. I pushed him from ship into the Gulf of Mexico and yet the waves did not claim him. Noble and Bundy dragged him into the strong Mississippi currents, and he was spewed onto the banks by a river that was reviled by his stinking flesh."

"Perhaps I would develop something of an attitude if everywhere I turned someone was trying to kill me."

"No, it is more than that. Even before, at some time in

253

his dark, evil past, he survived the flames of hell themselves, for his body is pitted and pocked and scarcely resembles that of a human . . ."

Diana inhaled a deep, ragged breath, all the terrors of her past suddenly dredged up by the young woman's story. Of course, it was too much of a coincidence, because the nemesis of her past had been consumed by the flames that had razed the east wing of Rourke House. Still, it was a shock to hear a man described so pitifully. She wanted to ask if the Junius Wade Carrie was describing had a missing left hand . . . but she feared the answer she would get.

"You are hardheaded, young lady," Diana said after a moment, "and you will do what you feel you must. If it is truly what you want, my husband will see that your passage is booked for Thursday morning." Rising, she released Carrie's hand. "I really believe, Carrie, that I could have loved you as a daughter-in-law."

Without further words, Diana Donovan moved from the room, closing the door quietly behind her.

The following two days were dreadfully lonely, even as the Donovans tried to make her stay comfortable. Carrie felt a little awkward in the home of Drew's parents, knowing how deeply she had hurt their son.

There was one thing she had to know for certain, though, before she sailed for England. Pleading the need to do a little shopping, Carrie slipped from the house and managed to talk Tuxford into driving her into Philadelphia. While he waited at a street corner for her to make the rounds, Carrie soon found Dr. Edwin Redding's small office on Market Street. Mrs. Donovan had mentioned the doctor in passing conversation the day before.

When she left the office, she had the answer she wanted. A confused Tuxford drove her back to Rourke House without boxes and other evidence of her shopping spree and yet asked no questions. She entered the house, pleaded a sour stomach and lack of appetite, then moved toward the bedchamber she'd been assigned. There she would pack her one bag for the long ocean voyage.

She slept fitfully that night and dreamed of Drew—away in his beloved Alleghenies, hating her and wanting her to be gone. The following morning, when she somberly boarded Cole Donovan's ship, *The Sea Lion*, she raised her hand in a trembling farewell and watched the Donovans quietly return to their carriage.

She did not want to envision the rest of her life without their loving son.

England now was nothing more than a depressing state of mind.

Chapter Sixteen

Cole stood at the one parlor window of Rourke House affording him an unobstructed view of the bay. *The Sea Lion,* her clean white sails clipping in the breeze, moved peacefully southward toward the Atlantic Ocean. He would not see the most majestic of his passenger ships for another five months, nor would he ever again see the prettiest of her passengers—who he had hoped would be his new daughter-in-law.

Who would ever understand women? he thought, fidgeting with his pocketwatch. Even after thirty-three years of marriage, he often found his beloved Diana somewhat of an enigma. She was always coming up with some new cog to wedge into the otherwise smoothly operating mechanics of his mind. Just when he was sure he knew her completely, a strange, unexplainable emotion would pop up to throw his mind into another dimension.

He could understand the emotion that flooded her this morning, though. She had seen Carrie Sherwood as Drew's last hope of salvation from bachelorhood. That they were deeply in love had been evident by the hostilities between them. Only love could breed such fire.

Cole had just exited the house through a back entrance when their servant Claudia entered the parlor where Diana sat with a book. The once-slender Claudia had put on the pleasant plumpness of middle age, and an irritated strength guided the feather duster she raked through the air. Disturbed from her household chores, she announced haughtily, "That lady is back, all teary-eyed and red-cheeked!" and quickly returned to the foyer to fetch her.

Surprised, Diana Donovan suddenly found herself facing a droop-shouldered Carrie Sherwood, her slim hands tightly holding the one canvas bag she'd carried with her aboard ship. Just an hour ago, Cole had dejectedly stood at the parlor window watching with unvoiced regret his gallant passenger ship leaving port with this young lady they had hoped to the last would decide to stay. Now she stood before Diana, tears filling her eyes and looking a bit dejected herself.

Taking the bag and tossing it aside, Diana took her hand in confusion and led her to the divan. "You have returned, Carrie. Dear Lord, you didn't walk?"

"Oh, no, Mrs. Donovan. I hired a carriage, hoping that you would not send me away."

"Claudia . . ." Diana Donovan's voice caught the attentions of the industrious servant. "Bring a tray of tea, will you?"

"Yes, ma'am," she replied with a curtsy.

"Now tell me, Carrie, why you left my husband's ship before her departure?"

A dreamy sigh touched the narrow space separating the two women. "I knew a girl once," Carrie began quietly, "raised alone by her mother after the father left them. I've never seen anyone adore a girl as did that woman. For seventeen years her world revolved around her daughter and every time she saw her, her heart swelled with pride. Even though they didn't have much money, she always tried to see that her girl had nice things to wear, as well as an education and little extras to please her. She worked to support them, and yet tried to bring happiness into her girl's life. Then, without warning, her daughter rebelled against

257

her moral teachings, left the home her mother had made for her, and took up with a poor, uneducated family. Unfortunate circumstances resulted in her forced marriage to one of their sons—a slobbering swill—and months later she gave birth to a girl child. My heart bled to see that woman deprived of her granddaughter. To this day, as far as I know, she has never laid eyes on the child. The daughter she had once adored, and who was the center of her being, has completely cut her off from her life."

Carrie looked up sadly.

"Oh, I do know I am rambling terribly, Mrs. Donovan, with this pitiful tale, but most is not at all relevant. What is relevant is that it is such a pity, don't you think, for a woman to be deprived of her grandchild? And the daughter who would do such a thing morally reprehensible?"

Diana Donovan took Carrie's slim hand from the folds of her cream-colored gown and held it warmly. "Why have you told me this story, Carrie?"

Tears rushed into Carrie's eyes. "Because, Mrs. Donovan . . ." A lump in her throat made it almost impossible to speak. Turning her hand over so that she could grasp Diana Donovan's, she attempted to restore herself to some semblance of order. Then in a tiny voice she continued. "I cannot do to you, my beloved Drew's mother, what my friend did to hers."

In the split second before comprehension clicked in her head, confusion settled upon Diana's brow. "You are bearing my grandchild," Diana murmured in stunned disbelief. "And that is why you chose not to sail to England, but returned to Rourke House instead."

"Yes." Tears stained Carrie's crimson cheeks. "I have no parents in England, though my dear uncle Penley loves me as a daughter. I cannot have the Atlantic Ocean part me from my beloved Drew. It would be unbearable and I could not live like that."

Taking her in her arms, Diana hugged her tightly.

"Dear, dear girl, do you realize you have contradicted your story? What you are doing to your uncle Penley is little different from what your friend did to her mother—"

Carrie drew back, horrified by her words. "Oh, but it is different! Were I to return to Holker Hall in my condition, it would cause a scandal to my dear uncle, who is a respected member of Parliament. It is entirely different!"

"It is not different, Carrie. But if you wish to stay, of course we will have you. We will see that you return to Andrew—"

"No!" Panic darkened Carrie's eyes. "No, I cannot return to Wills Creek. I cannot place Drew in danger."

"Because of that wicked man you told me about? How bad can he be, Carrie dear?"

Suddenly, Cole Donovan's dark-clothed form filled the doorway. He glared down at the two women in an expression both misread as disapproval.

"You heard, husband?" Diana asked cautiously.

"I saw the hired carriage leaving and reentered the house to see who had arrived. Then I became intrigued by Carrie's story," he said with some reserve. "I heard everything. Please forgive me for eavesdropping." The tall, imposing Scotsman took Carrie's hand and coaxed her to her feet. "Young lady, do you love my son?"

"Oh, yes . . . yes, Mr. Donovan. With all my heart and soul."

"And do you consider him a slobbering swill like the varmint in your story?"

Her face paling with embarrassment, she stammered, "N-no, of course not. I was rambling because I was so very nervous, Mr. Donovan."

"Are you up to traveling?" Carrie's gaze cut between the two Donovans, the gentle, feminine one suddenly surprised by her husband's question. "Are you?" Cole repeated.

"Yes, but are you going to send me away?"

259

With some consternation, Cole Donovan replied, "I am not, young lady. I am going to return you to Wills Creek where you belong and then I will—"

No one had heard the foyer door open or felt the cool morning air flood the room. Suddenly another form stood in the doorway—a familiar form with dark, brooding eyes. "What is going on here?" Cole Donovan's body had hid Carrie from Drew's view. When Cole turned, Carrie's eyes met Drew's. Before anyone could speak, Drew bellowed, "What the hell is she doing here? Blackmailing my family?" Torment and loathing mirrored in his eyes.

Diana rushed to her feet, approached her son, and was immediately assailed by the reeking smell of liquor on his breath. "Do not make accusations, Son, when you do not know what is happening."

With uncharacteristic arrogance, Drew produced a half-empty bottle of bourbon from the cover of his jacket. "Indeed, Mother?" Sarcasm laced his words. "Is my little princess telling you how pitiful she is, and how she deserves your sympathy?"

Carrie moved from Cole's shadow. When she attempted to approach Drew, his arm slung out at her, so close that the breeze it caused rustled her crisply ironed blouse. "Drew, please listen to me. I have much explaining to do."

"I'll hear none of it!" he slurred, slumping in the doorway. "You may be able to pull the wool over my parents' eyes with your innocent little act, but you won't get away with it with me!"

Without warning, Cole Donovan pulled his son up by the lapels of his jacket. The older man's eyes blazed with fury. "You will listen to her explanation, Andrew! You will be patient and tolerant and you will sensibly discuss the private matters existing between the two of you. Do you hear me?"

Drew had never before been disrespectful to either of his parents. Now, however, he made an exception. "I'm near thirty-three years old," Drew slurred in his drunken voice. "I'll be damned if my father is going to treat me like a young boy!"

"You will listen—"

As Cole snatched the bottle of liquor from his son, Carrie eased her slim body between the two men. "Please, Mr. Donovan, I am able to handle him when he's in this condition." Managing a small smile as she tried to dismiss the cruel words Drew had spoken just moments before, she continued. "The first time I met him he was like this, and almost as belligerent."

Cole set the bottle on a table, then roughly dragged down his own lapels in an attempt to straighten his appearance. His wife moved into his arms to calm his own fiery mood and watched as a much calmer Drew Donovan allowed himself to be coaxed into another room by the woman who had hurt him so deeply—the woman he had not been able to leave behind in Philadelphia. He had stayed at a local inn, hoping—dear God, hoping—that she would choose to stay in Pennsylvania. Now that she had, he was uncertain as to how to proceed. He was certainly suspicious of her motives.

As he slung himself into a chair in a small private office off the parlor, Drew was aware that his father stood at the ready, prepared to intercept if his son became a threat to the woman he was, thus far, unaware would give them their first grandchild.

For two days Carrie had thought of nothing but the words Diana Donovan had so softly spoken to her. "How would my son feel if he knew you did not trust him to take care of both of you?" Dear God, how right the sweet woman had been. Because they so dearly loved each other, any problems she and Drew had should be worked out together, and that included the problem of Junius Wade.

Drew was not nearly as drunk as he'd have her believe, though he was ired by the fact that his father had taken the bottle of bourbon from him. He sat silently in the chair, one leg outstretched, a passive cast to his ample mouth. He watched Carrie move about, pulling back the drapery to look out over Philadelphia, then pivot back, evading the searching of his eyes to flick her hand over the recently dusted table and straighten the lace doily lying there beneath an ornate wooden box.

When he could bear the silence no longer, he asked, "Why didn't you sail this morning?"

Drawing in a deep breath, Carrie replied, "Because I could not leave you."

"Why?" He sat forward, momentarily unbalancing himself in the move. "You said you loathed me, that you were just using me."

"I know what I said, Andrew—"

"Andrew!" He looked up. "You've never called me that before. It's always been Drew . . . darling . . . sickly sweet sentiments!"

"It is your name, isn't it? Andrew Cynric Donovan?"

"The last I checked." Arrogance stiffened his voice.

Carrie could bear his aloofness no longer. Flinging herself to the carpet at his feet, her tear-sheened eyes imploringly darted over his features. She half-choked out her words. "Oh, Drew . . . Drew, please forgive the cruelties I spoke to you. I have been foolish. I was so afraid of the danger I had brought upon you that I thought my absence would send it hither and yon, far away from you. I could not bear to have you hurt."

His eyebrows met in a perplexing frown. "What are you talking about?"

Stacking her hands, and finally her cheek, upon Drew's knee, she gave him the dreadful news. "Junius Wade was last seen in Louisville, doggedly determined to recapture me and . . ." She shuddered to speak the words, "kill you. It is all my fault this danger has been brought upon you!"

Taking her by the shoulders, Drew brought her gently

262

up. "Tell me that you love me, Carrie."

Her tear-sheened eyes darted over his passive features. "Oh, I do love you! I adore you, Drew Donovan. I would give up all my thoughts of England just to be with you forever."

His rough and drunken exterior suddenly masked his natural gentleness. Slinging her away as if the nearness of her was repulsive to him, he bellowed angrily, "I don't believe anything you say!"

Undaunted, she closed the distance between them once again, enveloping his protesting hand between her warm ones. "Then believe this, Drew Donovan, that I shall be the mother of your child—a child born of our love." His look was strangely stagnant, as though he had yet to comprehend her confession. "Did you hear me, Drew?"

A gleam of animation sprang into his blank gaze. "I heard you."

"And that is all you have to say?"

Dare he trust her? He wanted her, needed her—loved her—but would he be a fool to believe her easily offered confession? He certainly had seen the signs—the silent moods, her shrugs, at times, away from intimacy, the tears that never seemed to have an emotional tie. He could imagine nothing more wonderful than being a father and bouncing a fine baby boy or cherub-cheeked daughter upon his knee, and giving his physical and spiritual future over to a dear wife and the child his mind envisioned.

Drew moved gently forward. His elbows came to rest upon his knees, and he dropped his forehead against his hands. He was so quiet that it frightened the woman with him. As Carrie closed the distance between them, her hands rising to clutch at his own, she realized that tears rushed down his cheeks. When at last she coaxed his hands from his forehead, he drew her close and his deep, masculine sobs rushed against her soft, flaming hair.

"Forgive me, Drew," she whispered, her own emotions

scarcely more controlled than his. "I'll never hurt you again. Please give me one more chance. I know that you love me as much as I love you."

For a long while he held her, unable to give her the only answer echoing softly in his heart.

The bans were published in the Lutheran Church the following three Sundays of April. The large, somber house overlooking Philadelphia was suddenly transformed into a wedding chapel, with fresh coats of paint on the woodwork, floral garlands cascading over every window and across the upper portico, and enough pews, replacing the ornate furnishings in the long parlor, to seat three hundred guests.

During the planning weeks, guests arrived from throughout the states. Those who missed out on the personal accommodations of Rourke House were put up at the local hostelries. Reservations had been made in the house for Drew's special guests from Wills Creek—even old Hambone, who had sworn for years that he'd not miss his Andrew's wedding day, even to die.

Diana and Carrie busied themselves for more than a week with seamstresses and books of fashion from Paris, to put together the perfect wedding ensemble for Carrie's marriage to the man who had once been the most eligible bachelor in all of Pennsylvania. After long hours of mulling over the many fashions and samples of fabric brought daily to the house, Carrie chose her gown.

That Friday morning, with the drive and roads surrounding Rourke House lined with fine carriages and saddled horses, Diana fussed over her carefully dressed future daughter-in-law, who continued to find fault with her perfect appearance in the cheval mirror. Many voices buzzed from the floor below, intermingled with the melodic music of the organ, played to perfection by the minister's wife.

"Oh, do cease your fussing, Daughter-in-law," Diana laughed lightly, fluffing the bridal veil and positioning it over her lovely face for the long walk down the stairway.

"How do I look, Mrs. Donovan? Will he still want to marry me?" Though her cheeks were crimson, she pinched them, thinking she needed the color. Though her hair was perfect, pulled into soft waves and held with ivory combs, she flicked at an imaginary wisp she was sure would sabotage her careful appearance.

Diana clasped her shoulders and whispered against her flaming hair, "It is time you started calling me Mother, and—yes, he will still want to marry you. You are lovely."

The wedding march began to play. Drawing a breath into her lungs and attempting to still the wild pounding of her heart, Carrie turned, squeezed Diana's hand, and moved toward the bedchamber door.

Andrew Cynric Donovan thought the tight collar of his wedding suit would choke him. He wanted to tug at his cravat, but, meeting his father's controlled glare, kept his hands limply at his sides. Perspiration dotted his brow, despite the open windows and the cool breeze wafting through the room, which was filled beyond capacity with wedding guests. After all, Philadelphia's favorite son had finally decided to take a wife.

When the wedding march had begun to play, he'd slowly, nervously, turned to watch the stairway for the appearance of his bride, whom he'd not seen that morning. When finally she was all that filled his vision, her beauty took his breath away—her slim form wrapped in ivory taffeta, with a fitted basque bodice and a charming flounced skirt. Her velvet-and-taffeta sleeves were generously pouffed, tapering at her wrists. Bridal lace frosted her skirts and sleeves, which were accented with thousands of luminous faux pearls. A yoke of delicate lace swept her shoulders, flowing from a high collar trimmed with an ivory satin bow. Her lavish velvet train was lined with satin and trimmed with rosettes of softest peach. Her gossamer tulle veil flowed gently to the floor, elegantly finished with lace.

Drew swelled with pride at the graceful picture of her, and he smiled when a nervous moment threatened to deposit her rose bouquet, its heirloom lace and all, upon the floor. She composed herself immediately, and smiled timidly at him. When the wedding march ended and he took his place beside her, he wanted to pinch himself to make sure this morning was not just a wonderful dream.

Having eyes only for each other, neither Drew nor Carrie really heard the minister inquiring as to whether the union contemplated was in accordance with the Word of God and in accordance with the laws of the state. Later, they would both be sure they'd given the proper response, because the minister had continued:

"Andrew Cynric Donovan and Charissa Sherwood propose to enter into the holy estate of matrimony, according to God's ordinance. They desire that prayer be made for them, that they may enter into this union in the name of the Lord, and be prospered in it. If anyone can show just cause why they may not be joined together, I exhort him to make known such objection before the day of marriage. In the name of the Father, and of the Son, and of the Holy Ghost. Amen.

"Dearly Beloved, forasmuch as marriage is a holy estate, ordained of God, and to be held in honor by all, it becometh those who enter therein to weigh, with reverent minds . . ."

The words droned on like a toneless wind, through the heaven of their eyes holding each other's—hers covered by the veil of gossamer and his by the veil of his adoration for her. Andrew cut his eyes from those of his bride only when the minister spoke directly to him.

"Andrew, wilt thou have this woman to thy wedded wife, to live together after God's ordinance in the holy estate of matrimony? Wilt thou love her, comfort her, honor and keep her in sickness and in health, and forsaking all others, keep thee only unto her, so long as ye both shall live?"

Drew answered strongly, "I will."

"Charissa . . ." She could almost have repeated the words with him, because she had memorized them as he'd spoken them to her beloved.

In a very soft voice, she replied, "I will."

Opening Drew's right hand, the minister placed Carrie's within it. "Repeat after me, Andrew," which he did: "I, Andrew, take thee, Charissa, to my wedded wife, and plight thee my troth, till death us do part."

"Charissa, repeat after me: I, Charissa, take thee, Andrew, to my wedded husband, and plight thee my troth, till death us do part."

After she had so sweetly repeated his words, the tall, somber-browed minister took the ring and handed it to Drew. As he placed it on Carrie's finger, he said, "Receive this ring as a token of my wedded love and troth."

"Forasmuch as Andrew and Charissa have consented together in holy wedlock, and have declared the same before God and in the presence of this company, I pronounce them man and wife, in the name of the Father, and of the Son, and of the Holy Ghost. Amen. What God hath joined together, let not man put asunder."

After they had knelt and been blessed by the minister, they arose, man and wife, and gently kissed.

The reverence of the ceremony immediately erupted into revelry, as the wedding guests rose enthusiastically to the situation. Congratulations immediately followed, and Carrie felt her face stiffen painfully by the many smiles with which she greeted wellwishers. She was especially cordial to Jolie, though the woman's brown eyes glared with contempt and the few words she spoke were crisp and controlled. Noble, however, hugged her warmly and welcomed her to the Wills Creek family.

There would be much celebration that day, as banquet tables dotted the immaculate lawns of Rourke House for the grandest get-together held there in more than eighty years.

Only later, when she had collapsed into a weary bundle on the wide, spacious bed she would share with her new husband, was Carrie able to grasp the full meaning of the day. Her wedding gown was unbearably tight, the pins in her hair digging into her scalp. She might have flung her head in a wild attempt to free her flame-colored locks if Drew Donovan, absently loosening his cravat, had not sat upon the bed beside her.

Removing the headpiece and her gauze veil, he began to pluck the pins from her hair one by one. "One year for my true love . . ." he murmured, "two years. Three . . . four . . . and when I feel nothing but the sunset clouds of your halo beneath my fingers, I shall get right to work on those stays . . ." His eyes cut teasingly to her gently moving bodice.

A smile curled her mouth. "Drew Donovan . . ."

"Yes, Mrs. Donovan?"

It had not fully registered. She was, indeed, Mrs. Andrew Cynric Donovan. The marriage certificate they had signed was probably on its way to the registrar's office, even as they spoke. But suddenly a frown eased into their happy moment, halting the teasing movement of his fingers. "Oh, Andrew . . . Andrew," she whispered, taking his hand and holding it warmly to her chest, "would you have married me were I not carrying your child within me? Do tell me I have not trapped you into something that is not of your heart."

"Very well, you have not trapped me into something that is not of my heart. Is that what you want to hear?"

She pouted prettily. "Do say it more sincerely, Drew Donovan. Say it with the lusty emotion of a solicitor trying to convince the jury not to send a poor fellow to the gallows."

Andrew Cynric Donovan chuckled hoarsely, touching his mouth to her pouting one. "My pretty princess, your theatrics do amuse me. What a lucky, lucky fellow I am." Instantly, Drew found himself holding his breath, so absorbed was he in the beauty of her, in her delicate features, the gemlike twinkle of her emerald eyes, her attractive pout, the ever-so-slight heaving of her bodice confined within the tight taffeta bindings of her wedding dress. His body responded painfully to the nearness of her, to the seductive sigh that whispered upon his cool cheek. He wanted only to feel his own hard, sinewy body molded gently to her warm, willing one, to have her slender limbs twine among his own and fire him with her passions and her needs.

If any power on earth could have parted him from his prize, it could only have been Claudia, suddenly knocking at the bedchamber door, then entering without awaiting a response. She looked from one to the other of the Donovans and arched her graying eyebrows like gulls taking to flight over a windward ship. Drew found his feet in a haste that almost unbalanced him.

"The mistress said to bring you this tray of England's finest port, that you may sip together on this, your wedding day." Andrew could well imagine the simple-minded servant echoing the very words of his mother. "And Miss — do pardon . . . Mrs. Donovan . . ." Having set the tray upon a table, Claudia now stood with her hands propped upon her hips. "Shall I assist you in removing your gown so that you can tend to your wifely duties?"

A surprised choke caught in Carrie's throat. Quickly drawing her hand to her mouth, she stifled the laughter before it could reach her lips. "No . . . no, Claudia, I believe my husband and I can manage quite well."

"Are you sure . . . ?"

"Quite sure." Drew instantly closed the distance between them, took Claudia's hand, and gently coaxed her to the door. "Be assured, Claudia, that if the new Mrs. Donovan is in need of your assistance, she shall summon you without haste."

When the door closed and Drew had slipped the lock bolt, he himself found that he could not restrain his own chuckle of humor. "That woman! She keeps us all wondering from day to day what she will say next!"

"Where on earth did you get her?" Carrie asked, rising to her feet, allowing herself to be folded within Drew's waiting arms.

"She was born in this house. Remind me one day to tell you about some of her antics. You will be amused. But not today—not now . . ." His breath rushed hotly upon her cheek as his mouth claimed hers. "Now we have a warm and very lonely bed waiting to be pounced upon."

"Andrew Cynric Donovan . . ." The teasing reproof instantly became a seductive smile.

"Yes, Mrs. Donovan?"

Putting her hand to her ear, her eyes widening innocently, she asked, "Don't you hear it?"

"Hear what?"

Her head moved slightly. "The bed is calling our names."

"Then let us not keep it waiting."

"Let us not," she agreed, allowing his hands to lower from her shoulders to the stays of her ivory wedding dress with its fitted basque bodice.

Part Three
The Prowling

Chapter Seventeen

A colorful array of wildflowers flocked the ponds and lagoons of western Pennsylvania. The deep shades of the late afternoon reduced the underbrush, and the dense foliage overhead seemed to shut out all traces of the world.

Junius Wade was furious. He'd traveled too far atop the aging gelding he'd purchased in Louisville to have been thrown on his rump in six inches of bog. The snake that had spooked the beast now slithered across the toe of his boot and the horse itself was probably halfway back to Louisville by now, taking with it the extra change of clothing he'd purchased and a fifty-dollar rifle strapped to the saddle.

Picking himself up, he limped toward a fallen tree covered with moss and ferns. Since he'd crossed the Allegheny River two days before, he'd not met up with a single traveler. In his condition—teamed with the exhaustion of the long trip from New Orleans and having survived a murder attempt—he did not believe he would last the night.

Sitting calmly upon the moss-blanketed log, Junius extracted his sidearm from its holster and inspected it for damage. He took aim at the snake that had spooked his horse, missing it by scarcely an inch. At least his only weapon was still functional! he thought, returning it to the safety of its holster.

273

He used the stump of his left wrist to scratch at his itching scalp. Then he began bickering to himself about little things—the loss of his blanket, a torn seam in the sole of his left boot, his greasy, unkempt hair drawing pesky little flies. Looking around him, he realized he was surrounded on all sides by mountains. A wide stream flowed gently somewhere; he could hear the water churning over smooth, white rocks.

The beauty of his surroundings did not penetrate his black mood as he realized he was stuck in the middle of God only knew where without transportation. The least he could do was clean himself up until he decided what to do.

Unfortunately, he would spend two long days and nights in miserable hunger, refusing to waste the five bullets he had left in his sidearm to bring in a meal. On the morning of the third day a stroke of luck appeared in the form of a traveling preacher. Despite Junius Wade's hideous appearance and scowling countenance, the kindly gentleman stopped to offer his assistance.

"I'll give you a hundred dollars for your horse, Preacher," Junius offered.

The dark-clothed man was much too thin to fill out the oversized, long-tailed coat he wore. He tripped on the ridiculous garment as he dismounted his horse, removed a few strips of dried beef from a saddle pouch, and handed them to Junius Wade. "Sir, I cannot sell you my horse, but I will share with you both my humble meal and the word of our Almighty God."

Aggravation gripped Junius Wade in his gut. He took the strip of beef and gnawed hungrily upon it. When the preacher had completed a silent prayer, Junius implored him, "Then let me ride double on your horse until we reach a place where I might buy another."

"Sir, I will happily allow you to travel along with me, but the mare is old and could not bear the extra weight."

Without a moment's hesitation, Junius Wade pulled his

274

pistol. He did not so much as blink an eye as he fired the weapon. The stunned man, struck point blank in midforehead, was dead before his body hit the ground. "Should have sold me that horse," Junius mumbled, extracting the strip of beef still clutched in the dead man's fingers. "Don't you fret, Preacher. Almighty God'll take care of you now."

Now that the excitement of the wedding was over, Carrie had done a lot of thinking about her dear uncle at Holker Hall. Since he'd surely received the letter she'd sent from St. Louis, he knew she was alive. He had to be worried sick for her.

She and Drew had discussed a wedding trip, so her suggestion, when made, would not come as too great a shock to him. That early Wednesday morning, with Cole and Drew on their way to Wills Creek to see to business involving the trading post and Diana in her bedchamber nursing an annoying headache, Carrie requested that Tuxford drive her into Philadelphia to the office of Dr. Edwin Redding.

Carrie sat in the small outer office, pulling nervously on her wrist-high white gloves, smoothing down the wrinkles of her peacock-blue gown, and straightening her bonnet that really did not require it. A plump lady with a sniffling child had just gone in to see the doctor. Moments later, she heard the child's piercing wail from behind the curtain and Edwin Redding's soothing voice. When his young patient and her mother, weeping herself for the pain of her child, had exited the office, Edwin approached and hovered over Carrie with a concerned gaze in his eyes. Extending her hand in greeting, Carrie returned his smile.

Escorting her into his examination room, Edwin Redding took a chair across from her and held her hand in a paternal gesture. "And what can a humble physician do for the new Mrs. Donovan this lovely morning?"

She smiled warmly, feeling strangely at ease with the man she had met only a few weeks ago, and to whom she was making only her second visit in his professional capacity. "I would like for you to tell me I am as fit as a fiddle and that an immediate trip to England will not impair either my health or that of my baby so that I might be able to maintain a substantiated argument against my husband's protests." Her quickly spoken declaration left her breathless.

Again, the stocky gentleman patted her hand. "You are a very healthy young woman, Mrs. Donovan, and under most circumstances I would see nothing wrong with two months aboard ship in these early months—if, that is, you planned to give birth in England. I cannot, however, recommend travel to England, and a return trip before your child is born. I always insist on plenty of rest for my expecting mothers, even when they are as healthy as you."

A dreamy gaze suddenly met Edwin Redding's professional one. "If I gave birth in England, then you would have no argument against my travel?"

"None whatsoever."

Carrie rose gracefully to her feet, gently extracting her hand from Edwin's. "If necessary, will you talk to my husband about this and support my position?"

"Are you saying that you will give birth to your child in England?"

She nodded.

"Andrew Donovan is a hard-headed man, but I'll do what I can if the need arises," he assured her.

Smiling her sweetest smile, she said, "Good day to you then, Dr. Redding. Please send my husband the bill for the visit."

"No charge," he replied, accompanying her into his empty outer office. "But I'll take an invitation to dinner at your leisure. Claudia has the brain of a goose, but no woman in all of Pennsylvania prepares a feast like she does, especially my own dear wife!" His features contorted as he recalled some of the concoctions his dear Cora had set out for human consumption.

Moving onto the platform and the few stairs that would take her to Market Street, Carrie turned. "Then do come on Sunday, Dr. Redding. My mother-in-law was mentioning just yesterday that we needed to have you out soon. And do bring Mrs. Redding." Smiling mischievously, she continued. "Shall I have Claudia give her some tips in the kitchen?" Humor rocked him; he could imagine that going over quite well with his high-and-mighty wife! Returning to the subject that had brought her out this morning, Carrie said, "By Sunday I shall try to mellow my husband about the trip so that your efforts will not be wasted on needless argument."

Edwin Redding watched her move vibrantly toward the waiting Tuxford, her tall, slender form and flowing flame-colored hair turning several masculine heads.

She stopped into a ladies' shop and purchased a pair of gloves in the event she would have to justify her trip into Philadelphia when she returned to Rourke House. Half an hour later, entering the parlor and coming face-to-face with her mother-in-law, she found herself doing just that.

"A new pair of gloves?" Diana questioned dubiously. "There should have been several in the trousseau my husband and I gave you."

That certainly demanded an immediate explanation. With a small, nervous laugh, Carrie drew her hand to the slim column of her throat. "Oh, no, Mother, not for me. I . . . I purchased them for . . . for Claudia. Yes, for Claudia! To thank her for being so kind to me while I have been in Rourke House. I certainly did not wish to give her one of the pairs you and Mr. Donovan so generously gave me."

Pressing at her still-pained temple, Diana said, "It is a very kind gesture. Claudia will be pleased," and did not, for a minute, believe Carrie's explanation. She would not, however, press the issue.

Carrie bubbled over with enthusiasm and had to confide her plans in someone she trusted implicitly, someone like Diana Donovan. Tossing off her bonnet, then gathering her skirts and easing herself to the very edge of the settee, she dropped her hands among the folds. "Mrs. Donovan, would you be very displeased with me if I wanted to journey—with my dear husband, of course—to England and see my uncle before the birth of my child?"

The pain of her headache suddenly increased. Diana's slim form moved forward. "Before the birth? But surely it could wait until afterward when you have fully recovered."

Would Diana Donovan want to hear the tale of her tragic parting from England? She knew her Doubting Thomas husband had related her story to his mother, probably in a light moment. Carrie, however, was not up to a humiliation to parallel one she had once suffered at the hands of Drew, and therefore, she dropped her eyes. She lifted her gaze in surprise only when Diana asked, "Are you lonely for Uncle Penley and Holker Hall?"

Knitting her eyebrows, she asked, "Are you familiar with Holker Hall?"

Quietly, Diana replied, "Over the years my husband and I have traveled extensively throughout Scotland, England, and the Continent. I know that Holker Hall is the home of the Duke of Devonshire and is situated between Morecambe Bay and the Lakeland hills. A long walk meanders through the grounds and, Daughter, I have trod upon her paths with my own feet."

Carrie drew in a deep, surprised breath. "You have? But . . . surely I would have remembered you!" Then a flush of embarrassment claimed Carrie's cheeks. "You don't expect that you'd have seen me because . . ." Dropping her eyes, she continued softly, "you do not believe I have ever been a part of Holker Hall."

"I could not possibly have seen you." Tears rushed into Carrie's eyes—because Diana Donovan doubted her heritage, just as Drew did. In one graceful move, Diana Donovan took her hand and held it fondly. "I saw Holker Hall twenty-five years ago, before you were ever born. Carrie . . ." She paused as she waited for the younger woman to meet her gaze. "My son has told me the story you told him and . . . yes, I do believe it." She had sensed Carrie's homesickness, but had not thought it deep enough to have stirred within her the need to journey to England during the months of her pregnancy. Diana's thoughts revolved at a rapid speed. Perhaps she and Cole should make their trip to Europe soon so that they could visit Holker Hall on behalf of Carrie and assure him of her welfare. Diana quietly continued. "I'll be truthful, Carrie. I do not want you to journey to England before the birth of my grandchild, though, ultimately, that choice will be yours and Drew's, and not mine. Just remember that whatever you do, my blessings are with you."

Carrie hugged her tightly. "Oh, thank you, thank you, Mother. Then you will not mind that our child is born in England?"

"If that is what you and Drew want. And . . ." Drawing back slightly, she favored Carrie with a sad smile, "as long as you return to Pennsylvania with my grandchild. Remember your friend and her poor, embittered mother . . ."

When she posed her suggestion to him almost the moment he entered Rourke House, Drew Donovan hit the ceiling. Since his marriage to Carrie, he had existed in a dreamland of happiness and contentment, and he would not have believed that a mere few words, spoken so softly, could have had this effect on him.

"Damn, Carrie! I thought that once we were married you would have forgotten these ridiculous dreams of being an English duchess!" Giving her no moment to discount his false accusations, he continued hastily. "I expect you to be sensible, especially now that you are going to be a mother. I will not have you speak of these insane delusions again!"

"Andrew Cynric Donovan!" He spun rapidly as his mother hissed his full name. "You apologize to your wife this minute!"

Drawing himself up ramrod straight, Drew balled his hands and pounded them rhythmically against his hard thighs. "I am a married man now, Mother, not your little boy. I'll handle my affairs with my wife without your interference."

"Not when I have information that you do not," she argued firmly, approaching her son and holding his disapproving gaze with strength and dignity. Taking his hand, she forced a piece of heavy paper between his fingers. "A gross of these bulletins has just arrived aboard one of your father's ships. Look at it." When his gaze did not cut from hers to the handbill, she said more sharply, "Look at it!"

Though she did not interfere, Carrie was terribly concerned by the source of their argument.

Drew's eyes darted downward. He read the bold black lettering, "R-E-W-A-R-D. Five thousand pounds being offered for information leading to the recovery of Lady Charissa Sherwood, niece of Lord Penley Seymour, Duke of Devonshire, lost off the Isle of Wight June 26, 1821 . . ." and so on and so on, giving a full description of his beloved Carrie.

Sheer terror claimed Drew's silvery-gray eyes—a terror that immediately encompassed Carrie as well. Suddenly her hands rushed upon his chest, which was so tense and hard-muscled it was like a plate of armor. "Drew! Drew!"

she implored. "What have you read that has so filled you with emotion?"

He did not see his mother across Carrie's shoulder, standing with her fingers lightly entwined, her violet gaze dropped beneath finely arched brows. He saw the questions amassing in Carrie's eyes, and yet it was as if he was seeing past her—through her—as well. All he could think of was the marriage that had bound them together as man and wife, and his child which grew within her. If she had simply been a common English girl sold into white slavery—a common girl with the keen sense to escape her captors—there would have been little threat in that. But if, indeed, she was Lady Charissa Sherwood, niece of the present Duke of Devonshire, would that powerful political figure be able to take her away from him, her own husband? Andrew Cynric Donovan feared that he would. Damn her! Damn her for not convincing him of the truthfulness of her declarations! He could have ended all this in New Orleans!

With an angry set upon his sharp good looks, Andrew put her away from him, then turned and stormed from the house. Carrie, too shocked to go after him, turned her bewildered, beseeching gaze to the silent Diana Donovan. She did not, at first, see the bulletin that had seized Drew's emotions lying facedown on the parlor floor.

"What did I do to him?" Carrie asked quietly, holding back her tears with great effort.

Calmly, Diana approached, picked up the bulletin, and handed it to Carrie. "You've done nothing, Daughter."

Carrie's eyes flew over the bold black lettering that had sent her husband fleeing from Rourke House. "But I told him . . . From the very first I told him who I was."

"But he did not believe you."

"That is his fault. But now why does he show this emotion?"

Diana's satin-clothed arm slipped across her daughter-in-

281

law's shoulder. "I know my son very well, Carrie. He felt no threat believing you were like us—ordinary people. Now he must face the fact that you are, indeed, the niece of the Duke of Devonshire. He feels that he will lose you, because he cannot go up against so powerful a man."

"Uncle Penley is a gentle old puss! He would never separate me from my husband," Carrie assured her.

"Drew does not know that, Carrie. He has always been a loner, an adventurer, giving little thought to long-term commitments. Then he met you and his life turned around. I never thought I'd see my son love anyone as much as he loves you. I believe he would rather die than lose you."

"What can I do to reassure him, Mother?" Carrie asked, accepting the comfort of the woman's arms.

"I can think of only one way, though you may rebel against the idea."

"I will do anything."

Drawing away from the young woman's embrace, Diana turned away, approached the wide window, and looked out toward the stables. She was scarcely able to see the tall, slim form of a man standing in the shadows, gently stroking the soft muzzle of one of the horses. Her Andrew's heart was breaking; she could sense it. When she began to speak, her voice was soft and low. "Carrie, your marriage to Andrew is young. My suggestion to you is not to travel to England right away. Assure your dear uncle, of course, that you are all right, but remain here and strengthen your love and the vows you and Drew have made to each other. Only then, when he does not feel that your past will destroy your future, will you be able to return to Holker Hall for a visit."

Silence. Carrie's fingers wrapped firmly together, reddening her knuckles and causing a sharp pain to travel into her wrists. Drew and the child growing within her were more precious to her than anything. Nothing—and no one—would ever come before them, not even her dear uncle Penley.

Her silence compelled Diana Donovan to turn back. When their eyes met, a strange, encompassing understanding was shared between the two women.

"What a lucky woman I am," Carrie said quietly. "Not only have I won the most wonderful man in all the world as a husband, but the most wonderful in-laws as well. As I said, I will do anything to assure Drew of my love for him."

Touching her mouth in a gentle kiss against Diana's warm cheek, Carrie rushed from the house.

She found Drew at the stable, rubbing the horse so briskly it was certain to lose a few hairs. Linking her fingers loosely at her back, she strolled toward him, kicking up imaginary stones, her eyes coyly cutting between the hard-packed earth of the stables and her husband's firm profile. Though she knew emotion moved within him, his features were strangely blank.

"I believe we have travel arrangements to make, Husband," she said after a moment.

"I gathered that." He mumbled his reply. "The question is, do you wish that I accompany you?"

Forcing a small laugh, Carrie replied, "And how, Husband, do you propose that I find my way back to Wills Creek without your love and guidance?"

Surprise fleeted across his eyes as they turned to her. His jaw clenched so tightly that it became a sharp ridge. "Wills Creek?" he echoed her words. "What do you mean?"

"I mean, Husband," she said with hushed reverence, "that I believe it will be better if we wait a year or two before visiting my uncle in England."

"Carrie!" He gripped her arms firmly, and drew her to him. "Do you mean it? God! I never believed your story about who you were. I didn't want to believe it! I am an ordinary man and I wanted so much for you to be an ordinary girl. But, damn . . . even were you not the niece of the Duke of Devonshire, there is nothing—nothing!—ordinary about you!"

"That is because," she whispered with softly controlled happiness, "I am your wife."

Their gazes locked and held mutely, new vows being made in the adoring reflection of their eyes, in bodies softly molded together in the sweetest of embraces, in the promises they made to each other, without ever having uttered a word.

That evening at dinner, with Edwin and Cora Redding joining them, Cole Donovan announced that he and Diana had decided to journey to Scotland and England at the end of the week.

The two surprised young people made no reply, at which time, Diana took up the conversation, "Carrie, my husband and I will journey in your behalf to Holker Hall to meet with your uncle. I do hope you will not consider our visit there an intrusion into your private affairs. But we know, dear, how very important your relationship is with your uncle."

"So that is why Dr. and Mrs. Redding have come to dinner tonight rather than Sunday?" She smiled timidly at their two guests.

"Yes," Diana replied, briefly taking Cora's hand as she sat beside her. "They will be looking after the house while we are away. So, Daughter-in-law? Andrew? Are we intruding?"

Swallowing an imaginary lump in her throat, and aware that Drew was giving her the moment, Carrie replied, "Intruding? Goodness no! I do not presume to speak for your Andrew, but I do hope he will join me in considering it to be the sweetest of gestures. How happy my uncle Penley will be to know I am in the embrace of such a loving family!"

In her happiest mood since her wedding day, Carrie discussed with her new family and her new friends, the Reddings, every aspect of the journey to England, promising that a long letter would be written for delivery to her uncle and Drew promising to add a generous postscript. When, after enjoying a glass of after-dinner port in the parlor, she and Drew retired to their bedchamber, Carrie felt absolute exhaustion, so content was she with the turn of events.

The two lovers enjoyed a long, passion-filled night, falling asleep wrapped in each other's arms and the early May breeze wafting through the large chamber. Just past dawn, Drew prepared their horses for the trip back to Wills Creek while Carrie wrote her lengthy letter to Penley Seymour at Holker Hall, keeping it open at the bottom for the addition of Drew's postscript.

After tearful farewells with Cole and Diana Donovan, whom they would not see for perhaps a year, they began their eastern trek beneath warm, clear skies, their lazy pace hinting that they were in no great hurry to join their friends at the Wills Creek Trading Post.

Carrie's drab gray dress was more suited to winter than the warmth of this sad June day a year later. She stood solemnly beside Andrew, her hands folded reverently over her slightly rounded abdomen and studied the faces of her friends surrounding her while the preacher's solemn voice echoed in the early-morning stillness.

His last days had been peaceful and happy . . . the dear old man for whom Drew now quietly wept. Hambone had arisen earlier than usual that morning before, had summoned Jolie in his usual brusque, graveled tone, and had made a strange request. He had wanted to visit the grave of his dear wife, Rufina, a ritual he customarily performed only once a year, at Christmas.

Complying with his request, she had stood solemnly back while he'd spoken to his dead wife, then had returned him to the trading post within the hour. In his strangely sad yet happy mood, he had enjoyed the adoring company of Hester's children, with whom he had shared imaginary cakes and tea served in the youngest girl's new china playset. She had been anxious to break in the new treasure, given to her by her parents for her fourth birthday. Shortly thereafter, Hambone had engaged his family in tales of the old days back before the French and Indian War—his eyes twinkling with wicked remembrance as he'd told of being a scout under Major Washington's command. Then, while the women had hustled to and fro preparing for a picnic feast to be enjoyed at the pond, he had peacefully closed his eyes and drawn his last God-given breath.

Snapped from her thoughts by the melodic call of a songbird, Carrie wrapped her fingers through Drew's limply hanging ones. Immediately his grip tightened, so glad was he of the comfort. Across the timberline the early-morning sun streaked the pale blue skies with crimson, a sight that held Drew's melancholy gaze.

After the funeral, when everyone quietly returned to the trading post and their homes, Drew stood silently by while a local man filled in the grave. He did not leave until the dirt had been firmly tamped and a simple wooden cross erected. He would order a tombstone, but it would take several months to arrive.

When he finally turned away, he found Carrie pressed against an oak tree, her hands tucked behind her and her eyes quietly watching him. When he approached and his embrace made them as one, she held him for a long while until they heard Hester's mellow voice calling them home.

Drew was somber throughout the morning. He relaxed at the kitchen table behind the trading post, his chair tilted back, his boots drawn up to the back of another chair, his dark head dropped back against a trestle table. Occasionally he would look around . . . and remember. Hester, almost forty, her light hair peppered with long gray strands, had been one of his father's favorite children at Pine Creek. Cole had first met the precocious five-year-old child the night her little brother Garland had been born in an abondoned cabin, the same night Cole and Diana had formed a lasting friendship with Callie and Zebedee Ward, her parents. As he watched Hester move about, tending to her kitchen chores and occasionally scooting her own children out of harm's way, his mind wandered toward his own parents, whose ship should soon be pulling into port at Southampton after their long ocean journey.

Drew was well aware that his parents did not intend to remain in Philadelphia. Diana had long considered Rourke House something of a hindrance to the carefree lives she and her husband wished to live. She wanted only to return to Pine Creek, North Carolina, where she and Cole had lived their happiest moments and a settlement where Cole himself was a founding father.

Drew wasn't sure why his mind wandered, perhaps so that he would not have to think about dear old Hambone. Now, he turned his gaze to Noble and Bundy, entering through the rear door to partake of the noonday meal. Noble did not look particularly content, and Drew imagined that Jolie was not living up to his expectations as a wife. She'd complained miserably about the child growing within her, irritating complaints that usually compelled Noble to leave early in the mornings on hunting trips with some of the local Shawnees; he often did not return for a week or more. He was beginning to portray some of that cool indifference characteristic of his Indian brothers, though not with the women. To that gentle breed he usually gave his undivided attention, no matter how small the need.

Bundy was another matter! He had settled down to the boring, domestic life of Wills Creek. Drew managed a smile to himself. One good thing about Bundy was that it had been five years since he'd gotten into trouble. He had stolen no hogs from local settlers or gotten into any strapping good fights. Perhaps he'd finally left his rabblerousing days behind him.

A fire lit in Drew's eyes as his beloved Carrie emerged from the trading post area where she'd been assisting a local family in the purchase of practical yard goods for summer sewing. Her loose, rose-colored shift was attractive on her, betraying only a slight roundness where his child grew. Jolie, however, entering behind her, looked as though she would give birth any day, though she and Carrie were expected to deliver within a week of each other. Drew could tell by the severe set of Carrie's features that she and Jolie had again exchanged harsh words. He groaned inwardly, imagining the topic of their argument. Jolie simply would not give up!

Carrie approached, coaxed Drew into dropping the front legs of the chair back to the floor, then sat gently upon his lap to rest her cheek against his. His arms encircled her and he smiled, even as his eyes met those of the disapproving Jolie Ward. "How is my princess?" he asked Carrie as he held Jolie's look. "Tired?"

"A little," she replied, aware of Jolie's condemning scrutiny. "I thought I'd take a short nap back at our cabin."

Touching his mouth warmly to her cheek, he said, "I'll join you," and only now averted his gaze from Jolie's. He watched Noble's wife turn smartly on her heel and disappear into the trading area.

She would bloody well have to get used to the fact that he was married to Carrie—and happily so.

That evening Andrew visited Hambone's grave. There, resting across the loose dirt, his chin resting lightly on his crossed paws, was Sweet Boy. He lifted doleful eyes to

Drew, who bent to his knees and scratched at the bobcat's head.

"You miss him, do you, boy?"

He remained in the evening twilight for a long while trying, with his understanding silence, to convince the bobcat that his other human friends loved him every bit as much as had the old gentleman lying in peaceful repose beneath the Pennsylvania earth. He had gone to his rest, never having betrayed his true identity.

Wasn't that just like the lovable old scoundrel?

Chapter Eighteen

An impenetrable veil of darkness clung to the rooftops of Philadelphia. The heat that had shimmered in visible waves during the July afternoon continued to claim the night, compelling men to quench dry throats at the many taverns scattered throughout the historic bayside city. Edwin Redding was one of those men who found the taverns inviting that steaming summer night . . . thanks to the unplanned journey of his wife to Virginia to visit a sick sister. If Cora knew he was sitting in the smoke-filled room, nursing a glass of liquor between his fingers, she would have set a record returning to Philadelphia to snatch him from the scandalous iniquity.

Downing his drink, Edwin looked to the bartender. "Another one, Ben."

The big, burly man approached and expertly mixed the rum, pumpkin beer, and brown sugar commonly called Flip, into which he then plunged a red-hot poker from the coals behind him.

Of the taverns in and around Philadelphia, Edwin was partial to this one when the rare opportunity for patronage arose. Harry mixed the best Flip in Pennsylvania, and it was the one place where gentlemen could enjoy their bowl and bottle with satisfaction. Violence seldom rocked the peaceful atmosphere of this particular tavern — because, he supposed, of the quality of the patronage—professional men from about town. They played billiards and cards, whist, and punched at ombre. This tavern sported a skittle alley and shuffleboards, and an alley had been built in the rear especially for bowling.

Edwin came for the drinking and the sport; the heavy smoke, on the other hand, aggravated his delicate senses and was the one drawback to a perfect evening at this rarely partaken pleasure. Too many men had an intolerable itch for tobacco, smoked chiefly in pipes, the most common being the fine long-glazed pipes called churchwardens. A few men smoked cigars, a luxury that had only been available in America for the past twenty or so years.

Men entered the tavern all through the evening, and scarcely a head was picked up from their sport to watch the comings and goings. Now, however, just before the hour of midnight, a hush fell over the crowd as an almost skeletal form suddenly emerged from the street. Men's heads snapped around, pipes fell from between teeth, and even the sounds of the night beyond the tavern droned into silence.

Edwin Redding had never seen such a hideous sight. He had seen birth deformities in his practice as a physician, and he had seen grievous injuries, but he had never seen anything like that—a pitifully burned and mangled shell of a man who might once have been tall and imposing. He wondered what the stranger was doing in Philadelphia.

Junius Wade stooped in the doorway, wishing he could crawl into a crack, away from humanity. Dismounting the aging mare he'd coldly murdered the preacher for, he'd come face-to-face with a gang of young, taunting ruffians wielding short lengths of two-by-four boards as weapons. Trying to fight off the bold thugs, he'd taken a hit in mid-forehead. His pockets picked clean as he lay bleeding in a dark alleyway, he now sought out the doctor he'd been told was patronizing the establishment.

"Is there a Dr. Redding in here?" he called across the silence.

"I am Edwin Redding." Pushing himself up from his chair, Edwin hesitated to move toward the frightful man. Closing the distance with difficulty, he noticed the white length of handkerchief held to the man's head by a dirty hat. Blood oozed through the fabric.

"I am in need of a doctor," Junius growled. "I was attacked within the hour of entering your fair city and robbed of my money."

Adjusting himself to the sight of the unfortunate man, Edwin outstretched his hand, motioning the man to the outside. "My office is around the corner, sir. Accompany me there and I shall tend your wound."

Junius did not want to show physical weakness. Even though a cloud of darkness threatened him, he moved slowly yet confidently behind the short, balding physician. However, the moment he stepped through the curtain in the doctor's small, neatly furnished examination room, his knees crumbled. Edwin Redding scarcely had time to scoot a chair beneath him.

Removing the handkerchief, which had hidden not only the damage the young attackers had done but the full extent of his disfigurement, Edwin Redding carefully examined the wound. In the following moments he cleaned and stitched his forehead and rebandaged it with clean gauze. As he washed his hands in a white ceramic bowl, he was aware of Junius Wade's penetrating stare.

"You're wondering, sir, how I got to look like this, eh?" Junius queried.

Edwin tried to be as pleasant as possible. "I apologize for my curiosity. You apparently were the victim of unfortunate circumstances at some distant time. It is none of my business."

Junius managed a grin with what was left of his mouth. "Circumstances, blast! I'd imagine it must have been more like an inferno, Physician."

Edwin caught his meaning. "Sir, you do not remember the circumstances? Surely, that cannot be!"

" 'Tis a convenience of the mind, I would imagine," Junius mumbled. "And 'tis best sometimes not to remember."

Edwin wiped his hands dry on a small towel. "You have a point." He watched the pitiful man clinging to the chair as if it alone supported him. "Will you be able to make your way now, Mr. — ?"

"Wade . . . Junius Wade."

"Mr. Wade, I could recommend comfortable lodgings."

Junius waved his only hand. "No need. I'll take care of myself. Always have . . . always will."

"Shall I see you back to your transportation then?"

Junius Wade's eyes narrowed dubiously. "Why are you being kind to me? Don't you feel sick to your stomach just looking at me?"

"I feel sick to my stomach," Edwin countered flatly, "glaring at small, peeled potatoes bobbing in cooked spinach!"

Junius liked the man, which was something of an oddity for him. Considering himself cold, heartless, and dispassionate, he'd never liked anyone before, except Flame. "I'll repay your kindness later, Physician," he said, arising, "if you'll extend credit now." Reaching the outer office, a pain grabbed in his head, threatening to unfoot him. He cried out, clutching at his temples.

He would never fully recall what had happened after that — only bits and pieces, with the missing parts provided by Edwin Redding. He knew only that a bolt of darkness as quick as a bullet fired from a gun filled his brain. His body losing all control, he'd folded to the floor like a man with no spine. He would later learn that he'd lain in a state of delirium and half-consciousness for six long days and nights in the small, private antechamber of Edwin Redding's clinic.

When he came to in the midnight darkness of a hot July night, all those lost years came back in a rush of rapidly darting lights of crimson and gold and blue—year after year that had so long escaped him and whose loss had puzzled him for the past thirty years.

Rising weakly from the cot, he moved in an unsteady gait toward a washstand and mirror.

Though he was almost too weak to stand, mirth danced in his beady brown eyes. He stared at his hideous face without seeing it. What he saw in the mirror was the reflection of who he had been . . . before that gruesome night when the flames had licked at his flesh. In the netherworld of his evasive past, he had never claimed to be handsome but not ugly, either. He had modestly considered himself a somewhat plain man but tall and imposing and able to turn the eye of a few women. That is what he saw now.

A smirking grin clinging to his half-mouth, he whispered hoarsely, "Welcome home . . . Master Mayne."

Carrie moved along a shaded trail south of Wills Creek. She'd had another of those irritating verbal exchanges with Jolie and needed to get away from the trading post for a while. The trail emerged into a shady area overhung with viburnum and draped with wild grape. Here and there lay the ghostly white trunks of fallen trees.

Carrie usually did not pout, but thinking about Jolie made her do just that. She was aware that Drew was trying to be terribly patient in dealing with the woman's moods, but he did not have to spend as much time with Jolie as she did. Jolie complained constantly and found fault with every aspect of life at Wills Creek. And her ridiculous insinuations made Carrie want to rip her hair out by the handful.

Today she had gone a bit too far, hinting to Carrie that Drew would not have married her had she not been pregnant. It was the first time Carrie had raised her voice to Jolie. Hester had interrupted before the encounter could evolve into fisticuffs between the two screaming women.

That would have been a sight, Carrie thought, managing her first smile of the morning . . . two women soon to give birth tearing each other's hair out!

Oftentimes Carrie allowed herself to escape into a dreamworld away from Wills Creek and that dreadful Jolie. Now, as she moved absently along the trail, her fingers loosely linked and resting on the roundness of her abdomen, she scarcely noticed the scurrying of a rabbit or a startled quail taking flight. She heard only the echoing silence of the forest, an occasional breeze chiming through the topmasts of the firs. Here and there the sun's rays were like angel's wings. Silver shards of light touched upon her brow, warming her and easing the ugly melancholy that rested heavily upon her heart.

At that point, nothing but sheer necessity could have coaxed her back to the tense atmosphere of the trading post. She wanted only to relax in the shade of a favorite tree, close her eyes, and think only good thoughts. She was ashamed of her feelings about Jolie. Never before in her life had she despised anyone so much . . . with the exception, of course, of Junius Wade.

Quickening her pace along the path, she berated herself for allowing Junius to touch her thoughts. She wanted only a moment of happiness and solitude, not to dredge up unhappy memories. Now that he had become an unwelcome visitor in her thoughts, she couldn't help wondering where he might be now. The last time she had heard—in April—was that he had been seen in Louisville. Had he traveled eastward, or had he given up his quest in favor of the comforts of home—his murderous den in The Swamp district of New Orleans?

Thinking of Junius made her think of the other girls who had been purchased from the auction that cool October morning. She still grimaced with shame and guilt to remember what Junius might have done to little Kama. What had become of Topaz, the fiery Julia, and the others? A shudder touched her summer-warmed flesh as she remembered that morning she had stood, trembling, upon the auction block. She remembered tugging at the scant bodice of her cheap taffeta gown and having her hands slapped down by the auctioneer. She remembered staring over the sea of masculine heads, meeting leering, lusty eyes and watching their hands go up as the bids were called. Then she had seen Junius, stooped and ugly and vile, the wisps of hair clinging to his mottled scalp rustling in the cool island breeze, his half-mouth smiling a wicked smile as he continued to outbid every other man.

Thank God, that Drew had come along when he had. She remembered her first glance at the tall, dark-haired Pennsylvanian Solomon had pointed out in New Orleans. She remembered her terror believing the man wanted to beat her, until Solomon assured her it was simply a ruse to save her from a worse fate. Oh, how desperately she had pleaded with Drew in that gaudy room of sin and lust to save her from Junius! She smiled, remembering. Even though he'd been drunk, there'd been a certain charm about him. She'd seen salvation in him, even as he had tried his darndest to gain the intimacy he thought he'd paid twenty-five dollars for.

Now, less than a year later, she was the wife of that same dear man and soon to be the mother of his child. Before she'd been plucked from the waters of Wight she'd spent a carefree life caring about little else but her hairstyle, the latest fashions, or the next ball to be attended. Now a gentle Pennsylvanian had replaced those frivolous cares. She wanted only to be his wife and the mother of his child. She wanted to be these things, and yet not be at the mercy of Jolie day after day. She wondered if she could have one without the other.

Reaching her favorite spot beside the pond, Carrie eased down upon a moss-covered log, straightening her skirts around her as she did so. Upon seeing her, a snow goose took flight and a white-tailed deer turned and darted back into the forest, followed by a half-grown fawn. She liked it there, surrounded by peace and serenity, and the wild green forest that was, in itself, a blanket of security. She wished she'd brought a book with her.

A sudden movement on the other side of the pond caught her attention. Two dark figures emerged from the forest, a Shawnee leading a packhorse, upon which sat a woman with an infant strapped to her back. Recognizing the frequent visitors to the trading post, Carrie lifted her hand in greeting, a gesture that was timidly and immediately returned by the Indian woman.

She sighed dreamily as they disappeared onto the trail toward the settlement, where they would trade their village-made crafts for eastern goods. Every aspect of life at Wills Creek filled Carrie with awe. Everything she'd read back in England of America and the native Indians had been hostile and frightening. But the Indians she had met were strange and gentle people who made every effort to get along with the white people flooding across their land. There was, however, an exception in the savage Iroquois, who couldn't even get along with each other.

The sky caught Carrie's full attentions as a sudden, intense wind rushed through the treetops. Gray-black clouds tumbled across the heavens, appearing from nowhere, colliding with each other, taking away the mellow blue that had clung peacefully there before. A growl of thunder erupted from the timberline, its threat gaining in clarity as it rushed to take up a new position over the gentle pond.

Carrie had left the trading post a half mile behind her. As she watched the sky's activity, she wondered if she would be able to reach shelter before the unexpected storm. But even as she had asked herself the question, the first droplets of rain puddled upon her skin.

With the suddenness of a cannon exploding, the storm whirled around her, transforming the morning sky into the blackness of midnight, snapping off branches in the highest bows of the trees, sending the wildlife fleeing into the safety of the forest, and changing the ground into slippery mud beneath her feet. The wind tore at her hair, and the rain beat viciously upon her skin.

Gaining her footing, she turned to flee onto the trail toward the trading post, but her flight was immediately cut off by a branch ripped from a mighty oak by the force of the wind. Terror darkened her eyes. Caught between the pond and the felled tree, the storm lashing overhead and the earth shifting beneath her feet, Carrie's mind reeled in panic.

Her feet rushed from under her. With a scream tearing from her throat, Carrie's slim fingers dug frantically into the coat of mud beneath her body. She tried to get a grasp on something solid, but there was nothing, only the sheet of slick mud that now weighted down her cotton shift. Her long hair clung to the ground, and she was sure that it was ripping from her scalp.

Her footing caught in the mud's current, and she felt herself slipping . . . slipping into that now-swollen current of the pond that had been so peaceful just moments ago . . . the rain so dense she could not see her hands in front of her. Darkness whirled around her; she felt her body being pulled heavily down the incline.

Is this how my life shall go? she thought, desperately trying to cling to lucidity. *The calm before the storm, and then nothing? Am I to be denied the love of my husband and my darling baby — the evidence of our love — lying peacefully in my arms? Am I to have my life ended before I am allowed to fully enjoy it?*

Then the fog of half-consciousness became a heavy veil, the storm caught in a vortex of silence, and she remembered nothing after that.

The suddenness of the storm infuriated Drew. He and

Noble sought shelter in the barn of a settler half a dozen miles from the trading post. The furs they'd purchased from one of the Indian villages were drenched and would require many hours of drying before being sent to the furriers in Philadelphia.

He wanted only to return to Carrie and spend a few days with her without being required to go on the purchasing rounds. Perhaps he should put Bundy to the job; the man needed a little peace and quiet away from four rambunctious children.

He had thought that since the storm had come up so suddenly it would be of short duration. An hour later, though, as its intensity had not let up a shade, he reassessed his earlier presumption. He slumped lazily on a mound of hay and chewed a bit of straw between his teeth. Noble lay flat on his back on the hard-packed earth, his drenching-wet hat stretched across his face and his knees drawn up.

"You going to sleep, you lazy scoundrel?" Drew growled, irritated by the storm keeping them prisoner.

Nobel's dark eyes glared at him from beneath the rim of his hat. "I am already asleep, Donovan," he replied with husky annoyance. "This storm is going to hang on for a while longer. Why don't you get some shut-eye yourself?"

Dragging the bit of straw from between his teeth, he picked himself up from his resting place and arched his back. Despite the storm, the July heat hung on, and perspiration tickled down his spine. His long strides took him to the door of the barn, where he looked out at the darkly vicious sky. "Damn!"

Drew's single expletive brought another look from beneath the hat Noble wore. "What's your problem, Drew?"

"I don't like our travel being interrupted. And I don't like those furs being wet."

Noble pulled himself into a seated position. "The furs are not hurt. That's not what you're worried about. It's Carrie."

Noble's growl had been almost an accusation. "If I am

worried about Carrie, why should that bother you?"

"It doesn't bother me," he remarked absently. "I envy the fact that you care so much for her."

His friend's eyebrows met in a puzzled frown. "Are you saying, Noble, that you do not worry about your wife as I do about mine?"

Frustrated, Noble slapped his leg as he vaulted to his feet. "I'm beginning to think the biggest mistake I made was in not bringing a woman home from New Orleans the way you did."

"That was not something I planned, though I am happy things worked out as they did." Drew sat upon a low stable rail and eased his boot onto one below it. "Jolie's not making you happy, is she?"

"Happy! I'm so blasted miserable I'm thinking of taking to the woods with some of my renegade brothers!"

"I'd rather have Jolie escorted back to Pine Creek," Drew groaned, the sudden picture of Noble joining the most vicious of his heathen brethren causing a shudder to ripple the length of his spine. "I'll not have her upsetting life at the trading post."

Noble watched the rain, his arms crossed and his feet slightly apart. A deep sigh rent the air. "She's been upsetting life at Wills Creek for ten years," he remarked. "I don't know why the hell we didn't send her back the first time she caused trouble. For the time being, she will have to stay. I will not lose my child."

"It means a lot to you, does it?" Drew asked, approaching to stand beside him.

"It means everything." Silence.

Drew watched his Indian brother's dark profile, his severe frown, his mouth pressed firmly, the stiff stance of his body.

"Drew . . ." Noble finally said. "You might as well know. Jolie does not want the child because it is mine and not yours. I have asked Hester to take over its care at the moment of birth. I am going to suggest to Jolie that she return to Pine Creek. I do not want her here and if she does not go, then I will."

Drew's hand fell to his blood brother's shoulder. "I will not let you go, Noble. We are friends as well as brothers. If you give her a chance, perhaps she will adjust to being your wife—"

"Hell if she will!" Noble clipped the retort. "I just need you to know how things stand, Drew. She's making my life miserable, your life . . . and Carrie's. Never a day goes by she does not antagonize Carrie."

Drew's deep, weary sigh followed. He had known in his heart that it would come to this. "In the past ten years, her brother at Pine Creek has not failed to make his September visit to Pennsylvania," Drew reminded his comrade. "If he will agree to stay until after the birth of your child, he can escort his sister back to the home of her parents. Is that what you want, Noble?"

Silence again marked the moment. Noble's gaze held the blackness of the sky, the ferocity of the storm, reminding him of his brief marriage. Never a day had gone by that Jolie's vicious moods had not prevailed over their lives as man and wife. "It is what I want, Drew," he eventually replied.

It pained Drew to see his good friend so unhappy. He almost wished he hadn't forced Jolie to marry him but rather insisted that she return to Pine Creek. But enjoying his own happiness at the prospect of becoming a father, could he have deprived Noble of that joy? No, he thought not.

For the past ten years, Drew had been plagued by Jolie's amorous pursuits. Now that she was a married woman—and bearing her husband's child—why couldn't she let go of him and be a good wife to the man who truly loved her? Jolie's obsession was one reason Drew hated these moments away from Wills Creek. He never knew when control would be lost and Jolie would begin a cruel course of intimidation that might, ultimately, result in harm to Carrie.

Drew shuddered visibly. Damn! Why couldn't this rain let up? He wanted to return to Wills Creek and assure himself that Carrie was safe in their cabin and happily awaiting his return.

A frisky Claudia moved about Rourke House straightening throws upon the furniture, changing the wilted wildflowers for the fresh ones she had gathered earlier, sweeping and dusting and straightening pantries until a normal person might have worn herself down. Claudia, however, prided herself on not being normal, and as the evening wore on, she found herself searching for things to be done.

Her husband, Mr. Lundy, had long ago retired to their simple quarters at the rear of the kitchens, drunk on the best bourbon he had managed to pilfer from the liquor cabinet in the parlor. Thinking of him, Claudia began to sing gaily, "Mean Mr. Lundy, born upon a Monday. Why can't his die-day be upon a Friday." Then she snickered mischievously to herself, pleased at her quickly composed verse. "See, Mum," she said, thinking of her dead mother, Mrs. Sanders, "your Claudia isn't as addle-brained as you'd thought."

Looking at the bare spot in front of the parlor window affording the best view of the city, Claudia remembered the trip she had meant to make to the attic to retrieve one of the tall, ornate fern stands. Though it was late, she did not hesitate to take up her lantern and begin the three-story trek to the attic.

She remembered a time when the third-floor corridor of the house had opened onto dark, dank, dusty rooms. In the years that Cole and Diana Donovan had owned the house—even when they'd resided in Pine Creek, North Carolina—they had seen to the slow and painstaking chore of refurbishing the rooms, replacing old, unstable furniture with new, modern pieces, wallpapering the walls, adding new cornices and draperies, and generally chasing away the antique gloom. Today the house could easily accommodate a hundred guests in luxury.

Claudia moved onto the narrow stairway leading to the attic. She'd brought the key with her, and as she stood at the top of the stairs, she thought she heard a flurry of movement from within. Pressing her ear to the door, the annoyed servant said sharply, "Rats! I'll put out poison for the little beasts!" then opened the door and entered the huge, seldom-visited expanse.

A hundred and fifty years of collected pieces cluttered the attic. Moving among the history of Rourke House, looking for the fern stand she knew Tuxford had stored there earlier in the year, her eyes scanned every cobwebbed piece. Suddenly, something caught her attention. She moved toward a canvas-covered portrait, surprised that it was not on the wall of the parlor with the other Rourke and Donovan ancestors. Taking the edge of the canvas she ripped it off. So! That was what had happened to Master Webster Mayne's portrait. She had wondered why it hadn't been returned to its hanging place after the winter cleaning. But Claudia was much too clever to be perplexed for long. She was well aware of Mistress Donovan's animosity toward her long-departed cousin . . . dead, she would think, though Claudia did not agree. Still, she had thought the mistress's superstition—that the absence of the portrait would bring gloom upon the house—would have compelled her to return it to its rightful place. She suspected that Master Cole was responsible for its attic hiding.

Now Claudia had two things to struggle to take downstairs. Master Mayne, because he was family, deserved to be hung in the parlor, along with the portraits of his mother and father and the many others. And she still had not located the fern stand . . .

Ah! There it was, half reclining against one of the two attic windows. Clicking her tongue, she hoped the sun had not damaged the cherrywood as she moved carefully between the clutter to retrieve it.

Claudia managed to pry the delicate piece of furniture loose and eased it above her head for the short journey back to the attic door and the lantern she had brought with her. But as she turned, her eyes met small, dark, staring ones. She was not alarmed as she squinted to make out the form in the darkness. It certainly was not Tuxford; the illusion before her was only half her brother's size. "Ralph Lundy, is that you?" She could not believe her drunken husband would have attempted to climb three flights of stairs. But if not . . . who?

The pale, haunting figure moved into the light of the lantern. When, at last, the grotesque and twisted form of Webster Mayne stood in outline against the pale glow, Claudia smiled her biggest smile. "Master Mayne, what are you doing up here in this drafty old attic?"

Webster smiled wryly. He had expected the addle-brained servant to accept him without question. He remembered the fifteen years when, as a young girl, she had tended his mother's corpse as if she were still alive. Now Claudia accepted Webster's return after more than thirty years just as easily as she had accepted her service to a dead woman.

"Claudia . . ." The one word was emitted in high-pitched, maniacal suspension. "Will you do my bidding, girl?"

Without hesitation, Claudia replied, "Aye, you are the master here. It is my duty to do your bidding."

"Where is my cousin Diana?" Webster asked, attempting to arrest the mad thumping of his heart as he spoke that hated name.

Claudia carried on the conversation with him as though time had stood still, as though only yesterday he had criticized her maddening simplicity. "Mistress Donovan has journeyed to England and Scotland with her husband. They shan't return until early next summer. But their son, Master Andrew, and his new wife shall be visiting soon. She is expecting a child and he will wish that she be here in the house, near enough that a physician can be called when her time comes."

Upon regaining his memories, Webster had not believed his good luck, and the coincidence of a cool night in New Orleans, when a bold young Pennsylvanian named Donovan had taken his best girl to one of the back rooms. Now he stood firmly rooted to the floor of his dead mother's home, knowing that after all the years he would finally get his revenge, if not against his cousin Diana, then against her only son. He would gladly bide his time, though he would rather do it in comfort.

"Since the east wing of this house burned, Claudia . . ." Webster spoke with unhindered malevolence, "where would a good girl like you suggest that I sleep?" He liked the idea that the house was so enormous that hiding would be a simple task, requiring little effort.

"I'll prepare a room for you myself," she said, the perils of his presence lost within the innocence of her simple, unquestioning mind. "Come with me, Master, to the third floor where I shall see to your comfort and prepare a supper tray."

Her acceptance pleased him. Webster would delight in being served as he deserved to be—by a woman too simple-minded to question his grotesque appearance. He had not enjoyed sneaking to the kitchen in the darkness of the night to nibble at what had been left of the evening meal.

A vicious smile played upon what was left of his mouth. Webster's plan was falling perfectly into place.

Chapter Nineteen

As he entered the clearing and looked toward the familiar trading post, a momentary shiver caught the length of Drew's spine. Evening twilight had just wrapped the forest and its occupants in a veil of foggy gray and there was an unusual flurry of activity around the post for this late hour of the day.

While Drew sought the source of the activity, Noble saw to the horses and the wet furs that would have to be put on lines for drying. Seeing the older of Hester's girls moving toward a trail, Drew asked, "Dora, what is going on?"

Anxiety was a mask over her soft brown eyes, which she dropped from his view as she replied, "I am merely looking for Cawley. I saw him go this way."

"What is Cawley doing out in the forest this time of evening?"

Dragging her toe across the rain-soaked earth as she sought to buy extra time, Dora tucked her hands behind her and gently shrugged. "Mum wishes to see you," she said after a moment.

Dora's obvious anxiety now grabbed at Drew. "Did any of the children suffer the perils of the storm, Dora?"

"No, Mr. Donovan. Please . . ." Dragging up her skirt and darting a few feet into the forest, she said over her shoulder, "I really must find Cawley."

Drew attempted to still the tremble erupting from deep within him. His half-running footsteps carried him to the spacious cabin he shared with Carrie. Rushing onto the porch he threw open the door. "Carrie . . ." No lamp had been lit; the aroma of supper did not waft through the stillness of the immaculate cabin. Pulling the door open, he eased his hands to his hips and stood for a moment, attempting to inhale a deep breath into his burning lungs. As he moved in long strides toward the trading post, he reassured himself that Carrie was assisting Hester with the evening meal, that they would all dine together as they'd gotten into the habit of doing lately. But all the reassurances in the world could not silence that nagging little voice inside him that kept telling him something was terribly wrong.

As he closed the distance to the trading post, heated feminine voices from within gained in clarity. Drew stood at the entrance, unable to ascertain which woman was more furious, Hester or her younger sister, Jolie. Just before Drew made his presence known, Jolie growled angrily, "Why should we care about her? She shouldn't be here anyway!"

Drew slipped quietly into the room, and the gazes of the women lifted simultaneously to meet his questioning eyes. Jolie's cheeks paled and Hester, relief sweeping over her own freckled features, rushed toward him. "Drew! Thank God you've returned. Your Carrie was out when the storm hit and we cannot find her!"

Without a moment's hesitation, Drew turned a swift and accusing eye toward Jolie, who had moved into the shadow of a wall. "Are you responsible for this, Jolie?"

"Wh-what do you mean?" Her eyebrows met in a serious but obviously feigned frown of confusion.

Drew approached and clamped his hands viselike

around her upper arms. She winced from the pain. "Are you responsible for Carrie being out when the storm came in?"

She could lie, she supposed, but Hester stood silently by, very aware of the heated exchange of words the two women had shared earlier in the day. Hester had heard her sister's accusations toward Drew's wife, and she would not hesitate to set the record straight if Jolie evaded Drew's inquiry. She attempted to wrench her arms away from Drew, though with little success. His grip did, however, loosen ever so slightly. "We had words, I'll admit, but nothing worse than any other times. She doesn't like me." A pout, surely meant to solicit his sympathy, had softened those last words.

Drew released her as if he was disgusted by the mere presence of her. He wiped his hands down his shirt, grasping the coarse fabric and attempting to still the rage bubbling from within him. Carrie . . . his Carrie had been caught by the most furious storm he could remember in all his life, and that she still had not returned was a sign something was wrong. Standing near the back entrance, clutching at his forehead, he tried to imagine where she might have gone. Hester silently approached. She started to drop her hand to his shoulder but instantly withdrew.

Turning to hold Hester's gaze, Andrew asked, "Was the smokehouse checked?" She silently nodded. "The lean-to in the dale?" Again she nodded, at which time Drew continued. "The pond? The waterfall? The Widow Howland's place?" And to each query, Hester nodded her head of pumpkin-colored locks until Drew was sure he would lose his mind.

"They are all out searching," Hester assured him. "The children, Bundy, Cawley . . . and others from the region."

Drew felt a sick, sinking feeling in the pit of his stomach. The look he darted toward Jolie might have had the power to erase her from the face of the earth if he hadn't felt so drained of energy. He turned toward the darkness folding more heavily to the clearing and stepped out to the porch. He did not know which way to turn. He could hear the faraway voices of the children, and of Bundy and Cawley, calling Carrie's name. He also heard the deep, resonant voice of Noble, who must have gotten word from one of the other residents.

He tried to think, to grab at tenuous straws dropping randomly inside his head. Where would Carrie have gone? She never strayed farther than the pond in one direction, or the waterfall in the other. She often visited the Widow Howland, with whom she'd spent many hours sitting on her porch and chatting about their common English bonds.

Soon Drew separated himself from the porch and moved on a slow and deliberate course toward Carrie's favorite santuary—the pond. It did not matter that it had already been searched. It would be searched again.

A faint lump began to enlarge inside his tightly constricted throat. He couldn't imagine carrying on with life if his beloved Carrie . . .

"Drew!" He turned sharply, his rigid stance disrupted by Noble's voice sharply calling his name. He did not like the way Noble moved toward him, his hands hanging limply. What he didn't know was that Noble's eyes had dropped in spite of his determination to face this tragedy with some degree of strength. When he stood within touching distance of Drew, he held out his hand. "I just found this at the edge of the pond."

The eyes of the Pennsylvanian frantically scanned the bit of fabric. He recognized what had once been a part of Carrie's loose shift, the cream-colored one she wore most days because, as she explained, it was comfortable and allowed for expansion. "This doesn't mean anything," he said softly, then pulling his bottom lip between his teeth in a moment of silence. "It means only that she tore her dress."

Noble's dark eyes sheened with moisture. His hand closed over the tense strength of his blood brother's arm. "Damn, Drew! Debris from the forest slid down the embankments and filled the pond. The body of a fawn was found there, dragged to death by the fury of the storm. Your Carrie is . . ."

"No!" Grief raking his face, he ripped his arms from Noble's strong hand. "You are wrong! Carrie has not been claimed by the pond! She is safe somewhere, waiting for me to find her!"

"Drew . . ." Noble attempted to pull his friend around to face him but Drew resisted. "Two Shawnee entered the trading post shortly after the storm started. They had seen Carrie at the pond. The woman had waved to her as she had sat on the embankment. And that . . ." He pointed toward the limp piece of cloth draped across Drew's fingers, "that was found there. It is a fact, Drew. Carrie is lost." Noble turned, so sick and frustrated he did not know where his strength came from. As much as he loved Jolie, he wanted to throttle her. God! Could he wait until his child was born before he sent her back to her parents in North Carolina? "I've gathered some of the local men to assist me in recovering her body," he added after a moment. "It would be better if you did not—"

"Do what you must!" Drew thundered his response. "While you are wasting your time, I will be looking for my wife!" He knew his beloved Carrie was not dead. Tightening his bearing, Drew paced off toward the forest, aware of the sheening blackness of Noble's eyes as

310

he watched him disappear. Out of sight of his Indian brother, Drew fell to his knees on the rain-sogged earth and clutched madly at his temples. "God, Carrie . . . where are you? Reach me somehow—tell me where you are!" He half mumbled, half cried the words, tears turning his eyes into deep, impenetrable wells. "Don't you know how much I love you?"

Indeed she did. Carrie owed her life to sheer determination and her tremendous love for Drew. As she had felt her body being dragged down the embankment, she had thought only of her beloved returning to the trading post to discover that her corpse had been pulled from the rain-swollen pond. She was not sure where she was, only that blackness surrounded her. Sticks and twigs dug into her tender flesh and weeds twisted together with mud were like glue against the tattered remnants of her clothing. She tried to picture the landscape around the pond. Where could she possibly be?

There were only the bald cypress at the edge of the pond, the forest around its embankment, a trail here and there emerging from the woodland. There was the small boat the men used for fishing, but as she put her hand against the rough walls imprisoning her, she knew she was not surrounded by an overturned boat. In her half-consciousness just moments ago she vaguely recalled many voices calling her name and hearing the dull thud of footsteps upon the slick bank. She had to be near, yet so far, because they apparently had not been able to see her, and she had been much too weak to answer their calls.

She shivered from the dampness and the darkness that formed a fragile blanket around her. Her favorite dress was a tattered rag heavily weighted by the mud that

311

held her prison together. She lay very still, forming a pillow of her damp and muddy hair and tried again to envision the pond and the forest in those few moments before consciousness had been lost.

If only she could see! she thought, finding a loose twig to weakly jab at the strange cavern walls. Was there still a world? Or had she died and crossed a threshold that would take her to a new plane of existence? Was she simply awaiting that transition, for a bright, heavenly light to penetrate her darkness and guide her into that other world? But if that were so, would she be so damp and uncomfortable, lying upon the prickly bed, wrapping her arms around her bruised body? Would the child within her kick in protest, wishing, she liked to believe, for the warmth and comfort of the simple, rustic cabin she shared with her beloved Drew?

She had to believe that she was still alive, and that the residents of Wills Creek were out, even now, searching for her. She tried her voice so that she would be able to call out when she heard them again. Though she opened her mouth and strained to speak, nothing audible formed there. Perhaps if she lay very still, her strength would return.

Suddenly, she heard a long, melodious whisper on the wind somewhere beyond her prison walls, "Caaaaaaaareeee—"

Her head snapped up so quickly she collided with the mud roof. Grasping her throat, she tried to call, "I am here. I am here." But her words were no more than a strained whisper.

Then she heard muttering far, far away . . . angry, masculine voices, muted accusations . . . water splashing so close yet so far away. Again, the voice called her name. Recognizing its familiarity, she felt her heart suddenly begin to beat furiously.

"Drew. Drew . . ." The whisper hung onto her voice, no matter how hard she tried to shake it. Drawing in a deep, stale breath, she called again, "Drew . . ." and was pleased with the sudden return of some semblance of her strength. Still, she wondered how anyone could hear her beyond the wall of mud and sticks. She tried to push the offending barrier away, but it would not give an inch. "I am here, Husband. Please, I am here . . ."

Drew snatched at Noble's arm, stilling its angry flailing. He was sick to death of his blood brother trying to convince him Carrie was dead.

"Did you hear that?" Drew asked, turning his ear to the darkness of the pond.

"I heard nothing," Noble replied, frustrated by Drew's insistence that Carrie would be found alive.

"I heard something."

"You heard the wind in the trees!" Noble stormed, "Nothing more than that!"

Drew would hear none of it. He moved unsteadily toward the edge of the pond. Cupping his hands to his mouth, he called again. "Caaaaaareeeee!" When the tiny voice he was sure he'd heard did not again move across the pond, he called her name again.

Noble had drawn his hands to his narrow hips. He stood staring at Drew, then swept his gaze over the men with boats on the pond. In a loud, gruff voice, he called, "Come in, men. We're suspending the search until tomorrow morning."

Drew turned swiftly, his narrow eyes holding his Indian brother's plaintive features. "You cannot do that. I heard something. I heard Carrie!"

Noble countered with irritation, "And you are the

only one who claims to have heard something. The other men did not, and they are in a better position to hear Carrie if she were still alive!"

Drew pinched his mouth, frustrated by Noble's declaration. In his own grief, he could not see that his friend's heart was breaking for him, and for the lovely English girl who had finally made him happy. "Very well!" Drew's reply was biting annoyance. "Call in the men! Go to your warm beds for the night. I will find her myself."

The exhausted men were pulling their boats onto the embankment. As they passed near Drew some lifted their eyes compassionately, others spoke a sympathetic word to him. Though he did not respond with words, his eyes softened in deference to their individual kindnesses.

Before the passage of five more minutes, Drew found himself alone at the pond. The darkness was a damp, gloomy veil upon him, the only light to be seen that of a lantern Noble had left on the bank. Turning sharply, he approached and took up the lantern, then began moving silently around the pond. A tender-hearted Noble had removed the drowned fawn from the waters and had buried it; Drew came upon the grave scarcely fifty feet into his journey. He moved slowly around the pond, calling Carrie's name over and over and over again. She was out there; it was only a matter of time before he heard her response to his call.

Carrie flailed her fists against the walls of the cavern that she had only now recognized as the long-abandoned beaver mound at the east side of the pond. Her heart thumped madly as she tried to push her back up against the walls in a feeble attempt to free herself. The beavers

314

had been masters of engineering; she could not so much as budge a twig. Desperation clung to her as she heard Drew calling her name. The pitch of his voice now gained in clarity and she knew he was moving in her direction.

"Andrew . . ." The mere calling of his name took away her breath. She sat for a moment, stilling the tremble that erupted from deep within her. Closing her eyes tightly against the darkness, she called in a somewhat stronger voice, "Andrew. Andrew, I am here!"

As the dark clouds parted, Drew suddenly found the pond drenched in moonlight. The slight breeze had stopped rustling among the treetops and he knew he had heard her familiar, melodic voice calling his name.

Desperation pinched his brow. Placing the lantern on a felled tree he surged into the storm-cooled waters of the pond and moved toward the beaver mound. When he felt the sharp twigs beneath his palms, he called hoarsely, "Carrie. Carrie, are you in there?" Tears sheened his eyes when a tiny, trembling feminine voice answered him.

He began tearing at the twigs and branches until his fingers were sore and raw. An animal growl erupted from his throat as he tried to maintain his footing in the shallow current of the pond. It seemed that hours passed, rather than the few minutes it took to break a hole in the beaver mound. And there, kneeling in the dank darkness, her own fingers working frantically to break through from her side, was his beloved Carrie. Pulling her up and into his arms he hugged her tightly, laughing and weeping simultaneously and enjoying her happy tears mingled with his own.

"They thought you were dead," he managed in a low,

315

weak voice. "The men were dragging the pond for you!"

"I heard them," she murmured in reply, relishing the musky, manly scent of him pressed to her. She had thought she'd never again enjoy this intimacy with him. "I just couldn't find my voice to call out to them. But your voice gave me the strength."

A thought occurred to him. Putting a brief space between them, his glazed, worried eyes darted over her mud-caked form. "The baby! Is the baby all right?"

Pulling herself back into his arms, she whispered against his wet hair, "Mother and baby are both fine. I assure you, Husband."

Over the next few minutes, Drew managed to separate her from the confines of the abandoned beaver mound that had drawn her in from the swollen current of the pond. Thank God it had been there! he thought. As he moved with Carrie toward the bank, the cool current cleaned the mud from her scratched and bruised flesh and the remnants of her gown. But she didn't seem to notice as she lay comfortably in his strong arms.

When he started to emerge onto the trail, Carrie struggled against him. "Allow me to walk, Husband. It is much too far for you to carry me."

"Allow me the pleasure," he remarked, suppressing the emotion digging at his throat. "I feared I'd never do this again."

Elation and relief strengthened him on the long walk to the cabin. As he dropped her to their comfortable, quilt-covered bed, he instantly busied himself around the cabin, preparing her a cup of hot tea and a meal of bread and beef, warming water for the bath she would want to take in the large iron tub behind the sheer curtain. There was nothing he didn't think of that she might need.

Still weak from her ordeal, Carrie watched his tall,

muscular form ambling about the cabin, his eyes turned deliberately from her, his busy preparations performed methodically. Moisture sheened his eyes, even now when he knew she was safe.

That troubled her. "Drew?" His gray-black gaze cut to her in anticipation. "Do you know why I was out in the storm?"

His eyes became vials of wrath. "I do," he replied curtly.

Carrie sprang from the bed with much more agility than she thought she possessed. Her arms slid around his taut back. "You cannot entirely blame Jolie, Drew. Were I not so hot-blooded also, I would not have fled from our problems. I would have stayed and faced them."

Her entreaties did not dull his anger. Mention of Jolie only heightened it, but he deliberately kept his reply calm and evasive. "Eat your meal and drink your tea, Carrie," he lightly ordered, his hands massaging her arms through the tattered remnants of her gown. "Your bath is almost ready."

With a pout, Carrie gained more intimate contact to him. Though anger clung to his eyes, his body relaxed beneath her gentle touch. "Don't brood, my love." Carrie spoke softly. "I won't ever again let her prickle me. If I find that I must part from her company, then I will return to our cabin. I will never go to the woods where such dangers lurk. Oh, Drew . . . Drew, do not look at me with such bitterness."

"I'm taking you to Philadelphia for the duration of your term," he quietly advised her. "I'll not take any more chances. You'll be safer in the city, with Claudia and her girls to take care of you. I'll hire a special nurse—"

"No!" Carrie swiftly broke contact. "It is the height of

317

the trading season. You said we would not go to the city until early October."

Recapturing her to his embrace, Drew spoke huskily. "The trading post is a mere hobby to me! Noble and Bundy are here! Hester is here! I have other enterprises to keep me occupied in Philadelphia. I have my father's shipping business—"

"Regardless of your arguments, I know the trading post is the most important aspect of your life."

His grip tightened. His glaring eyes connected to her surprised ones. *"You* are the most important aspect of my life, Carrie. Not a building of logs and mortar and a business as easily run by Noble and Bundy as by me. We will journey to Philadelphia within the week or I will not wait until after Jolie's child is born to send her back to North Carolina."

Her surprise deepened. "You are sending Jolie and her child away?"

Drew realized he'd said more than he should. He and Noble had spoken in confidence, and Drew was not sure just how much of their conversation Noble would expect him to divulge. But surely his good friend would not expect him to keep secrets from his wife. "Jolie does not want her child," Drew said after a moment. "After its birth, it will be given over to the care of Hester, and Jolie will accompany her brother back to Pine Creek."

"Her brother? Who is her brother?"

Shrugging, easing down into a chair and coaxing her to his lap, he said, "His name is Garland Ward and he shows up here every September without fail. I'll ask him to take Jolie back with him. It's best for everyone concerned."

"Noble? Is that what he wants?"

"He is very aware that Jolie does not want to be his wife. If she will not go, then he will. I will not allow

Noble to leave."

Rising sharply, Carrie retorted, "Allow it? What are you, Drew? His owner?"

"I did not mean it like that," he said patiently, also coming to his feet as he realized how his words had sounded. "I meant only that I do not want Noble to leave. If there is anything I can do to prevent it, I will do it, even sending Jolie away."

Clutching at her temples, Carrie said, "This is my fault! Oh, if only I hadn't been so childish today!"

"You had nothing to do with it. Today when the storm came up—before I knew you were in danger—Noble told me his plans. I will stand by his decision."

His words had the capacity to darken her mood. She did not wish it; she wanted only to enjoy her husband and to be thankful the pond had not claimed her life. "We will discuss it in more detail tomorrow, Drew. For now, I shall enjoy that warm bath you've prepared for me."

She hesitated to withdraw from him. As she stepped away, her hand moved fluidly down his arm, grasping his hand gently just as final contact was broken. Moving behind the thin veil of gauze, she began removing her tattered gown. A deep, pensive sigh touched the moment.

Drew began shedding his own wet clothing in exchange for a pair of loose trousers. Then he sat upon the mattress and relaxed against the headboard. He watched Carrie in silence as she deposited the ruined gown to the floor, her still-damp underthings moving the length of her ivory form and her narrow feet stepping from them. When her fingers tried to comb through her disheveled, flaming tresses, he heard her little cry of protest as they caught in knots. As she stepped into the bath, her eyes turned to his own, veiled by the sheer fabric of the curtain separating them.

How lovely she was, Drew thought, her rounded abdomen alive with his child who would be born in three months, her body milk-white and smooth. When she began to struggle down into the soapy water, Drew pushed himself from the bed and moved through the opening of the gossamer fabric. Kneeling, he took up a cup to wet her hair. "It may take several washings to get your hair clean," he remarked, twining the wet strands through his fingers while he applied the soap.

Carrie enjoyed the warmth of the tub and his hands gently massaging her scalp. She closed her eyes dreamily and replied, "I don't mind, as long as you are willing to assist me with it."

Dropping the soap, Drew pulled her into his arms, almost crushing her to him. "God, Carrie! We speak so lightly of little things that we have failed to grasp the full import of what almost happened today. I almost lost you, Carrie. When Noble tried to convince me you were dead — when the men were dragging the pond for you — I felt like an empty shell of a man. I felt that I wanted to flee into the forest and die. My living defied logic. Without you, I was only half a man." Tears rushed into his eyes but did not touch his cheeks.

Hugging him Carrie replied, "But I did not die, my husband. I am here in the tub . . ." She managed the tiniest laugh, "soaking wet, your gentle hands washing the mud from my hair, your child growing in my body, and our love as bright and fresh as the day it first appeared from the deepest recesses of our hearts. And a person doesn't *almost* die. Either she dies or she doesn't. It's as simple as that. We were not meant to be apart. God knew that when he saved me."

Drew attempted to laugh off the emotion that had risen in him. "Let's get this soap out of your hair, woman, and get you to bed where you belong."

"*We* belong," she softly amended, gathering her hair from his hands to drag it gently through the water. Moments later, with her hair clean and wet and straight, he cradled her in his arms and soon dropped her to the plush covers of their bed. "Drew . . ." she laughed, "I am soaking. The bed will be drenched!"

Easing to the bed beside her, he folded her soft, damp form to his body. He had brought a towel to her, with which he gently dabbed the length of her body, pausing lovingly at her abdomen where his child grew. When she gathered her gown from under the pillow where she kept it and started to pull it on, he halted her movement. "No, just let me feel you against me . . . like this." He had dropped his head tenderly to her abdomen. "I can hear my child's heartbeat," he murmured. "Thump, thump . . . "

Carrie laughed softly. "That is probably *my* heartbeat, Andrew Cynric Donovan!"

His arm moved to form a pillow for her head. "Rest against me, Carrie. I promise I will never let harm come to you again."

"I know that," she whispered in reply, a long sigh touching his cheek. "Drew?"

"Hmm?"

"Are we still going to travel to Philadelphia?"

His grip tightened. "We will discuss it at length tomorrow."

"Drew, I love you enough, not to argue with you, but to journey to the city when you wish it. I know that your only concern is for my welfare."

A pleased grin raked his features. "Good! You always know just what to say." Turning to his side, he studied her sweet face, her love-softened emerald eyes, the delicate spread of her hips, her gently rounded abdomen, and long, lithe legs. He had never imagined that a pregnant woman could be so astoundingly beautiful. It pleased him immensely to know that she was his woman, his love and his life.

Drawing her to him for the long night ahead, he vowed that he would protect her from all danger, that he would never let anything or anyone cause her harm again.

Chapter Twenty

Drew arose before dawn the following morning, touched his mouth gently to Carrie's forehead so as not to awaken her, then dressed and moved out into the humid morning. Tightening his muscles, he relieved the stiffness of the long night, then ambled toward the solitary light shining from the kitchen area of the trading post. When he entered, he encountered a dozen gloomy souls, including Noble and Bundy.

"I'm famished, Hester," he said to the woman cooking eggs and fatback over the black stove. "That smells mighty good." Noble gave him a strange look, then shared one with his half-brother. Drew turned, a grin widening his mouth. "What are you two fellows up to this morning? By the way, Hester . . ." Again, he turned toward the stove. "Could you prepare a breakfast tray that I could take over to Carrie . . ."

Noisily dropping her spatula, Hester drew her hands to her face and wept, stirring her children into nervous action. Bundy shot up from the table and approached his trembling wife. "Damn it, Drew, why'd you have to upset her?"

Drew scratched at his dark head. "I didn't ask her to take it over. I said I'd do it myself." He was genuinely perplexed by Hester's show of emotion.

Noble rose to the situation. "You know damn well what he means, Drew."

"No, I don't!" Drew shot back with equal vehemence. "I came over here to have breakfast and to take a tray back to my . . ." It hit him suddenly. Last evening when he'd rescued Carrie from the pond, he had taken her straight away to their cabin. He had not informed the men of the rescue, and as far as they were concerned, dragging the pond for Carrie's body was top priority of the morning. "Oh, hell," he droned, his eyes sweeping apologetically over the occupants of the kitchen. Approaching Hester, he dropped his hand to her shoulder. "Forgive me. I brought Carrie back to our cabin last evening."

"You're dreaming!" Noble accused.

"Is Miss Carrie alive?" Dora asked with nervous expectation, tears sheening her eyes.

At almost the same time, Jolie wailed "You're all trying to make me feel guilty!" and fled into the trading area.

"Hell!" An exuberant Cawley Perth, not wishing to be left out of the excitement, suddenly jumped into action. "I'll take the breakfast tray over to Miss Carrie . . . but not if she's a spook!"

"I'm not a spook!" Carrie laughed, entering the living quarters. The occupants—managing to survive their stunned disbelief—gathered around, touching her to make sure she was real. Explanations immediately followed and, gathering the happy children around her, Carrie moved out to the porch to watch the first glint of the sun's rays crest the horizon. She did not see Jolie's silent, lethal glare from the trading area. Drew approached from the rear, wrapping his arms about her in a firm embrace.

"I'm glad you showed up when you did," he murmured. "I was afraid Noble and Bundy were going to dissect me!"

Wrapping her fingers loosely around his wrists, Carrie replied, "I wouldn't let it go that far, Husband."

Reading the silent message in Drew's gaze, Dora gathered her sisters and herded them back into the kitchen for breakfast. Cawley, lovestruck over the pretty Dora Duncan, trailed her like a faithful pup. Carrie and Drew both heard Cawley say to Dora, "One day you're goin' to be all over me like that." He cared not a whit that Dora's mother turned a disapproving eye to the amorous attentions paid her daughter.

The pretty Dora smiled a smile much more mature than her sixteen years.

Left to themselves, Carrie turned and placed her hands gently upon Drew's arms. Her eyes did not meet his. "Have you given any further thought to our leaving Wills Creek?"

"It is what I wish to do," he replied soberly.

Her gaze met his own. "Please, won't you reconsider? It'll be so dreary, cooped up in that big, gloomy house until after our baby is born. Especially since your parents are abroad. You will be engaged in business and I will be cooped up with Claudia and her girls and that drunken Mr. Lundy—and that frightening Tuxford! Here on the creek life is so exciting—"

"Exciting, yes!" he smarted. "Exciting enough to get my wife killed. I would much rather subject you to three months of absolute boredom than to endanger your life here."

"Please, Drew, give it more thought."

Silence. Drew's smoky gaze moved over his wife's pale features, the thick masses of her hair which drew the attention of his fingers like a magnet. Her mouth was petulant this morning, as if an argument would be an easy accomplishment. "I'll tell you what," he said after a moment. "I will have a long, private talk with Jolie, and then I will decide whether we travel to Philadelphia this week, or whether we wait."

Holding back her groan of protest, Carrie reluctantly let him go. She feared his facing Jolie at a moment when he was much too vulnerable to his own anger.

As he moved silently into the trading area, Carrie returned to the kitchen, which was filled with the aroma of Hester's breakfast. Sitting at the table with the children, she propped her chin on her palm and looked dreamily at their faces. The children, ranging in age from four to sixteen years, made her think about her own baby.

When Hester brought a plate of food and placed it in front of her, breaking her concentration, Carrie looked up guiltily. "Hester, you do not have to wait on me."

"Don't mind," the freckled woman replied, sweeping back her sun-colored hair. "Just glad I don't have to be wasting this time attending your funeral."

Rising rapidly to her feet, Carrie hugged her tightly. "Me, too, Hester. Thank you for being so kind to me. I'll never forget you."

Hester separated from the younger woman, giving her a dubious look. "Not going somewhere, are you, Carrie?"

Shrugging her slim shoulders, she replied, "I don't know. It all depends on Drew's conversation with your sister."

Both women wanted to press their ears to the curtain separating the kitchen from the trading area, but both had too much pride. Thus, Carrie returned to the table and began to pick at her breakfast.

Drew had come upon Jolie in the large pantry, dragging a feather duster over the shelves and stored goods with a vengeance. Meeting Drew's silent gaze, her eyes narrowed hatefully and her nose lifted in a haughty air. "What do you want?" she shot at him.

"You're a remarkable woman," Drew said, leaning in the doorway and crossing one boot over the other, undaunted by her viciousness. "When you thought Carrie was dead, you feigned sympathy and shame, then when

326

she walked through the door, alive and well, jealousy glared in your eyes. Why, Jolie, can't you try to get along with her?"

Flinging up her arms in mock despair, Jolie continued in her same venomous tone. "Why does life have to revolve around her? We had a happy life on Wills Creek before *she* came along! You had no right to bring her here, Drew, and disrupt everyone's lives! I was not pleased thinking she was dead. But I would be very pleased if she would just go away!" Her declarations became a choking sob. Her palms pressed firmly against her tear-stained cheeks. "Oh, I hate her! Hate her!"

Were it not for her vicious words, Drew would have made an effort to soothe her tears against his shoulder. But to do so would only encourage her obsession, and it would do neither of them any good. Rather than call on his tenderness, he kept a cool tone in his voice and replied, "I will take Carrie to Philadelphia this week. It is the only thing to be done."

His shocking statement immediately halted her emotions. Drawing a deep breath, she knew she had a choice to make: either Drew would remain with the English tart and she would have to accept her, or he would himself go away because of her. Giving little thought to a carefully composed reply, Jolie said quickly, lest she lose the nerve, "You did not allow me to finish, Drew. Though I dislike her immensely, I am willing to get along, for your sake. I could not bear the thought that you would flee Wills Creek because of my dislike of Carrie Sherwood—"

"*Donovan!*" Carrie Donovan!" he shot back in frustration, though he immediately softened his voice. "She is my wife, Jolie. And don't you ever forget it. I demand peace here. If you cannot ensure it, then my wife and I will leave."

Carrie had heard Drew call her name. She moved toward the trading area, pausing before reaching the door which led to the pantry. She saw Jolie's hand move out toward Drew and his arm withdraw from her touch. She stood in the shadows, aware that she had merely heard her name in conversation—though why it was sharply spoken she couldn't imagine—and that he had not called her. She could not very well retreat without detection, and so stood silently by, hoping for the opportunity to ease back into the kitchen.

Though Jolie was willing to meet Drew halfway, she was not willing to completely relent. Throwing herself into Drew's arms so quickly he could not evade the intimacy, she whispered so that only he could have heard, "Oh, Andrew, Andrew, don't you think I would give my right arm for the baby growing inside me to be yours, and not Noble's?" Forcing tears with the talent of an actress, her voice gained in depth as she added, "What a wonderful revelation, Andrew! Your baby . . . your baby growing inside me!"

These last few words were all that Carrie's keen hearing had caught. Her breath stilled as she pressed herself against the wall and watched Jolie firmly embrace her husband, her hands moving smoothly over his broad back. Then, in stunned horror—hardly able to believe Jolie's confession—she turned and fled through the front entrance and toward the peaceful cabin where she had spent her happiest moments with her husband.

Drew turned sharply. "Who was that?"

Jolie had seen Carrie. Her mouth twisted in wry satisfaction as she mentally patted herself for her cleverness. She had deliberately raised her voice so that the wrong impression had been left with Drew's English wife. "It was just one of Hester's children," she lied, flicking away one of the forced tears clinging to her cheek.

Shrugging off her disclosure, Drew returned his attentions to the pretty wife of his blood brother. "So what do you say, Jolie? Are you going to continue to make trouble, or do I have to take Carrie to Philadelphia?"

Jolie pouted prettily, cutting her eyes from Andrew Cynric Donovan. "Oh . . . I'll behave."

"And you'll try to get along?"

She tried her best to be sincere. "I'll try my best."

"Good!"

Drew's hand fell briefly to Jolie's shoulder, but she shrugged it off, even though she'd liked to have enjoyed it lingering there. That she dearly loved Drew did nothing to quell her annoyance with his English wife. She wished she could be in the same room with the two of them when Carrie told him what she had overheard. That she might possibly harbor doubts about the true parentage of Jolie's child filled her with wicked joy.

Carrie threw herself upon the bed and pulled a fat, feathered pillow to her. Hugging it tightly, she pressed her cheek to its downy softness and breathed a most delicate sigh.

The very idea that Drew might be the father of Jolie's child caused pain to grab at her heart. Could he have left her to go to the bed of the pretty, brown-haired woman? The times he had left in the early mornings to hunt, had he actually gone to Jolie?

She wanted to be angry and hurt, to scream her indignation at the very idea of Drew being intimate with Jolie. But she felt empty inside, like nothing in the world could come as a surprise to her after everything that had happened in the past year.

She had to think rationally, to try to picture Drew and Jolie together, embracing, Jolie making the harsh declarations against Drew's shoulder seem plausible. *Your child, Andrew!* Those are the words she had uttered. What else could they mean? Carrie again sighed pensively. She might be young, but she wasn't naive.

Drew had spent ten years on Wills Creek with Jolie. How was she to know what had gone on between them? Had Drew and Jolie been lovers—he and Noble sharing the most attractive unattached woman in the region? But Carrie couldn't imagine either man sharing a woman; they were both too hot-blooded and possessive.

But if Drew had, indeed, taken to Jolie's bed before his last journey to New Orleans, would he have been enticed back to it when they returned to Wills Creek?

Jealousy seethed deep within her. She could not bear the thought of her Drew slipping into Jolie's bed and being the father of the child she was carrying. Closing her eyes tightly, she tried to chase away the green giant gnawing at her heartstrings.

She clutched the pillow madly, trying to remember that she was a lady and that Noble's wife was a vicious troublemaker. For the first time in a long while she found her dear uncle Penley filling her thoughts. Had his unexpected visit with her in-laws gone smoothly? Had they made a good impression on her staid politician of an uncle? But, of course, they had! Cole and Diana Donovan could not possibly leave a bad impression with anyone, even the elite of English society. The two impressive Americans probably had managed to intimidate her uncle Penley just a little.

Thinking of Drew's parents helped alleviate her black mood. She could not wait to see them again and wished they could be at Rourke House when their first grandchild was born.

Rourke House! Now there was an enigma! Drew had told her so much of his family history, how the house had changed names as it had changed family surnames. It had first been Donovan House, then Rourke House, so named by Drew's murdered grandfather, Standish Rourke,

330

so why had its name not been returned to Donovan House? There was a question she would have to put to her husband, when and if this latest circumstance of misfortune was solved.

Speaking of murder, Carrie still puzzled over the gruesome story her husband had told her of his mother's first cousin, the evil Webster Mayne, who had murdered his uncle Standish and hid his dead mother's mummified remains in her private suite for fifteen years so that they would not have to move from the wealthy family estate. She imagined the horror of the simple-minded servant Claudia, taking meals to that dry-rotting suite all those years and never telling—indeed, never even noticing—that her mistress had long been dead. Standish Rourke might have been alive to this day if he had not accidentally discovered the grisly secret the two Mayne men had attempted to keep. What had happened to Webster Mayne? It was one of the greater mysteries to come out of Philadelphia. Because he had not died in the house, the case seemed to be a prime example of evil that did not die easily. But Carrie could not imagine Webster Mayne being any more evil than Junius Wade.

Oh, how desperate she was to avoid thoughts of Jolie! If she was willing to allow Junius Wade to fill her thoughts, she would allow even the vilest invasion into the privacy of her mind. Still, he deserved at least a small measure of thought. She and Drew had both expected him to show up at Wills Creek by now; that he hadn't indicated that some misfortune might have befallen him. She shuddered to think of the gentle Noble and his half-brother dragging the vile man into the currents of the Mississippi, and for the sake of Noble she was glad the act had failed. Bundy could easily come to grips with committing murder, but Noble would surely have allowed it to fester for the remainder of his life . . .

So deep was she in her thoughts that she had not heard

the door open. She had not heard masculine bootsteps or steady breathing obliterate the silence. She started when she felt pressure upon the mattress beside her. Flinging open her eyes, her gaze met her husband's. Her mouth pressed into a thin line. "You could warn me when you enter so that you will not frighten me, Andrew Donovan!"

His eyebrows met in a hooded frown. "Are you angry with me? What have I done this time?"

Should she tell him what she had overheard, or should she allow her own anger to fester? As she held his look, transfixed, she knew she had to make a decision. Anger and jealousy were ugly beasts, but could she tolerate him knowing, once again, that she had eavesdropped, no matter how innocently? Since her thoughts were at odds, she asked, "Did you reach a decision?"

"About Philadelphia?"

"No, about who was really responsible for your revolution!" she retorted sarcastically, moving from the bed with the agility of a tigress. "Of course, about Philadelphia!"

Silence. Drew stood, tucked his fingers into the waist of his trousers, and looked down at her. "Well, aren't you in a mood," he said matter-of-factly. "Shall I go away and come back when you can be more civil?"

Shame rushed upon her. Tucking herself into Drew's embrace, she dropped her head to his chest. "Oh, do tell me it isn't true, Andrew."

She seldom called him Andrew; it was usually a sign that he didn't, at present, stand in her favor. "Tell you what isn't true, Carrie?"

"That you did not sire Jolie's child . . ."

"What?" Surprise forced him to put a breath of space between their bodies. His gaze was a strange mixture of emotions. "Why would you think that?"

"I thought you called my name when you were speaking to Jolie." Shamefully, she dropped her eyes. "I tried to withdraw when I realized you had not meant for me to respond, but . . . I heard Jolie say that—"

"You heard Jolie say that she *wished* I was the father of her child, Carrie. That is what you heard. My naughty little English wife," he said sharply, and yet with an understanding softness. "You are always misunderstanding."

"Then you are saying that Jolie's child could not possibly be yours?"

"Not unless the nature of things recently changed without my noticing. Believe me, Carrie . . ." His fingers rose to gently touch her chin, forcing her gaze to connect to his own. "Jolie has never enjoyed the favors of my body."

Lightly slapping him, she shot back, "Pooh! Drew Donovan! You are an egotistical man!"

"But the man you love, eh, Princess?"

"That I cannot deny." Though she spoke lightly, the frown still sat upon her brow.

"Now, have we put this matter of Jolie and the paternity of her child to rest?"

Her shoulders moved in a childlike shrug. "Let's just forget about it, Drew."

"But *will* you forget about it?"

Managing a small smile, she responded, "I'll try." When she started to walk away, Drew grasped her wrist and pulled her to him. She seemed rigid against him, her eyes dropped and her cheeks strangely pink.

Drawn by his silence, Carrie lifted her face to study his darkly handsome features.

Drew looked deeply into the emerald pools of her eyes. He didn't like what he saw there. "Don't look at me with questions in your eyes, Carrie," he whispered. "You must know how I feel about you. You must know that I would not—could not—take to the bed of another woman. Not after I have known and loved you. Now . . . " Grinning with masculine appeal, he said on a note of finality, "I'll not have my wife suspicious of me, by George! Either you are with me or you are agin me!"

333

Carrie detected his humor. Lacing her arms through his, she gently massaged his strong back. "I would have to be with you, Husband, since I am certainly not agin you! How about you and me . . ." She spoke in the careless American brogue common on the creek, "gettin' this cabin ready for the appearance of our wee one in a couple of months."

"That's a long way off," he remarked.

"It isn't as long off as you might think, Andrew Cynric Donovan. Before you can blink an eye, there'll be a bonny lad or lass lying in that pretty crib you brought from Philadelphia on your last trip."

"But that's for when we get back with our babe, Carrie. We may not be traveling to the city right now, but we *will* go before the babe comes. Time will pass quickly, Princess. Very soon I'll tell you to pack your bags and we'll be traveling eastward."

Two months passed quickly and Carrie's babe did not allow her parents to tell her when it was time to make an appearance but came into the world three weeks before Dr. Edwin Redding had predicted that she would. Hester and one of the women from the Indian village sat with Carrie for the twelve hours it took to deliver her baby. As twilight fell on a warm September evening, Carrie rested in exquisite exhaustion with the cherub-cheeked angel resting in the crook of her arm. Her proud and beaming husband gently sat on the mattress beside them both.

. Drew did not want to downplay his wedding day, but he was almost certain this was the happiest day in his life. The immense pride echoed in his voice as he asked his beloved wife, "What shall we name her?"

She was almost too exhausted to speak. "What would you like to name her, Husband?" After doing all of the work bringing forth the new life, she did not mind assigning this duty to Drew.

Drew touched his index finger to the tiny dimple in his new daughter's cheek, then smoothed the silky ebony locks. As he eased his finger between her tiny ones and they locked firmly around it, he smiled broadly. "Blast, this lass has a grip!"

"Don't swear in front of our daughter," she admonished, managing the smallest smile. "Now, about that name?"

"I knew we'd have a girl," Drew reflected thoughtfully. "It came to me in a dream the other night." His chest swelled with pride; he wanted to take his child and hold her close to him and feel the new warmth of her tiny body against his own. But she looked so natural and sweet lying in the crook of her mother's arm.

"And did her name come to you, also, in this dream?"

"It did." Grinning boastfully, he said, "What do you think of Hannah? Hannah Emilia Donovan?"

Fighting sleep so that she could spend these special moments with her husband and new baby, Carrie looked down into the child's own sleeping face. "Hannah . . . yes, I like it. Welcome to the world and Wills Creek, little Hannah Emilia Donovan."

Kissing her forehead, Drew said, "You get some sleep, mother of my daughter. I shall sleep on the settee tonight."

"Pull it close enough that I might touch you."

While Hester sent her children through the settlement to spread the news of the birth, Drew settled his tall, slim frame on the narrow settee, his fingers lightly touching Carrie's damp, disheveled hair. He could scarcely fall asleep for the excitement of the new life lying peacefully between them and was content to lie quietly on the divan, watching the light fluttering of Carrie's eyelashes as she slept, and the funny little faces made by their infant daughter.

He felt so blessed. Two months ago he had been trying

to keep peace on Wills Creek between two feuding women. Tonight the one he loved lay in exhaustion upon their bed, holding her newborn daughter to her, and the other . . . God only knew how she'd taken the news. Drew did not want to think gloomy thoughts. He wanted only to savor this tender moment, to enjoy the first day of his daughter's life, a day that initiated him into the special order of fatherhood. He felt different—more mature and responsible. From this point on, he had a new life to take under his wing. A year ago he had been an adventurous bachelor traveling by steamboat to New Orleans. Tonight he was a husband and father.

His Carrie was like an angel sleeping so peacefully upon the mound of pillows. Every once in a while she would cradle the child to her in her sleep, then touch her cheek to Hannah's tiny forehead. Occasionally her hand would ease across the pillow where Drew should be sleeping, and a frown would gather upon her brow as her hand met the emptiness. That was when Drew's hand would warmly cover her searching one. She would smile her angel's smile and her fingers would close lovingly over his own.

"I love you," she murmured in her sleep, bringing his hand against her ashen cheek.

"Not as much as I love you, Carrie Sherwood Donovan," he replied. "Sleep peacefully, Princess." Touching his free hand to the plump cheek of his daughter, Drew closed his eyes and forced sleep upon him. He had a lot of boasting to do when the sun came up in the morning.

Jolie was not really sure what she expected of the day, but upon hearing that Carrie and Drew had a healthy baby girl, she cried, screamed, threw things, and cursed the Almighty heavens. Disgusted by her theatrics, Noble left their cabin in pursuit of sporting pleasures. He and Bundy and his recently arrived brother-in-law, Garland Ward, headed north toward the Susquehanna River to do some fishing. Perhaps while he was gone, Jolie would give birth to his child and thereafter he could send her south with her brother. By now he hated the woman almost as much as he loved her.

Autumn would soon be in the air. Already the nights had begun to cool off and Noble was glad they had not waited until the morning to travel. He shifted his backpack and looked behind him on the trail at the tall, thin Garland and his own brother, Bundy, who had decided to ride rather than walk.

The three men had scarcely entered the dense foliage of the forest before Jolie rushed out to the porch, clutching at her huge abdomen and screaming his name. "Noble . . . Noble, you Indian bastard! How dare you leave me like this!" The way Jolie carried on, one would have thought she herself had gone into labor. But she simply needed someone upon whom to vent her anger and frustration. When Hester attempted to coax her up from her knees where she'd dropped, Jolie's right hand flayed the air. "Get away from me, big sister! Your husband encouraged Noble to leave! I am about to spew his Indian bastard and he decides to go fishing! Well, damn him!"

The scornful Hester crossed her arms and tapped her toe, angering Jolie and forcing her eyes to meet her own in something of a sisterly challenge. "You are so pitiful, Jolie," Hester said with all the venom she could muster from her gentle heart. "You have a man every bit as good as Drew and you are chasing him off! I'll be glad to see you go back home to . . ." Hester's words trailed into silence. Perhaps she had said too much. No one had told Jolie the plans made for her to travel to North Carolina with their brother after the birth of her child, and it wasn't her place to say anything. But there had been no

337

need to halt in midsentence. The infuriated Jolie hadn't heard a word she'd said. Exhausted by the heated words, she now solicited her sister's assistance.

"Help me up, will you, Hester?"

Hester firmly grasped her arm. When the two sisters met face-to-face, Hester gave her a small, knowing smile. "Will you be all right now, Jolie?"

"Yes. Not that you would care!"

With a long, deep sigh, Hester turned and sauntered slowly back to the living quarters.

Chapter Twenty-one

Edwin Redding left Lancaster two miles behind him. He moved at a leisurely pace that did not fit the seriousness of his mission and occasionally dismounted his gelding to stretch his legs. He would rather have traveled by carriage or coach but felt that a good horse, even coaxed along at this easy speed, would carry him to Wills Creek quicker than either of his preferred modes of transportation.

He felt sick to his stomach. He'd scarcely eaten a bite in three days and the thought of doing so now almost doubled him over. He wanted to get this ghastly duty over with. He had been to Rourke House, hoping that Andrew and his new bride would be in residence, but they had delayed their journey eastward for reasons not made known to him by the housekeeper, Claudia.

He kept rehearsing in his mind, over and over and over, the news he had to give Andrew Donovan, news he had gotten quite by accident from a patient just arrived from England who'd had in his possession a written account of the tragedy.

Andrew and his wife were expecting a child. Could he dampen their joy with such tragic news? This was the hardest thing he'd ever in his life been required to do.

As he remounted his horse after a fifteen-minute rest,

Edwin tried to put his thoughts elsewhere. Claudia had acted rather strangely when he'd seen her several days ago. He'd thought she had put all her ghosts to rest, but now she had dredged up a new one — Webster Mayne, a man Edwin scarcely remembered, since he had been just a boy when the fire had destroyed the east wing of Rourke House. Why, after all these years, would Claudia start talking about the ill-favored cousin as if he were still alive? She had even answered his knock carrying a tray which she'd said was destined for Webster's private suite.

He remembered how his father, John, had enjoyed taking meals at Rourke House, since Claudia's mother, by his own declaration, had been the best cook in all of Pennsylvania. John Redding had been active in Webster Mayne's downfall on that fateful night the house had burned, and to the day he died he had been adamant that Webster had escaped with his life. If he was alive, then where was he? Could he have voluntarily separated himself from the Rourke wealth for more than thirty years? Edwin had to agree with his Pennsylvania brethren that this was one mystery that would never be solved.

For the remainder of his journey, Edwin tried not to think. He was weary from travel, weak from hunger, and sick at heart. When he eventually emerged into the wide, spacious clearing where the trading post nestled, he sat for a moment astride his horse, his eyes sweeping over the serene, domestic scene. It had been several months since he'd visited this favorite spot of Drew Donovan's. Since his last visit, a wing had been built onto the trading post, probably to accommodate the growing family of Bundy and Hester Duncan. Off to the right were several cabins, and beyond, sheds, barns, and a curing house where smoke, blending with the aroma of pork, swirled into the warm September air. A group of children, including several of Indian heritage, played a game of hide-and-seek while their Indian parents bartered within the trading post. Coaxing his horse ahead, a weary Edwin Redding hoped a nice hot meal might be awaiting him in Hester Duncan's friendly kitchen.

When he dismounted, he was immediately surrounded by Hester's three younger children, anticipating the hard candies he always brought from Philadelphia. Although the trading post carried sweets, the imported English candies especially appealed to the children. As he emptied his pockets into their hands, and into the hands of the Indian children wishing to share in the bounty, Edwin was eventually able to ease between their small bodies and enter the trading post. Immediately he was greeted by the pleasant Hester Duncan.

"Dr. Redding, we weren't expecting you. Are you hungry? I have a nice dinner in the kitchen."

"I am famished," he replied, bringing his palm to his empty stomach. "But first I need to talk to Andrew. Is he about, or has he gone off hunting?"

Hester smiled. "He's at home, sir. His Carrie has given birth to a fine baby daughter."

"Indeed?" Edwin was surprised. "I had expected to deliver Carrie's baby in Philadelphia."

"That wee one wasn't willing to wait until reaching your Philadelphia, Dr. Redding." Hester smiled her biggest smile as she continued. "Andrew is so proud. Except to make his rounds along the creek boasting of his new daughter, he hasn't left Carrie's side. He'll be happy to see you."

Edwin Redding felt that ten pounds of his ample frame had probably been lost in the journey to Wills Creek. Surely he'd be more prepared to meet with Drew and give him the dreadful news if he were not weak from hunger. "I think I'll accept your kind offer of a meal first, Hester, and give Drew a little more time with his wife and daughter." Actually, he dreaded seeing him and having to dampen the joy and elation that a new life brought to proud parents.

Junius was immensely enjoying his recaptured identity of Webster Mayne. During the two months he had secreted himself in the family mansion, with Claudia waiting on him hand and foot, he had managed to gather together many of his personal belongings from the attic, including a favorite pocketwatch that miraculously had survived the inferno, and various other items of jewelry. He basked in the wealth of Rourke House, sunned himself in the day room which had been placed off limits to Claudia's children, and, at night, roamed the grounds and the cemetery, kept immaculately neat against the hedgerow. Ah, this was the life!

Claudia had just brought his dinner tray. He sat at the small, round table and uncovered the dishes one at a time. The simple-minded girl had learned her culinary art well under the tutelage of her mother.

As he ate his meal in silence, he found the tall, imposing figure of Cole Donovan filling his thoughts. He remembered a day many, many years ago when Cole had looked him square in the eyes and said, "God have mercy on your black soul! Because one day I will see you dead!"

His half-mouth smiled its wicked smile. If he had to wait another year . . . or . . . ten . . . or twenty, he would turn the tables on the man who had uttered that threat. Claudia kept him informed on the whereabouts of the family. He knew that his Flame had married the younger Donovan and had spoiled herself with a pregnancy, and that Cole was in Europe with his wife. He was going to strike Cole and Diana where it would hurt the most — at their son. He had escaped justice after murdering his uncle Standish thirty-five years ago and could certainly do so again. He could hide for years in the enormous family mansion with its secret panels and passageways and never be caught.

He had made a list of books to be brought to him from the downstairs library. When Claudia appeared to take down his dinner tray, he gave it to her. He enjoyed ridiculing the simple-minded woman who did not have the sense to realize she was the butt of a joke. "Do you remember a long time ago, Claudia, that you told me you were addlebrained?"

Smiling widely and innocently, Claudia replied, "Aye, that I do, Master Mayne!"

"And are you still addlebrained?"

"Aye, that I am, Master Mayne! More so than ever, or so Tuxford and Mr. Lundy say. Though now . . ." She frowned her disapproval. "I know it isn't such a good thing to be."

"Tell me, Claudia . . ." The servant gave him her full attention. "That oldest girl of yours . . . Liddy, is it?"

"Aye, Master Mayne . . . Liddy. A good girl she is, but blind as a bat. Can't even assist with the household chores."

"Is she discreet?"

Claudia looked at the grotesque man in horror. "No, Master Mayne, she's blind, to be sure, but she has no diseases that I know of."

Rising, fidgeting with the ties of the forty-year-old smoking jacket he had salvaged from the attic, Webster clicked his tongue in annoyance. "I didn't ask if she had any diseases, woman! I asked if she would keep the secret of my being in the house."

"Who is she to tell, sir? She hasn't left this house in the thirty years of her life, even to attend church. She doesn't even go outside."

Webster turned back, his eyes sparkling with ungodliness. "Indeed? I'll tell you what, Claudia. You allow your daughter to be . . . friends with me, and I'll see to it that she always has nice things." After all, he thought, grinning to himself, what was better than a little fun between friends.

"My Liddy would like that, Master Mayne." A thought came to her. "But you've been in this house a few weeks and you've not requested the pleasure of my Liddy's company before. Why is that?"

I didn't know the wench was blind! The hateful response flew through Webster's brain as he recalled seeing the pretty, petite girl feeling her way down the corridor just the day before. Rather, he replied, "It has taken this long to become lonely in my seclusion, Claudia. Would you like your girl to have pretty things . . . and my special attentions?"

With complete trust, Claudia replied, "I'll bring my girl to you. When do you wish to see her?"

His eyes black with lust and greed, Webster pressed his one palm to the windowsill and looked out over the immaculate lawns. "Bring her to me tonight, after I have enjoyed my supper." *And she shall be my dessert!* he thought wickedly.

"Aye, sir. By the way, sir, my brother Tuxford has been asking a lot of questions about that old mare you left at the stable the night he was at the tavern. I obeyed your order not to tell him you were here, but he's been advertising the beast here and about trying to find the owner. What do you suggest I do?"

"Let him ramble, Claudia," replied Webster, his tone flat, "He'll get tired of it and put the beast out of her misery."

"Tuxford would never do that, sir. Tuxford likes the beasts, big and small, better than people, he says. He'll

344

turn her out to pasture, but he'll not put her down."

"Let him do what he will," he replied in that same indifferent tone, thinking, at the moment, that there were better subjects to be discussed than horses. "Meanwhile, you get that pretty girl of yours prepared to keep me company this evening. And . . ." His wicked eyes raked the plump servant's features. "You instruct her to be nice to me, Claudia. You might even ply her with a tad of opium."

Puzzlement pinched her brows. Why should she feed opium to her Liddy simply to prepare her for the master's company?

President James Monroe sat quietly in his office, his fingers linked and his cleft chin resting firmly upon them. The passage of time had not dented his raw-boned physique which, at the age of sixty-one, was still straight and well proportioned. He'd had a bit of a row with Mr. John Quincy Adams, his secretary of state, over the criticisms the cabinet wives showered on his own wife, Elizabeth, renowned for her snobbishness. They were still miffed that they'd been left off the guest list last year for their daughter Sarah's wedding to Samuel L. Gouverneur.

He did not rise when his secretary entered, though he did spin his chair away from the open window through which he'd been absently gazing. "Yes, Boden, what is it."

The secretary was tall and slim, with a needle-thin nose and eyes that appeared much too small for his face. He had a habit of sucking in his bottom lip, a habit the President deplored. "Sir, I happened upon a news article in the *London Times* which has just arrived in the office. I thought you would be interested."

Monroe dropped his linked fingers upon his cluttered desk. "Well, what is it, Boden?" he finally asked.

"An American ship has been lost off the coast of Scotland."

"Indeed? And what is the special significance of this ship?"

"It is one owned by the Donovan family."

"The Philadelphia Donovans?" Monroe shot from his chair as if he'd been stung. The Donovans had been among the very few guests invited to attend their daughter's private wedding ceremony. Monroe very much liked the tall, imposing Scotsman and his beautiful wife, Diana, one of a select group of women his wife considered socially acceptable.

"Yes, sir. The ship's manifest is also printed on the front page."

"Give it to me." Monroe's eyes quickly scanned the list of passengers aboard the ill-fated American passenger ship. Then, dropping the paper from his trembling fingers he mumbled, "My God . . ." His thin, pale eyebrows met in a regretful frown. Raising his hand, he tapped his index finger to his chin. Then, as the secretary turned to discreetly leave his formidable employer to his thoughts, Monroe bellowed loudly, "Send a team of investigators to the Islands right away! I want to know exactly what happened! I want statements from survivors—"

"There is no report of survivors, Mr. President."

Andrew simply could not get enough of his baby daughter. While Carrie bathed, Drew held the sleeping child across his shoulder and spoke to her in a mellow, soothing tone that only a loving father could accomplish. When a light rap sounded at the door, he gently laid Hannah in her crib, threw a blanket over the thin gauze curtain with assurances to Carrie that she was well covered, then answered the call of the visitor. He was shocked to see Edwin Redding standing there, his hands

346

drawn to his hips.

"Edwin, what a pleasure," Drew greeted, taking the man's arm as he stepped out to the porch. "Carrie is bathing. I hope you don't mind sitting out on the porch until she dresses."

"Don't mind a bit," replied Edwin, his tone so flat it alarmed Drew. His voice was naturally alive and jubilant.

"Something's wrong, isn't it?" Drew crossed his arms. "You usually send word when you plan to visit."

Extending his hand, Edwin replied, "Let's sit, Drew."

"No, Edwin . . ." A chill crept through the younger man's shoulders, traveling the length of his spine. Dropping his hand heavily to Edwin's shoulder, he suggested, "Let's talk over there . . . in the privacy of the oak. If you have bad news, I do not want Carrie to overhear."

"I'm sorry, my friend. It isn't good news."

The pending gloom formed an invisible shield around Drew as he moved toward the oak, the shorter man struggling to match his pace. When he reached the massive monument he lifted one hand to his hip and supported himself by placing the other on the smooth bark. "What is wrong, Edwin? Rourke House has burned?"

"No, the house is fine. It's—"

"My bank has closed its doors, then? Our family is bankrupt?"

"The bank is solid, Drew—"

"Then what!" No, dear God, he didn't want to hear it. A horrible feeling grabbed at his heart. He did not want to hear the news that had sent Edwin Redding on this trip, and yet he knew that it was inevitable. Edwin would not have made the long ride and leave without accomplishing his mission.

Momentarily, Edwin Redding, choking back a lump in his throat, said, "It is your parents, Andrew—lost with their ship off the coast of Scotland."

Drew sank heavily to his knees, then battered his back against the bark of the oak where he had played many times as a child visiting a doting great-aunt. He did not feel the pain; dread and disbelief had numbed his body. He clutched at his temples, his eyes closed tightly as if to shut out Edwin's declaration.

At that point, the stocky man dropped to one knee and his hand closed comfortingly over Drew's forearm. "I am so sorry to have to bring you this news, Andrew."

"I don't believe it," Drew murmured, his strength threatened by the hopelessness he felt. "I just don't believe it."

"Their names were on the manifest filed at the docks in Southampton."

His tear-sheened eyes slowly opened. "Have you told anyone else here, Edwin?"

"Of course not."

"Then don't. Carrie is still recovering from the birth of our daughter. I'll tell her in my own way, and when I feel the time is right."

"Damn, Drew!" He immediately softened his knifelike tone. "The only way for Carrie *not* to know is if you carry on as if nothing has happened. Do you really believe you can do that?"

"I must do it. Please . . ." Waving his hand in a display of impatience he did not intend, Drew said quietly, "Leave me alone for a while, Edwin. I . . ." Emotion threatened his voice. "I need to think things out."

As a slump-shouldered Edwin Redding moved toward Carrie Donovan, who had stepped out to the porch of her cabin, Andrew arose as if in a daze and strolled onto the shady trail eastward from the trading post.

Half a mile into the forest—he cared not where his feet carried him—Drew dropped against another massive oak in a secluded spot where he could vent his tears without the need for explanation. His face rested heavily upon his palms as his inconsolable rage and heartbreak veiled the warm September air all around him. Dear Mother . . . dear Father . . . how can this be? You were alive and happy, wanting only to make your trip and take Carrie's good wishes to her uncle, then return and hold your first grandchild in your arms and touch your lips gently to her love-kissed forehead. Oh, how proud you would have been of our little Hannah . . . your little Hannah.

A numb, impenetrable silence enveloped him. He was a boy again, hiding in the forest, dashing about with boundless energy, his high-pitched laughter filling the air and mingling with that of his parents as they searched for him. His father took him fishing and hunting; his mother held him lovingly on her lap in those rare moments that he did not squirm to get free. How staunch he'd been as a boy, wanting only to be a man! He certainly would not have crawled into his mother's lap then! When he had made the transition from a cuddly little boy to a young man approaching adulthood, the transition had often left his mother wishing that she could turn back the hands of time. She had missed the moments he had snuggled in her lap, her darling boy who was her life and her love.

How he wished he could hold his mother near this very minute. When was the last time he had told her how much he loved her? When was the last time he had engaged in a long chat with his father, sharing a brandy and laughing about the old days when the elder Donovan had threatened to take a strap to him?

Had he let them slip away without telling them one last time how precious they were to him?

Tuxford Sanders busied himself around the stables, putting away saddles and tack, scrubbing down the carriage horses, filling feed bins, and gathering the scraps from the kitchen for his seventeen cats. His favorite, an eight-year-old she-cat he called Maisie, always got the best scraps of meat. Putting her aside with her special treat, he knocked a saddle off an unused stall enclosure that had escaped his domestic sweep earlier in the evening.

Slinging the old saddle across his shoulder, he moved toward the tackroom. "Don't know where the blasted mare came from," he mumbled with irritation, "and don't know where you came from, either." He spoke to the saddle as easily as he spoke to his cats. As he found a place for it in the overcrowded tackroom, the saddle cases slipped from their ties and landed in a bundle at his feet. He picked them up so hastily their contents spilled onto the floor.

He began to pick up the items . . . letters to and from a man named Reverend Uriah Wakefield, notes of wedding and funeral services, a well-worn Bible, and a circuit map X'd and marked by days of the week. The map was of the western area of Pennsylvania. How then, had the saddle and mare gotten so far eastward, and how had it ended up in the Rourke stables? Where, Tuxford wondered, was this Reverend Wakefield?

Because of his past record—and the fifteen years he had spent in prison—Tuxford decided he'd better cover himself in the event criminal mischief had resulted in the appearance of the abandoned mare. Stuffing the letters and documents back into the cases, he saddled his favorite horse, tied the cases across its rump, and headed for the constabulary in Philadelphia.

The present constable was a reserved, impeccable police officer who knew Tuxford by sight. He'd often hired the man to perform carpenter chores around his house and had extensively studied his background. Thirty years ago, the gullible young servant had merely fallen in with the wrong person, a wicked, licentious bastard by whom he had been employed. Given other circumstances, Tuxford Sanders might never have ended up the pawn of Webster Mayne.

Constable Thorpe offered his hand when Tuxford entered his small, stone-walled office. "What is the pleasure of this late-night visit, Tuxford?"

Taking a chair before Thorpe's desk, Tuxford slid the saddle cases across his desk, smoothing a path between the clutter of papers. "I have run across these in the Rourke stables, Mr. Thorpe, and do not know where they have come from. They accompanied an aging mare I found penned behind the stables."

"When was this?"

"The mare?" Thorpe nodded imperceptibly. "Late in July, as I recall."

"And why are you just now coming forward?" As he questioned Tuxford, he dragged the letters and other documents from the saddle cases and scrutinized them. "Do you know this man . . . this Reverend Wakefield?"

"I do not . . ."

Suddenly, a memory stirred in the police constable's mind. Dropping the items belonging to Reverend Wakefield, he began scouring among the clutter on his desk, stirring papers, half of which fell to an equally cluttered floor. There it was—correspondence from the Lawrence County constabulary in the village of New Castle, located in the extreme west of Pennsylvania. He hastily reread the letter addressed to the Philadelphia constable's office to refresh his memory.

"August 16th inst.
Sir:
Please be made aware of the murder of Reverend Uriah Wakefield, whose corpse was discovered in the

vicinity of the Alleghany River some miles east of New Castle. Reverend Wakefield was reported overdue on his circuit and an extensive search undertaken. Missing were an aging mare identifiable by a scar on her left shoulder and his personal effects contained in a deer hide saddle case marked with his initials. This office begs your cooperation in its investigation of the murder of Reverend Wakefield, a much-revered gentleman of New Castle and a friend of the Christians he humbly served."

The missive was signed "Edgar Lott, Constable, Lawrence County."

Constable Thorpe slid the single sheet of paper across the desk toward Tuxford. Then, remembering the man's difficulty in reading, briefly related to him the details of the report.

"I am not guilty." Tuxford immediately defended himself, his memories of the fifteen years he'd spent in prison horrifyingly vivid.

"I am aware of that," Thorpe replied. "In the latter part of July, when the crime would have been committed, you were installing a new roof on my house. I would never in a minute have suspected you, regardless, Tuxford. Could Andrew Donovan have brought the mare from Wills Creek?"

"His last visit to Rourke House was before the appearance of the mare."

Thorpe frowned darkly. "We have a mystery here, Tuxford. I shall respond to Constable Lott that the horse and personal effects have been located. I shall keep these items and take the mare into my custody while I await his response."

"I have taken good care of the horse, sir. She was poor and underfed when first she appeared and has gained

352

considerable health. I would beg your leave to allow the beast to remain in my care."

"Very well, Tuxford."

Taking his leave after the required amenities and assurances of his full cooperation, Tuxford mounted his horse and returned to Rourke House. He went straight away to the kitchen where his sister was cleaning the last of the dinner dishes. "Tuxford! Where have you been? You missed a fine supper."

"Claudia . . ." Tuxford approached and picked absently at the remains of the roast she had spent the day cooking. "I asked you once if you knew where that old mare came from, and I ask you again."

Claudia had a way of lifting her chin that made her appear almost childlike. "I told you I don't know," she lied, shrugging her dark-clothed shoulders. "Why are you now troubled about it?"

Tuxford had always been gentle with his sister, but he firmly gripped her arms and forced her to meet his gaze. "Claudia, this is very serious. If you know where the horse came from, you must tell me. If you don't tell me the truth God will punish you."

Her eyes widened in fear. She had always attended her church services, because God was the only thing in the world the simple-minded servant had the good sense to fear. The prospect of being punished by her God sent a shiver down her spine. "He will punish me?"

"If you lie about the horse, Claudia. Yes, He will."

"If that is the way of it, Tuxford, then the mare belongs to Master Mayne."

The big, burly man dropped her arms and fixed her with a grave look. "What do you mean, Master Mayne? Philip has been dead these twenty years."

"Not Philip. Master Webster. Yes, it is his horse. But . . ." Her finger waved in a childlike warning. "I am not supposed to tell that he is here, though I let it slip to Dr. Redding earlier in the week."

Tuxford never ceased to be amazed at his sister's strange declarations. With an indulgent sigh, he replied, "And where is Master Mayne at this time?"

Claudia shrugged with renewed vibrancy. "He is entertaining my poor, lonely Liddy in his chamber."

"Which chamber?"

"The brown room on the third floor."

Tuxford stepped away, then pivoted on the heel of his well-worn boot. He traversed the stairs three at a time and his heavy steps paused just outside the room commonly called the brown room. He tried the door, finding it locked. Then, with a mighty groan and a swift kick of his right foot, the door crashed upon its ancient hinges. There, in the light of the single lamp lay the slim form of his eldest niece, clutching a sheet to her nakedness.

"Who is there?" she called out timorously.

"It is your Uncle Tuxford, Liddy. Why are you here?"

The blind girl had been warned three nights ago when the secret resident of Rourke House had initiated her into womanhood that she was not ever to mention him. As her uncle's heavy bootsteps approached the foot of the bed, she could only slide down deeper into her shame and embarrassment. "I am pretending, dear uncle, that I am awaiting a lover. I am doing no harm."

Tuxford's dark eyes scanned the niches and crannies of the large, masculine chamber. "No one is with you, girl?"

"No, Uncle . . . no one." She silently prayed her uncle would not make a search of the room, which would certainly yield the man who had fled upon hearing the heavy bootsteps in the corridor. She was not sure where he had secreted himself, but wherever it was, Tuxford apparently could not see him. The diffident downcast of her blind eyes did not go unnoticed by her uncle.

354

"What you are doing, girl, is a scandal and a disgrace. I will leave you now. Dress and return to your own room or I'll take a strap to your wicked shame. If you crave a man, I shall find one for you, but don't ever again lock yourself alone in a chamber of this house."

Tears stained the girl's ashen cheeks, her heart pained by the cruel and stinging accusations written upon the words her uncle had uttered. "Yes, Uncle."

Backing into the corridor, his own gaze of disappointment holding the form of his favorite niece, Tuxford quickly rushed from the house.

Liddy was sobbing uncontrollably as the grotesque form of Webster Mayne emerged from its hiding place. "You did very well, girl," he chuckled, pulling back the sheet to roughly cover her body. Wasting no time, he quickly took his pleasure from the one woman who could not be repulsed by his appearance. When she continued to sob, clutching the sheets as he raked her body, he yelled hoarsely, "Shut up, girl, or I'll tear your hide to pieces!"

Infuriated by Tuxford's interference, Webster knew he might prove something of a problem and would have to be dealt with accordingly.

Chapter Twenty-two

Half a week later the news of the Donovans' loss officially reached Philadelphia. On a warm Friday morning, the Lutheran church was filled to capacity with mourners—a few, the locals suspected, attending the memorial service in hopes of seeing the President of the United States, Mr. James Monroe.

Andrew and Carrie Donovan felt sure the minister had done great honor to the elder Donovans, though neither could recall much of the service he had spoken.

Sympathetic exchanges with friends ended none too soon, and Drew eventually stood alone with his wife. "Shall we return to Rourke House, Carrie?"

"Must we, Drew?" She drew in a trembling sigh. "If we cannot continue to stay with Edwin and Cora, then let us collect our Hannah from their daughter and return to Wills Creek."

Drew's dark eyebrows met in a thoughtful frown. "I indulged you, Carrie, when you did not want to stay at Rourke House—and thank God for Edwin's hospitality—but these sinister feelings you are having about the house are very troublesome to me. We had scarcely stepped into the foyer earlier in the week before you were backing out to the carriage. What has happened? You did not feel that way before—"

"Your parents were there," she replied without a moment's hesitation. "No place on earth could have been gloomy with their smiling faces gracing it. I could not bear to stay there without them."

"My parents would not want you to feel that way."

Shrugging apologetically, Carrie met his warm gaze. She had just given him her sweetest smile when an unexpected greeting came their way. "Mr. and Mrs. Donovan . . ."

Andrew Donovan turned sharply to find himself face-to-face with Mr. James Monroe. "Mr. President, how very kind of you to have attended my parents' service."

"I regarded them highly," he said, his eyes cutting to the guards circling him, silently requesting them to give him privacy. "I want you to know, Andrew, that I have sent a team to investigate the sinking of the *Isadora*."

"That is very kind of you." Unconsciously, Andrew brought the black-clothed Carrie into the protection of his arm. "From the information I have gathered, a fire broke out and spread out of control. I have received no evidence of foul play."

"I'll still send that team." Taking Andrew's hand in a gesture of sympathy, then covering it with his other hand, Monroe said, "Elizabeth, too, sends her condolences. She was very fond of your mother."

"And mother was fond of her." Emotion once again became a threat to his composure. As James Monroe withdrew, he took Carrie's hand, gave her a brief smile, then returned to the company of his guards to begin the first leg of his return trip to Washington.

"Were it not for the situation," said Carrie, tugging at the ties of her bonnet, "I might very much have enjoyed meeting your President."

"*Our* President," he softly amended, watching the approach of Edwin and Cora Redding. "Well, my friends,

357

are you ready to be rid of your houseguests?" Andrew was very aware of Carrie's quickly drawn breath and her unspoken apprehension at the prospect of returning to Rourke House. He could not allow her fear to gain strength, and though it went against the grain of his consideration for her feelings, he would have to force the issue. "Carrie and I will return to Rourke House this morning."

Cora's gaze cut to the younger woman's. Though Carrie said nothing, Cora noticed her anxiety. She didn't blame Carrie Donovan for viewing the house with trepidation. It was a drab, dreary place, and too many terrible things had happened there. Its history was black and formidable. But rather than fuel Carrie's apprehension with her own fancies, Cora smiled sweetly and said, "We shall miss you, but we certainly understand your need to surround yourselves with familiarity. And . . ." Her mouth pressed into a thin line as she spoke with mild reproof, "I am very aware that Claudia puts a meal on the table such as Edwin could only dream of appearing on our own."

Edwin cleared his throat. "Now, Cora . . ." he spoke patiently, "I've never said any such thing."

"You didn't have to!" she admonished without true feeling, trying to defuse the sadness of the occasion. "But enough of your nutritional needs, Husband. Let us concern ourselves with Andrew and Carrie, and that darling little girl of theirs."

While her husband exchanged words with their good friends, Carrie studied his profile thoughtfully. Of course she was being foolish not to want to reside at Rourke House. That it was his family home should make all the difference in the world. Why then did an invisible shudder crawl through her spine at the very thought of being ensconced within those dreadful walls?

358

Later in the morning, with amenities nurtured, gratitude expressed, and farewells tendered, Andrew, Carrie, and their infant daughter began the short carriage ride to Rourke House. A very important part of their lives that had been fed and nourished by Andrew's loving parents had ended. Now, they would have to go on with the future.

Carrie might have given her husband a good piece of her mind for making the decision to return to Rourke House had it not been for his profound sadness over the loss of his parents. As she cradled the blanket-covered Hannah in her arms, she watched the dreary house looming in the distance, gaining size and depth, like a giant spider slowly lowering to her face from above. Claudia's husband pruned the bushes running the length of the porch, and Tuxford exercised a horse in a small pen beside the stable. The domestic tranquility did not support Carrie's fear of the house.

Tuxford released the mare and approached when the carriage halted at the stable. He had been absent earlier in the week when Andrew and Carrie had decided not to stay at the house. "I offer my deepest sympathies over the loss of your parents, Mr. Donovan. They were decent people."

"Thank you, Tuxford." Drew alit the carriage, offered his support to Carrie, then politely requested of Tuxford that he bring their bags into the foyer.

With her husband's hand gently holding her elbow, Carrie moved toward the house. As she looked up, though, she immediately paused and drew in a quick gasp of air. "What is it, Carrie?"

Hugging her sleeping child to her shoulder, Carrie replied, "I saw someone at an upstairs window . . ."

"Perhaps Claudia or one of her girls."

"No . . . I am sure it was a man."

"It couldn't have been," he argued firmly. "Both Tuxford and Mr. Lundy are outside."

Tuxford had heard the exchange of words, but before he could respond to the situation, a tall, dark-clothed Noble vaulted from the porch. "Andrew . . ." He ran toward his friend. "I'm sorry I did not get here in time for the service."

As Carrie gave her husband a look of relief, Drew firmly clasped Noble's hand. "It couldn't be helped. I am grateful that you have come."

Noble nodded politely to Carrie. "I came as soon as I returned to Wills Creek and learned of the tragedy. I'll miss them dearly. They were my parents, too — the only ones I ever truly knew."

"I'll go on to the house," Carrie intervened politely, "and leave you two to talk."

"When my wife saw you at the upstairs window, she was alarmed," Drew told Noble. "Everything about this house spooks her."

"I wasn't upstairs, Drew."

A scowl crossed Drew's darkly handsome features. "Then my little wife is seeing things," he replied succinctly. The two men progressed to the house, entered the parlor, then followed the aroma of freshly baked bread coming from the kitchen. A heavy-hearted Claudia, sniffing back tears, had just taken a pan of steaming rolls from the oven.

Overlooking his own sadness, Drew was disheartened by the gloom permeating the house. His parents had lived for each day, enjoying life and taking from it as much pleasure as possible, even in the worst of times. Were they able to look down upon the occupants of the house at this very minute, they would have been disappointed.

"I would be grateful, Claudia . . ." A deliberate vibrancy moved his words, "if you would be so gloomy."

"As you wish, Master Donovan."

"I wish you wouldn't call me Master."

Her shoulders moved upward in a careless shrug as she took plates from the cupboard to fill for the two men. "Forgive me . . . old habits die hard." Putting their meal on the table, as well as a basket of bread and bowl of fresh butter, Claudia moved off to other chores.

Settling down to his first full meal in several days, Drew enjoyed the atmosphere of the kitchen and chatted pleasantly with his good friend. He tried not to think about the tragedy that had struck Rourke House, but that was like asking him not to love Carrie.

The fact that Claudia and her two younger girls had put together a cheerful nursery in the chamber adjoining hers and Drew's suite helped to alleviate some of Carrie's melancholy. The cradle was very old, probably brought to the house when the first Donovan had seen the birth of his little daughter . . . the same little girl from whom Hannah's middle name—Emilia—had been taken. Claudia had sewn lovely sheets, adorning them with cotton lace and pink rosettes, and matching draperies for the one long window. She had gone to considerable lengths to welcome the newest Donovan to Rourke House. Carrie would have to remember to express her gratitude.

She put the sleeping Hannah into her cradle, then propped open the connecting door. She had already tossed her dark, funereal bonnet upon the Queen Anne chair and could not wait to get out of the equally depressing black dress she'd purchased especially for the memorial service.

She had just slipped into a loose, comfortable daygown when an almost imperceptible knock sounded at the door. Calling, "Come in," she immediately turned to face Claudia's oldest daughter, Liddy. She smiled in greeting, her face gaining a crimson hue as she realized the girl could not possibly enjoy the favor.

"Mrs. Donovan?"

Though she looked tired, with shadows beneath her sightless eyes, Carrie noticed how pretty she looked, with her brown hair softly swept back and held by a velvet ribbon. "Yes, what is it, Liddy?"

"Mrs. Donovan, may I see your little girl?"

Remembering all the times she'd fussed over a tiny blemish or a recalcitrant lock, Carrie paled with shame. The woman standing serenely in the doorway had never enjoyed the wonders of sight—or even her own pretty reflection—and yet she had so naturally asked her question. "Yes, come in, Liddy." Carrie closed the distance and offered her support to the pale, slim woman. "I'll take you to her."

Within moments, Liddy's fingers gently traced a path along Hannah's cheek. Her own cheeks became rosettes as she smiled. "Mrs. Donovan, may I hold her?"

"Of course. Come, sit in the chair right here and I shall hand her to you."

Listening to the movements of the new mother, Liddy's arms went out in preparation for receiving the child. When the tiny, warm body came to rest in the crook of her arms, she gently touched her mouth to Hannah's forehead. "Oh, she's beautiful, Mrs. Donovan . . . so very beautiful."

Without warning, tears flooded Liddy's eyes. Carrie dropped to one knee before the woman. "What is the matter, Liddy?"

"Please, forgive me." Liddy smiled sadly as she thought about the man in the upstairs room. Though she could not see, she knew him to be a vile creature. Because of the nature of the man she had to service with her body, she did not feel that she was good enough to be sitting in the same room with the kind Mrs. Donovan, holding her innocent babe in her arms.

"Tell me, Liddy, what is the matter? Has someone in the household hurt your feelings?"

"Oh, no . . ." Sniffing back her tears and regaining her composure, Liddy let the matter drop, knowing the young master's wife was too much a lady to be persistent. "Would it be all right if I sit here for a while and hold your daughter? I'll watch her while you nap, if you like."

Carrie certainly needed a rest, since she had slept fitfully last evening. Covering the woman's shoulder with her hand, she replied, "That would be very nice, Liddy. You'll wake me when she wishes to be fed?"

Liddy managed the tiniest laugh as she shifted the child to her shoulder. "I'm sure she'll let you know that without any assistance from me, mistress."

As Carrie left to go to her suite, Liddy gently rubbed Hannah's back. How dear was this little girl, she thought, as she tried unsuccessfully to put out of her mind the image of the vile, grunting body of her mother's strange houseguest covering her own.

Liddy wanted to die. In her mind revolved the idea of enjoying these precious moments holding the mistress's new baby, then saying her silent farewells to the house where she had been born. How would she do it? she wondered. Plummet from an upper-floor window? Shoot herself? No, she did not know how to load a gun. She knew where her mother kept the opiates. Would that be the easiest way to escape the immoral prison to which her mother had unwittingly condemned her? It was something to seriously consider.

Try as she might, she could not put from her mind her thoughts of that miscreant upstairs. After all, he would be expecting her favors later in the evening and once again she would spend the night in silent tears.

Webster was reasonably sure that Flame had seen him. When their eyes had met; he was also sure that he couldn't have appeared as much more than a blur to her. His heart beat quickly at the thought of Flame being so near. Her new role as a mother appeared to have softened the fire within her that had been his primary reason for purchasing her at the slave auction. Although he did not believe he would return to his former life as Junius Wade, Webster still considered Flame to be his property. He had bought and paid for her, and she was his.

His mind revolved in a mad progression of plans to recapture his stolen treasure. He had no use for the child . . . it was simply a burden to be gotten rid of. And his second cousin—the irascible Andrew Donovan into whose arms Flame had ironically fled . . . he would gain immense pleasure from seeing him die one day.

He enjoyed being the only resident on the third floor of Rourke House; it minimized the chances of discovery. If necessary, he could always flee into the maze of corridors between the walls, though he did not relish the discomfort and cold dampness of those narrow, neglected passageways. He remembered with a malevolent grin on his half-mouth a time when the late Cole Donovan had crept through those connecting stairways to frighten Diana Rourke, the woman destined to become his wife.

Webster had wanted to drive his cousin Diana mad, the only way he and his father could have claimed her inheritance, and he had blackmailed Cole Donovan into entering the conspiracy. His plan had backfired, and he had lost everything, including his hand. But he would not lose again!

Cole and Diana Donovan were now dead. And as soon as he disposed of the rest of the Donovans—except his Flame—he would wallow in the luxury of the wealth that had been robbed from him for too many years. He was Webster Mayne, and he had wasted a lot of good years in the despicable identity of the nobody, Junius Wade.

A knock sounded at the door . . . one rap, then two, then one again—the secret knock of Claudia and Liddy, the only two people who knew he was in the house. He did not worry about Claudia's loose tongue. Because she had been seeing her ghosts for years, no one would believe her if she let it slip that Webster was in the house. As for Liddy . . . she knew what was good for her.

Removing the chair jammed beneath the doorknob—Tuxford had broken the lock when he'd caught his niece in her state of undress—Webster admitted Claudia. She had brought a tray containing a goblet and a bottle of port that he'd requested earlier in the morning.

"What took you so long, woman?"

Claudia set down the tray. "The young master and his wife have returned to the house. I could not get away."

Grabbing her wrist with his one hand, Webster's eyes glared threateningly. "I come first, Claudia! Remember that! My wishes will always come first!"

"Aye, master," she replied, extricating her wrist from his firm grasp. "Is there anything else you'll be needing?"

"Yes. I want Liddy!"

"She's with the young mistress."

"I said, 'I want Liddy!' "

Despite her slow-wittedness, Claudia had begun to think that everything wasn't as it should be with Liddy. Mere companionship should not have made her dear girl so despondent. Though blind and reclusive, Liddy had been reasonably happy. But Claudia could not presume to argue with the master. "Very well, Master Mayne."

His half-mouth twisted into a wry grin as he realized that for the first time in her life Claudia might have allowed a moment of sensible thought to fleet through her brain. She was beginning to suspect that Liddy wasn't *just* a companion. It might be an enjoyable game to see how long it took the simpleton to realize just what Liddy's true role was when she came to her master's chamber. "Go about my orders, Claudia."

Taking short, quick steps, Claudia moved into the wide corridor and turned toward the stairs. Something wasn't right. What was it the master wanted from her Liddy? She felt he was too old to seek the pleasures of a woman's flesh, and poor Liddy was not able to read to him or engage him in a game or cards or backgammon. Did the master just want to talk? But what could an unworldly girl like Liddy say that he might want to hear?

Moving about the house in search of Liddy, Claudia wondered all these things. When she eventually located her daughter in the nursery, she still had not found an answer. "Liddy, does the young mistress know you are here?"

Liddy had heard the familiar footfalls of her mother upon the plush carpet. "Shhh . . . you'll awaken little Hannah. Of course her mother knows I am here."

"You must come with me, Liddy."

The younger woman's face paled. "Why? The mistress said I could sit with her child."

"The master wants you."

A cold chill dropped upon Liddy's thin shoulders. She

shuddered visibly. "H-he wants me now?"

"That he does, girl. You must obey the master."

"But . . ." Rebellion pinched Liddy's mouth. "He is not the master of this house. Mr. Donovan is master, and from this moment on I'll take my orders only from him. In fact . . ." When the child stirred against her shoulder, Liddy softened her voice as she continued to speak to her astonished mother. "I'm going to tell the young master about that old man on the third floor!"

Linking her suddenly perspiring fingers, Claudia countered, "What has the master done to you that has made you so hateful, Daughter?" When Liddy did not respond, her mother pleaded with her. "Won't you at least step into the corridor and discuss it with me?"

"Why not here? Are you afraid Mrs. Donovan will overhear?"

Claudia was surprised by her daughter's show of bravado when she'd always been such a humble, obedient girl. Drawing her hands to her plump hips, Claudia tapped her toe. "Liddy, are you disobeying your mother?"

Touching her mouth gently to little Hannah's warm forehead, Liddy politely replied, "Yes, Mother."

The news Claudia brought Webster Mayne wasn't at all what he wanted to hear. He viciously slapped her face, sending her fleeing from the room in tears. How dare that blind wench disobey his summons!

He had an ache in his groin that would not wait while Liddy's rebellion slipped away. The woman had asked for it. When she came to his chamber tonight—and she had better do so—she was going to beg for mercy!

Meanwhile, he needed to do a little looking about.

The exchange of words between Liddy and her mother did not awaken Carrie. She scarcely stirred in the two hours before Hannah cried in a way that hinted at hunger.

After seeing to her child's needs and leaving her in the care of the gentle Liddy—who was thrilled that Carrie had appointed her private nanny to Hannah—Carrie tidied her hair, changed her clothing, and moved out into the corridor. But an immediate chill crept upon her. Pausing in her journey to the first floor, she looked both ways in the corridor, sure that someone lurked about. Drawing her fingers to the slim column of her throat, the chill crept down her spine and into her legs, threatening her equilibrium.

Suddenly the corridor seemed to darken. She looked at the lamps flickering along the walls; their brightness remained and yet the shadows deepened. It was eerie and frightening and . . .

A hand landed heavily on her shoulder. Crying out, she turned quickly, falling into Drew's arms in her fright. "You just startled ten years' growth out of me!" she accused, pummeling his chest.

"You looked as though you'd seen a ghost," he said somberly. "I thought you'd want to see Noble before his departure."

Surprised, Carrie forgot her moment of annoyance. "He is leaving so soon?"

"Yes. Jolie will deliver any day, and he wants to be there since she is so hostile toward the child. He anticipates trouble when he tells her she will journey to North Carolina with her brother."

"No one has told her yet?"

"Not yet."

"Oh, Drew . . ." Carrie's fingers locked around the lapels of his shirt. "Couldn't we travel back to Wills Creek with Noble?"

His impenetrable eyes glared at her from the shadows

of his dark eyebrows. "Carrie, I have many duties to attend because of the death of my parents. I have to get affairs in order, and that will take a few months. If you will bear with me, I promise we'll return to Wills Creek with the first thaw of the spring."

"Not that long, Drew, please . . ." Desperation colored her words in shades of gray and black. "I couldn't bear it."

Drew was tired of this stupidity! It was simply a house overlooking Philadelphia . . . nothing more sinister than that! "I'll not discuss it further, Carrie. If you wish to return to Wills Creek without me, then go!"

Had she not been so surprised by his lofty declaration, tears of hurt and outrage might have flooded her eyes. When he turned to depart, her hand scooted out to his arm, halting him. "Andrew, I wouldn't leave you. If I have said something to annoy you, I apologize. I hate this house—I'll not say that I don't—but if you remain here, then I shall stay with you. Unless, of course, you want me to go."

His staunch anger suddenly vanished. He turned with such pain in his eyes that it momentarily took Carrie off her guard. "Carrie, I couldn't bear to be parted from you for five months." Taking her in his arms, he warmly massaged her back through the silky fabric of her gown. "Let's not fight. Come downstairs and bid Noble farewell. Then we'll enjoy a peaceful afternoon with our daughter and try not to let the tragedies get us down. Please believe that there is nothing—absolutely nothing!—in this house that could cause you any danger."

Webster had crept through the secret passageway and into a vacant chamber within hearing distance of the two Donovans. He pressed his ear firmly to the door and absorbed every word spoken, every sigh, every assurance spoken by the man to the woman. It was all he could do to keep from leaping into the corridor and prying their two bodies apart. Flame was his property, not Donovan's! Damn them to hell and back!

Webster made a decision at that moment. The Donovans would be in the house for five months. Claudia—and Liddy—were providing him all the comforts his body needed. The blood sport of stalking them appealed to his sense of adventure.

He waited until the two moved down the corridor and he heard their footsteps on the stairs before he crossed over into the nursery. He was amazed at how little the house appeared to have changed over the past thirty years, despite the new furnishings and superficial renovations.

Liddy raised her head as the footfalls sounded on the floor and then were muffled by the carpet. "Who is there?"

Webster stood with his feet apart, his one hand tucked between the buttons of his waistcoat. He looked down on the child sleeping in her crib. His mouth twisted. At least his Flame had birthed a lovely child. "You disobeyed my summons, Liddy."

A pain grabbed in her chest at the unexpected and very familiar voice. "M-master, what are you doing here?" She had been so adamant to tell her mother that he was *not* master, and now she found herself a stammering, trembling fool before him.

"I came to warn you, Liddy, that if you do not come to me tonight, I am going to kill your mother and dump her body between the walls of the house."

Tears flooded Liddy's sightless eyes. She sank heavily into the chair she had vacated just moments ago when she had put Hannah to sleep in her crib. "Please . . .

370

please. Don't say that."

"Will you come to my chamber?"

Fear flooded her. She dearly loved her mother and could not bear the thought of harm coming to her. "Y-yes, I will come to you." She wished she could see his loathsome face so that she could spit in it.

"And do you know what will happen if you tell anyone else I am in this house?" When she did not answer, he continued viciously. "When I hear their footsteps in the corridor, I will flee into the walls. Always I will keep one step ahead and I will come to the rooms occupied by you and your family. I could snuff your lives one at a time, Liddy, and never be caught, so you had better be nice to me. I have made you mine, and you shall remain mine."

Without thinking, she blurted out, "Not if I kill myself!"

"Ah, so that is on your mind, is it? Am I that dreadful, Liddy?" She did not respond, nor did she attempt to wrest her arm free when he grappled for it. "Kill yourself then, girl, and you'll take your mother to hell with you. I promise you that! Now . . ." Liddy knew he was withdrawing, because his footsteps again echoed on the hardwood floor. "Remember what I said . . . and come to me tonight. My bed will be cold without you."

As he departed, Liddy turned, picked up the babe, and held her sleeping body close. Tears rushed upon her cheeks, which she did not attempt to flick away.

There was absolutely no place to hide.

She was a prisoner to the monster on the third floor.

Chapter Twenty-three

Too many strange things happened in the weeks to follow to soothe Carrie's feelings concerning the house. The despondent Liddy suddenly decided she was not competent to serve as nanny to little Hannah and withdrew once again into her own private world, Drew was short-tempered and tired of the constant visits of the Philadelphia constable with his questions about a blasted horse, and Carrie could not shake the feeling that someone—or something—sinister and brooding was lurking in the niches and crannies of the house, nor could she discount the feeling that someone often watched her sleep when Drew was away. That one might be directly linked to the other—Liddy's insecurities and her own constant complaining about the house—had not really occurred to her. She knew only that she wanted to return to Wills Creek.

Noble had made several visits to Philadelphia since the memorial service for Cole and Diana Donovan. In mid-October, Jolie had given birth to twin sons, dark with the Indian blood of their father. Struggling for life, Jolie had died three days later from complications following the difficult birth. Noble, somber and brooding, had still not come to grips with her death. He had loved her, regardless of everything.

Hester, who had just learned that she was expecting her

fifth child in the early summer, now had Noble's two sons to care for. Dora and Cawley Perth had crept off into the night to be secretly married, then had returned to Wills Creek to make their home together beneath the critical eye of Dora's parents. If only she could have waited a year, until she was eighteen, Hester's short letter to Carrie had stated. But they had to make the best of the situation. Ah, young love! Carrie felt she had left her own youth many years behind her. It was this house, blackening her moods just as surely as it blackened everyone else's.

Christmas was only a week away. Leaving Hannah in the care of a new nanny, Mrs. Marwood, Carrie had made several trips into the city to do her Christmas shopping and to visit Edwin Redding's office. She had been concerned for the past two days that she could not nurse her own child, but rather than the remedy she hoped would be forthcoming, Edwin had simply advised her, "These things happen sometimes. Tell Tuxford to purchase a good, healthy cow."

"We have a good cow," she had replied. "Who do you think has nourished my daughter?" She had left his office, disappointed in his inability to "cure" her.

Now she had to go on to other worries. She hoped that the recent loss of Drew's beloved parents and the gloom they were all feeling would not dampen Hannah's first Christmas.

She had extended an invitation to all their friends at Wills Creek to spend the holidays at Rourke House, an invitation that had been accepted. They would have a full house between Christmas Eve and New Year's Day, and Carrie hoped those few short days would chase away all the ghosts and ugly moods. She wanted it to be a festive holiday, and she was going to considerable lengths to make it just that.

Nothing in Carrie's power, however, could have been as instrumental to making it a monumental day as the passengers aboard the French passenger ship, *Luxueus*, slowly narrowing the distance to her berth in Long Island Sound.

Lady Anne had just fed her seven-month-old daughter and put her in the crib. A cold blast of Atlantic air compelled her to stretch a blanket over the cabin door before she set about straightening the mess she'd made in packing their valises and traveling trunks. They were only three days out of New York, their point of debarkation, and she was anxious to begin the last leg of their journey to Philadelphia, the new home of their beloved Carrie.

Anne had just finished packing when Penley entered the cabin, knocking down the blanket she had so carefully stretched there. "What is this?" he asked, humor lacing his voice. Anne gave him a reproving look, because she was sure he would chastise her for being overly cautious where their little Rebecca's health was concerned. She was immediately behind him, restretching the blanket over the doorway.

"Just don't say a thing, Penley Seymour," she gently admonished. "We can never be too careful."

Drawing his wife into his arms, the English lord gave her his warmest smile. "Anne, what did I ever do to deserve you?"

"Deserve me!" She tried pouting but found it terribly unladylike. "I believe I spent most of my younger years just chasing you down, Husband! Now, let us put our efforts elsewhere . . ."

A knock sounded at the door, dull and hollow against the veneer. Penley repositioned the blanket and opened the door to their traveling companions.

Cole Donovan held his cold and shivering wife beneath the protective wing of his arm. "Are you ready to go to dinner?" he asked his newfound friends.

"Come in . . ." Penley outstretched his hand. "Rebecca's nanny has not yet returned from her meal. Come in from that blasted cold."

Rubbing her hands briskly to warm them, Diana soon touched her fingertips to the sleeping Rebecca's temple. "I cannot wait to see our new grandchild," she reflected softly. "If she came on time, she will be almost three months old."

"Or he," Cole softly amended. "It could always be a lad, rather than the bonny lass you'll be wishing for."

"I still cannot imagine my adventurous Carrie being a mother," Penley replied.

"She's a good wife to our Andrew . . ." Diana immediately responded, "and she'll be a good mother."

Sitting beside her husband on a narrow divan, Diana closed her eyes dreamily. It seemed like years since they had sailed for England, disembarked in Southampton, and traveled overland to Holker Hall, only to find that the Seymour family was in France gathering together forces to begin a massive search of America for the missing Carrie Sherwood. Rather than journey on to Scotland, as had been their initial plan, they had traveled instead to France in the hope of halting the preposterous search and to attempt to enumerate to the Seymours the qualities that made their Andrew the perfect husband for Carrie. Diana was glad that they had gone to the effort. The look on Penley Seymour's face when he'd received the news of his niece had been well worth the change in plans.

To this day they did not know of the loss of the *Isadora* off the coast of Scotland and of the unfortunate listing of their names on the manifest. Had the Seymours not journeyed to France, the Donovans would have been aboard the ill-fated *Isadora*.

A happy Christmas reunion with their loved ones was

the only thing on all their minds.

Carrie was sure she'd bought out all the shops in Philadelphia in anticipation of her two dozen expected guests. She especially enjoyed shopping for the children, including her own little Hannah, who was much too young to comprehend the joy of Christmas.

By the time she returned to the house at midafternoon she was exhausted. Her new nanny, Mrs. Marwood, had taken Hannah down to the kitchen while Claudia and her girls were doing the Christmas baking. The nanny had taken to tasting the cuisine as it came out of the ovens, an act Claudia viewed as a compliment to her cooking.

Leaving Tuxford to remove the wrapped presents from the carriage to the parlor where the tree would be erected on Christmas Eve, Carrie went straight to her suite, shed her bonnet and cape, and dropped wearily to her bed. A warm fire burned in the hearth, its golden flames casting dancing reflections upon the cream-colored walls.

Rising just long enough to pull on her favorite bedgown, she might have fallen sound asleep if a sudden pressure on the mattress had not startled her. Drew perched over her, his smile warming as her emerald eyes gazed into his own. "You frightened me, Husband!" said Carrie, drawing her hand up to his shoulder to pull him close, no censure reflecting in her voice. "Have you come to tell me what you want for Christmas, since yours is the only gift I have not purchased?"

Fond reflection sat upon his brow as he said, "I would like for my parents to walk down the stairs on Christmas morning." He had not meant to sadden her, as her lovely features instantly betrayed, and his voice gained inflection. "Since that is not possible, I would like . . ." The merest space separated his mouth from her own, "an early gift — soft, warm flesh and a seductive smile from my fa-

376

vorite girl . . . teasing affection and . . ." He gave her that devilish smile she had not seen in several months, "a good tumble beneath the sheets!"

"Oof, you rogue!" Even as her words were sharp, she returned his smile, linking her fingers around his neck to pull him close. "I thought you would be at your shipping office, Andrew Cynric Donovan. You have been so busy these past few weeks that I did not think you even remembered who I was. Just that woman from your past who might be an aggravating thorn in your future—"

"Thorn? I've thought you anything but that. Now, please me, wife. I've been busy at the office. Tuxford is complaining to the high heavens about the sudden disappearance of that blasted old mare early this morning and I need a little loving care from my favorite darling."

"Well, I've been terribly neglected," she pouted.

Drew's body physically responded to her sensual warmth. He could not resist lowering his eyes to her supple, milk-white breasts straining against the fabric of her satin gown. Tunneling his fingers through the clouds of her flaming hair spread upon the pillow, he lightly covered her slender, womanly frame with his own body. "How about that early Christmas gift, Princess?" he solicited enticingly.

"What do you want?" she teased, walking the fingers of her left hand across his chest, then flicking lightly at his chin. "I'm just an 'umble lass with narry a bloomin' copper in me bosom for a fine lad such as you."

With a throaty chuckle, Drew responded, "I'll take what *is* there, me 'umble lass. It is a better treasure, I'll wager, than a blasted copper."

Continuing her teasing tone, she asked, "Would you like to see?" Arching a dark eyebrow, he took the fingers resting against his chin and tucked one between his lips. He nodded imperceptibly, and Carrie feigned an exasperated sigh. "Oh . . . I don't think so. I'm really not in a mood—"

"Hell . . ." Grabbing her wrists, he playfully pinned them to the bed on either side of her flaming hair. "You're in a mood, all right, my princess. Your lovely body is as hot right now as Claudia's kitchen."

"I beg the comparison!" she laughed, her emerald eyes flickering mischievously, her cheeks rushing with color, and her mouth parting to accept the kiss she hoped would soon be forthcoming. But even as she teased her husband, her lover, she was surprised to find herself slipping into a hungry, magical vortex that knew only one pleasure . . . that of man and woman together, embracing in love and want. His masculine strength devoured her, stirring a river of fire within her, causing a deep, familiar ache to radiate outward, enveloping both of their bodies in the warm nest she was creating for them. Suddenly the sounds of the house were gone . . . the children stirring about downstairs, the servants giving brisk orders—it all flew off with a wind that had ceased to blow.

Drew had captured her face between his gentle hands, her flaming tresses lying like thunderous clouds upon the pillow. Fire leaped through every inch of her slender frame.

Their mouths met in a deep, wonderfully tormenting kiss, frantic and unending, blending the sweetness and the rapture that had set their bodies simultaneously into a raging whirlwind.

His gray eyes darkening, Drew's hand slid beneath her satin-clothed body. Absorbing her beauty and radiance with his love-glazed eyes, he cupped a gently exposed breast in his hand, then teased the hardened crest beneath his searching mouth. Then with a deep, throaty groan he pulled the single tie and swept the scant material down the length of her body.

Had it been weeks or just the day or two since they had last been together like this . . . loving each other with the

378

fervent need of young lovers? A sudden need rippled through Carrie's body as he lingeringly, tormentingly aroused her feminine curves with soft, masterful explorations, his fingers traveling a deliberate path downward with two goals in mind—searing her most intimate flesh with his loving caresses and freeing his own body from the confines of his tight clothing. Both were accomplished almost before either was aware of it.

He lay naked against her, upon her, wrapped around her—his hard-muscled arms imprisoning her, loving and arousing her, his mouth teasing the sweetest kisses from her . . . slowly, slowly—one kiss, one caress, one flaming, erotic move after the other until Carrie thought her body would explode with the sheer want of him.

When at last Andrew could no longer hold back his own riveting need, he eased atop her, braced himself on his elbows and, meeting her passion-glazed eyes, joined to the treasure so willingly offered him.

A tiny moan escaped Carrie's mouth as she accepted his kiss, given at the same moment he took willing possession of her. She could tell how he tried to maintain control, to delay the wondrous torment of their fused bodies so that he could carry her into the blinding world with its magnificent lights, there to enjoy the sweet, consuming passion that rushed through him.

When at last the wild locking and joining of their bodies expanded into rapturous explosion, they lay in exquisitely sweet and consuming satisfaction, trying as they might to catch their breaths.

As their breathing stilled in unison, the sounds of the house slowly came back. They lay together, their bodies entwined, their hearts pulsing at a similar rhythm, their mouths mere inches from each other's, and their sweet breaths blending.

"Damn . . ." Drew spoke the single word in a hushed whisper.

"What is it, Husband?"

"Damn . . ." he whispered again. "If that isn't worth twenty-five dollars, I don't know what is."

Webster Mayne decided to overlook his dislike of the holidays and buy a few Christmas gifts himself. Since it had taken the past four months to have his personal funds transferred from his bank in New Orleans to the prestigious Bank of North America in Philadelphia in the name of Junius Wade, he'd had to make do with his old clothing from the attic and whatever necessities Claudia had been able to afford from her housekeeping fund. Now, not only could he purchase the new and fashionable clothing he had always been accustomed to, but he could buy the frivolous gifts he was sure would please his Flame.

The residents of Philadelphia should have grown used to seeing his face about town by now, and Webster was surprised that reports had not been made to the Donovans of his presence. After all, his was a face that could not be easily forgotten. He was especially surprised that Edwin Redding, whom he frequently visited for his medical needs, had not brought him up in idle conversation. The man was discreet; Webster could not deny that.

Having slipped from the house in the predawn hours, Webster idled away his time about town, waiting for the shops to open. By ten o'clock the town had been all abustle with Christmas shoppers and gentlemen tending last-minute business needs so that holiday leisure could be spent with family.

With the assistance of a kindly and sympathetic shopkeeper, Webster had chosen what he considered the perfect gifts for his Flame. Then he had visited a jeweler on Market Street, who had promised the completion of a custom-made brooch by Christmas Eve. His last stop was a shop specializing in toys for children.

Webster had never enjoyed life more than he had these past two months, living beneath the same roof with the unsuspecting Flame. He was fairly certain he could live like this for whatever years he had left and be perfectly content. By Christmas morning she would know that he was close by. His carefully chosen gifts would be as clear as his handwriting on the wall.

Since he could not return to Rourke House until well after dark when the house was quiet and the man Tuxford at his bed, Webster made rounds at the taverns in and about town. It pleased him to see aging gentlemen he recognized from his younger days but who did not recognize him in return, and to occasionally hear talk of the mystery of Rourke House.

What had happened to Webster Mayne? *He is sitting beside you in this tavern, you ass!* But he said nothing as he curled his half-mouth into a devious smile and leisurely sipped his whiskey.

Caught up in the revelry and mood of the taverns, Webster did not return to Rourke House until well past midnight. He unsaddled and turned the mare into the pen and crept into the house through a cellar entrance. He made his way up the maze of stairs between the walls, and on the first floor, he stirred Liddy from her peaceful sleep by stepping into her small room. She did not scream when his footsteps crunched beside her bed, but when she recognized his voice, her features, in the semidarkness of the room, paled visibly.

"Your master is home, Liddy," Webster announced, viciousness playing upon his tone, "and wanting your attentions." When he slipped back into the secret passageway, Liddy turned upon her bed, dropped her forehead to her arm, and wept gently.

On the second floor, Webster peered into the nursery where Flame's child and nanny slept. He did not have access to the Donovans' suite except from the corridor in the high dark of night so he resumed the short trek to his private rooms on the third floor. He knew that many guests were expected for the holidays but felt reasonably sure none would be housed on the third floor.

His own malice strengthened him and made him look forward, almost impatiently, to the coming days when family and friends would gather together in the spacious parlor below, and his Flame would open the special gifts he had purchased for her.

By Christmas Eve, all the expected guests had flooded the house and settled into their individual accommodations on the second floor of Rourke House. Though it was the first Christmas without his parents, Andrew was making a special effort to join in the holiday festivities. He and Edwin had gone into the forest south of Philadelphia and had cut a twelve-foot tree to be decorated by the children, who were busy making colorful decorations and popcorn and holly garlands to add to the many treasures collected over the past Christmases by the elder Donovans in their worldwide travels. There were brightly colored wooden elves from Germany, a porcelain treetop angel from England, miniature china dolls from Switzerland and paper ones from France, and sachets from Spain, their fragrance long spent on their first Christmas in Rourke House.

Mrs. Marwood found her nursery filled for the holidays with Hester's two youngest, ages four and six, and Noble's two-month-old twins, in addition to her own charge, Carrie's little Hannah. She had asked Liddy to assist her, but she had sullenly and politely declined. So Mrs. Marwood had shrugged her shoulders indifferently and decided to make the best of it. She would, she supposed, be adequately compensated by the Donovans for her extra duties.

That Christmas Eve she packed up her three infant charges in one oversize pram, ordered the two older children to hang on to her skirts, and journeyed downstairs to spend time with the Donovans and their friends from Wills Creek. Edwin and Cora and their two children were part of the gathering, and Mrs. Marwood implored the Redding girl to assist her in her care of the children so that she could be free to sample the dishes.

A fine Christmas Eve was spent on the hill overlooking Philadelphia. Even the recent loss of Cole and Diana Donovan did not veil the gaiety and festivities. Throughout the evening they sang Christmas carols, the children opened one gift each, saving the rest for Christmas morning, and Claudia and her girls had set a buffet feast to be enjoyed by all, family and servants alike. Even Tuxford, renowned for his reclusiveness, joined the family that evening . . . which worked to Webster's advantage. As early darkness fell over the cold evening, he saddled the mare and journeyed into the city to pick up his special purchase from the jeweler. He admired the man's exquisite work . . . the diamond-and-emerald brooch was exactly as he had envisioned.

Returning to Rourke House, he paused on the road when a wagon rumbled near the stable. Hidden in the shade of a fir, he watched a deliveryman unload a barrel of oysters at the kitchen entrance of the house. As the heavy wagon began its return trip to Philadelphia, Webster moved from his hiding place. He enjoyed the solitude of the stable as he unsaddled the mare and turned her into the pen. Then he pivoted back, preparing to creep back into hiding through the cellar entrance.

When a massive shadow suddenly loomed before him, Webster halted. What a time to be discovered, he thought, meeting the glaring, contemptuous gaze of the stableman. "Well, Tuxford," Webster said after a moment, "how did you know?"

If Tuxford was surprised, his face did not betray it. "I did not know it was you, Mayne. I knew only that the mare was gone again, and I was determined to find out who was taking her." As an afterthought, he added, "You're supposed to be dead these thirty years."

"So I understand." As he spoke, Webster's hand rose to the handle of the knife he kept sheathed against his thigh. "What do you propose to do with me now?"

"What am I supposed to do? You are the one who killed the preacher on the river a few months ago. Thirty-four years ago you killed your uncle, and twice you tried to kill Mrs. Donovan. You got off scot-free while I spent fifteen years in prison."

"You call *this* scot-free?" Webster hissed, his only hand raking down the length of his twisted body, then back up again, covering his hideously burned face. "I paid a price far worse than your years in prison." The sounds of many voices lifting in harmony drifted from the house. Webster looked past Tuxford to the parlor window where the candles of the Christmas tree flickered hypnotically against the darkness. His gravelly voice softened considerably as he continued. "Will you ruin Christmas for these people, Tuxford, by dealing with me tonight? I have secreted myself in the house for half a year and I have done no one any harm." All the while he spoke, his fingers flexed nervously over the knife handle. "Come, let us go to your quarters and talk about this."

With only the slightest hesitation and complete, if not foolish, trust, Tuxford moved toward his room in the rear of the stables, followed by the grotesquely disfigured man whose wishes he had once obeyed, without question.

Andrew and Carrie were both disappointed that Tuxford had elected not to remain and enjoy the evening with his family. "I wish he'd stop worrying about that old horse," Drew remarked.

"At least he is gentle toward the four-legged beasts," Carrie reflected, keeping her voice deliberately low so that it would not rise above the singing of the children. "He's a terribly strange man."

"The whole family is strange," Drew was quick to point out. "I had once thought Liddy was the most sensible of the bunch, but even she has been acting in a peculiar fashion. Look at her there . . ." He pointed toward the blind woman sitting away from the others, her eyes lowered and her hands resting limply in the folds of her skirt. "She has not even joined in the singing, and she does have a beautiful voice."

Carrie had certainly been aware of Liddy's somber moods of late. She had at first shown such interest in taking care of little Hannah, had joyfully accepted the position of nanny, then almost immediately had declined it, saying she was not suitable. Carrie wondered if it was something she had said or done, though she couldn't think of anything that might have offended Claudia's eldest daughter.

If Drew had expected an answer to his latest observation, his face did not betray it. He watched the young singers, the corners of his mouth lifted in an admiring smile, and his hands gently and absently caressing Carrie's shoulders between them.

Carrie was happy with her husband and child and all their wonderful friends. She dropped her head of flaming hair against Drew's shoulder and enjoyed the melodic voices of the children and their parents now joining in the harmony.

Oh, if only Cole and Diana Donovan could have been there with them, enjoying the love and devotion of family and friends united, she thought.

Christmas Eve in Rourke House would have been perfect if the public coach from New York had not broken an axle just across the border into Pennsylvania. While repairs had been made, the travelers had spent five long hours enjoying the hospitality of a farm family, and were now less than a half dozen hours away from Philadelphia. They were all tired and wanting only to enjoy warm beds. The Seymours' little girl slept in peaceful exhaustion in the nanny's arms, and Cole had eventually dropped his head against the plush leather seat to catch a few minutes' rest. Diana could not sleep, though; she was much too excited about seeing her family.

They entered their hometown at just past three in the morning. Because Philadelphia was the end of the line and they were the only passengers, the coachman agreed for a price to take them the mile westward toward the house overlooking the sleepy town.

Though excitement flooded her veins as their family home came into view, a sense of dread also grabbed Diana Donovan's heart. She had hoped the months away from the house would have quelled the sinister feelings it produced, but they were even stronger now. Though the bitter-cold wind stung her tender cheeks, nervous perspiration suddenly beaded her brow.

When she shivered, Cole's arm, resting across her shoulder, tightened comfortingly. "Anxious to see our family?" he questioned, unaware of the sinister foreboding guiding the tremble of her slender frame.

Diana was aware that her husband would not want to hear that her old feelings had returned. Quietly, she replied, "Yes," then gave the Seymours a warm smile. "Though it cannot compare to your magnificent Holker Hall, Lord and Lady Seymour, I do hope you'll be comfortable at Rourke House."

"I'd be comfortable in a shabby greenhouse," Lord Penley replied, reflecting the sentiments of both him and his wife, "as long as our dear Carrie was there."

Alighting at Rourke House, where not a single light shone in the enormous structure, Cole Donovan apologized to his guests when the usually prompt Tuxford did not appear from the stable to assist with their trunks. Claudia, however, the only person stirred from the house by their very quiet arrival, opened the front door before Cole Donovan could use his key.

"Shh!" Claudia drew her finger to her mouth and admonished them, much to the surprise of Anne and Penley Seymour who would not have allowed such insolence from their own servants. "Everyone was up late and is sleeping soundly. Master Donovan, you could have had the good graces to arrive earlier with the missus and your ghostly friends."

To the surprised English couple, Diana said, "Forgive Claudia, she has always seen her share of ghosts," and to Claudia, "These people are just as alive as you and me."

"Perhaps *you*," Claudia replied indulgently, "but *I*, Mrs. Donovan, am *very* much alive. Now, do be quiet, sir and madame, and not wake the household."

Again, Diana's eyes cut apologetically to her guests. Entering the house, she excitedly asked Claudia, "Did I have a grandson or granddaughter?"

"A granddaughter," she replied shortly.

"A granddaughter!" she echoed proudly. "What did they name her?"

"Hannah Emilia Donovan, sleeping peacefully in the nursery on the second floor."

"Where?"

"The chamber adjoining that of her parents," Claudia replied brusquely, a little annoyed by the persistent interrogation of mere ghosts. "Now, Mrs. Donovan, you really must retire. We've a busy day ahead of us tomorrow."

"Did you hear that, all? A little girl." Diana drew in a quick breath to still her excitement. "Thank the Lord the children are at Rourke House."

"Andrew is usually here for Christmas." Again Claudia drew her finger to her mouth. "Now, shh, you'll wake the house!"

Indulging the longtime servant her strange ways and leaving the main bulk of their heavy bags and trunks in the security of the stable, Cole directed that Lord and Lady Seymour be shown to the comfort of a guest chamber and the nanny and her charge to an adjoining one. But the four adults could not bear it, as simultaneously they returned to the corridor from their separate suites.

Mrs. Marwood had eaten so much that evening that Claudia had given her a bit of opium to help her sleep. When the four adults crept into the nursery to admire all the babies, then surrounded Hannah's crib, not a breath of movement could be detected.

"She's so lovely," Diana whispered, touching her fingers to the cherub-cheeked child.

"I'll be the first to hold her in the morning," Cole chuckled softly.

"She *is* lovely," Anne agreed, taking her husband's hand to share the proud moment.

Hearing a stir from within the chamber of Hannah's parents, the four adults quickly withdrew to the corridor.

Carrie pulled open the adjoining door so quickly she almost lost her balance. She stared around the large chamber lit by a single lamp, her breathing so heavy she felt weak.

"What is the matter, Carrie?" Drew asked, stirring lightly from his sleep.

"I thought I heard voices," she whispered harshly.

Drew turned on his stomach, and his hand patted the pillow Carrie had just vacated. "Come back to bed . . . it was just the nanny talking in her sleep."

The nanny almost looked dead to Carrie. But no, that was not where the voices had come from. Seeing only the peacefulness of the nursery, she quietly withdrew and returned to bed.

She had a strange feeling that everything wasn't as it ought to be.

The four adults who had barely escaped being caught in the nursery shared parting amenities in the corridor between their chambers, then retired for a few hours' sleep before the dawn.

What a grand and glorious Christmas morning it would be! The elder Donovans thought their separate and yet identical thoughts, resisting the urge to announce, right there and then, their return to their dear Andrew and Carrie.

Chapter Twenty-four

The church bells rang across Philadelphia, signaling the arrival of Christmas Day. The children of Rourke House were up at the crack of dawn, scattered about the tree in their bed clothing, watching the glimmer of the lights against the frosty dawn outside the parlor window and anticipating the treasures their nimble fingers would soon unwrap. Cawley and Dora, scarcely above the age of childhood themselves, held hands and frequently, but lovingly, restrained the excitement of the children, admonishing their impatience as little fingers eased toward wrapped gifts bearing their names.

Spying a large, gaily wrapped package, Dora leaned forward. "Who is this one for?" she asked.

Cawley scooted forward on his knees. "It's for Miss Carrie," he replied. "Prob'ly somethin' fancy from Mr. Drew . . ."

But Cawley had heard Miss Carrie complain about the color green too many times. Knowing how much she detested it, would Mr. Drew have placed his gifts for her in a box of that color? His youthful instincts told him no.

On the second floor, Penley Seymour and his wife had just introduced themselves and their personal nanny to Mrs. Marwood. After they'd fawned over the children for a respectable length of time they left Mrs. Cullen-White to assist Mrs. Marwood, since their Rebecca would comprise a part of the nursery population while the Seymours were in Rourke House. Having arisen early, anxious for their reunion with Carrie, they had just exited the nursery when Carrie entered through another door, missing them by scarcely a second. Seeing four babies in residence, rather than three, Carrie approached the unknown child, a lovely, dimpled blonde who was fretting miserably over the parting of her mother.

Taking her up in her arms, Carrie asked Mrs. Marwood who the child belonged to.

"It is the English lady's," Mrs. Marwood replied, wrapping her shawl firmly about her as she prepared to feed a bottle to one of Noble's twins.

Carrie's mouth puckered. Puzzlement touched her brow. "What English lady?"

Mrs. Marwood was still feeling the effects of yesterday's holiday gluttony. Not only did she look a little ashen, a symptom of her ills, but her memory wasn't up to par. "She told me her name—her and her mister—but I don't remember. An odd name, I recall. But if you'll wait a minute, madame, their private nanny is occasioning the water closet and will be back presently."

"That's all right, Mrs. Marwood. It must be someone my husband invited for Christmas. I'll ask him about it."

Carrie thought it odd that Drew would invite guests he did not first tell her about. She returned Rebecca to her crib, then bent lovingly over the one where her Hannah slept.

Returning to her suite where Drew was just finishing his dressing, she asked, "Did you invite anyone else for Christmas?" then began tugging at the stays of her gown to finish her own dressing as if an answer really didn't matter.

"Not me."

Carrie dragged her fingers through the thick masses of her hair, tugged one last time at the bodice of her blue velvet gown, then turned an admiring eye to her husband. "I would imagine we have an impatient lot waiting downstairs to open gifts," she reminded him, "and if I know Claudia, she'll have hot cocoa and her famous sweetbreads." When he continued to tug at his boot, Carrie approached, knelt before him, and linked her fingers over his knee. "You aren't melancholy, are you, Andrew?"

He smiled sadly. He was, of course, but he did not wish to burden his wife and all their friends and family gathered together for the holidays. He forced a look of contentment over his features and took Carrie's hands between his own. "I'll be wanting some of that cocoa and sweetbread, little wife, because I am famished!"

Together they moved into the corridor, then toward the stairway. After the babies were fed, Mrs. Marwood would tuck them into the pram and bring them to the parlor. Though they were much too small to enjoy the opening of gifts, Carrie wanted them present nonetheless. Christmas was for children, regardless of age.

They had just entered the parlor when Claudia placed a tray of cups and plates on a trestle table. When she pivoted, preparing to return to the kitchen for the other tray, she spied the young Donovans. "You're up. Good," she remarked. "Shall I await the arrival of your parents, Mr. Andrew, before pouring the cocoa?"

He tried not to register shock at her words. Closing his eyes, he immediately regained the moment. He would not let Claudia upset him on Christmas morning. If her ghosts included those of his parents, he did not want to hear it. He also did not want to respond with anger to her innocently delivered question and dampen the moods of the children. "Claudia, you may pour the cocoa now," he said, surprising himself with the temper of his words. "Everyone will be up and about in a few minutes."

"But your parents were late getting in—"

"Claudia!" He immediately softened his tone, restraining the annoyance he felt. There were times that he literally wanted to throttle the woman. "Pour the cocoa."

"As you wish." The servant moved toward the kitchen entrance but soon turned back, "Master Andrew, have you seen Tuxford?"

Absently, he replied, "Isn't he at the stable?"

"No. And he hasn't put sweet feed out for the horses this morning."

"Odd . . ." Drew reflected thoughtfully. "Could he have ridden into town?"

"I don't know why he would." Shrugging as if her brother's absence would remedy itself, Claudia resumed her journey.

Watching her move toward the kitchen, Carrie linked her arm through Drew's stiff one. "She can be so persistent about her ghosts," she said. "Thank you for not letting her upset the day."

"If she hadn't been here most of her life, I'd send her packing without a prayer," Drew immediately responded, turning to favor his wife with a renewed smile. "I'll go out to the stable and feed the horses. It won't take long."

Before he could leave, Carrie wrapped her fingers lightly around his arm. Her emerald eyes lifted to his smoky ones. "Happy Christmas, Andrew Donovan."

Gently, he patted her hands, then drew her into his arms and touched his mouth to hers in the sweetest of kisses. "And to you, Princess."

Moments later, Drew stepped into the brisk December air, immediately wishing that he'd thought to pull on his

393

wool coat. The children were hoping for snow today, but from the appearance of the sky—gray-black and overcast—he imagined they'd get little more than sleet. He moved carefully down the steps, trying to maintain his balance on the thick blanket of ice.

The moment he entered the stable he felt a strange foreboding. These past few days Tuxford had been in one of his better moods and he could not understand why he'd have chosen this time to neglect the horses and his cats that now gathered hungrily and expectantly around his boots. In the next few minutes he threw scraps of meat from a small barrel along a wall for the cats, then began filling the individual bins in the stalls with sweet feed. A gutter from a handpump at the back of the stable routed off into the different stalls; Drew pumped fresh water, his narrowed eyes scanning the perimeter of the building for the missing Tuxford Sanders.

"What're you doin', Mr. Donovan?"

A jolt of surprise enflamed Drew's spine. He spun rapidly to face Cawley Perth. "Damn, boy. Don't sneak up on a thinking man!"

Undaunted by his admonishment, Cawley merely shrugged his shoulders. "What're you thinkin' so heavy about, Mr. Donovan?"

"Tuxford . . . Come with me, boy. Let's check his quarters."

The two men moved toward the large room that served Tuxford Sanders as living quarters. Like the stable, it was immaculate, except for a corner where he'd apparently been working on a torn saddle, the rawhide strips and large needles still lying on the top of a pork barrel serving as a table. The cot where Tuxford slept was still made up, its patchwork quilt carefully tucked beneath two feather pillows. He had not slept there last night.

"Look here, Mr. Donovan."

Andrew turned toward Cawley, who had dropped to his knees on a small braided rug. Drew bent beside him. "What is it, boy?"

Cawley's long, bony finger pointed to a stain on the planked floor. "This here blood, Mr. Donovan?"

Drew touched his fingers to the dark, dry patch. "Could be . . ." Although his instinct was to jump to a dire conclusion, he continued quietly. "But Tuxford's always fixing up a hurt critter, and he's had a fair share of accidents himself."

"But what does yer guts tell you, Mr. Donovan?"

Drew pressed his mouth into a thin line. "I have a feeling this'll be a Christmas we won't soon forget."

Carrie had seen to the preparations of Christmas dinner, then had returned to the parlor to watch the children attempting to restrain their excitement over the Christmas treasures beneath the tree. Small fingers were itching to get into boxes and packages.

"Carrie!" At the sound of a familiar voice calling her name, Carrie turned sharply. She could scarcely believe her eyes. Her dear uncle Penley, and her good friend, Anne stood before her. Attempting to gather together her wits that had blown to the wind, she rushed up from her comfortable seat at the end of the divan and into her uncle's arms. "My girl!" he continued, embracing her warmly. "How good it is to see you."

Carrie laughed and cried in the same moment, hugging them both. "Uncle Penley . . . Anne . . ." She managed to gasp their names between her joyful sniffles. "Dear Anne, how did you manage to talk your father into allowing you to take this trip?"

"He had no say in the matter," the slim woman replied

in between her own gentle tears. "Your dear uncle and I are husband and wife."

Carrie was in a whirlwind of happiness and disbelief. She hugged Anne, bounced about like a joyful child—a glee that caught the children in its exuberance—hugged her uncle, and congratulated them until her words twisted incoherently. Renewed tears came to her emerald eyes when she learned that the new little girl in the nursery belonged to her uncle and his new wife.

"And where is this charming husband of yours?" Penley found the moment to ask.

"He's at the stable feeding the horses."

Just at that moment Drew entered, followed closely by Cawley. Both wore worried frowns. But Carrie seemed not to notice as she proudly invited Drew into her arms. "This is my husband, Andrew Cynric Donovan . . . Drew, my uncle Penley Seymour and his wife, Anne."

"A pleasure to meet you, Mr. and Mrs. Seymour," Drew greeted cordially, taking the older man's proffered hand. He was, of course, surprised by their arrival.

While Anne and Carrie got reacquainted after two long years, Penley urged Drew aside. "I want you to know, young man, that after I met your parents, I wasn't at all worried about my Carrie's choice of a husband."

"You met my parents?" he asked, stunned by the man's declaration.

"Of course. Good people they are. Good people, indeed!"

He spoke of them in the present, rather than the past. "Then I guess you do not know that my parents are—"

"Here is the cocoa!" Claudia interrupted Drew's statement. "Drink it, all, before it grows cold."

"Come . . ." Drew outstretched his hand, glad of the diversion from the subject of his dear parents. He did not want Christmas dampened with gloom. "We'd better

396

enjoy the cocoa before Claudia has one of her usual fits."

Remembering the woman's attitude when they'd arrived that morning, Penley Seymour asked, "Why do you put up with such a servant?"

Drew managed a half smile. "We put up with her because she was born in this house. I'm sure she'll die here, because I am not making her go anywhere."

"In England, we would deal harshly with such insolence."

"This is America, and we put up with a lot." Drew smiled, relaying to the English lord that he was not complaining, merely making a statement.

As Claudia poured the cocoa from a large silver pitcher, Anne spoke up. "Shouldn't we await your—"

"It's poured," Claudia announced, setting the still-steaming pitcher back on a small embroidered towel. "Shall I tell the children they may begin to open their gifts?"

Watching Mrs. Marwood and her own nanny enter with the pram of babies, Anne again spoke up. "But shouldn't we await your—"

Carrie had not meant to be rude when she cut Anne off by announcing, "Yes, tell them to go ahead."

The children, their ears tuned to the adults, released joyful yelps as Dora began passing out the gifts.

Anne merely shrugged her shoulders. Cole and Diana Donovan would just have to miss the excitement of the children opening their gifts.

Diana had not slept a wink since slipping between the sheets of the bed she and Cole shared. She had spent the past three hours listening to Cole's gentle breathing, staring into the darkness of their chamber and seeing horrible, swirling visions that could not gain clarity. The tension was heavy through her shoulders, her eyes wide, and her mind alert. Somewhere inside this house a manifestation of evil was about to make itself known.

She had risen before dawn, dressed in a comfortable day dress, and paced the room, her fingers gently linked. She had pulled her loose hair back into a velvet ribbon, and its wheat-colored locks rested against her back. She wanted only to be with her family, though she would not leave the chamber without Cole at her side. Their reunion with the children was a moment to be shared.

As the sun began to make its appearance this chilly Christmas morning, so began Diana's entreaties that her husband arise. She certainly understood his reluctance, since he had gotten scarcely three hours of sleep. Nevertheless, she wanted him up. There would be plenty of time later for catching up on rest.

Finally, Cole stirred into full wakefulness. Drawing himself up ramrod straight, he stretched widely, then focused his eyes in the semidark chamber. "Blast, is it dawn already?"

"It's past dawn, dreary and overcast . . . a wonderful day!" Diana replied elatedly, "and I am anxious to join our family downstairs." She had heard footfalls in the corridor earlier, and now, dropping to the mattress beside Cole, she heard others—Noble and Bundy, their footsteps disappearing onto the stairway. "Quickly arise, Husband. I am sure I heard Penley and Anne going downstairs a little while ago. I did not want to be the last downstairs, though I think it is now too late to worry about that."

Pulling her into his arms, a very sleepy Cole Donovan whispered, "Lass . . . I'm getting to be an old man. I need my sleep. But . . ." He grinned boyishly, sweeping back his lightly peppered hair, "I'll be a wantin' to see everyone, so give me a few minutes to dress."

Webster Mayne had arisen early in his secret chamber of horror, enjoyed the cocoa and teacakes Claudia had brought him, and had crept into the stairwell between the walls. While there was no entrance into the parlor, he was able to see into the large, brightly lit room through a narrow crack in the paneling of the east wall. His eyes greedily raked over the domestic scene — the children gathered round the tree tearing into boxes and squealing over unwrapped treasures, the reunion of his Flame with people unknown to him who had apparently intruded during the night. His eyes caught the stairway as that blasted blood and half-blood who'd tried to drown him in the Mississippi emerged into the happy scene. There, against the wall, was the large box he had secreted beneath the tree in the dead of night. How surprised his unwary Flame would be! He hoped it produced the proper effect — terror!

He was still irate over the unfortunate circumstances the evening before. If only Tuxford hadn't discovered him! If only he'd stayed in the house with the celebrating family and ignored the disappearance of the old mare. Perhaps if he had, he would still be alive.

After his well-placed knife thrust into Tuxford's back, Webster had tried very hard to dispose of him. He had struggled to get the man's dead body down the steps and into the wide chamber of the cellar, then had found the ground too hard to take the thrusts of the spade. Rolling Tuxford's body against a wall, he had covered him with canvas and left him there to rot. There he lay, dead because he hadn't minded his own blasted business!

Webster looked about the parlor, eventually settling his gaze once again on Flame. He gritted his teeth as his eyes cut briefly to Andrew Donovan before returning to his Flame. How lovely she looked this morning, in her modestly cut day gown of blue velvet, a matching sapphire brooch pinned between her exquisite breasts, her flaming hair long and loose, like puffs of clouds caught by the rays of a brilliant red sun.

"Open your gift, Flame." His rasping voice carried no farther than his own ears. "Surely you did not think you could escape your master."

Chatting pleasantly with the Seymours, and with Noble and Bundy—whose Indian darkness fascinated the English lord—Andrew sipped the steaming cocoa slowly. Carrie nestled softly against him, holding his free hand, her own cup still upon the tray because she was much to excited to drink it.

Penley and Anne were both a little surprised that Andrew had not brought up the subject of his parents. If either of them started to mention their names, he immediately cut them off, bringing up an unrelated subject for discussion.

Occasionally, either Penley or Anne would cut their gaze to the direction of the stairway, expecting the elder Donovans to saunter casually into the parlor. Perhaps it would be a greater surprise without any warning from them. Diana had, after all, said that the children would not expect them back until the summertime.

When the children scattered with their various Christmas treasures and the still-ailing Mrs. Marwood returned to the nursery with her charges and the English nanny, Claudia, joined by her husband and two oldest girls, began sorting through the gifts for the ones bearing their names. Finding one for Mrs. Marwood, Claudia arose with the gift and moved across the parlor. "I'll take this one upstairs to Mrs. Marwood," she announced. Halfway

400

in her ascension of the stairs, she met the elder Donovans. Nodding pleasantly, she said, "Good Christmas morning to you," then continued on her short journey to the nursery.

As Cole and Diana reached the last stair, a sudden hush fell over the occupants of Rourke House. Claudia's husband, on his knees before the tree passing the gifts to his family, widened his bloodshot eyes, his mouth falling open in his shock at seeing the elder Donovans alive.

Watching the faces of his two Indian brothers pale, Andrew, seated with his back to the stairs, felt the same apprehension he had felt moments ago at the stable. His grip tightened, causing Carrie's eyes to lift inquiringly to his own.

Penley and his wife were a little surprised by the reaction of the household to the entrance of Cole and Diana Donovan.

Drew felt the penetrating chill accompanying the expressions of horror and disbelief surrounding him. He gently pressed Carrie to him, watching the direction of Noble and Bundy's dark, moisture-sheened eyes, afraid to turn around lest he see something that would not settle well with him.

Cole and Diana, standing quietly just a few feet from them, were themselves surprised by the reactions of the household. When, at last, Andrew shifted in his chair and his eyes lifted to their faces, they felt they'd done something terribly wrong.

While Carrie, just now seeing them, released a startled cry and brought her trembling hands to her mouth, Andrew rose hypnotically and without expression, drawing himself up to his full height to slowly approach them. He said nothing—indeed, he could not find the words—but stared at them as if he expected them to disappear.

Then, in a scarcely audible whisper, tears sheening his

gray-black eyes, said, "Mother . . . Father?"

That was the all the greeting the elder Donovans needed to lovingly draw their son into their embrace. But he was stiff and unyielding, his eyes glazed more with shock and disbelief than with emotion and happiness at seeing them again.

"My God . . ." Drew could scarcely speak, his emotion was so thick. "I thought you were both dead."

As a happy and very disorganized reunion followed, and loving embraces made the rounds, details of the shipwreck were related to the very stunned Cole and Diana Donovan. No wonder the household had received them as they might the sudden materialization of Claudia's ghosts!

Hugging Carrie to him, Andrew remembered his reply to her when she'd asked what he wanted for Christmas. He had gotten his wish. His dear parents, believed by all of them to be dead, had walked down the stairs on Christmas morning!

Webster was furious. Seeing the faces of the elder Donovans—alive, damn it, alive!—he had moved at a pace far swifter than he'd thought possible and pummeled the walls of his suite on the third floor with his fist until he was sure he'd cracked all the bones in his hand. When the rage had held on, he had beaten the stump of his left wrist against the wall. Not only were the two people he hated most of all alive, but the sticky-sweet reunion being carried on in the parlor had delayed Flame opening his special gift to her. He didn't like his plans going awry!

He wanted everyone to be gone! Those two damned Indians who'd tried to drown him in the river . . . those blasted children giggling over Christmas presents . . .

that damned Liddy who'd evaded him for the past few days! He hated them all! He wanted to be alone in the house with the Donovans! He wanted to go on a bloody rampage and empty the guns he'd ordered Claudia to bring to him over the months from the gun cabinet below—guns he kept loaded and lined up inside the armoire. He wanted to recapture his prize—Flame. She had, after all, cost him fifteen hundred dollars on the auction block.

The rage rose within him like a storm. He paced in a frenzied circle, clutching his fingers through the thin strands of hair across his mottled scalp. The sounds drifting up from the first floor—the sounds of gaiety and laughter and grand reunions—slowly drifted off with what remained of sensible thought. The crazed beast within him knew no control. Quickly traversing the room, taking his loaded weapons up in one swift sweep, he turned toward the exit door.

He halted. No . . . no, he had to be sensible! There was a house full of men who could cut him down without a prayer, no matter how many loaded weapons he had. He could do his fair share of damage beforehand, but what purpose would it accomplish? He might leave a few dead bodies scattered about, including his own. He might leave behind a bloody Christmas the Donovans would never forget. But was he ready to die to accomplish it?

No! If ever there was a time he had to think and act rationally, it was now. Dropping his weapons in a noisy clatter, he moved back into the dark, narrow passageway between the walls.

Dora Perth timidly interrupted the pleasant chatting of the adults. "Mrs. Donovan, may I take charge of little

403

Hannah for the morning?"

Carrie looked up. "If you wish, Dora. But don't disturb her if she's asleep."

The children were playing with their Christmas presents, Cawley had returned to the stable, and Claudia and her twelve-year-old girl were busy in the kitchen, preparing the noontime meal. When a disappointed Dora found Hannah soundly sleeping in her crib—and Mrs. Marwood snoozing lazily upon a spacious bed—she elected to assist Claudia in the kitchen. She did not see the dark, glaring eyes raking the hearth-warmed chamber where the babies slept.

Webster Mayne had crept out to the stable and had saddled the old mare, coaxing her to the fir-shaded privacy of the west side of the house and narrowly missing being caught by that raggamuffin boy he'd heard called Cawley.

He had then reentered the mansion, moved through the passageways staking out the location of every person, and now stood outside the chamber. He had to hurt all the Donovans, and there was only one way to accomplish that.

Mrs. Marwood was snoring upon the feather mattress and the English nanny had slipped into the corridor just moments ago. The babies were all quiet. Slowly pushing open the secret door, disguised by an eight-foot still-life painting of flowers in a vase, Webster stealthily approached the crib of Flame's little girl.

How lovely she looked in her white lace frock, her dark hair curled at the nape and forehead, her cheeks round and crimson, her little fingers tightly clenched in her moment of baby dreams. As he took two woolly blankets from a small table, another baby grunted in its sleep, stirring the nanny. Webster held his breath as the child quieted again and the light breathing of the nanny betrayed her sleep.

He had to act quickly, before the English nanny returned. Even as he struggled to turn the child over with his one hand and ease her into the crook of his other arm, she did not awaken. He bundled her in the blankets, smiled wickedly to himself, and moved back into the passageway of the walls. He had just pulled the door to when the Seymours' nanny returned and began making a head count of the babies.

Her eyes widened in alarm as she found Hannah's crib empty. "Mrs. Marwood?" The lady stirred in her rest. "Where is the Donovan child?"

"Hmm? The twins?"

"No . . . the little girl." The English nanny did not take at all well to Mrs. Marwood's inattentiveness to duty.

Mrs. Marwood's feet shifted to the floor. "Isn't she in her crib?"

"She is not!" While she crossed her arms and tapped her foot in disapproval, Mrs. Marwood toddled toward the corridor. Opening the door, she spied Hester's six-year-old girl passing by with a gaily dressed china doll. "Child, do you know where the Donovan's little girl is?"

The child cocked her head. "Little Hannah?" she asked. "I heard my sister ask if she could take charge of her for the morning."

A moment of relief settled on Mrs. Marwood's features. "And did Mrs. Donovan give her approval?"

"Yes, ma'am," the wide-eyed child replied politely. "My sister was told not to disturb her if she was asleep."

"Then go about yourself, child." Reclosing the door, Mrs. Marwood met the stern features of the English nanny. "It is all right. The girl, Dora, has charge of little Hannah. She must have come in while I was sleeping." When the nanny opened her mouth to scold Mrs. Marwood, the older woman raised a threatening finger. "I always hear the children when they stir. And I'll have none of your scolding, lady."

With that last word she set about waking the twins for their scheduled feedings.

Chapter Twenty-five

Cawley had heard the stirrings of a horse at the west side of the house. Taking short, cautious steps over the ice-coated ground, he just caught the tail end of the beast disappearing into the woodline two hundred yards to the west.

Scratching his head, he wondered if the horse had carried Mr. Tuxford, then turned back to the house. He met Claudia turning onto the stairs descending to the cellar. "Where're you goin', Miss Claudia?"

Drawing her hands up to wipe them on her apron, she quipped, "Help me, boy. The young master wants a bottle of 1783 French port to celebrate the return of his parents and it'll take some hunting." As they moved down the narrow steps, Claudia asked, "Did you and the master find my brother, Tuxford?"

"No, ma'am . . . saw somebody a leavin' to the west, but don't know if it was him." In an effort to avoid the unpleasant subject of the missing Tuxford, Cawley added with a mischievous chuckle, "If my Dora's a helpin' you in the kitchen, you be sure to warn me the victuals she had her hands in so's I can avoid 'em. I'm too young to die, Miss Claudia."

With the tiniest smile, she replied, "I'll do that, boy."

The search began for the elusive port. While Claudia

searched the wine racks, Cawley scanned through the wood crates stacked along the wall. The one lamp Claudia had brought did not emit enough light to make the search easier, and Cawley soon found himself facedown on the hard-packed dirt floor.

"Hell, what'd I trip over?" he grumbled, pulling himself to his knees to study his skinned palm. He had just run his hand down the bulge beneath the dusty canvas when Claudia spoke sharply.

"Found it! Come along, boy." Studying the label of the rare port, Claudia moved toward the stairs.

Shrugging his shoulders, Cawley fell in behind her, forgetting the mystery of the strange bulge—probably just rolls of canvas used to cushion the port in the wine racks, he thought, closing the door to the dark, dank cellar chamber.

The atmosphere of thrill and surprise was settling into a pattern of tranquility in the parlor. Cole and Diana had exhausted themselves telling of their adventures in England and France, adventures embellished by the Seymours. Joined by Edwin Redding, Noble and Bundy had just moments before retired to the outdoors for a game of horseshoes and had excused themselves from participation in the rare port Drew had been saving for a special occasion.

Claudia's shuffling footsteps broke into the gaiety of their laughter. "I've found it, Master Drew, though it was an unpleasant search in that dusty old chamber."

Her tone elicited an apology. Drew was much too content to deny her that. "I appreciate your effort, Claudia," he replied, arising, "and I apologize that you had to go to so much trouble."

Mrs. Marwood entered. She stood silently by, awaiting Carrie's attention. "Yes, what is it, Mrs. Marwood?"

"The girl Dora has little Hannah. It is past her feeding time and I have warmed her bottle."

Carrie was immediately embarrassed in the company of her friends. These past few weeks she had been forced to put Hannah on cow's milk—a necessity Edwin Redding had not been able to explain—and Carrie did not want her family and friends aware of her inadequacy. Pulling Mrs. Marwood aside, she gently admonished her. "There is no need for advertisement, Mrs. Marwood. I'll find the girl and send her to you with my daughter."

Just as Claudia was about to round the corner toward the kitchen, Carrie called to her. "Claudia, will you kindly send Dora upstairs with Hannah for her midmorning feeding?"

Claudia turned and took a few steps into the parlor. "Ma'am? What do you mean?"

Carrie's eyebrows suddenly met in a frown of annoyance. "Just what I said, Claudia."

"But Dora's helping me with the meal preparations. She does not have your little girl."

A gnarl of panic twisted in Carrie's chest, and as the fright settled upon her brow, Andrew immediately responded. "Don't worry, Carrie. Someone has taken charge of her. Claudia . . ." Again, the servant turned, annoyed that she had once again been detained. "Send Dora immediately."

Diana had calmly risen from the divan, and now moved toward the stairs with an equally controlled Anne Seymour only a footstep behind her. As though Drew's assurances were not strong enough, Cole had eased between the two young people and gently clasped Carrie's shoulder. "Do not worry, Daughter, your little girl cannot come to harm in this house."

But Carrie was not so sure. A dread had settled like a lead weight in her chest.

Dora sauntered into the parlor, the tones of the voices

409

surrounding her as unsettling as one of her mother's firm scoldings. Immediately, the adults were swarming over her, causing her to press her hands against her chest to still a sudden tremble.

"Who have you left Hannah with?" Carrie spoke sharply.

"Ma'am? I . . . I didn't have Hannah . . ."

With faltering control, Carrie took the younger woman's shoulders and roughly shook her. "Yes . . . yes, you did. You asked earlier if you could take charge of her."

Because she was quickly losing all control, Drew pried Carrie's fingers loose from Dora's shoulders and pulled her against him. Cole took over the interrogation. "Dora, didn't you have Hannah with you this morning?"

Tears flooded the young woman's eyes as she realized the severity of the situation. "No . . . no, Mr. Donovan. The young mistress said not to disturb her if she was sleeping. I left her sleeping." In an effort to shift the blame, she hastily added, "Mrs. Marwood is the nanny! The babies are her responsibility!"

Of course Dora was right. Cole turned his interrogation toward the silently waiting Mrs. Marwood. "When was the last time Hannah was in the nursery?"

"I tended her at eight-thirty, sir. I left for a moment to occasion the—well, you know—and when I returned, the little one was gone from her crib." That was a blatant lie, meant to cover her tracks. She had been sound asleep at the time Hannah had been taken from her crib. "A child playing in the corridor said that Hannah had asked to take charge of her. Therefore I assumed—"

Losing complete control himself, Cole snapped, "You should never assume, woman! If you cannot be responsible for one wee bairn, then perhaps you should seek another kind of employment."

Mrs. Marwood drew in a surprised breath. "Are you dismissing me, sir?"

410

"I am! But you shall remain in this household until my granddaughter is found! For the time being, you do have other charges, and if they go missing as well, I'll have your hide!"

"Well, I never . . ."

Cole shook his finger in the nanny's face, immediately silencing her. "And you never shall again, madame!"

Webster Mayne had made good time, despite the old horse and a foot of snow covering the ground. He held the child firmly between his chest and his crippled arm and guided the mare on a steady course to the west. He had accomplished his purpose. He had gotten revenge both on Flame and his old nemesis, Cole Donovan! It pleased him immensely that the household was in a panic looking for the child. He was, however, disappointed that he could not be present when Flame opened her gift and realized what had happened to her cherub-cheeked babe. He grinned wickedly. As soon as he disposed of the child, he would return to Rourke House. Since he would be the only person aware of the child's fate, no one — no one! — would touch a hair on his head!

The rocking motion of the horse had put little Hannah to sleep. Well covered by the blankets he had grabbed from the nursery, she was warm and comfortable and did not realize the tremendous loss she had suffered that day. She was too young to be anything but trusting . . . too innocent to sense the danger her third cousin Webster was to her.

As the mare half slid on her haunches into a wide ravine shielded from the winter wind, Webster came upon a stalled wagon. Four harness mares stood grouped together in a roped-off area among the pines, and a nanny goat tied to the disabled wheel of the wagon nibbled on an ample portion of hay. Immediately, the barrel of a weapon emerged from the canvas opening at the back of the wagon. "Who'll be there?" a masculine voice called.

To which Webster politely replied, "A fellow traveler, sir, greatly in need of hospitality."

A heavyset man of about thirty jumped to the frozen ground, steadying his musket as he regained his footing. "What'll you be wantin', mister?" First and foremost in his mind was protecting his wife from the stranger.

Webster dismounted his horse. In the move, Hannah awoke and released a piercing wail. When he heard a woman's voice from within the canvas covering, Webster smiled, the fragments of a plan beginning to form in his mind. He certainly did not intend to cause the child harm. He wanted only to separate her from her parents and her family, for her to live a life as someone else's child and never know her true roots.

"You have a missus, eh, mister?"

The gun slightly rose. "I do."

"Children, eh?"

The young man's eyes had settled on the crying child. "My missus and me ain't got no young'uns. What'll be your interest, mister?"

"I've got a bit of a problem, sir." Turning back the corner of Hannah's blanket, he continued. "I just returned from Philadelphia where I was delivering this orphaned child to her remaining living relative, only to find that the poor woman had died just a month ago. Now I must return to Louisville, and I've no way of providing for the child."

The suspicious young man again raised his weapon. "How'd you manage on your trip *to* Philadelphia, mister?"

Webster had always prided himself on his ability to think quickly, to lie convincingly. "Had a woman traveler destined for that fair city to take charge of the child. You have a goat there, mister. The child needs milk and the goat appears heavy."

412

When Hannah again wailed, a slim young woman emerged from the cover of the wagon. She moved against her husband's side and attempted to see beyond the barrier of the blanket where the crying Hannah lay. "Your child cries with the pain of hunger," she said softly. "My husband will draw milk." Wrapping her fingers around the barrel of the gun, the woman slowly forced it down. "The gentleman will do us no harm, Timothy. He merely seeks nourishment for the child."

When she approached, Webster allowed her to take Hannah from him. "You're very kind," he said, painfully aware of the woman's eyes fixed on the disfigurement of his face.

Lowering her eyes to the distressed child, she asked, "Male or female?"

" 'Tis a female child."

The woman felt beneath the blanket. "She is wet. Do you mind if I change her into something dry?"

"Don't mind," Webster replied. He watched the woman disappear into the wagon, then turned his gaze to the man drawing milk into a tin bowl. Quietly, so as not to disturb his concentration, Webster remounted the old mare. The young husband looked up only when the mare's hooves crunched in the snow.

Instantly, panic rose in his voice. "Where you going, mister?"

Webster nudged the mare into a lope. "Got some traveling to do and no time to waste."

"But . . ." The bowl of milk spilled into the crisp white snow. "What about your child?"

Over his shoulder a snarling Webster Mayne called, "Congratulations. She is your child now!"

Carrie's grief had slowly crumbled into a veil of stunned silence. She was scarcely aware of the approach of Dora,

413

who eased against her and drew her arm across Carrie's shoulder. "It'll be all right, Miss Carrie. We'll find your wee Hannah." With gentle admonishment, Dora attempted to still the rambunctious play of her two young sisters at the Christmas tree.

The little girls, however, had discovered that the lid of the big green box had not been secured. At four and six years of age, they had not yet fully grasped the courtesy of respecting another's property and were awed by the lovely treasures within. The fingers of the six-year-old gently stroked the rich satin bodice of the gown, while the youngest held the expensive emerald-and-diamond brooch to her own simple pinafore.

When Dora realized that her sisters were invading Carrie's Christmas gift, she slipped from the divan and approached them. But she halted what would have been a firm lecture. As she knelt to tidy the contents of the box, she became immediately suspicious of the items: the green satin dress with its low bodice that a lady such as Carrie Donovan would never wear, the expensive brooch spelling out the word "Flame", and a richly carved wooden box. Curiosity compelled Dora to open it. When she saw the lovely porcelain baby doll in a christening gown and bonnet, she snapped the lid shut, gathered up the box and its contents and ran from the house.

A frowning Andrew Donovan stood at the stable with the men, planning a strategy. He would be able to make sense of this strange box of gifts.

Saddled horses stood the length of the stable interior. The men huddled together, talking, gesturing with their hands, occasionally mulling over the suggestions and speculations of one of the men. Dora approached. When Drew took no notice of her, she gently cleared her throat.

Turning, he asked, with mild trepidation, "Yes, what is it, Dora?"

"This was under the tree," she said quietly, "and Mrs.

414

Donovan's name is on it."

He immediately responded, "I have no time for non-sense, Dora."

"But . . ." When he turned away to rejoin the men, her hand went out to tug at his jacket. "Please, Mr. Drew, there's something strange about the contents . . ."

Taking the box, Drew bent to the ground and removed the lid. His gaze flew rapidly over the contents. It was all the answer he needed—Junius Wade was behind the disappearance of his and Carrie's precious daughter. Attempting to regain the moment, he dropped his forehead against the back of his hand.

"What is it, Son?" Cole Donovan kneeled beside Drew and placed his hand on his shoulder.

"The man I told you about, Father . . . the man who pursued Carrie up the Mississippi. He is responsible. Somehow he got into Rourke House undetected. God! Why does the place have to be so big . . . so damned secretive! I've a mind to burn it!"

At that point, Cawley stepped forward. "Mr. Donovan, when I was down in the cellar with Miss Claudia . . ." Immediately, he stopped to think about it. If he voiced his suspicions, the other men would think him a bit daft not to have investigated when the opportunity was his. With that thought in mind, he concluded. "Ain't nothin' but my ramblin', Mr. Donovan. I apologize fer wastin' your time."

Cawley turned and moved quickly toward the rear entrance of the house, then he traversed the narrow cellar stairs toward the dark corner. He wished he'd brought a lantern, for the one small cellar window did not permit clear visibility. Allowing his eyes to focus in the semidark chamber, he scanned the bulge of canvas. Then, with his heart rising into his throat, he bent, slowly folded back the canvas, and stared at the object it covered.

With a hoarse cry, Cawley fell backward, landing full upon his backside. Immediately gathering his trembling legs beneath him, he scrambled across the floor and up the stairs. Moments later, when he stumbled into the group of men, he could scarcely find his voice.

"Why are you so clumsy, boy?" Drew asked with a note of irritation raking his voice.

"M-mister Donovan . . ." Cawley pointed toward the house, then clawed his fingers down the length of his throat, forcing himself to recapture his composure. "In the cellar . . . Mr. Tuxford—dead in the cellar."

At that moment, Constable Thorpe rode up on a dappled mare. He dismounted. "What's the problem here, men?"

Calmly, Drew replied, "You were summoned because my daughter is missing. Now the boy says he found Tuxford dead."

Moments later, the body of Tuxford Sanders was brought up to the carriage house and the family informed. Armed with the news of Cawley witnessing a rider moving into the forest to the west, Drew entered the house, separated Carrie from the other women, and said softly, "We believe we know who has taken our daughter."

Carrie's emerald eyes lifted in hopeful anticipation. "Who? Who, Andrew?"

He had deliberately left the box containing the gifts at the stable. He did not want her to see the items, especially the carved box containing the porcelain doll. Its vicious symbols would only alarm her as it had him. He wished to spare her that agony. "I believe it is Junius. Cawley saw—"

Her eyes widened in horror. "Junius? He has taken our daughter?"

Drawing her to him in a gesture of comfort, Drew's hand gently massaged her back. "Cawley saw a man enter the forest. We are going after him. Promise me, Carrie . . ." He lifted her chin, so that her tear-sheened eyes met his own. He wanted to solicit her promise to be

416

strong, but he knew, looking into her lovely eyes, that he could expect nothing less. She trusted him. And for that, he had to bring back their daughter and place her in her mother's adoring arms. Before he could lose his composure, he touched his mouth to hers in the briefest of kisses and pivoted on his heel, away from her, away from the sole source of his own strength.

Six armed men mounted horses and easily picked up the trail in the snow. Mr. Lundy remained behind with the household of women and children, and to comfort Claudia on the death of her brother.

Their happy day had turned topsy-turvy. There wasn't a single dry eye in the entire household, even the children had melded into the sea of melancholy permeating the rambling old house. Each of the women sought solitude in their separate chambers; Carrie, especially, needed to be alone, to think her private thoughts and worry her private worries without the smothering attentions of the other women.

But her thoughts were scattered, disconnected, refusing to form into a single sensible word or phrase that could distinguish her need for sanity from the darkness of insanity. Her fears for little Hannah were tearing her apart, creating a dreaded vortex of uncertainty, a mother's fears so strong that she was but an empty shell. She was not even a wife; that part of her existence had been separated from her by the winter forest. Where was Andrew? Was he as confused and lost as she was? Did he fear the worst fate had befallen their darling Hannah, and was he even now bringing home her lifeless body?

No . . . no! Carrie linked her fingers and squeezed her palms together until pain shot up through her wrists. No, Andrew would bring their daughter back to Rourke House, back to the nursery where she had been safe and

417

warm and comfortable. No harm could befall their child. She had to believe that . . . believe it with all her might and all her soul. With that thought in mind, she was scarcely aware of her rapid pacing upon the Oriental carpet, and the shadows of the afternoon laying claim to the cream-colored walls and ornate Queen Anne furnishings within the chamber she shared with her beloved Drew. Had only a few seconds passed, or hours . . . two or three or four? The shadows and the failing light indicated that much more time had passed than she could actually account for.

"Flame?"

Carrie Donovan spun toward the single, graveled word spoken from the darkness of the far corner. When she faced those evil eyes and watched that vicious half-mouth turn upward in a smile, she should have pounced and killed. But she was almost relieved by the sight of him. She ran toward him, scattering the box he balanced precariously upon his left arm. "Junius! Junius, have you brought back my little girl?" Carrie's fingers held his lapels with a strength that reflected in her imploring emerald eyes as she awaited his reply.

"Your little girl, Flame? Your little girl will be returned to you when you admit that you belong to me. I paid good money for you, and you belong with no one but me."

Logically, Carrie should have felt the threat of him standing so near, telling her that he did not have her daughter with him, his one hand moving fishlike upon the satin sleeve of her left arm. She should have struck out at him or, at the very least, shuddered in her revulsion of him, but no emotion moved her, not even fear.

Webster Mayne thought how lovely his favorite girl looked, though her blue gown was not as complementary to her fair coloring as the emerald gown she had just knocked from his arm. Slowly, he bent, retrieved it from

418

the floor, and held it out to her. He took advantage of the stunned silence enveloping her, the almost blank look upon her lovely features that indicated sensible thought was far, far away, upon a vast plane that, for the moment, posed no threat to him. He felt that she was in his power, his girl, willing to obey his every command in exchange for the safety of her daughter. She was like a puppet, and he held the strings.

Holding the dress out to her, Webster ordered with insincere sweetness, "Put this on, Flame. I want to see how beautiful you will be in it."

Her voice was childlike as she inquired, "Then, Junius? Then you will bring my daughter to me?"

Junius smiled his wicked smile, his lecherous eyes raking over her slender form. "Of course . . . of course I will, Flame."

The puppet strings were still attached. Slowly, she took the dress from him and turned, her eyes darting over the bedchamber. Her movements were stilted and awkward as she closed the distance to a delicate Oriental divider and slipped into its darkness. Within moments she emerged, in full, emerald bloom, the gaudy yet beautiful brooch spelling out the word "Flame" pinned firmly to the bodice of the scant gown.

Webster's heartbeat all but ceased as his eyes raked over her youthful, feminine form. He had never seen anything so enchanting, so desirable, and so innocent as the vision of her, standing in semidarkness, her senses so far away that she did not even bother to tug at the bodice of the gown scarcely covering her full, supple breasts. Then he outstretched his hand and waited for her slim one to come to rest within it. He liked her this way, trapped in a netherworld by fright for her young daughter, belonging more to him at this very moment than ever before.

Webster Mayne felt that he could never feel safer in this house than he felt right now. He was the only one — save

God and a couple of travelers—who knew where little Hannah Donovan was. No one would be a threat to him. He wielded a powerful force over the household and no one—no one!—would dare threaten his life. If anyone so much as harmed a hair on his head, they would never learn the whereabouts of the Donovan baby.

He was, at long last—and the way it should always have been—the supreme master of Rourke House.

Feeling a deep sadness at the loss of her little granddaughter, Diana Donovan looked in on the tiny residents of the nursery. Anne was assisting the still-sniffling Mrs. Marwood with the feeding of Noble's twins while her own little daughter slept peacefully in her crib. Rourke House was its usual harbinger of creaks and groans and strange noises and voices that seemed to sift through the walls themselves. She could hear children far, far away, beginning again to enjoy their Christmas treasures. Beyond the walls of the mighty house, the few remaining horses stirred in their stables and carriages moved precariously over the icy roads in the distance.

Suddenly, a distinct masculine voice caught her attention, so tormenting, like a twisted memory from days long past, that her heart began to pound violently. She approached the door leading into the chamber shared by her son and daughter-in-law. While the other women tended the business of the nursery, Diana Donovan's sweating fingers closed over the door handle.

The dark stillness on the other side of the door suddenly rushed upon her, and yet a frigid wind seemed to whip all around her, drawing her within. A chill crept through her shoulders and down her spine, despite the thick shawl she wore. As she closed the door behind her, she called gently, "Carrie . . . are you here?" In that same moment, she saw the shimmering green form of her daughter-in-law, then the stooped shadow of the man whose hand gently rested upon her sleeve. Drawing her hand to her slim throat, Diana Donovan felt her shawl suddenly slip away.

Her eyes only then connected to that of the malevolent cousin of her past . . . his small, glaring eyes watching her from the pockets of burned flesh that had once been a gaunt human face. She felt sick to her stomach, scarcely able to gain her bearing enough to cut her attention to her daughter-in-law, standing so still in the shadows of the large room that she might have been an emerald-draped marble statuette. The beauty of the younger woman glowed through the darkness, even as an ashen fear suddenly rushed upon her. At that moment, Carrie's emerald eyes caught Diana's violet ones.

"Well, my dear Diana . . ." The raspy, sarcastic voice once again drew the older woman's attention. "I trust that I have never ceased to bear the distinction of being your worst nightmare?"

Only now did she find her voice. "No, Cousin, you have never lost that distinction. I always knew you would return."

"How astute you are . . . Cousin!"

Diana would never fully understand from where the strength came to approach and draw Carrie away from that black-hearted rogue. She stood just out of touching distance of Webster Mayne, hugging Carrie to her. She felt her shiver; she knew Carrie was paralyzed with fear, both for this evil man and for the fate of her missing daughter. "Where is my granddaughter, Webster?"

The vicious man looked from one woman to the other. How beautiful his cousin Diana had grown in her mature years, her slim loveliness as youthful as he had last seen her more than thirty years ago. She gently held the trembling shoulders of her new daughter-in-law, her violet eyes holding his gaze with feminine bravado. He could see murder in those exquisite orbs. She would like to kill him without prelude—if only she could be assured that such an act would produce her missing granddaughter. But Webster felt safe. Diana was much too smart to threaten the one link to the cherubic child he had taken away from Rourke House that day.

Ah, yes . . . he was definitely master of the house again, and master of their minds, controlling their every movement as skillfully as the most accomplished puppeteer.

Chapter Twenty-six

Seven miles to the west, the hastily organized posse had just come upon Tim Farthingham's stalled wagon deep in a shaded dale. The burly young man dropped an armload of collected wood and retrieved his musket as the mounted men took up positions. He had not only a wife to protect now, but a tiny girl as well.

"What'll you men be wantin'?" he asked the lead man, Andrew Donovan, hoping to conclude whatever business they might have as soon as possible. He couldn't help but notice the similarities between this rider and the older one coming up on his right.

"We're tracking a man," Andrew said, dismounting, the cold of the late afternoon shivering through his shoulders. "A rather conspicuous man—tall, thin, about seventy years old, skin mottled and burned, a missing left hand . . ." Andrew did not see his father visibly shudder at the description.

Tim Farthingham narrowed his eyes, his gaze sweeping over the group of men. "What's he done?"

Constable Thorpe spoke up. "He's wanted for murder, and he kidnapped Mr. Donovan's daughter."

Tim had never seen his wife happier than in the moments she had held the child before putting her down to sleep. He could not break her heart. He and his wife had been unable to conceive a child in the thirteen year of their marriage. If the man Donovan had fathered the child and his wife had given birth to her, then they could do so again. Putting his conscience aside for the moment, Tim replied, "I've seen no one, mister."

Andrew Donovan squeezed the reins so firmly the rawhide cut into his palm. Moisture sheened his gray-black gaze as he attempted to still the emotion choking in his throat. "The child belongs to my wife and me, and we love her very much." He was not sure why he felt compelled to offer that information. "If you see the man we're looking for, I implore you to send word to Constable Thorpe in Philadelphia, or to my home, Rourke House, near there. You will be well compensated for your trouble."

Though Tim Farthingham had lowered his musket, he kept his finger on the trigger. "Sure, mister. If I see the man . . ." Guilt riddled him; emotion had trembled in the man's voice. But he had a choice to make—between his wife and a stranger. "If I see him, I'll send word somehow. Good day."

Although Andrew remounted his horse, he sat huddled with the men, conversing in muted tones, making plans and decisions with the ultimate goal of rescuing little Hannah from the clutches of her kidnapper. Tim Farthingham held his breath, praying to God that the infant within the canvas covering did not choose that moment to wail. When at last the group moved up the hill, he breathed a sigh of relief, then returned to the wagon where the glow of burning coal in an iron pot had warmed the interior.

Scarcely had he allowed the canvas covering to fall before his wife, her hand gently stroking the sleeping child's hair, said, "It is a wicked thing we have done, Husband. I heard the love in his voice when he spoke of his child."

"He can have other children . . . he and his wife!"

424

Tim retorted sharply. "You have proved yourself barren and have given me no offspring."

Though her features remained gentle and kind, a firm accusation sat upon her voice as she replied, "It is sometimes the stallion at fault, Tim, and not the mare."

Without a moment's hesitation, the force of his right palm stung her pale cheek. She staggered from the blow. By the time she dared look again at the place where he had been, he had made a hasty retreat. As the heaviness of his boots upon the crisp snow blanketing the glen echoed toward her, she dropped her face into her hands and gently wept.

Webster was enjoying himself immensely. He sauntered back and forth in the chamber usually shared by Flame and the man who had taken her from him and watched the expressions on the faces of the two women—the older one, her features pale and frightened, the younger one, strangely devoid of expression, as if she were sure she would awaken from a terrible nightmare and find that none of this was actually happening. Diana held Carrie comfortingly, her glistening gaze catching Webster's every movement. Webster could almost see the sequence of events flooding her thoughts as she made her plans to extract herself and her daughter-in-law from the situation.

Webster smiled wryly as he considered the advantage he held over the two women. He knew the whereabouts of little Hannah Donovan. Neither his cousin nor Flame shared that knowledge.

"What are you going to do now?" Diana asked after a moment, the firmness of her voice certainly not matching her trembling within. She felt all aflutter, as if she might faint. "You are a criminal, and you are evil. Our family will not tolerate you on these premises. When my husband and my son return . . ."

"Ah, yes . . . Cole Cynric Donovan. I'll never understand why that troublemaking bastard didn't remain in Scotland. And your son, madame! He'll pay for taking what is mine. He'll pay dearly. Just as I paid dearly when this blasted house singed my hide thirty years ago. Tell me, Cousin, are you not the least bit curious as to how I escaped?"

"I couldn't care less, Webster Mayne," she stated flatly.

He laughed maniacally. "When the floor collapsed beneath me, I was pitched headfirst and half naked into that blasted stream. I saw all of you watching what you thought was my death, and even in my pain I was able to crawl through the shallow waters for two miles before collapsing. I was so badly burned I couldn't even feel the cold when I was found by a Bible-thumping Quaker, whose wife took care of my wounds all the way to North Carolina. Then I was quite rudely deposited on the steps of the Junius Wade Institute for the Mentally Deranged, where I spent two long years before escaping. I had no idea who I was, but I proved my worth by amassing a fortune."

Neither Webster nor the women had heard the door open. Standing against the window at an angle that kept the doorway in semidarkness, Webster was aware of Claudia's presence only when her stocky frame suddenly loomed before him. Because she cut off his view from the two women, he clicked his tongue and ordered viciously, "Get out of my sight, you addlebrained old cow!"

Claudia had a strangely judicious look upon her face belying her usual inappropriate smiles or ridiculously stammered unhinged statements. "You killed my brother," she said quietly. "Poor old Tuxford, who always did your bidding without question. You probably didn't bat an eye when you thrust your dagger into his heart. Who'll feed his cats now, Master Mayne?"

"Blast it, woman!" Webster bellowed, his eyes narrow

426

and black. "I give less than a damn about cats. Get out!"

"Claudia, this isn't the time," Diana intervened.

"But it *is* the time, mistress," Claudia countered in her same soft, dull tone. Without warning, she released a high-pitched scream, then dashed toward Webster with both hands extended in front of her. Before the startled man could react, she had pushed him through the floor-to-ceiling window. Smashed and splintered glass clinked upon the circular drive thirty feet below.

Carrie's senses returned in a rush. She hastened toward the window, Diana close behind her, while Claudia stood to the side, staring in horror at what she had done. When Carrie leaned out the window, Diana's hand clutched her shoulder. "Be careful, Daughter. It is a long drop."

Penley and Anne Seymour, jarred from their solitude in the room to which they'd been assigned just down the corridor, rushed into the room. "What has happened?" Penley inquired, to which no answer seemed forthcoming.

Webster had more lives than the most agile of cats. With his one good hand, though badly cut on the glass, he clung precariously to the windowsill, his spindly legs raking at the frigid air. "Help me! For God's sake, help me."

Carrie attempted to hold fast to his wrist, a difficulty considering the blood flowing freely from Webster's cut palm. She was aware of her uncle Penley's presence. "Help me, Uncle, I cannot get a good grip on him."

As the staid Englishman leaned across the windowsill, his first instinct was to recoil from the grotesque human form hanging in midair. Rather, he managed to get the coarse material of Webster's coat between his fingers. "I'll need you to help me some, man!" Penley bellowed.

Webster looked up at the human faces surrounded by jagged glass clinging to the frame of the window. He knew he could not hold on much longer, and neither

Carrie nor her uncle was able to get a firm grip. He knew he was only moments away from dying. Looking up at his beloved Flame's pale, anguished features, he whispered hoarsely, "Flame, do you wish that I tell you the whereabouts of your daughter?"

Hope fleeted into Carrie's fear-darkened gaze. "Yes, yes—please, tell me."

At that moment, Webster heard the sound of horses emerging from the woods. Aware that the men had returned and he had very little time, he did not avert his gaze from Carrie. He could not have planned his revenge more perfectly. His vicious half-mouth curled into a smile as he said, "Dear, dear Flame, your lovely little daughter is . . ." Smiling his evil smile, he calmly let go of the sill, never cutting his gaze from her own as the collision with the shelled drive crushed the brittle bones of his body.

His last vision in life was of the circle of horses surrounding him, the last sound to reach his ears that of Flame's high-pitched scream of fear that her daughter was forever lost to her.

Ah, what a perfect ending to a less-than-perfect life . . .

People rushed to and fro, half colliding in corridors and rooms before eventually emerging into the freezing December afternoon. The children moved cautiously toward the twisted body upon the circular drive, morbidly drawn to the first evidence of death they'd ever faced.

Carrie did not recall the hasty trip downstairs; she knew only that one moment she had been leaning far out an upstairs window, pleading for news of her daughter, and the next she was on her knees before the man she'd known as Junius Wade, shaking his limp body in a desperate attempt to rouse him. "Where is my daughter, Junius? Where is my daughter?" Then she felt Andrew's hands firmly at her shoulders, attempting to draw her back. Slapping at the intruders in a distraught rage, she demanded, "Let me go, Andrew! He'll tell me where Hannah is if you will all leave us alone!"

Undaunted by her tone, he again attempted to coax her to her feet. "He is dead, Carrie. We will have to find Hannah on our own. He will provide us no assistance." Even as he spoke, Drew was well aware that locating Hannah was a remote possibility. They would have to rely on chance and God, but the chances were that she would not be found alive in this frigid weather. But when he saw his beloved Carrie's face grimace in desperation, he knew he had to give her hope. "Come back to the house, Princess . . ." he ordered, willing his tone to reflect strength, his gaze cutting to his mother in an effort to solicit her assistance. "The men will search the house. There are any number of places he may have hidden Hannah."

His words accomplished their purpose. Hope sparkled in her sea-green eyes. "Do you think she might be nearby, Drew? Oh, do you?"

"There is always a chance," he replied noncommittally, directing his next statement to his mother, "We have had quite a day. Why don't you have Claudia make a tray of tea."

"Claudia!" The abrupt word was immediately followed by Diana Donovan's gaze locking to that of her son. "She is the one who pushed him out the window."

"Son, I need to talk to you." Andrew turned at the sound of his father's voice. "Send everyone to the house."

Hearing the urgency of her husband's voice, Diana took control of the situation. She called the children to her, and they all entered the warm interior of Rourke House.

Only then did Andrew turn to his father, who was on his knees in silence beside the body. Andrew, too, dropped to one knee. "I know he is a hideous sight. Believe me, Father, Junius Wade is — was — every bit as evil as he looks, even in death."

Cole's eyes scanned that hideous form, the twisted arm with its missing hand, the wide-eyed terror in lifeless eyes surrounded by the scarred remains of burned flesh. "Andrew, I don't know who you think this man is, but it is Webster Mayne."

"Mother's cousin?" Drew merely hissed the two words in disbelief.

Cole was morbidly fascinated. His Diana had known all along that this maniac would return to Rourke House! He could scarcely force himself up from his knees when Constable Thorpe brusquely spoke his name.

"Are you saying, Mr. Donovan, that this is the same man who . . ."

Andrew's hooded eyes narrowed. He knew the fear his mother had had for this man. Men had been speculating on the fate of Webster Mayne for more than thirty years. "That is, indeed, what my father is saying," he answered the constable's inquiry. "The man I knew as Junius Wade is, in fact, my mother's first cousin, believed dead all these years. But this news must go no further than our group," he continued, absently watching his two Indian brothers dismount their horses. "We shall bury Junius Wade . . . not Webster Mayne. I'll not have that bastard buried with our family here on the grounds."

The men shared a conspiratorial look. "Let's get the body of" — Constable Thorpe's gaze moved fluidly over the men he had ridden with — "Junius Wade taken care of. Then let's find that little girl of yours."

A thorough search of the house and grounds of the rich estate overlooking Philadelphia failed to yield even the smallest clue as to the whereabouts of Hannah

430

Donovan. By nightfall of the following day, with every settlement, farmhouse, and residence within a twenty-mile radius of Philadelphia searched by the hundred local volunteers, hope for Hannah being found alive slowly diminished.

Two days later the murderous miscreant, Junius Wade, was buried in the pauper's cemetery. Though Claudia was summoned to the constabulary in Philadelphia to give her account of his death, no charges were brought against her in connection with the killing. The constable recorded the act as "accidental" and closed the books on the murders of the Reverend Mr. Wakefield and of Tuxford Sanders. Whatever else the man had done, the devil would see that he paid his dues.

That same morning, Tuxford Sanders was laid to rest in the Donovan family cemetery. His had been a life of unexpected turns. He had once been nothing more than a thug, taking his orders directly from Webster Mayne. Then he had spent fifteen years in prison because of his association with that same man to whom he had sworn his loyalty. Thereafter, he had settled down to life at Rourke House, taking care of the horses and his odd assortment of cats. Ironic that he should have been killed by Webster Mayne thirty years after the latter should have died.

Moving back up the lawn toward the house after the funeral, Carrie tucked her dark-clothed arm through her husband's. Cole and Diana, accompanied by the Penleys, spoke their condolences to Claudia and her family. One way of life was ending; another had to begin.

Carrie, however, knew that her life was at a standstill until her beloved Hannah was returned to her. She would not give up hope, not until someone, somewhere, confirmed beyond all measure of doubt that her daughter was no longer alive.

When they entered the warm parlor of Rourke House,

431

Carrie shed her somber black bonnet and dropped wearily onto the divan. One by one the rest of the family drifted in and assumed quiet places around the parlor.

After amenities and condolences, a shared brunch, and exchanged promises between Carrie and Andrew to never stop looking for Hannah, they departed to their chamber for a few hours' rest before Andrew joined the still-hopeful men to continue the search. The men of Rourke House would be with him; most of the locals had formed dismal conclusions on the fate of Hannah Emilia Donovan.

It had been a long, weary two days since hell had reclaimed the blackest soul of all . . . and heaven had returned to earth—and Rourke House—the purest souls in the form of Cole and Diana Donovan.

But one more little soul was missing . . . and the house would be cold and dark and empty until she was returned to the antique cradle in the nursery with its rose-colored poufs and drapes of the finest gossamer.

Three weeks later, Rourke House returned to some degree of normalcy. After Bundy, Hester, Noble, and their children returned to Wills Creek, and the Seymours began the return trip to their estate in England, the silence within the house was almost unnerving. Carrie spent much of her time within the chamber she shared with her husband, engaging in needlepoint that did not quite have her full attentions. She found herself ripping out more times than her needle actually pierced the fabric.

Cole and Andrew had ridden away from the house every morning, scouring the countryside for Hannah. The last few days they had steadily left later in the morning and returned earlier in the afternoon. Even for the Donovan men, the time was soon approaching when all hope would be declared lost and the search abandoned.

It came as something of a shock when Diana Donovan calmly made her announcement at the dinner table that Thursday evening: "Before tomorrow, you'd better freshen the linens in the cradle. It'll have an occupant."

Drawing in a trembling breath, Carrie fled to her chamber in tears. Andrew, throwing down his napkin, shot to his feet and bellowed, "That is the most vicious thing you have ever said, Mother! How could you hurt Carrie like that!" then rushed up the stairway to comfort her.

Cole, who had only recently forced himself to recognize his wife's gift of insight, gently covered her hand with his own. "Are you sure, lass?"

"I am very sure," she replied, tears sheening her violet eyes. "Our little Hannah will be home well before the hour of noon."

Tim Farthingham had not needed those accusing looks of his wife of thirteen years to realize the cruelty of his actions. He'd spent two days repairing the wagon wheel, then, with men scouring the woods for the infant safely tucked in his care, had beat a hasty retreat toward the Susquehanna River to the west. Travel had been slowed because of the inclement weather, but within days he had managed to reach the outer perimeters of the area being searched. He and Jewel, with their new daughter, had been well out of harm's way before he'd decided to turn back.

That evening they settled down in the same glen where the dark-haired little girl had been handed over to them. It seemed a fitting place to spend a final night with the child they had agreed to return to her rightful parents. They'd had three wonderful weeks with her; now it was time to clear their consciences.

Early the following morning, Tim harnessed the horses and began the last leg of the journey toward Philadelphia. He wasn't sure just how much trouble he would be in, but he imagined the punishment would fit the severity of the crime. Thank God Jewel had a sister living in Philadelphia. When they sent him to jail, she would need someone to take care of her until his release.

His chest tightened as the majestic city against the bay came into view. Halting the horses, he inquired of a traveler walking slowly along the road, "Where might be a place called Rourke House?"

To which the old gentleman replied, "Right yonder through the trees. Ye'll be findin' a road a hundred yards farther on."

Tim Farthingham nodded appreciatively, then flicked the reins at the heavy geldings.

In the back of the wagon, Jewel fed Hannah a bottle of goat's milk Tim had drawn earlier in the morning. The angelic child smiled as she met Jewel's pleasant face, and her little fingers closed over the woman's extended finger. "Soon, oh, so soon, little cherub, you will be back in your mama's arms."

The slush of the roadway soon yielded to the crisp, shelled drive ribboning through the trees. A large, somber brick house loomed against the gray-black sky. As they pulled up to the carriage house, a gaunt man emerged from the darkness.

"What'll you people be wantin'?" Mr. Lundy inquired. "You lost?"

Tim Farthingham pressed his foot upon the brake and tied off the reins. "If this is Rourke House, then I've reached my destination."

"The family's not accepting visitors."

Tim Farthingham turned his mouth up in a half-smile. "Believe me, sir, they'll certainly not turn away a certain young lady traveling with us."

The window where Carrie sat afforded her view only of the rooftops of Philadelphia far off in the distance. She rocked back and forth, paying little attention to the rumblings of her stomach and the nagging little headache she'd had upon awakening that morning. Her needlepoint had fallen to the floor and she had yet to retrieve it. The needle, which she held absently between her thumb and index finger, stabbed lightly at the arm of her chair.

Perhaps it was time to return to Wills Creek. There, at least, she would be able to put the past behind her and make an effort to go on with life. Everywhere she looked in Rourke House, she was reminded her of something unpleasant.

The door opened. Andrew carried a silver tray, upon which sat covered dishes and a crystal vase, into which he'd stuck the only red rose brave enough to bloom in the frigid weather. Placing the tray on a footed table, he approached her, his hand touching softly upon her shoulder. "You did not come downstairs for breakfast and I know you must be hungry."

"I really couldn't eat a bite," she replied, managing the smallest smile as her eyes met his own. "Do you think we might return to Wills Creek soon?"

He had been evading such inquiries from his parents these past few days. Returning to Wills Creek was a final admission of their daughter's death. While they remained in residence, there was always a chance . . .

But there wasn't, he thought glumly. Almost a month had passed since that fateful day their dear daughter had been spirited away by the devil incarnate. If only he could utter the words, "Hannah is dead," perhaps he could come to grips with his grief and go on with life.

Just as he would have answered Carrie's question, a sharp rap sounded at the door. "Yes, what is it?"

Claudia pushed the door open. "Visitors downstairs, wantin' to see the two of you."

"Blast!" Drawing in a breath, Andrew fought to restrain his moment of annoyance. "I told you we are accepting no visitors, Claudia."

"The gentleman and his lady insist." Claudia smiled. "I really believe you should see them, young Master Andrew."

"Blast," he mumbled again, sweeping back his dark hair as his eyes cut to the silent Carrie, "I'll be rid of these pesky intruders and return shortly. We'll share a brunch."

Before he moved from her, Carrie took his hand and held it gently. Linking her fingers through his, she brought it in a tender caress against her cheek. "I love you," she whispered, her smile as sad as any he'd ever witnessed.

His ample mouth touched her forehead. "And I love you, Carrie Sherwood Donovan."

The door closed behind him. In that last, full glimpse of him, Carrie was sure of one thing . . . their love would endure, even when life was its bleakest.

Diana Donovan must have been awaiting the departure of her son from the chamber he shared with Carrie. Only a few moments had passed when she gently knocked at the door, then entered. "Carrie, are you all right?"

Carrie was still a little upset with her mother-in-law. She'd been unnecessarily cruel at dinner the night before, and Carrie had yet to forgive her. "I just needed the solitude," she replied a little more curtly than she'd intended, hoping that her tone would keep Diana's visit short. "Andrew is rushing away uninvited guests and will return in a moment." Rising to her feet, she upset her basket of threads and sewing notions. "Oh, dear . . ."

Bending to retrieve the items gave Diana a moment to

436

study her melancholy young daughter-in-law. She wished that Carrie's uncle Penley and his new wife might have stayed longer, in view of the circumstances, but Diana had understood Penley's need to return to home and business. In the days of turmoil and trial so recently in their past, Penley's long walks with Carrie on the frigid grounds of Rourke House had been a tremendous comfort to her when all their other efforts had failed. He had been able to give her hope, when it had been all but lost.

Carrie righted the basket of notions, retrieved her fallen needlepoint in its wood hoop, and dropped it, too, into the basket. Then she approached the tray Andrew had brought. "Would you care for tea, Mother?" she asked, pouring herself a cup while she awaited Diana's reply.

The tension was thick between them. Diana was almost certain Carrie, whose eyes had suddenly darkened, would any moment voice her dismay and disapproval of Diana's visit to her chamber. But just as the words might have been spoken, Andrew's roll of laughter reverberated through the corridors of the great house and caught their attention.

"What is this?" Carrie turned, shock, bewilderment and anger reflecting in her gaze as she looked at her mother-in-law. "How can he laugh? How can he be happy when we have suffered such a tragic loss?" Even as she spoke, her father-in-law's deep, resonant laughter joined that of his son in the parlor downstairs.

Carrie was furious and hurt and determined to stop any show of merriment in the gloomy old house. She paid no attention when Diana suggested, "Carrie, don't be so quick to condemn," but hastened into the corridor and down the stairs.

Her attention was first distracted by the beaming Claudia, then by the timid young man and woman seated together on the divan. She fought to control her rioting feelings; how could the Donovan men be so happy? She might have been a riled bull, so angry was she as she charged past Claudia and the strangers and into the brightly lit parlor where the maddening laughter instantly faded into silence.

Her body suddenly trembling, Carrie took a frantic step, unable to fully fathom the sight of the cherub-cheeked child being juggled between the two men. When she was sure that her legs would melt like molten lead from beneath her, she turned, rushed into Diana's arms, and held her tightly. "Please . . . please tell me, Mother, that I have not gone mad."

The brightness of the crystal chandelier was suddenly magnified by the moisture sheening Diana's exquisite violet eyes. "Dear, dear Daughter, you have not gone mad. Truly, you have not."

Their two men surrounded them, and the precious little one, whose loss had broken her young parents' hearts, found her way into her mother's trembling arms. Carrie crushed the babe to her, laughing and crying in the same moment, and was scarcely able to lend strength to her legs long enough to find a comfortable place on the divan.

"Oh, Hannah . . . Hannah . . ." Carrie kissed the tiny fingers suddenly thrust into her mouth. "What good soul has brought you back to our arms and our hearts?"

The rush of attentions as the adults surrounded her suddenly brought a moment of apprehension to Hannah. Her piercing wail rocked the room as Carrie drew her comfortingly to her shoulder. Oh, how good it was to hear her cry, to see her alive and well and scarcely changed since Christmas Day!

Across the room, another young woman, Jewel Farthingham, was kept in her seat by her husband when her first instinct was to comfort the crying Hannah.

438

Tim and Jewel Farthingham might have slipped, unnoticed, into the brisk morning air if Cole Donovan had not interrupted their retreat. While Diana remained with Andrew and Carrie and enjoyed the happy reunion with her granddaughter, Cole caught the two young people just as they prepared to board their wagon.

"You there . . ."

Tim had assisted his wife up, but now turned at the sharp reverberation of the elder Donovan's voice. "Sir, I know we did wrong," he immediately defended himself, "but sending me to jail will accomplish naught. I have a wife to care for . . ."

Cole's eyes narrowed beneath frowning gray-black brows. "It'll not be sending you to jail that brings me out, but to thank you for returning my granddaughter."

"Don't thank me," he replied somberly. "She was with my wife and me the first time you stopped at my wagon. I was prepared to keep the child—"

"But you did not," Cole instantly cut him off. "Now . . . be on your way before my son decides that some action is, indeed, warranted against you."

He stood there in his muslin shirt, shivering against the cold while the noisy, canvas-covered wagon disappeared into the Pennsylvania countryside.

Wills Creek,
Four Months Later

An eagle dipped low on the horizon, its wings stationary against the gentle winds of springs. Holding her seven-month-old daughter firmly to the saddle in front of her, Carrie pointed out the magnificent sight. Hannah's guttural exclamations caused her father, riding ahead of them on the trail, to turn his head in their direction.

439

"Is that girl muttering expletives?" he asked, his feigned frown of disapproval bringing a smile to Carrie's lips.

"Indeed not! She was just telling me how handsome her father is, as handsome, in fact, as the eagle soaring on the horizon."

Just at that moment, the two horses emerged into the clearing at the bend of Wills Creek. Since they'd been expected, Dora, who had been watching for them on the trail, yelled toward the trading post, "They're here — Mr. Drew and Miss Carrie and little Hannah . . . they're here."

Before more than a minute had passed, they were surrounded by the residents of Wills Creek, welcoming them home.

After the required amenities, a waddling and very pregnant Hester took Hannah from Carrie's arms. Her immediate retreat from the Donovans drew a caravan of children into the trading post. While Andrew exchanged a few words with Noble and Bundy, and promises to go hunting with them as soon as the grounds dried up after the heavy rains, Carrie moved toward the comfortable cabin where she, Andrew, and their daughter would live. She had never been so happy. Songbirds filled the air and love filled her heart.

Andrew soon managed to break away from his blood brothers. He quickly dismounted his horse, then offered his support to Carrie. When she moved into his arms, he held her closely. "Let's you and me go see if our favorite spot on the pond is just as we left it."

Her fingers traveling up the warm fabric of his shirt, she laughed lightly. "I've got a little one to pry away from Hester and the children, Andrew Cynric Donovan. I've no time for your playfulness." Smiling her most appealing smile, she lightly accused, "I suppose you fellows have already made plans to go hunting and leave us ladies alone?"

His smile might have been a rebellious refusal to answer had he not loved her too much to deny her such a small requirement. "Noble's stalling. Says the ground is too wet, but I believe he wants to return to Rourke House . . ."

"Poof! That man! He has been to Rourke House half a dozen times in the past three months. And I know why . . . Liddy is acting the dizzy schoolgirl because of Noble's attentions."

His fingers loosely linked at her back, his gray-black eyes narrowed. "I'll wager, lass, that we'll soon have a marriage between those two."

"Oh, I do hope so!" Excitement bubbled in Carrie's voice. "Liddy deserves to be happy and she does so love the twins."

Across Carrie's slender shoulder, Drew watched the slow approach of Cawley Perth. He grinned when the boy met his gaze. "Where have you been, boy?"

Cawley smiled his pleasure at seeing the two people who had changed his life. "Where I was ain't fittin' fer discussion in front of your missy. I'm here now and I'll take care of your horses and put your things inside."

When Cawley sauntered away, followed by the two mares, Andrew dropped his hands across Carrie's shoulders. "Hannah is being smothered by attention. Let's go for a nice long walk and I'll smother you, too."

"Promise?"

He grinned rakishly. "Sure do."

Relishing the strength of his arms, Carrie fell into his warm embrace. Then she turned against him and coaxed him toward the trail and the large pond to the north. Moments later they emerged from the shadows of the forest into the sun-bathed clearing. The aroma of wild violets and honeysuckle growing in profusion wafted on the gentle wind, a largemouth bass leaped into the swirling darkness of the pond, and all around, the melodic harmony of songbirds filled the air.

Dropping to a patch of sweet clover, Carrie leaned into Andrew's strong embrace and accepted his gentle caresses, his fingers loosely entwined through the clouds of her hair, a teasing wind plying upon their sun-warmed faces.

They might have enjoyed the gentle enclosure of the pond all morning had deeper passions not compelled them back to the cozy little cabin sitting peacefully in the bend of Wills Creek.

The bed with its large downy quilts and pillows was every bit as comfortable as the thick patch of clover . . . and as comfortable a domain for the fulfillment of their mutual love and adoration.

Part Four
Fulfillment

Epilogue

Carrie stood on the narrow street, her eyes scanning the tavern and brothel that had now fallen to neglect and decay. She couldn't help but wonder about those who had stayed behind—the kindly slave Solomon, the feisty Julia, and the others. She imagined them to be long gone by now, blending into the wild American land and never again allowing anyone to lay claim to their lives.

Her soulful eyes briefly scanned the quiet street. At scarcely past dawn, even the hawkers had not flooded the streets with their wares. Occasionally, a flatboatman would emerge from a dark alley where he might have passed out from drinking and debauchery the night before. Otherwise, the street belonged to her, and to her husband who now approached and gently enfolded her within his arms.

"Have you seen what you wanted to see, little wife?"

She managed the sweetest of smiles. "I have seen the place where I first met you, Andrew Cynric Donovan!" she replied. "And whether that is good or bad I still have not decided!"

Andrew turned her into his arms, his dark eyes scanning her youthful figure . . . her pretty cream-colored gown with its tightly pinched waist, her fashionable bonnet scarcely able to contain the rich masses of her flowing copper-colored hair, her eyes lovingly, teasingly, lifted to his.

"Come, Princess . . ." he said, coaxing her away from the late Junius Wade's abandoned den of iniquity, "we've promised a certain little soul that we'd take her to Circus Square this morning."

As they moved back toward *Donovan's Dream*, where a hired Creole lady took care of Hannah, Carrie thought of the renovations Andrew had made to the boat last year. The ladies' cabin belowdeck was elegantly fitted, with ornamented windows and beds, with bombazette curtains, fringes, and mosquito bars, an elegant carpet upon the floor. The cabin where Hannah most liked to play was thirty feet in length, affording her plenty of scampering room.

Abovedeck an elegant roundhouse for the gentlemen was forty-two feet in length and twenty-eight in breadth. Each sleeping berth had a window. Sofas and chairs, two large tables, a large gilt-framed mirror, and several elegantly finished recommendation cards in gilt frames adorned the room.

Since the renovations, Andrew had started taking on passengers between Louisville and New Orleans. Hannah enjoyed the gay assortment of people who frequented the boat on the long trips up and down the Mississippi. Noble had brought his young wife Libby on two of their recent trips, giving her a first taste of life beyond the borders of Pennsylvania.

Soon, Carrie and her beloved Drew reached *Donovan's Dream*. The dark-haired, emerald-eyed Hannah squealed her delight as she spied them and scarcely could be restrained by the nanny as her parents traversed the gangplank. Then she rushed into her mother's arms and hugged her tightly.

"And a hug for Papa?" Drew laughed, taking his

squirming little girl.

"A hug for Papa, too," she greeted, giving him her most precocious smile.

"You'd better run along with Nanny and get ready for . . ." He smiled teasingly, halting his words.

"The circus, Papa?" the little girl finished his words with unrestrained excitement.

Handing her over to the Creole woman, Drew gently folded Carrie within his arms. "Shall we go to our cabin and take a short nap? We really shouldn't have stayed out, dancing away the whole blasted night."

"Didn't you have a good time, Drew? I've never seen such a gay assortment of people in one hotel dancing parlor. But . . ." Lightly, she shrugged her shoulders, "we've promised Hannah the morning so we can only take a short nap." Together they strolled toward their large, private cabin with its elegant furnishings. "We haven't gotten much sleep since arriving in New Orleans, have we?"

He laughed. "When we do try to sleep, we have rabble shooting it up on the docks. How could anyone sleep?"

"Hannah thinks it's all terribly exciting."

Again, Drew laughed. "Yes, I know."

Entering their cabin, Drew turned and shut the door. He poured a goblet of port and sat in a plush leather chair, watching Carrie move about the cabin, tending little needs, loosening her tight clothing and then eventually discarding it for something more lightweight and comfortable.

He knew she was anxious to return home to Wills Creek, and in a way, he was, too. They missed their friends . . . Noble and Liddy and two mischievous sons, Hester and Bundy and their brood, Cawley and Dora and their new daughter.

He'd missed his parents since their return to Pine Creek, though they had promised to visit Philadelphia this summer. Their visit should correspond closely with that of

Lord and Lady Seymour, who had sent word they would arrive in July. It would be a grand reunion; they hadn't all been together since Christmas of that fateful year.

Drew had not realized how deeply he'd lost himself in his thoughts until Carrie stood before him, wearing a comfortable daygown and tapping her foot upon the planked floor. Setting down his untouched glass of port, his hand went out and grasped her own.

"Come here, Princess." Pulling her into his lap, his arms went about her tiny waist. "Love me?"

"You? Poof!" She tried to be flippant, but the warmth of him, his hand gently massaging the length of her spine, grappled feelings from her that were reserved only for him. "Andrew Cynric Donovan, I think I do love you."

"Think, hell!" He rose to his feet, shifting her in his arms as he did so. He dropped to the bed with her and lovingly held her gaze.

"What do you think you're doing, Andrew Donovan!" she gently admonished, fighting the smile that would only serve to betray her delight.

Drew dropped the mask of teasing affection, and his expression was now a mirror of the moments to come. His gaze moved over her emerald eyes, her petulant mouth inviting a kiss, her cheeks that rushed with the color of her own feminine wants.

"Carrie Sherwood Donovan, I love you."

"Do you, Andrew? And how do you propose to prove it?"

A grin raked his masculine good looks. "Like this, Princess . . ." His mouth brushed each of her translucent eyelids, her willing mouth, the slim column of her throat, "and this . . . and this . . ."

Who cared that it was morning and a busy day awaited them? All duties would be attended in good time. But for now the moments were their own—upon their bed of love and exquisite happiness . . .